All the Love Songs

by

NICOLE PYLAND

All the Love Songs

Celebrities Series Book #2

Peyton Gloss is the world's most famous and popular singer & songwriter, known for her chart-topping hits as well as her famous girl squad and July 4th events, inviting all of her famous friends to celebrate. This year, she did something even more extravagant than ever, and invited her friends to join her for a week-long adult summer camp experience.

Mackenzie Smyth was dared to audition for a TV show. Thinking she had no chance of getting the part, she went along with it. Five years later, she's one of the most popular young actresses in Hollywood. She's also socially awkward and struggles with getting to know new people and spending time with her peers.

Lennox Owen is Hollywood royalty and has been famous since birth. She's remained in the business because she didn't know what else, if anything, she could do, and because it was what was expected of her.

When Lennox and Kenzie meet, there's electricity between them. And the camp is the perfect opportunity for them to explore what might be. But after the magic of their week away from the world dissipates, can they still find that spark and make their relationship work?

To contact the author or for any additional information, visit: **https://nicolepyland.com**

This is a work of fiction. Any names or characters, businesses or places, events or incidents, are fictitious. Any resemblance to actual persons, living or dead, or actual events is purely coincidental. No part of this book may be reproduced or transmitted in any form or by any means, electronic or mechanical, including photocopying, recording or by any information storage and retrieval system, without written permission from the author.

Copyright © 2017 Nicole Pyland

All rights reserved.

ISBN-13: 978-0-9996221-2-4

BY THE AUTHOR

Chicago Series:

- Introduction – Fresh Start
- Book #1 – The Best Lines
- Book #2 – Just Tell Her
- Book #3 – Love Walked into The Lantern
- Series Finale – What Happened After

San Francisco Series:

- Book #1 – Checking the Right Box
- Book #2 – Macon's Heart
- Book #3 – This Above All
- Series Finale – What Happened After

Tahoe Series:

- Book #1 – Keep Tahoe Blue
- Book #2 – Time of Day
- Book #3 – The Perfect View
- Book #4 – Begin Again
- Series Finale – What Happened After

Boston Series:

- Book #1 – Let Go
- Book #2 – The Right Fit
- Book #3 – All Good Plans
- Book #4 – Around the World
- Series Finale – What Happened After

Sports Series:

- Book #1 – Always More
- Book #2 – A Shot at Gold
- Book #3 – The Unexpected Dream
- Book #4 – Finding a Keeper

Celebrities Series:

- Book #1 – No After You
- Book #2 – All the Love Songs
- Book #3 – Midnight Tradition
- Book #4 – Path Forward
- Series Finale – What Happened After

Holiday Series:

- Book #1 – The Writing on the Wall
- Book #2 – The Block Party
- Book #3 – The Fireworks
- Book #4 – The Sweet Escape
- Book #5 – The Misperception
- Book #6 – The Wait is Over
- Series Finale – What Happened After

Stand-alone books:

- The Fire
- The Disappeared
- The Moments
- Reality Check
- Love Forged
- The Show Must Go On
- The Meet Cute Café
- Pride Festival

CONTENTS

CHAPTER 1	1
CHAPTER 2	11
CHAPTER 3	23
CHAPTER 4	29
CHAPTER 5	36
CHAPTER 6	43
CHAPTER 7	51
CHAPTER 8	60
CHAPTER 9	69
CHAPTER 10	78
CHAPTER 11	102
CHAPTER 12	122
CHAPTER 13	132
CHAPTER 14	145
CHAPTER 15	157
CHAPTER 16	166
CHAPTER 17	184
CHAPTER 18	191
CHAPTER 19	204
CHAPTER 20	215
CHAPTER 21	226
CHAPTER 22	236
CHAPTER 23	247

CHAPTER 24	255
CHAPTER 25	267
CHAPTER 26	279
CHAPTER 27	292
CHAPTER 28	301
CHAPTER 29	311
CHAPTER 30	320
CHAPTER 31	329
CHAPTER 32	339
EPILOGUE	353

CHAPTER 1

MACKENZIE SMYTH had no idea how she had gotten here. She stood in the parking lot, away from all the chaos she would be walking into, and inhaled the sticky summer air that came every year in the deep south. That part she knew well. She'd grown up only about two hours from where she was standing. And, as she listened to the laughter and loud conversations about one hundred yards away from her, she also paid close attention to the sound of the crickets and birds in the trees as their leaves moved with the slight breeze.

The past two years of her life had been such a blur. She turned twenty-six only a month earlier and had taken the summer off from work, after having worked non-stop for five years. She had auditioned for a role on a television show that no one thought would go past the pilot. She'd done it on a dare. She had been in school at the time; about a year shy of a degree in political science, having no idea what she would do with it after graduation. She had acted a little in high school and enjoyed it, but that was high school. She hadn't taken it seriously nor thought she was any good. And high school was her only acting experience prior to that night of drunken truth or dare with her friends.

***

"Kenz, you have to audition. You were dared." Kathleen pointed at Mackenzie with one finger while using her other hand to lift her beer to her lips. "You can't get out of it. You already passed on the dare to make out with Mark." Her finger moved to Mark.

"I'm gay, Kat," Mackenzie professed. "Sorry, Mark." She shrugged at her friend from her philosophy and law course. "No offense."

"Also, I'm right here," Mackenzie's girlfriend, Annabelle, added with a wave.

"You know the rules. You only get one pass," Kat insisted.

"Why are we playing truth or dare on a futon?" Mackenzie stared at Annabelle for a moment before resting her head on her shoulder.

"We are playing truth or dare because it's our last night of fun before Emily leaves us, and it's Emily's favorite game," Kat explained.

"So, are you going to go through with the dare or not?" Mark asked Kenzie.

"She has to go through with it," Kat encouraged. "My dad's a producer. Come on, Kenz. Just like all his other shows, it's not going to go anywhere. There's a part for a girl who is about our age, and you fit the bill." Kat rolled her eyes at her own father, who had worked in Hollywood for more than two decades in a variety of capacities and only just started producing.

"If age is the only requirement, then all four of us fit the bill," Kenzie reminded.

"Yes, but you were the one that I dared," Kat smirked and winked back.

"Come on, babe. Just agree to it so this game can end." Annabelle patted her thigh.

"Fine. Fine." Kenzie finally relented. "I'll do it. Can we just watch a movie or something? Emily?"

"Movie is fine with me," Emily agreed.

***

Three days later, Kenzie had made it to the audition, with Kat driving her to make sure Kenzie went through with it. Kenzie had been given the sides and sat in a stark-cold waiting room, surrounded by a lot of other girls that looked eerily similar to her. She was twenty-one, 5'8", and thin, thanks to her mostly healthy diet and the fact that she ran track in school. Her long brown hair was typically wavy and unmanaged, and she had left it that way today as well. She had worn it down and looked around to see that most of the other girls had done the same with their locks.

"Mackenzie Smyth?" A woman, with short dark hair and black-rimmed glasses, leaned out the door and looked around.

"That's me." Kenzie stood and, for the millionth time, rolled her eyes at her friend, who smiled and laughed at her silently. "I will get you back for this." She reminded Kat and headed off into the audition.

Her entire life had changed that day. She had read the script they had given her, and then, they had called her back two days later to do it again. Four days after that, they'd had her read with Doug Waverly, the male star of the show. Kenzie had gone because by then, Kat's father had gotten involved and asked her to read. That day she said goodbye to Annabelle, due to Annabelle's graduation and her new job in Sacramento. And with their future in question, it was the day they had offered Kenzie the lead role on the show. It was one of those teen dramas, on a network filled with teen dramas, and involved the world of the supernatural, like four of the other dramas on the network.

She signed on for the pilot because they were paying her, and she thought that would be the end of it. Kenzie didn't exactly have money as a starving college student, and her parents weren't an option, so anything she could make would make her life a little easier. She'd had a part-time job in a café since she first moved to LA, and she survived on her scholarship and the tips she made there more than the actual paycheck.

Filming was unlike anything she'd seen, and they spent eight days shooting the pilot. When it was all said and done, Kenzie put the money in the bank and went back to work at the café. She figured that would be the end of it, and her almost accidental career in Hollywood was over. Kenzie actually laughed about the whole thing with Annabelle over the phone one night in July. They had attempted a long-distance relationship, but Kenzie was already sensing the strain. They had no idea when they would see each other again. And, once Kenzie was told that the pilot had been picked up, and they would start filming the rest of the first season in August, that was it for school and for Annabelle.

Kenzie had thought they could make it work, at first. But, once the filming took off, and Kenzie was working fourteen hours a day, Annabelle ended it and met someone else shortly after; which Kat had been kind enough to tell Kenzie after she had learned it on Facebook. Her whole world shifted then. Once the show aired, it was an instant success, and she was thrust into the spotlight she had never craved nor sought. Suddenly, Kenzie was giving interviews and showing up at events and award shows. Her face was on a billboard a block away from the apartment she still shared with Emily and Kat, because though she was making money now, Kenzie wasn't dumb. She knew this fame thing was fleeting, and she'd go back to school and need that money to help her get through.

The first season led to the second and so on. Four seasons later, the show had wrapped for good. They'd all thought they'd had another two or maybe three seasons in them. The network disagreed. And though the show was performing well in ratings, Doug Waverly's movie career had taken off, and he hadn't renewed his contract. The showrunner left as well, to pursue another show on a cable network. All that left Kenzie and the supporting cast wondering about the future, while the network considered everything and decided not to renew the show for the fifth season.

Kenzie thought that was the end, and she would go back to finish her degree. She only had one year left. And though Emily and Kat had both moved on, they no longer lived together, and she'd be a twenty-five-year-old senior, Kenzie still wanted to finish. She was looking into getting enrolled again when her agent, Carson, called and told her about another show that wanted her to audition, and that he had three movie scripts on his desk for her to read. She considered all her options, and after reading the pilot script and the movie screenplays, Kenzie decided to try the TV show and audition for the movie that would film on the show's hiatus.

Kenzie had just wrapped the show's first season, and they'd been renewed for season two and three already. She had two days off after this camp session before she had to report to London, where she would be filming for two months before returning to film in New York for another month. She would be back to the show a week later. And with her only real vacation time, she'd been talked into attending this adult summer camp for six days, with a bunch of other famous women.

***

"Hey! There she is." Peyton Gloss stood about twenty feet in front of her and waved her over to the group. "You're late, Kenzie. We've been waiting for you."

"Sorry… I just have to get my stuff," Kenzie replied and turned to walk to the back of her car to get her luggage from the trunk.

"Need any help?" Peyton asked. "I can send Dani. She's super strong."

Peyton Gloss was the host of this event and also a massive superstar. She was twenty-seven and had six albums to her name already. She had been in the music business since she was fourteen, and had started in country before moving over into pop. Her last album had been her most successful to date. She had wrapped a world tour only a month prior and was taking the next several months off to relax. Peyton Gloss was also gorgeous and actually born with the name

Peyton Gloss. She had blonde hair that was usually wavy, and she'd only just cut it short to just above shoulder-length. She had bright blue eyes and was 5'11" without the heels that she normally wore when she was working. Peyton was also bright, funny, and incredibly generous with everyone, but especially, with her friends. And Kenzie Smyth could now count herself among that group.

They'd met at a charity event in March. After a few minutes of talking, Kenzie knew she liked Peyton. And when she observed how Peyton was with Dani Wilder, Kenzie felt like she understood something that likely not many others did.

Peyton and Dani had become friends when Dani, a supermodel, joined her then-boyfriend at a gala, to support his work in technology. Peyton had performed that night, and they clicked immediately, according to their interviews later and all the rumors. Those rumors also indicated that their friendship was more than just a friendship, but that had never been confirmed. As far as the world knew, Peyton had dated two actors since then, and Dani was still with her boyfriend of now four years.

In truth, the two were an item; and had been for over two years. Everyone at this week-long event knew that. And their families, of course, were also aware, including Peyton's three sisters and Dani's younger brother. Outside of that select group, though, no one else knew that within a few months of starting their friendship, Dani had ended her relationship with her boyfriend, and she and Peyton were in love.

"No, I'm okay," Kenzie replied.

"I *am* strong." Dani wrapped her arms around her girlfriend from behind. She was 6'1" and, therefore, two inches taller than Peyton. "I work out," she added.

"She does. Every single day, she's up at five," Peyton agreed. "It's annoying," she teased.

"She loves me." Dani kissed her cheek.

"I'm okay," Kenzie repeated. She lifted her large roller

out of the trunk and settled it onto the gravel of the parking lot that gave way to dirt and grass and the large grouping of trees.

Beyond that laid the campground Peyton had rented for the week for her massive group of female friends to celebrate July 4th and spend much-needed time together. This group consisted of actresses, musicians, and models. Rarely all of them could get together like this, due to their schedules. In total, Kenzie had heard that there were eighteen women at this adult summer camp. She'd met a few of the women through work or events, but most, she had never had the chance to meet. She had never been particularly outgoing, and that was especially true with women, once Kenzie had gotten the role. Her agent and manager, along with her publicist, all asked Kenzie to keep her sexuality to herself when the show first started airing. She was playing a teenager who fell in love with a boy. And, apparently, in their mind, she could act, but she couldn't possibly act straight enough if the world knew she was a lesbian.

"You brought a roller bag?" Peyton laughed. "I thought you grew up around here. Didn't you ever go camping?"

"I grew up around here, yes. But no, we never went camping. And you said we would be in cabins. I didn't know I'd have to wheel this thing through gravel," Kenzie replied as she tried to pull the bag along.

"There are four supermodels here with the reputation of being divas, and even they brought duffel bags."

"Honey, you're not helping," Dani told her girlfriend and pulled back. "I will." She moved in the direction of Kenzie.

"I got it." The voice came from behind her, which surprised Kenzie, because, a moment ago, there had been no one behind her.

The parking lot sat between two campgrounds. Behind the long row of cars, there were more trees and grass. Beyond that, she couldn't see anything. But she was sure that only a moment prior, she had been alone.

"Go for it, Len," Peyton told the voice. "We'll head back. We're about to do s'mores. Head toward the fire pit, and I'll show you where to put your stuff."

Peyton and Dani practically jogged back to the rest of the group, which must have been beyond the row of trees. Kenzie turned around to see someone she recognized but had never met, standing behind her. Lennox Owen was more beautiful in person than she was on screen, or in the pictures Kenzie had seen of her in magazines, or on the billboards plastered all over Los Angeles in preparation for her movie release next month. The woman was a little taller than Kenzie, but only by an inch or so. She had long light-blonde hair that had dark lights of brown in it and was pulled back into a ponytail. Her eyes were bright blue, but a deeper blue than Peyton's. They sparkled. That was how Kenzie would describe them. As Lennox approached, she could see them even clearer. And yeah, they sparkled, as did the smile she was currently delivering in Kenzie's direction. Lennox wore a white tank top, with denim cut-off shorts, white tennis shoes, and white ankle socks. Kenzie gulped as she felt Lennox's hand slightly cover her own as the woman gripped the handle of the large roller bag.

"Hi, I'm Lennox. Everyone calls me Len or Lex. So, take your pick," she greeted.

"Mackenzie. Everyone calls me Kenzie or Kenz. So, take *your* pick," Kenzie replied and removed her hand from her bag.

Lennox lifted the bag off the gravel and began tugging it in the direction of the grass and dirt path, where it would roll smoother.

"Have you ever noticed that everyone in the show business – which I hate calling it that, by the way – has a name meant for show business?" Lennox asked as Kenzie walked next to her, trying to figure out if she should help Lennox carry the bag or just stay out of her way.

"I guess not," Kenzie returned and opted to let Lennox carry it on her own and just watch the biceps that were clearly defined but not so much so as to be intimidating.

"Seriously, though, Peyton Gloss? Dani Wilder? Mackenzie Smyth?" Lennox turned and smiled at Kenzie. "Unless you changed your name when you got famous."

"No, I was born with this one." Kenzie smiled back shyly. "What about you?"

"I was named after my mom's maiden name," the woman answered and dropped the bag onto the dirt, to pull it the rest of the way. "What about Jack?"

"Oh, she's Jackie. Born with Jackie. I learned that when we worked together," Kenzie paused. "April was April, and Carlie was born Carlie. Those are the only ones I know for sure."

"Well, I know that Mandy is actually Amanda, but Amanda is technically her middle name, and her first name is Ethel. She's named after her great-grandmother. Don't tell her I told you." Lennox stopped rolling the bag when they had made it to the clearing. "And I know Sarah was Sarah, Jenna was Jenna, but Quinn is actually her middle name. And Tiana is actually Christina."

"That's a lot," Kenzie offered.

"I guess I've been a member of the squad for a while." Lennox nodded in the direction of the fire pit, where Kenzie could see the group chatting away, laughing, and attempting to build a large fire. "Welcome to the squad, rookie." She lifted her left eyebrow, and Kenzie had to swallow at the sight.

"Thanks."

"Ladies, I have cabin assignments." One of the girls yelled, but Kenzie hadn't recognized the voice.

"I guess we should go." Lennox pulled Kenzie's bag again, and Kenzie walked next to her.

Kenzie didn't respond. She couldn't believe she had been talking to *the* Lennox Owen. She couldn't believe she was going to be spending the next six days in the same space as her. Kenzie hadn't known the woman would be here.

Peyton had left her name off the list of confirmed attendees. Had she known, Kenzie could have mentally prepared herself for spending time with her crush. Only Peyton knew about the fact that Kenzie had a crush on Lennox.

Peyton and Dani both knew Kenzie was gay, but no one else at this event was aware. Kenzie had been crushing on Lennox since high school, when Lennox had her own show. Her show had lasted for seven seasons, and Kenzie had seen every episode multiple times. After the show, she had moved on to movies, and she was now a thirty-one-year-old Oscar nominee and Golden Globe winner, three times over. Kenzie had seen every one of Lennox's films and watched many of her interviews. She considered it light and completely innocent stalking, and she was nervous now, as she stood next to the woman she'd often fantasized about, even when she'd been lying next to a woman she was dating.

CHAPTER 2

LENNOX Owen was the oldest person at this shindig. She had arrived over an hour ago and had dropped her stuff by the fire, after saying her hellos to the women who had already shown up for this grown-up summer camp experience. Truthfully, if she wasn't so close to Peyton, she probably would have turned down the invitation. But the two of them had grown up together in a way; Lennox considered Peyton to be like a younger sister to her, and she'd adopted many of Peyton's friends as her own as a result.

She loved Dani and loved Dani for Peyton. She had been there the night they'd met and recalled how they clicked so instantly, it left Dani's boyfriend confused and alone, checking his iPhone every thirty seconds to appear to be busy and distracted. Lennox had laughed at the whole thing and waited until Peyton told her, months later, that she was madly in love with a woman. Peyton hadn't needed to reveal the name. Lennox had guessed, to Peyton's surprise, and the three of them had been friends ever since.

For Lennox, the child of two well-known movie stars, events like this camp were things she'd normally either decline or fake-smile her way through. But it had been so important to Peyton to get her friends together once a year and to include new friends in the group as often as possible, that Lennox always obliged and usually had a good time. There were always a few girls she would avoid during whatever event Peyton was putting on. But, for the most part, Peyton's friends were smart, kind, and fun to be around. The few divas Lennox encountered, she'd just steer clear of whenever possible.

"Okay… Everyone here?" Peyton stood in front of the fire pit that Mandy and Cleo, members of an alternative girl band, were piling logs onto. "Everyone's here." She didn't wait for a response.

The fire pit was surrounded by six picnic tables. Lennox stood next to the newest arrival, Kenzie Smyth, while the other women, not helping with the fire, were sitting around the circle, either on the benches or on the tops of the tables themselves.

"You wanna sit?" Lennox asked Kenzie.

"Sure," she replied and then moved away from her toward a picnic table to her immediate right.

Lennox left Kenzie's bag where it was and walked over to join her, sitting next to Bobby Jane, the drummer of the girl band.

"Hey, Len. Where'd you go?" she asked when Lennox sat next to her.

"I had to take a call," Lennox returned and placed her hands between her legs as she sat on top of the table, noting that Kenzie sat on Bobby's other side and on the bench.

"Hey, there's no work while we're here. That's the one rule." Brooke Williams, the supermodel and sometimes-actress, joined in from her position at the next table over from them.

"It wasn't work," Lennox retorted with a smile in her direction. "It was my sister. She's at basic training and only gets one phone call a week."

"Oh, right," Brooke relented.

"Basic training?" Bobby checked.

"She joined the army," Lennox shared with Bobby and noticed that Kenzie had turned to listen as well.

"Ladies, are we ready?" Peyton asked the group, encouraging them to quiet down.

ALL THE LOVE SONGS

"How'd your parents feel about that?" Bobby asked.

"I'll tell you later. Peyton looks like she's about to pop a vein." Lennox motioned to Peyton, who was glaring at them.

"Welcome to your first annual adult summer camp experience," Peyton greeted them all together for the first time. "If you're here – you are someone that is very important to me. You're family. And I want us to spend a week having fun, learning more about each other, and taking a break from the crazy world we all live in," she added. "If you're here, that also means you've agreed to the one rule: there's no work here. No calls from managers or agents. No reading scripts on your phone, Quinn." She nodded and pointed at Quinn Harris, the twenty-nine-year-old movie star, who'd won an Oscar at age thirteen for her breakout role and had worked steadily in the industry ever since.

"I'm not reading a script. I'm on Instagram," Quinn responded to the rule.

"Better not be," Dani said. "PG's crazy about the one rule," she said of her girlfriend she sometimes referred to by her initials.

"I am," Peyton added and smiled at Dani. "I think it's important that we all have a chance to get away from it for a while. And since it's way too hard to get us all together for longer than a week, and it was damn near impossible to schedule and rent this whole place over the 4th of July holiday weekend, you all better stick to the damn rule," she issued but had a playful smile on her face.

Lennox had no idea how much this must have set Peyton back, but she'd guess it was hundreds of thousands of dollars. She had rented the entire campground on this side of the lake and the one on the other side of the parking lot, where her security would be staying for the duration of the event. Peyton's career and her success meant that she had to have security around her at all times, and, as a result, so did Dani and anyone else who spent time with her. She'd rented out the four cabins on the other side of the parking lot and the six on this side, along with the cafeteria and other parts of the campground she wanted them to have solo access to.

They'd have staff prepare their meals, and that staff would stay in one of the cabins on the security side. But, outside of that, they were completely alone. They had access to two open fields, where there would be archery and softball or other sporting events, if they chose to play. They had the lake on one side of them, with access to two rowboats and the boathouse on the opposite side of the lake as well. The bathroom was one long building with six stalls, four sinks, and four showers. Lennox could only imagine how that would work with eighteen women, who were all more than used to their own expansive bathrooms with plenty of room for their products and their egos.

"Are there any more rules, boss?" Davica asked.

Davica was the group's pop star. Well, she was one of them. She went only by Davica, and Lennox wasn't even sure of her last name. The other pop star in the group was Lynn Erickson. She used her full name and was more of a singer/songwriter than a pop star, but because she sang mostly pop songs, she was grouped along with them.

"No more official rules," Peyton explained. "I would like everyone to participate in the events, though, and other than that, just have fun."

"And what's the first event?" That question came from Carlie, on the table directly across from Lennox.

"A round of getting to know one another over s'mores, if those two can get a fire going sometime this century," Dani answered for her girlfriend.

"I don't see you being helpful," Mandy argued while she attempted to strike a match. "Weren't you an actual girl scout?" she asked of Dani.

"I was. I still remember the pledge and everything." Dani stood and approached the fire. "On my honor, I will try…" Dani began, but Lennox didn't hear the rest of it, because the space almost immediately broke out into the sounds of girls talking to one another.

"So, s'mores with a group of models," Bobby offered her as she stood up. "I'm taking bets. How many do you think they'll actually eat? How many will ask if they're gluten-free or low-carb?" She rolled her eyes and walked off to help her bandmates with the fire.

That left Lennox and Kenzie alone at the table, while others had either stood to begin rifling through bags of graham crackers and chocolate, or remained at their tables to talk in smaller groups. Lennox turned to see Kenzie's eyes on her, but, the moment their eyes connected, Kenzie turned away and stood. Her eyes were green. They were a deep dark-green, from what Lennox could tell, and they appeared to her to hold secrets. She had no reason to suspect that, of course, but it was her initial impression in the parking lot. And when Kenzie turned away and stood, that impression had remained.

"Oh, and I almost forgot!" Peyton nearly yelled over the group. "There are eighteen of us and six cabins. There are four beds in each cabin. Dani and I are in one of our own because–"

"You want to have sex," Carlie yelled, and everyone laughed.

"Because we're the only couple, and because I'm hosting," Peyton returned with an eye-roll.

"And so that they can have sex," Carlie repeated, though with less enthusiasm this time.

"Anyway, that means there are five cabins for the sixteen of you. I decided it would be fun for everyone to rotate, though, so that people can get to know one another a little bit better. And I've put you in cabins for tonight with people I don't think you know well."

"I feel like I'm at some corporate team-building retreat," Maddox, a thirty-year-old famous photographer, shared. "When are the trust falls so I can skip them?" She smiled.

"No one would catch you anyway, Mad," Peyton fired

back and earned a laugh from the group. "All right, here's the list for the first two nights. Then, we'll switch." She pulled out her phone and scrolled. "Kenzie, Carlie, and April are in cabin one. Sarah, Tiana, and Jack are in two. Brooke, Mandy, and Mad are in three. Lynn, Bobby, Quinn, and Jenna are in four. Davica, Cleo, Len are in five." She completed the list. "Those are your roomies for night one and two, and then, we'll switch things up. Good?" She waited, and everyone nodded along.

Lennox looked over toward Kenzie, who appeared to be looking around at the cabins, which were in a circle around the campsite. She was likely trying to find cabin one. Lennox would be rooming with Cleo and Davica. She knew them, but only somewhat, and decided she'd give this whole get to know each other thing a chance, since it seemed to be so important to Peyton. She would do anything for Peyton Gloss.

Peyton had been a part of her life since the girl auditioned at age fifteen for a small part in a movie Lennox was staring in. Despite their near five-year age difference, they struck up a conversation and friendship that began at the beginning of Peyton's career before it took off. Peyton had since been in a couple of movies in small roles and had a few appearances on TV shows. She had also been there for Lennox when Lennox had lost her older brother to a mountain biking accident. She had been twenty-two, and Will had been twenty-four. He'd been in a coma for a few weeks, and it was splashed all over the tabloids and on every entertainment show. Her parents were from a long line of Hollywood royalty. Her grandmother had been in the pictures when they were still called *pictures*. She'd worked alongside Shirley Temple and then raised her daughter in the business. Her mother hadn't been planned and was a late-in-life baby for her grandmother, which meant she was raised by nannies more than her mother. She had started acting as a child as well and met Lennox's father, Brian Owen, on set. Brian was unknown at the time. After his breakout role in the movie they co-starred in, he was highly sought-after, and it had been that way ever since. Will had been a child star himself. He started in commercials and then was on a kid's show as a child. Then, after not having much luck beyond that, he had given it up as a career and lived mostly off his trust fund, traveling the world in search of the next adrenaline high.

When he died, Peyton was there for Lennox, and Lennox would never be able to thank her enough for that friendship. Peyton had helped her get through filming the movie she'd been working on right after it happened, and even arranged movers for her when Lennox had bought her first house only days before the accident and, a month after, had to move out of her apartment and into her new home. She couldn't function without Peyton's help for weeks after the loss of the brother she'd loved so much. And Lennox would always be especially grateful to her friend for helping with her baby sister.

Jamie had been the accidental child after her parents thought they were done having kids. She was twenty now but had been only thirteen when their brother died. Peyton had been amazing with her. When their parents decided that the best way for them to grieve, was to work more than ever, and moved to Monaco to live there whenever they weren't on set, Jamie moved with them for a year – until she was so depressed and unhappy, that Lennox told her parents Jamie would live with her instead. Lennox had essentially been Jamie's guardian from that moment on. And while she'd kept Jamie out of the spotlight – because that was Jamie's preference – every now and then, her parents tried to get Jamie to audition for a part or appear in a movie one of them was working on. Jamie was no actress and wanted nothing to do with that life.

Lennox hadn't been given the chance to find her own dream. Her parents had her in commercials, like her brother, from the age of three, and she'd moved on to small roles after that. In her teens, things had taken off, and she'd never looked back. She'd attended school on set with tutors and hadn't ever thought about college. She had enough money and always had constant work to keep it that way. Lennox liked acting. She had entered the profession because of her parents but stuck with it because she enjoyed it. It was also all she'd ever known, and that was probably the main reason she continued doing it, if she was being completely honest with herself.

"Hey, you cool with the roomies I assigned you?" Peyton approached with a s'more she held between two fingers while licking the fingers on her other hand to get rid of the melted chocolate.

"Yeah, I'm good."

"Hey, Kenz!" Peyton turned to Kenzie, who was standing off to the side of the group.

"Yeah?" Kenzie turned her attention to Peyton, then her eyes met Lennox's again and quickly flitted away.

"I got those things we talked about. There are three of them behind cabin five, if you want to check them out."

"Oh, cool." Kenzie smiled.

"What things?" Lennox asked and kept her eyes on Kenzie's smile.

"These cabana things. Kenz saw them online and thought they would be great for this week," Peyton explained. "They hang from the trees and are comfortable inside for, like, three or four people. They swing, too."

"Did you get the—" Kenzie began.

"I did," Peyton interrupted. "They're bug proof. And they had this canvas you can hang over them for privacy, so I just got that, too. It all came together."

"Awesome." Kenzie's smile grew. "Can I go—"

"Have fun!" Peyton waved her off.

Kenzie first went to her bag and pulled on it, while Lennox half-listened to Peyton talk and watched Kenzie drop it by the entrance to her cabin. She then headed in the direction of cabin five, which was by the lake they could just make out a little of through the trees, and she disappeared behind it.

"So, how's Jamie?" Peyton asked, and at the mention of her sister's name, Lennox returned her attention to her friend.

"She's good. She's getting used to it now and seems to really like it."

"That's great news. I know how much you worry about her."

"She's my kid sister. It comes with the territory. Will and I used to share the job, but now it falls on me."

"She'll be fine," Peyton encouraged. "You going to grab a s'more?"

"I think I'll pass now," Lennox answered. "I have a feeling we'll be eating a lot of those this week," she added.

"Dinner is in an hour in the large cabin." Peyton pointed in the direction of the cafeteria cabin, which was the largest by far and had both indoor and outdoor seating, enough for at least a hundred people. "We would have had it earlier, but Kenzie couldn't get here until now. She was in LA and had a meeting."

"She seems nice," Lennox shared and found herself looking at cabin five.

"She's great. She's a little shy at times, but she opens up once you get to know her. I was kind of hoping you'd actually spend some time with her this week. I have you two rooming together twice."

"But not tonight?"

"She knows April and Carlie. They've hung out at my place before, so I thought it would be an easier first couple of nights for her."

"She's that shy?" Lennox lifted an eyebrow.

"Not *that* shy. She just needs time to get to know people first, and there are a lot of people here she doesn't know yet."

"Like me," Lennox reminded. "And you want me to get to know her. Why?"

"Because I love you like a sister, and you're the best friend a girl could ask for, and I'd like you to help me make her comfortable here. It's the first time she's been to one of these things, and you know how crazy they can get."

"I do," Lennox recalled the last one they had spent in The Hamptons, at Peyton's beachfront property.

Back then, Peyton and Dani had disappeared to Peyton's room, where everyone just assumed they were having sex, and the rest of the attendees were still swimming in the water or playing on the beach around the illegal fire they'd built. Music was being played by the musicians, and some people were singing along. Others were doing shots and lighting fireworks in between. Lennox had been surprised that no one nearby had called the cops on them. By morning, half of them were passed out on the sand, and the rest were either on the deck in the patio furniture, or inside on the sofas. No one, save Dani and Peyton, had made it to one of the thirteen bedrooms the house supplied.

"She's still kind of new to this whole business, and she doesn't really socialize a lot with people she doesn't know, outside of the appearances she's contractually obligated to make."

"She's been doing this for, like, five years now," Lennox said.

"She has. How did you know that?" Peyton quirked an eyebrow this time.

"It's a small world. You know that," she explained. "It's not like I don't know who she is, Peyton."

"Fan of her old show?"

"Fan of her current show," Lennox offered back and looked to see Carlie trying to shove a marshmallow into April's mouth while many others looked on and laughed. "It's a big hit; kind of hard to miss it. And she's great in it."

"She is. I just didn't know you watched it."

"I caught it on a flight once and liked it, so I've watched the whole first season. And I'm interested in seeing where they'll go with it the next season. Happy?" She jested.

"Yes, I am." Peyton laughed. "How's Aaron, by the way?"

"Oh, about that..." Lennox returned her full attention to Peyton.

"No! Already, Len?" she exclaimed.

"Hey! I take offense to that." She pointed at Peyton. "It's not like we were dating that long. He's a nice guy. I just don't see it going beyond what it was."

"I thought you really liked him."

"I did. I do," Lennox replied. "I just don't want to date him anymore."

"Fine. Whatever you say. I just thought you two hit it off so well."

"We did," she offered. "Like I said, he was a nice guy, but I don't think he wanted it to go any further, either. He didn't exactly put up a fight when I ended it last week."

"He's not exactly someone that fights. He's kind of quiet, isn't he?"

"I guess I hope that, one day, I'll find someone that's willing to fight for me because they don't want what we have to end. He didn't seem to care. And he's in Brazil, filming, for the next four months. So, I shouldn't run into him awkwardly anywhere. The timing was right."

"Whatever you say. Listen, can you go find her?" Peyton nodded toward the cabin. "She'll stay out there by herself for hours, if we don't pull her back in."

"Oh, sure." Lennox watched Peyton smile gratefully and then walk off to join her girlfriend and her other friends.

Lennox grabbed her duffel bag off the ground and carried it in the direction of her cabin. She dropped it by the door and headed toward cabin one. When she arrived, she lifted Kenzie's bag up the stairs and carried it inside, placing it beside one of the twin beds before leaving and walking around to the back of the cabins where she saw three large circular objects hanging from three different trees by their sturdy branches. She could see inside the one closest to her, and it was open inside, with a cushion on the bottom and four square pillows on top of that. It was screened all around and had an entrance that could be pulled apart or pieced back together with Velcro. She glanced up and noticed there was a rolled canvas that could be unfurled to cover the screens if the occupant or occupants wanted privacy. She moved around the first one and toward the second one, about twenty feet away, and found Kenzie lying back inside of it, facing the lake, with her headphones in her ears. Kenzie had her eyes closed and hadn't realized she was being watched. She seemed peaceful and had a small smile on her face. Lennox just stared.

CHAPTER 3

KENZIE needed a moment to herself. And, thankfully, Peyton had provided one. The moment she'd seen the swinging cabana, she had climbed inside, took a moment to stare out at the calm lake, and put in her headphones. Her eyes closed almost instantly, and she relaxed into the breeze and the music.

"Hey."

Kenzie's eyes shot open as she took in Lennox Owen standing at the entrance of the cabana.

"Sorry, I didn't know you were there." She pulled out her headphones and turned off her music.

"It's okay. I kind of snuck up on you. Peyton wanted me to bring you back over when you're ready."

Kenzie looked at the water and then back at Lennox, but not into her eyes. She looked just beyond her earlobe.

"Oh, okay. I guess I have been out here for too long." She went to move.

"Hey, I said when you're ready. Take your time," Lennox offered back. "Stay out here all night, for all I care. I'm just obeying the master of ceremonies over there."

"Oh." Kenzie looked at the ground and then back out at the water.

"You okay?" Lennox leaned into the opening of the cabana a little.

"Yeah, I'm good. I'm just not always great with people."

"Why's that?"

"Born this way, I guess," Kenzie replied, not wanting to give the real reason.

"Okay. I guess I'll take that." Lennox laughed a little. "Mind if I join you?" she asked. "I could get my own, technically, but then, I'd have to yell at you through it." She smiled at Kenzie.

"Sure. Sorry, I should have asked." Kenzie slid over to the side, making space for Lennox to climb in.

Before she did, though, Kenzie watched Lennox give the thing a push, causing it to swing back and forth toward the water, and then, she climbed inside.

"Is that okay? I wanted to experience that."

"It's fine. I didn't do that when I got here."

"So, we're both swinging cabana virgins then?" she teased.

"Not anymore," Kenzie replied and watched as Lennox smiled back at her, causing Kenzie to finally release a nervous smile of her own.

"It's nice out here." Lennox sank into the pillows next to Kenzie, and Kenzie tried to slide a little farther away.

There was enough space in the cabana for them to sit next to each other, legs outstretched in the direction of the water, and still have a foot between them, which Kenzie needed because she couldn't be this close to Lennox Owen and not embarrass herself.

"It is."

"And, I understand, you grew up here, right?" Lennox turned just her head to Kenzie.

"Not here. Nearby."

"How nearby?"

"Two hours."

"And you liked it?"

"Yes."

"I'm back to one-word responses. We were doing so well there." Lennox laughed and turned back to the lake.

"What?" Kenzie looked over at her.

"When we met earlier, you spoke in complete sentences. And, just a second ago, I had you up to three whole words. Now, you're down to one-word answers. I'm going backward. Care to tell me why?" Lennox seemed to genuinely want to know the answer to her question.

"Don't take offense. I'm like this with most people."

"Because you were born this way, right?" Lennox questioned.

"Yes."

"Can I ask you a question?"

"Sure."

"I don't want you to take this the wrong way, okay?" Lennox turned completely toward her and moved her legs under her body.

"Oh, okay." Kenzie gulped, worried now at what Lennox might say or ask.

"I've seen a few interviews you've done for your show. I'm kind of a fan," she admitted. "I've seen all thirteen episodes and can't wait for the premiere of season two. But, I've watched some of the behind-the-scenes stuff, and now, I've met you in person, so... I'm wondering something."

"You're a fan of the show?" Kenzie asked in wonder.

"I am," Lennox said. "And of you, too. You make that show, Kenzie," she added.

"Thank you." Kenzie's coy smile couldn't be hidden.

"I have a younger sister. She's twenty. And I've pretty much raised her since she was fourteen."

"I didn't know that." Kenzie hadn't known that, and she'd been pretty sure she'd known everything about Lennox Owen.

"I don't talk about it in the press. Part of the reason is because Jamie is autistic," she revealed. "Well, she has Asperger's. She's in the army now and is thriving there. She's a whiz with numbers and plans to work in engineering there."

"Oh." Kenzie turned to the lake again.

"And, I've offended you." Lennox moved to sit back the way she was only a moment earlier, with her legs stretched out. "I'm sorry. I just thought maybe–"

"I am," Kenzie admitted. "I mean, I'm the same," she said it before she could stop herself. "Borderline, technically. I scored thirty on the official test three times. Twenty-six to thirty-one gives a borderline indication of an autism spectrum disorder. It is also possible to have Asperger's or mild autism within this range. Thirty-two to fifty indicates a strong likelihood of Asperger's syndrome or autism," Kenzie recited the text she had read a thousand times on the assessments she had taken.

She had been tested when she was six years old, again at ten, and again at fifteen, and she'd always scored thirty. She had also taken online assessments about a hundred times. That was probably part of the spectrum disorder. She liked repetition and often found herself taking the assessments over and over because of that, but her score had never wavered out of that borderline range. She had scored twenty-nine a few times and thirty-one a few times, but thirty was where she'd ended up most consistently.

"Sorry, I shouldn't have said anything. I didn't mean to make you feel uncomfortable," Lennox commented.

"That's the thing – I'm pretty much always uncomfortable. Well, around new people, at least. Once I get to know them, though, I'm usually okay." Kenzie lowered her phone, at the same time, wrapping her headphones around it.

"Jamie got the affinity for numbers thing," Lennox added. "She can remember almost any number, where she saw it, and figure out patterns. What did you get along with the discomfort? If you don't mind me asking, that is."

"Nothing, really. I don't have the numbers thing. I like routine when I can get it."

"I bet that's hard in our line of work."

"It's part of the reason I do it," Kenzie told Lennox and wondered why she was telling a stranger and her long-time crush something she'd never told anyone before; and that included Kat and even Annabelle back then.

"What do you mean?"

"Do you know how I got the part on my first show?" Kenzie turned to Lennox but still didn't dare to look directly into her eyes.

"No."

"It was a dare." Kenzie smiled at the memory.

"What?" Lennox laughed.

"My friend's dad was a producer. One night in college, my friends and I were playing truth or dare," Kenzie began. "She dared me to audition, and I had no choice."

"You were dared to audition, and you ended up with the part?"

"I did."

"Wow! How have I never heard that story before?"

"I've never told it," Kenzie revealed. "No one outside of that group of friends knows."

"And, does anyone here know abou–"

"No," Kenzie interrupted her. "I've never told anyone about the Asperger's," she explained. "My parents know, and that's it. Well, and now, you."

"I'm sorry. I shouldn't have said anything. I just recognized…"

"It's okay. Just please don't say anything to anyone else."

"Of course not." Lennox sat up at that. "I'd never do that."

"Thank you."

Lennox turned then, to stare out at the water, and Kenzie took a moment to enjoy her features. She had seen them from almost every angle in pictures, but this was the first time she had seen them up close, and they were remarkable. Her face was symmetrical, which was the definition of beauty. Her nose was the perfect size for her face; her eyes were just the right distance apart; and her forehead was the perfect size as well. And, as Lennox glanced at the water thoughtfully, there were small wrinkles there that Kenzie thought only made her more beautiful. Lennox's eyes were that amazing blue, and wide open, as if to take in the entirety of the world. And her lips were kissable. They were full, and just on this side of pouty most of the time. They were natural right now, as was the rest of her face; devoid entirely of the makeup people in their industry were often forced to wear. Kenzie felt a pull toward that clean face she had to resist, because Lennox Owen was notoriously straight. But she was Lennox Owen, and she was perfect.

"I have an idea," Lennox said after a moment, and Kenzie pulled her eyes away.

"Yeah?"

"You should sleep out here tonight." The woman turned to face her.

"Out here?" Kenzie looked around.

"In this thing," Lennox added. "It's cool, and it's going to be a warm night tonight. You can pull down the canvas and have your own little space."

"Peyton wouldn't like that."

"Peyton doesn't have to know." Lennox lifted an eyebrow. "Come out here after your new roommates go to sleep, and go back in the morning. I can promise those two won't be up early."

Kenzie looked around for a moment, considering Lennox's idea.

"I don't think I can. It's important to Peyton that we get to know each other. And I'm not sure I could sleep out here on my own, anyway."

"But, you'd like to?" Lennox posited.

"I grew up around crickets, and it's nice to hear them again," Kenzie shared. "We don't exactly have them in LA."

"That's true."

"It would be nice, but I think I'll stay in the cabin," she stated.

"Okay. Sure." Lennox slid out of the cabana and stood in front of it. "I'm going to head back now. Dinner's going to be ready soon, and I know Peyton will want you there for that. But, stay out here as long as you need, okay?"

"Okay," Kenzie agreed and watched as Lennox smiled, turned, and walked off, but not before giving the cabana one more push so Kenzie could swing through the trees as she stared out at the lake.

CHAPTER 4

LENNOX made her way to the outdoor table with her plate of camp-inspired but five-star chef-prepared food. It was an interesting combination, to say the least, but it looked delicious. So, as she sat down between April and Bobby, she dove in. She'd flown in from New York that morning and had only eaten snacks so far. She was starving. She had water and a beer because everyone else had a beer, too. She watched as Kenzie made her way outside to join the rest of them, and there was something about the way she moved through the crowd of women, angling to grab drinks or food and silverware. She was graceful, somehow. Every step she took, every move she made with her hands to pick something up or place it down was efficient and deliberate. Lennox loved watching her. She had been watching her since the woman arrived and parked her car.

Lennox had been on the phone with Jamie and watched the security team set up on the other side of the parking lot when she heard a car pull up. She'd turned just in time to see the driver remain inside for a long moment, exit the vehicle, and then, stand almost completely still for another long moment. Once Peyton and Dani had noticed her, she relaxed a little and then moved smoothly back to her trunk, reached inside, and lifted her large bag out; all in one clean motion. It was strangely beautiful to Lennox. She'd wrapped up her call with her sister and approached, wanting to meet this woman. And now, here she sat, with Kenzie on the other side of the table and off to the end.

"What's on tap for tonight?" Mandy asked the group.

"Nothing tonight," Peyton revealed. "I thought you'd all just want to get settled. We can hang around the fire. And then, tomorrow, we'll have some fun."

Lennox watched Kenzie. She couldn't stop watching the woman. She ate the food on her own plate, but she didn't taste it. She watched as Kenzie delicately lifted her fork to her lips, and then placed it back down, lifting asparagus up and then back to her mouth again and again. Lennox wasn't sure she heard any part of the conversations going on around her. And when she had finished her food, she hadn't even noticed and took a stab with her fork to food that wasn't there.

"You all right there, Len?" Peyton asked her from her own position directly across from Lennox.

Kenzie seemed to hear that and turned to notice Lennox staring at her. Lennox turned quickly to Peyton.

"I'm good, yeah," she lied.

***

The next few hours went by slowly for Lennox. She enjoyed being with her friends and catching up with all of them. She didn't enjoy having to tell them that she'd ended her most recent relationship, though, and listening to them tell her how great Aaron was and that she should give it another chance. She didn't notice when Kenzie left the group initially, but she did notice there was a shift in her own mood around eleven. She resonated with something. Was it longing or loneliness, she wasn't exactly sure, but it had her looking around the fire at the women who had grouped off. Some were playing cards, with a lantern next to them supplying light. Others were sitting by the fire with guitars, playing softly and talking. Lennox had been sitting next to Dani for the past half-hour, talking about how her friend's brother had gotten a new job in Seattle. Lennox didn't see Kenzie, though, and that made her sad.

By midnight, Lennox was more than ready for bed, as were most of the women gathered. Many had already made their way to their cabins, including Kenzie's roommates, around eleven-thirty. Lennox went to her own cabin, grabbed her things, and headed to the bathroom. After wrapping up, she returned to her cabin, chatted with her cabin mates for a few minutes, changed into her sweats and a T-shirt, and slid into the sleeping bag on top of the bare twin bed. A few minutes later, she heard the sound of sleeping girls and lifted herself up. She checked by the light from the outside tall lanterns, streaming in lightly through the window, that they were indeed asleep. She made her way stealthily out of the cabin and headed toward cabin one, where she considered not doing what she was about to do for a moment. Then, Lennox sighed and opened the door to the cabin. It gave an unhelpful squeal as she did.

"Len?"

"Go back to sleep, April," Lennox whispered after April, the closest to the door, woke with a start.

"What are you—"

"Sleep." Lennox pointed at her and gave her a wink.

April did as she was told. She'd had a few drinks that night, so Lennox was fairly certain the woman fell right back to sleep. Lennox looked at the other beds and found Kenzie was the closest to the back of the cabin. She approached and sat on the empty bed to her right. She watched Kenzie for only a moment before snapping herself out of it. She undoubtedly looked like a creepy stalker.

"Lennox?" Kenzie stirred and looked up at her.

"Hey," she whispered.

"What are you doing here?"

"Let's go," Lennox encouraged and lifted back at the sleeping bag Kenzie had up to her chin.

"What? Go where?"

"Trust me." Lennox smiled at her and silently hoped that Kenzie did trust her.

It took a moment, but Kenzie slid the sleeping bag down a little farther, climbed out of it, and stood. Lennox stood up with her and grabbed at the sleeping bag and Kenzie's phone. She walked toward the door, with Kenzie in tow, after the woman had put on her shoes, and they left the cabin.

"Where are we going?" Kenzie whispered into the night.

"To the cabanas."

"Oh, no, I told you…" Kenzie stopped walking. "I can't sleep out there."

"You said you couldn't sleep out there alone. I'm coming with you, so it's fine," Lennox offered back and watched Kenzie consider it. "I'll protect you, Mackenzie Smyth," she added.

Kenzie bit her lower lip and then let it go. Lennox watched it, and found herself swallowing and hoping she hid it well with a smile.

"Okay," Kenzie replied simply, and they walked on.

They made their way behind cabin five and toward the cabanas. When they arrived, Lennox placed Kenzie's sleeping bag next to her own, which was already in place.

"I can sleep in another one," she told Kenzie when she noticed the woman's wide eyes at Lennox's sleeping bag next to her own.

"What? No, it's okay," Kenzie somewhat stammered. "I didn't expect it. I didn't expect this, I mean."

"Climb in." Lennox motioned for Kenzie to climb in.

Kenzie did and settled to the right, where her sleeping bag was laid out. She climbed inside a little but appeared to be uncomfortable. Lennox smiled at her and reached for the strings that held the canvas. She pulled down on one after the other and then slid inside next to Kenzie. She had brought one of the small battery-operated lanterns, and it was on the low setting to allow them some light. She slid into her own sleeping bag and then handed Kenzie her phone.

"Thanks?"

"Set your alarm, if you're worried about Peyton. No one will be up before eight."

"Oh, right." Kenzie set the alarm on her phone and placed it to her right while sliding down a little into the sleeping bag. "You didn't have to do this."

"I wanted to. Honestly, I think these things are pretty cool. And if we're going to camp, we might as well sleep outdoors, right?"

"Not on the ground, though?" Kenzie turned to face her, but Lennox noticed – and not for the first time today – that Kenzie wasn't meeting her eye.

"I draw the line at sleeping on the ground." Lennox smiled back. "You have this thing about you, you know?" she said after a moment.

"I do?" Kenzie asked.

"Yeah, you move differently than most people." Lennox turned on her side to face Kenzie completely.

"Oh."

"I keep putting you off, don't I? I swear, I'm normally a polite person. I don't mean to say these things."

Kenzie laughed and rolled over on her back. It made the cabana swing slightly, and Lennox started to wonder if sleeping out here was a good idea. If every movement caused the thing to swing, she would likely be awake all night.

"It's okay. You're observant."

"That, I am."

"That's what I got," Kenzie stated.

"Huh?" Lennox questioned.

"I move efficiently," she revealed. "I didn't get the numbers thing or the genius thing. I just move efficiently; sometimes, quickly. Quicker than most, actually. It's a nervous system thing."

"Oh, wow. How does that work?"

"The nervous system?" Kenzie turned her face to Lennox, and Lennox took in the lantern light in those green eyes.

"No, I mean how does that work for you?" Lennox smiled.

"Oh, I don't know. The doctors just told me it responds faster in me than in most people. So, I have quick reflexes. I never really knew what to do with it until I got to high school."

"What happened then?"

"I joined the track team."

"You run?"

"I used to. I haven't in a long time, but I ran in high school and got a college scholarship."

"I didn't know that," Lennox revealed.

"Why would you?" Kenzie asked curiously.

"So, what distance did you run?" Lennox changed the subject from the fact that she knew more about Kenzie than she had let on.

"I was a sprinter for a while. But, in college, I switched to long distances."

"Why?"

"We had one of the top sprinters in the nation on the team, and I decided to try something else when I realized I'd never be able to beat her. I tried the eight hundred and liked that, so I decided to stick to distances."

"And your nervous system helped with that?"

"That and training, yeah. I didn't know how else to use it. I couldn't dance. I tried ballet, but I didn't have the discipline. I had the grace, though, according to my first and only teacher. I switched to contemporary when I failed at ballet, but I just didn't like it. I tried playing an instrument, but got bored with guitar and piano. Running was the only thing I actually enjoyed."

"Why don't you run anymore then?"

"Because I don't have the time," Kenzie shared. "I

guess that's an excuse. It's not the same when it's not outdoors, though. I'm not a fan of treadmills, and running outside is problematic."

"You get recognized."

"Yeah."

"I can understand that."

"I thought a beach house would be a good idea. I wanted to live close to the water, so I bought something in Venice a couple of years ago. I love it, but that turned out to be a mistake, because it's tourist central most of the time, and if I want to go for a run, I have to get in my car and drive to a private place. I don't bother."

"You're in private here," Lennox proposed. "You should run while you can."

Kenzie smiled at her and looked out toward the lake that they could still see through the screen Lennox hadn't covered with the canvas.

"I don't know. Peyton seems to have the whole week planned, and I don't want to break any of her rules."

Lennox sat up, reached through the Velcro that was still slightly open, pulled down the final string, and let the canvas shield them the rest of the way before making sure the Velcro was tightly together. She laid back down next to Kenzie.

"You're already breaking one. Why not another?" she suggested.

CHAPTER 5

LENNOX Owen was sleeping next to her. Kenzie couldn't believe it. She was lying in a cabana behind the cabins and in front of the expansive lake, listening to the familiar sounds of her childhood alongside the sounds of Lennox's breathing. Kenzie was on her side, facing away from Lennox, because she couldn't fall asleep facing her. She worried that maybe she'd drool in her sleep or sleep with her mouth wide open, and Lennox would catch her. That would be way too embarrassing. She had rolled onto her other side, and, after only a few minutes, the cabana grew hot, thanks to the closed canvas giving them privacy but not a lot of fresh air, and probably, also the heat coming from their bodies, which weren't pressed together but were only about six inches apart. She pulled down at the sleeping bag so that it rested at her hips instead and enjoyed the cool sensation as a result.

Kenzie wondered if she'd ever fall asleep. She pulled her phone from its position next to her and held it so the light wouldn't wake Lennox, to check the time. It was four in the morning. They had talked until at least two. Outside of Peyton and Dani, Lennox was the only person she'd spoken to for that long in a very long time.

On set, Kenzie was often viewed as someone that didn't like to socialize with the other actors and the crew. And while that was partially true, and she couldn't help that part of her brain, she also wished more than anything that she could just grab a plate at lunchtime, sit down next to the rest of the cast, and strike up a casual conversation.

Growing up in the south and in the middle of nowhere, at that, didn't exactly help her socialize properly. And her parents – though understanding – were also somewhat impatient with her inability to make friends easily. Her mother left her father when Kenzie was nine years old. Kenzie had stayed with her dad for the school year and spent the summer with her mom an hour away. It was a strange custody arrangement, and that was especially true in the south, where mothers tended to get full custody. But her mother hadn't fought for her, while her father had. During her sophomore year in high school, she stopped going away for the summer. Track took over her life at that point, and Kenzie couldn't go back and forth. Her mother didn't seem to mind. By then, she had a new husband and his three kids, and that seemed to be enough for her.

Kenzie's dad did his best, but he was a mechanic and owned his own auto body shop. He spent most of his time at work, once Kenzie was old enough to take care of herself. In fact, she had often wondered at her father's personality. He seemed just as awkward as Kenzie felt most of the time and buried himself in his work. He loved cars and had a collection of models he built himself, along with books about classic cars. He specialized in their restoration and seemed to get the enjoyment in how the parts fit together to make the vehicles run. Kenzie had never asked him if he might also be on the spectrum growing up and hadn't gotten the chance later, either, because he had died before her twenty-fourth birthday.

Now, though, Kenzie was lying next to Lennox and closing her eyes to try to force her brain to calm itself enough to find sleep. She had a long six days ahead of her, and staying up all night wasn't the best way to start things off. She just needed to not think about Lennox next to her, and she would be able to get some sleep. She exhaled and inhaled deeply and thought back to her last race in school.

"You okay?" Lennox's groggy voice snapped her out of the recollection, and she felt a hand on her back through her sleeping bag.

Kenzie didn't know what to say, so she didn't say anything. She just remained still and pretended to be asleep.

The hand moved away, and she figured she'd pulled off the lie. But then, the hand moved back; and it didn't merely move back – it snaked around her waist, and Lennox was moving into her. She was spooning Kenzie from behind.

'Holy shit,' she thought. Lennox Owen was spooning her. The hand rested on Kenzie's stomach, and Lennox's breath could be felt on her neck.

"I know you're awake," Lennox whispered. "Can you not sleep?"

"I'm okay," Kenzie replied with a shaky voice.

"I've got you," Lennox said after a moment. "Is this okay?" She pressed the palm of her hand slightly into Kenzie's stomach.

"Oh. Sure," Kenzie both told the truth and lied.

Truthfully, it was more than okay. It had been a long time since Kenzie had been spooned like this by a woman. It had been a long time since she'd done anything with a woman. So, this touch was miraculous in more ways than one. It was also a lie because it wasn't okay that Lennox Owen, Hollywood's golden girl and heterosexual beauty, was touching her like this when nothing would come of it.

"Maybe we should go back to the cabins." Lennox pulled back slightly.

Kenzie turned over at that to face her, and Lennox's hand ended up on her back.

"No, it's okay. I'm just not great at sleeping in new places. It wouldn't matter if I was in the cabin or not," she lied. She had no problem sleeping in new places and had been asleep earlier, when Lennox had woken her for their little adventure. "I'm sorry I woke you up."

Lennox smiled at her and closed her eyes again, but her hand remained on Kenzie's back.

"Can you get to sleep like this?" she asked after a moment, with her eyes still closed.

"I think so." Kenzie wasn't sure if she'd be able to sleep with Lennox's lips only inches from her own, but she'd try. "You can go back to sleep. I'm fine now."

"Okay," Lennox agreed with a small, sleepy voice.

Kenzie smiled at it and bit her lower lip, which was a nervous tick she'd had since she was young. Annabelle and her last real girlfriend, Kelly, had both thought it juvenile and commented as much. As Kenzie watched Lennox fall back to sleep, she thought about Annabelle. Kenzie hadn't kept in touch with her, but they had become friends on social media. Annabelle had done well at work. She was working in the Capitol building and had a fiancée she was about to marry. Kelly was a different story. They'd dated during the filming of Kenzie's first show. Kelly had been an Assistant Director and about ten years older than Kenzie's twenty-two. It had been mild flirtations at first, and then, there was a kiss; the kiss led to a date, and that date led to more. They had dated for the entire season of the show before Kenzie had ended it. Kelly wanted more than Kenzie could offer at twenty-two; the woman was ready for a life with someone. She wanted them to move in together and tell everyone on the show they were a couple. They had dated in secret, and Kenzie had always been honest with Kelly: she wasn't someone who dated around; she had no problem with being with only one woman. But Kenzie was young. And when Kelly started pressuring her to come out in public – which Kenzie was not ready for, Kenzie thought it best to end their relationship. Kelly had worked on the show until it ended, and things had been amicable at best between them.

Kelly had been her last official girlfriend. She'd dated, but rarely since then because she still wasn't out. There was a vetting process for her before she could go on a date with a woman. Kenzie had to trust them as a friend first and know that they wouldn't out her if things ended badly. In the past three years, she'd probably been on ten total dates with four different women, and the last had been over four months ago.

She had Lennox Owen's lips in front of her, and her hand on her lower back, holding her close. Kenzie gulped and let out a small breath at the continued realization. She watched as Lennox opened her eyes, and she bit her lower lip again when she saw their deep blue emerge from beneath eyelids.

"It's cute when you do that," Lennox muttered.

"What?" Kenzie wasn't sure she'd heard her properly.

"That lip thing. It's cute," Lennox added and seemed to move an inch closer, but that couldn't be right. "You bite it."

"Oh, yeah." Kenzie realized. "It's juvenile; I've been told."

"Who told you that?" Lennox seemed to wake completely.

"Oh, just people I've..." Kenzie paused. "No one," she lied again.

Lennox's hand on her back moved up and down and didn't stop.

"Well, whoever told you that was wrong. It's not juvenile. It's kind of adorable," she paused. "Captivating really," she added.

Kenzie wasn't sure what was happening. Lennox was staring at her eyes, and then her lips, and then her eyes. Her hand was still moving up and down on her back, and Lennox Owen appeared to be nervous. She was making *the* Lennox Owen nervous. How had she managed that?

"I..." Kenzie stopped herself when Lennox's hand stopped moving.

"You're magnetic, Kenzie," Lennox said as she stared into Kenzie's eyes.

"No, I'm just me," Kenzie said back and bit her lip again.

"That's–" Lennox stopped herself this time. "We should get some sleep," she said after a moment and rolled over onto her back, removing her hand from Kenzie's body. "I'm going to go to the bathroom, though. I'll be right back." Lennox sat up quickly and seemed to shake her head before opening the screen and pushing the canvas aside.

She climbed out of the cabana, which caused it to swing a little, and then, she disappeared into the night. Kenzie sat up and touched her lips with her fingers. She didn't know why, but it felt like Lennox had touched them. She hadn't, of course. Lennox's hand had only been on her back. They hadn't touched in any other way. But it felt to Kenzie as if she'd just had the best kiss of her life without having actually kissed anyone.

"What the hell just happened?" she whispered before flopping backward, causing the cabana to swing more.

She closed her eyes and felt like several minutes had passed. She wondered if maybe Lennox had decided to sleep in her cabin or, perhaps, one of the other two cabanas, and decided to check the time on her phone to see how long she'd been gone. Just as she was about to pull it out, she heard footsteps and rolled onto her side, facing away from where Lennox would be. She heard the screen being pulled open and then felt the body move beside her. She heard a deep sigh and faked slumber until she recognized the even breathing and gave up on falling asleep herself.

***

Kenzie woke to her alarm and found herself alone in the cabana. Lennox, the sleeping bag, and the lantern she'd brought for them were all gone. Kenzie must have fallen asleep around six, or maybe it was seven. Either way, she hadn't gotten enough. And she would regret that later, she thought to herself as she slid out of her sleeping bag, gathered it along with her phone, and climbed out of the cabana to find Lennox sitting at the edge of the lake, with her sleeping bag rolled up beside her.

"Hey," Kenzie greeted, feeling like she couldn't just walk away without saying something.

"Hi." Lennox turned around. "I woke up a little while ago and was kind of restless. I didn't want to wake you, so I got my stuff and came out here."

Kenzie moved toward her and sat down in the small patch of grass that led to the rocky bit of beach before the water.

"I feel like I got no sleep at all." Kenzie chanced after a moment of watching Lennox staring out at the water that was again calm, save the movements of the birds diving for their breakfast.

"Sorry, that's probably my fault. I should have just let you sleep in the cabin." Lennox still wasn't looking at her, and Kenzie found herself wondering how they'd managed to switch places. Just yesterday, she'd been unable to meet Lennox's eyes. And now, it appeared Lennox wouldn't or couldn't meet her own. "I think breakfast is at nine. We should probably make a run for the bathroom before everyone else wakes up and storms in."

"Right. Good idea," Kenzie said, recognizing the deflection as something she often did when she was uncomfortable.

She stood and grabbed her sleeping bag. She then watched another moment as Lennox just stared before she, too, stood, and they walked in silence toward their cabins, separating when necessary, and then both ending up in the bathroom at the same time. They managed to brush their teeth and shower in silence as well. Then, thankfully, Dani and Peyton joined them to make things less awkward. After that, they separated again to go to their cabins to ready themselves for the day.

CHAPTER 6

WHAT the hell had happened last night? Lennox ate her breakfast, which was French toast – and it shouldn't have been French toast because they were camping; but leave it to Peyton to have good food. She sat next to Jack and at the end of the table so that she could have more time for her thoughts. She had to gather them. She had to think about why gravity appeared to be pulling her or maybe pushing her in the direction of Kenzie Smyth.

Kenzie sat at another table, next to Peyton and Mandy, with Dani and Bobby on the other side. She appeared not to be participating in whatever conversation was going on between the other three, but instead, was again moving her hands gracefully from the strips of bacon to her toast with what looked to be jelly. She moved quickly and efficiently, and though she'd explained why to her, Lennox preferred to believe it wasn't a function of the woman's nervous system but just a part of the whole that was Kenzie.

"Everyone, let the games begin." Peyton stood on the picnic table after the group had finished their breakfast.

"Games? Really, Peyton?" Jenna questioned as she sipped on her coffee.

"Not games, exactly," Peyton corrected. "Look, I know and love all of you. And some of you aren't exactly the most athletic and would prefer to lay out all week."

"Yes," Lynn agreed and then looked around at everyone who was staring at her. "What? I know who I am."

"Everything's optional, obviously," Peyton continued. "We have boats, archery is set up on the field over there, and I brought enough gloves, bats, and balls to play softball, if anyone is interested in that. You can hike around the lake or through the woods. I have maps of the trails for anyone interested. And we have just about every card and board game known to man inside here." She motioned to the cafeteria cabin behind her. "Lunch is at one, and dinner is at seven every night. Snacks are inside whenever you want. And if you're going on a hike or swim alone – don't." Peyton smiled and earned a laugh. "No, seriously, don't. It's dangerous. And the point of this week is to hang out with everyone, so take a buddy."

"What are you doing first?" Jack asked Lennox once the group disbanded.

"I don't know yet." She glanced over at Kenzie's seat, which was no longer occupied, and looked around to see that she was heading toward cabin five. "You?"

"I'm thinking about taking a boat out. They fit four. You in?" Jack stood up.

"Maybe later."

"Okay. I'll grab Jenna and Bobby then. Maybe Davica will want to go." The woman waved Lennox off and went to round up a boat party.

"Hey, where's Kenzie?" Peyton asked as she sat in front of Lennox.

"I don't know. Why?"

"Just checking on her. She isn't exactly being social. And I had hoped she'd get to know everyone."

"It's been a day, Peyton. Really, less than a day. The girl just got here. And she's surrounded by a bunch of people she doesn't know. Give her a chance to get used to it."

Peyton lifted an eyebrow at her.

"Well, okay, then. I guess I will. When did you get so protective of Kenz, there, Len?"

"I'm not."

"Yes, you are." Peyton laughed lightly and nodded at Dani, who motioned for Peyton to join her in the cafeteria cabin. "It's nice. I'm glad someone else is watching out for her. She can be completely invisible sometimes. I don't know how she does it."

"Invisible?" Lennox queried.

"Yeah, she's a freaking star, and she's gorgeous, but she has this way of disappearing into the crowd no matter how big when she wants."

"Really?"

"You haven't noticed?" Peyton stood. "She just sits there, and if you're not careful, you can forget she's there." She turned to smile at Dani, who was holding the door open for her. "By the way, I have a secret," she said and looked back down at Lennox.

"You do?"

"Yeah, I'll tell you later, though. Dani's watching."

"Why can't–"

"It's about her, dumbass." She winked at Lennox and headed off toward Dani.

Lennox was left wondering about Kenzie's apparent ability to be invisible. She hadn't noticed it at all, and she wasn't sure how it was even possible for that woman to be invisible. Lennox couldn't stop looking at her when she was anywhere nearby, or wondering where Kenzie had gone when she couldn't feel her there. She'd known her less than twenty-four hours, but she could safely say that Kenzie could never be invisible to her.

Lennox meandered around the different groups of her friends for the next few hours. She spent time with Peyton and Dani, who played Monopoly, and then, were joined by Carlie and Lynn, and the five of them played Scrabble, with Lennox partnering with Dani, and Carlie and Lynn being on the other side. Peyton insisted she needed no help and promptly lost to Dani and Lennox, which made everyone, save Peyton, laugh. Then, Lennox made her way outside to the picnic tables, where April, Cleo, Jenna, Tiana, and Jack were all lying out. They'd placed their towels on top of a picnic table each and talked while they absorbed the sun's harmful rays. Lennox sat with Quinn and Maddox at the free table and chatted for a while with the whole group before lunchtime.

It was ten after one when Lennox finally gave up on Kenzie joining them for lunch and decided to chance the awkwardness that had grown between them and go find her. Peyton nodded and gave her a wink when she figured out what Lennox was doing without words. Lennox just smiled back, rolling her eyes as she grabbed a second plate and a bottle of water, along with her own half-eaten plate and water she had shoved under her arm, and headed in the direction of where she had guessed she would find Kenzie. When she approached, she found Bobby and Mandy playing with squirt guns, aiming them out at the lake to see who could make their stream of water go the farthest.

"Hey, it's lunchtime," she informed them.

"Oh, shit." Bobby dropped the squirt gun, and Mandy followed suit. "Peyton's gonna be pissed," she added.

"She does love her schedules." Mandy set her gun on the ground next to Bobby's. "Coming?" she asked Lennox as they approached her.

"Did you bring us lunch?" Bobby asked when she noticed the plates in her hand.

"Uh, no. This is not for you. Your food is at the cabin." Lennox nodded back. "And I'll be there in a few."

"Okay." Mandy pulled on Bobby's shirt. "Let's go. I'm hungry."

Lennox waited for the two women to make their way past her, and then, headed toward the cabana covered in canvas. She couldn't exactly pull the screen apart with her hands full.

"Knock, knock." She greeted and hoped Kenzie would open it for her. "Kenzie?" It took a moment, but the cabana swung a little, two hands pulled apart the screen from just beyond the canvas covering it, and she saw Kenzie's face. "Were you asleep?"

Kenzie's green eyes were only half-open, and she had a line down one side of her face, suggesting she'd been sleeping on that side.

"Sorry, yeah," the woman replied and wiped her face with her hand.

"I brought you lunch." Lennox lifted the plate on her right.

"You didn't have to do that." Kenzie held open the screen.

"I figured you'd prefer to eat out here. I didn't know you were sleeping, though."

"I didn't sleep well last night," Kenzie reminded.

"My fault," Lennox replied to that. "And I've come with a gift to make up for it." She lifted the plate again. "Or, you can come back to the tables and eat with us."

"I don't know that I'm up for that just yet." Kenzie took the plate Lennox held out for her and made her way out of the cabana. "I'll just eat by the water, if that's okay. Is Peyton mad?" She glanced in Lennox's direction.

"No, I told her to back off. So, she's okay." She handed Kenzie the water.

"You told her to back off?" Kenzie asked and made her way down to the grassy patch they'd sat in this morning.

"I suggested you might need some time to get used to everyone and that she shouldn't pressure you," Lennox admitted.

"Oh, thanks." Kenzie sat down before looking up at Lennox, who still held her own plate and water. "Are you staying?"

"I don't have to." Lennox shrugged.

"You don't have to leave, either," Kenzie pointed out.

Lennox noticed that Kenzie had given her a non-committal answer. She hadn't exactly said that she wanted her to stay, nor had she sent her away. Things were weird between them now, and Lennox didn't like that. She decided to sit down and try to talk her way through the strangeness. She also had to admit to herself that she wasn't quite ready to not be around Kenzie, either.

"So, how was your nap?" Lennox spoke into the silence after a moment.

"It was okay. I guess you didn't take one?"

"No, I played Monopoly and Scrabble."

"Did you win?" Kenzie asked.

"Lost at Monopoly, but Dani and I won at Scrabble. And we beat Peyton, which is the best part. That girl is crazy competitive."

"You've known her for a long time, huh?" Kenzie took a bite of her sandwich and looked onward.

"Forever, it feels like," Lennox revealed. "We met when we were both teenagers. She's been with me through almost everything. And I guess it's the same for her with me."

"She's great." Kenzie smiled.

"She's like a sister to me. And Dani is perfect for her. I'm so glad they found each other and had the guts to admit what they felt," Lennox commented.

"She told me about what it was like when they first met," Kenzie started. "She said she felt it right away but hadn't ever felt anything for another woman before, so she didn't recognize it at first."

"Plus, Dani had a boyfriend," Lennox remarked. "Didn't take long for her to end that."

"It's amazing what they found." Kenzie shared, and Lennox looked over at her.

Kenzie's hair was down and wavy. The breeze from the water blew it into her face, and Lennox couldn't help herself. She took her hand and gently moved it out of Kenzie's face behind her ear.

"It is," Lennox agreed. "Do you have anyone like that?" she asked and looked away immediately.

"A girlfriend?" Kenzie's voice was high-pitched and louder than it had been only moments before.

"Oh, no. I didn't mean girlfriend. I meant boyfriend

or just someone," she rambled. "I just meant anyone. Are you dating someone, or – I don't know – with someone?" She internally smacked herself.

"No, I don't. I'm not dating anyone. I haven't for a while." Kenzie turned back out to the lake.

"Why not?"

Kenzie guffawed at that question and placed her plate on the ground in front of her.

"You've met me. Guess," she said and looked down.

"I have met you. That's why I'm asking," Lennox returned with a confused expression. "Kenz, have you seen you?" She chuckled.

Kenzie looked over at her, and their eyes met briefly before she turned away.

"Seeing is one thing. Try being with me," Kenzie said after a moment. "No one wants to be with the bumbling awkward girl, who has a hard time being around people. The last person I dated, well, I guess they wanted it to be more. But, whenever we fought, it was always because I wouldn't go somewhere or couldn't just make small talk with people at events. It caused a lot of problems."

"Probably just the wrong guy for you, then," Lennox stated and finished her sandwich.

"Yeah, something like that," Kenzie replied. "What about you? I heard from Peyton that you're dating Aaron Wilkes. I met him at a function once. He seemed nice."

"He is nice," Lennox concurred. "But we're not together anymore," she shared. "We weren't technically official, but we're not seeing each other."

"Oh, sorry. I didn't know."

"Nothing to be sorry about. It just didn't work out."

"Why not?" Kenzie asked and finally met her eye for more than a moment.

"Because he's not the one for me," Lennox said into those deep green orbs. "Your eyes are…" she faded and turned her attention to the water instead.

"Lennox, can I ask you something?" Kenzie pushed

the plate away and turned to face Lennox, moving her legs underneath her.

"Sure." Lennox gulped and remained facing the water.

"Did Peyton tell you about me or something?"

That was not the question Lennox had been prepared for. She had thought maybe Kenzie would ask about the comments she kept making about her eyes and her cute lip thing, and that she'd want to know if Lennox was attracted to her; and Lennox had never been attracted to another woman in her life. She had no clue what was happening or how to handle these kinds of situations.

"What?" She turned her face to Kenzie. "What about you?"

Kenzie did that lip thing, and it nearly broke Lennox. She wanted to kiss her. She wanted to lean in and kiss another woman.

"That I'm gay," Kenzie finally said.

Lennox's eyes went big, and her jaw dropped slightly. She couldn't stop it from happening, and she knew Kenzie noticed and was likely thinking it was for a completely different reason than the fact that Lennox's heart just skipped three beats, at least, at that revelation. Kenzie Smyth was gay, and Lennox was attracted to her.

"Hey, lovebirds!" Sarah yelled from her position next to the cabin. "You two planning on joining the rest of the group any time this week?" She laughed.

"It's time for those trust falls." Jack was standing next to Sarah and laughing alongside her.

"We'll be there in a minute," Lennox replied for the both of them.

"No, I'm good," Kenzie disagreed and stood.

She picked up her plate and the water and started in their direction. Lennox remained on the ground, wishing she could do that whole moment all over again.

CHAPTER 7

KENZIE had taken a chance and told Lennox about the biggest part of herself. Being gay wasn't all she was, but it was an important part. It was out there now, though, and Lennox's reaction told her everything she needed to know. She hadn't said anything. Her jaw had dropped, and her eyes had gotten big. That was enough to tell Kenzie she didn't need to stick around. She rejoined the other women around the picnic tables and decided to play cards with Carlie, April, and Lynn for a while, or until they got bored with her and left the table.

She hadn't noticed Lennox join the group next to her, the one that was planning the softball game that would be happening the next day, but she did notice Lennox and Peyton walking off together around four in the afternoon. Kenzie had fun playing cards and actually found herself joining in the conversations about work and travel. By five, they were done playing cards, and she had opted to go back to her cabin to change into some warmer clothes as the evening had begun to chill.

"Hey, I noticed you participating out there." Peyton entered as Kenzie was sliding on her sweatpants.

"Yeah." Kenzie nodded.

"Are you having fun?"

"Sure. It's different, but I'm having fun, yeah."

"Good. I was hoping you'd make some new friends out of this week." Peyton sat on the edge of Kenzie's bed.

"Did Lennox tell you to check on me or something?" Kenzie snapped at her friend and sat down on the bed across from her.

"What? No. Why?"

"I saw you two walking off together earlier."

"Oh, that wasn't about you." Peyton looked toward

the door of the cabin and then back to her. "I kind of needed her help with something."

"So, she didn't tell you that I came out to her?"

"What?" the woman exclaimed. "No, she didn't say anything about that. You came out to her?"

"It was kind of on accident."

"How do you accidentally–" Peyton stopped herself. "Pronoun slip?" she guessed.

"No, I was careful there. I said *they*. I just asked her if you'd told her."

"Why? You know I'd never tell someone *that* about you, unless you told me it was okay."

"I know. She's just…" Kenzie wasn't sure how to express what she'd been feeling about Lennox's words and actions. "Never mind." She exhaled deeply. "It's just me, thinking there's something where there's not because I'm gay and haven't had a date in forever, and she's the nice straight girl I'm imagining is flirting with me."

"Lennox is flirting with you?" Peyton jumped up. "Lennox Owen? *That* Lennox?" She pointed outside.

"No, she's not. She's just being really nice, and I'm reading into things." Kenzie stood, too. "Let's just get back out there."

"No, hold on." Peyton put her hand on Kenzie's forearm to stop her.

"When I told her, she freaked out. So that's probably the end of her being nice to me, anyway."

"She did not." Peyton didn't believe her.

"Her jaw hit the ground, and her eyes got crazy big, Peyton. She freaked out."

"Because she didn't know *you* were gay, but not because she has a problem with it. Look at Dani and me. She loves us together. She helped me realize I couldn't live without that girl, and that it wasn't friendship. I wanted way more than friendship." Peyton seemed to go into herself there for a moment.

"Are you thinking about having sex with your girlfriend right now, Peyton?" she guessed.

"Sorry." Peyton shrugged. "I was just thinking about our first time together," she admitted and blushed. "It was like, 'Yeah, that's what I was missing.'"

"Girl parts?" Kenzie lifted an eyebrow at her and smiled.

"Not girl parts, specifically… But I do love her girl parts." Peyton laughed. "Her." Peyton shrugged again. "I was missing her. And she happened to have girl parts."

"Well, I only like the girl parts, and she only likes the boy parts. So, it's better for me if I just pretend she has a problem with it–"

"Because you have a crush on Lennox," Peyton finished for her.

"Yes. And you knew that before this week. So, why didn't you tell me she was coming?"

"Two reasons." Peyton held up two fingers. "One – I didn't know until the day before, when Lennox actually confirmed she could come. And two – because I knew that if you knew she would be here, you would've dropped out. You got so nervous when I told you I knew her and considered her family, that one time. I knew you and your awkward self would refuse to come."

"I would have."

"See? I'm very smart." Peyton pulled her along.

"I knew that already."

"Is your crush more than just a crush now, though? You've spent a few minutes with her at best."

"I've spent a lot more than a few minutes with her, Peyton."

"Explain." Peyton stopped when they were right outside the cabin.

"Don't be mad."

"What did you two do?" She lifted both eyebrows.

"Nothing. We didn't *do* anything," Kenzie began. "She helped me with my bag."

"Fast forward," Peyton instructed. "I was there for

that part."

"She came to check on me, I was in the cabana, and we talked a little." Kenzie pulled out her headphones and put her phone in her pocket. "She said I should sleep in there, and I said no because you wanted me to get to know people this week. But, she came and got me last night, and we slept out there together."

"That little devil," Peyton commented.

"It was sweet, Peyton. I'd told her I didn't think I could sleep out there alone, and she stayed with me. She told me she had me; and she did."

"She told you she *had* you? Who is this person, and what has she done with Lennox Owen?" Peyton asked the world.

"Is she not normally like that?"

"Lennox is the best. I love her like crazy. But I don't think I've ever heard her say something like that or take someone on a little outdoor adventure."

"We talked for hours, and she told me about how she grew up in the business."

"Did you tell her how you knew that already because you've been obsessed with her forever?" Peyton teased.

"No, obviously not," Kenzie returned and slid the earbuds into her ears. "It was just hard. I couldn't fall asleep with her there, and she knew it. She felt that I was awake, even though she'd already fallen asleep. And she pulled me back into her, Pey."

"Huh?"

"She spooned me. She wrapped her arm around me and pulled me into her. It was nice, and I tried to not think about it being anything more than nice. But then, she said I was cute – or that this lip thing I do is cute, and I had to do everything to not kiss her."

"She called you cute?" Peyton smiled.

"No, she said biting my bottom lip was cute."

"Wow." Peyton looked down and then back up.

"I'm just reading into things. And now that she knows

I'm gay – it'll stop, and she'll pull away, like all straight women seem to do around me once they know; and it'll be fine."

"I know her. She won't pull away from you, Kenz. She's not that person."

"It doesn't matter. I am going for a run. I need to get into a different headspace. I can't stop thinking about her looking at me last night, and then, the completely different reaction I got a few hours ago."

"You're going for a run?"

"I memorized the trail map. I'll be fine."

"When was the last time you went running? Dani has asked you, like, ten times to run with her."

"It's been a while. I'd ask her now, but I think I need to be alone."

"Okay. But if you're gone longer than an hour, I'm sending security to find you."

"Give me until dinner, okay?" Kenzie requested. "I ran long-distance, remember?" She pulled out her phone and clicked on her music. "I'm taking trail eight and then four on the way back, just in case."

"Okay," Peyton agreed and nodded. "Be safe."

"I will. I'll see you at dinner." Kenzie turned and ran off in the direction of trail eight, which would lead her along the lake, and then, into the woods, before connecting to trail four, which would bring her back along the side of an open field, and then, through the woods again.

***

Kenzie's run lasted an hour and a half, and it felt amazing. She would pay for it tomorrow when she wakes up, because even though she worked out regularly, she hadn't worked those particular muscles in a long time. She made her way to her cabin to grab her toiletry bag and clothes to change into before moving to the shower. Thankfully, the room was empty. She showered in peace, choosing not to dry her hair, since it would take forever, and joined the group for dinner.

"How was the run?" Peyton asked when Kenzie sat at her left with her plate.

"It was good. I'm going to hurt tomorrow, though."

"Tomorrow's the softball game," Carlie added from across from her. "You're on my team, and I play to win, there, Kenz." She squinted playfully at her.

"Noted." Kenzie smiled back and then glanced over at the table to the right, where she found Lennox in conversation with Jack and Quinn about something.

"You're staring," Peyton whispered in her ear.

"I am not." Kenzie turned back to her.

"I thought the run was supposed to help with that."

"It did. I'm over it. It's nothing. There's nothing to get over."

"Which is it? You're over it, or there's nothing to get over?"

"Shut up." Kenzie stabbed at the red potato on her plate and shoved it into her mouth unceremoniously.

With dinner finished, the group moved to the pit, where Kenzie actually worked with Lynn, Jenna, and Sarah to build a fire. She sat at the picnic table next to Cleo and Maddox, attempting to get to know them.

"How do you become a famous photographer?" she asked Maddox.

"How do you become a famous actress?" Maddox tossed back.

"No, I mean… I don't know how you get into photography. With acting – you audition. How do you audition with photography?"

"I guess you just take a lot of pictures and hope the right people see them."

"Who are the right people, though?" Kenzie pressed.

"Gallery owners, anyone who has visibility, and people who have money," Maddox shared. "I owe at least some of my success to Dani. She saw one of my pictures online. I'd just done a show in New York. It was one of my first ones, and a friend sent her the link to the info after. She liked the picture so much that she asked about buying the print. Then, she hung it on the wall of her apartment, took a picture of it, posted it on Instagram, and her helpful girlfriend Peyton, the queen of all social media, commented on it. Then, suddenly, the world wanted to know who I was."

"Cool," Kenzie said after a moment.

"Yeah, it was pretty cool." Maddox laughed lightly in her direction and took a drink of her soda.

"How'd you guys meet, though?"

Kenzie nodded as she listened to the story. And while she was interested and enjoyed talking to Maddox and the other women, she couldn't help but notice that Lennox had left the group and made her way toward her cabin. Kenzie wanted to talk to her. She wanted to ask her questions and tell her things. But she also didn't want to talk to her. Because, if Peyton was wrong, and Lennox did have a problem with her being gay, that would be depressing. And if Peyton was right, and Lennox didn't have a problem with it, she still might want to pull away. And that was possibly more depressing to Kenzie.

"I'm getting another drink. You guys want anything?" Cleo asked.

"No, I'm okay," Maddox replied.

"No, thanks." Kenzie stood. "I think I'm going to turn in, actually. I didn't sleep well last night."

"Those beds are terrible, aren't they?" Cleo asked without waiting for a response and walked away.

Kenzie went back to her cabin and realized she was already in her sleep clothes. She took care of what she needed to do in the bathroom and grabbed April to tell her not to worry, but she'd be sleeping elsewhere that night. Kenzie grabbed her phone and a few other things before heading for the cabanas. When she arrived, she was surprised to find Lennox sitting on the end of the long dock, where the boats were tied up. Kenzie placed her stuff inside the middle cabana and made her way out, hearing the squeak of the boards beneath her feet as she moved. Lennox turned at the sound and met her eyes. She smiled politely and turned back to the water. It was after nine, and the sun had set only an hour ago, thanks to the long days of summer. They were lit by the two lights at the end of the dock, that were there to warn people that the water was just beyond them, and a few light poles at the campground that automatically turned on at seven.

"I was going to sleep out here again," Kenzie said when she arrived behind Lennox.

"I won't be long. I just wanted a few minutes to myself. I can't have that back at my cabin."

"Everything okay?" Kenzie asked, still standing behind the other woman.

"You can sit down." Lennox offered and moved over a few inches to make room at the end of the dock.

"I don't want to interrupt your alone time. I just wanted to check."

"It's okay. You're kind of the reason I need it," Lennox confessed. "Sit, please."

"I'm the reason you need to be alone?" Kenzie sat down next to her, placing her hands on her own knees.

"I met you yesterday," Lennox said to herself more than Kenzie.

"Yeah…" Kenzie wasn't sure what else to say to that.

"I'm back to one-word responses." Lennox smiled at her and knocked Kenzie's shoulder with her own.

"What else was I supposed to say to that?"

"Did you tell Peyton I have a problem with you being gay?" Lennox looked at her then.

"You heard about that?"

"She smacked me on the shoulder and told me to make sure you knew I don't have a problem with you being gay; or anyone being gay, for that matter."

"Sorry. I didn't mean to get you smacked," Kenzie offered with a laugh and stared out at the water. "It just seemed like we were really getting along last night, and then things got awkward between us this morning. I told you I was gay, and you just stared at me, and it seemed like it might be something you had a problem with."

"I don't." Lennox rested her hand on top of Kenzie's, which was still on her own knee.

"Okay. That's good." Kenzie bit her lower lip. "Can you not pull away from me? Now that you know…"

"What?"

"Sometimes, when I tell a straight woman I'm a lesbian, she pulls away. It's like they think I'm attracted to every woman on the planet or something, and they want to avoid that."

Lennox laughed and removed her hand before turning her body toward Kenzie and looking at her.

"I didn't pull away because you're gay and I'm straight, Kenz," she shared.

"Why did you?"

"Because I *am* straight." Lennox shook her head.

Kenzie squinted at her inquisitively and then turned her head toward the cabana, wishing she could just disappear inside it and avoid the rest of the conversation. This was too important, though, so she'd handle it like a normal person.

"I don't get it."

"I've never thought of another woman in that way before. I've never been attracted to a woman." Lennox tried to explain and stopped herself. She then stood. "I'm going to pull away right now, but it's not because of you, okay?"

"Wait. What?"

"I need to think, and I can't do that near you."

"You can't think near me?" Kenzie stood just as Lennox started walking off the dock.

"Not about anything other than you, no." Lennox jogged away.

"Well, that's new. She actually ran away from me. *Literally* ran," Kenzie muttered to herself.

CHAPTER 8

"IF you're having sex – stop and cover up, because I'm coming in," Lennox said to the closed door of the cabin Dani and Peyton were sharing.

"Len?" Peyton opened the door.

"Thank God, you're fully clothed." Lennox entered without being invited.

"What's wrong?" Peyton asked, and Lennox watched Dani glance at her girlfriend in confusion.

"How did you two know?" She pointed at Dani and then Peyton before sitting on one of the empty beds.

They had pushed two of the twin beds together to share, and the other two were off to the side.

"Know what?" Dani asked her and sat on the edge of their bed.

Peyton joined her, and they linked hands.

"That you were into each other."

"Huh?" Dani questioned and glanced at Peyton. "You were there. You know."

"I know the story, yeah. But… How did you know about the girl thing?"

"Oh, my God! You *are* into her." Peyton accused, and her eyes got big.

"What am I missing?" Dani questioned.

"Peyton, answer the question," Lennox insisted.

"You're into Kenzie, aren't you?"

"What are you talking about?" Lennox diverted.

She'd gone there to get information from her best friend, who had been in this near-exact situation a couple of years ago.

"She told me you were flirting with her, and I couldn't believe it."

"She told you I flirted with her?" Lennox pressed, suddenly much more interested in this line of questioning.

"She mentioned that you two slept in a cabana together, and that you were nice."

"Nice, or that I flirted?"

"Len, she's gay. You're straight. She wondered if maybe she was mistaking your niceness for flirting. And she's been trying to talk herself into that. That's why she went for a run earlier."

"She went for a run?"

"You didn't notice she was gone for, like, two hours?" Peyton lifted an eyebrow.

"Of course, I noticed."

"*Of course*, you noticed?" Dani joined in.

"All right. That's enough." Lennox pointed at her. "Yes, I noticed. I've noticed her since she first got here. It's kind of hard not to notice her. She's beautiful," Lennox admitted. "She's, like, crazy beautiful."

"Oh, Lenny." Dani put her hand to her mouth.

"You like her, don't you?" Peyton asked.

"I don't know what's going on." Lennox flopped back onto the bare mattress. "I met her yesterday."

"I met Dani and knew after three seconds."

"You did not. You told me it took you forever to figure it out. Your words," Lennox argued.

"No, I told you I knew immediately. The feelings were there. I just had to work them out. We had some complications."

"She's a girl," Lennox suggested.

"No. She had a boyfriend," Peyton corrected. "The girl part was something I had to figure out later, but I knew I had feelings for her right away. I just wasn't going to say anything to someone who had someone else." She paused, and then Lennox felt the bed she was on dip. She looked up to see Peyton sitting on the end. "You are not with Aaron, and Kenzie hasn't been with anyone in a long time. You two don't have that complication."

"Do you like her?" Dani stood and looked down to Lennox.

"I don't even know her."

"But, do you like what you know so far?" Peyton asked.

"I don't like you two ganging up on me," Lennox grumbled as she sat up. "I've never even kissed a girl for a part, let alone a girl I actually like in real life."

"But, you're thinking about kissing her?"

"Peyton, I can *only* think about kissing her," Lennox professed. "She does this thing where she bites her lower lip, and I about lose my shit."

Peyton and Dani both burst out laughing at that.

"You've got it bad, girl," Dani remarked.

"You want to kiss her?" Peyton pressed on.

"Yes."

"Do you want to do more than just kiss her? Because you can't kiss her, Len, if you don't think you might want more than that, too."

"She's not suggesting you sleep with her tonight, though," Dani added.

"No, definitely don't do that," Peyton agreed. "I'm only saying that it wouldn't be fair to her if you kissed her and got her hopes up."

"Her hopes are up?" Lennox asked.

"Yeah, you need to talk to her about this." Peyton smiled at her, patted her leg, and stood. "You're in it, Len."

"In it?" Lennox stood up.

"You came to us because we've been there before. But you need to talk to her, if you feel something you want to explore. If you don't think you want to explore it, though, I wouldn't say anything. That wouldn't be fair to her."

"So, if I like her but don't think I would be into the physical stuff – I shouldn't say anything. But, if I think I might want to, maybe, do more than just kiss her – I should tell her?"

"Could you have sex with Kenzie Smyth, Lennox

Owen? Hot, passionate sex? Like, up against a wall kind of sex? And then, also the sweet, slow kind of sex, where it's not really sex, it's making love? Could you do that?"

Lennox's eyes got big for the second time that day, and she swallowed as she pictured almost frame by frame the things Peyton was presenting to her. She had Kenzie up against a wall; Kenzie was topless, and Lennox's hand was doing something, but she couldn't see what exactly because of the next image that appeared in front of her, where she was on top of Kenzie, and they were both naked. Her body was pressed into Kenzie's, and she was kissing her slowly, reveling in it.

"Fuck!" she said out loud and then quickly blushed.

"Yeah?" Peyton asked after a moment, with shock reading on her face. "That good, huh?"

"*Fuck*," Lennox repeated, though, this time, not with the same vigor.

***

When Lennox approached the cabana at midnight, she considered turning back and not going through with it. But after she'd walked practically the entire campsite and sat in front of the dying fire, she couldn't just go to sleep without talking to Kenzie.

"Kenz?" Lennox said in a soft voice. She had made a deal with herself: she'd say Kenzie's name twice, and if she was already asleep and didn't open up, she'd walk away, think more about whatever was going on inside her head, and force herself to sleep.

"Yeah?" Kenzie's voice came from inside, but nothing moved to indicate she was opening the screen.

"It's Lennox."

"I know."

"Right," Lennox said more to herself than Kenzie. "Can we talk?"

"Are you going to run away again?" Kenzie questioned

after a moment that felt like forever.

Lennox thought about the answer to that question and decided she should just be honest.

"I don't know," she finally admitted. "I don't want to."

"Then, why did you, earlier?" The voice grew a little closer, and Lennox could sense Kenzie was just inside the screen and canvas cover.

"Because you scare me," she revealed.

"I scare you?" Kenzie was louder now.

"*This* scares me." Lennox pulled the canvas toward her because she needed something to hold on to.

A moment passed, and she wondered if Kenzie was going to respond, when she felt a soft hand on her own, pulling it through the screen. Lennox used her free hand to tug on the string and hesitated for a moment when she realized that, once she pulled the canvas up, she would be able to see Kenzie. But, more importantly, Kenzie would be able to see her. Lennox wouldn't be able to hide.

"Hi," Kenzie greeted once the canvas was rolled up and she could meet Lennox's eyes.

"Hey," Lennox replied and looked down to their still joined hands.

"You can come in," Kenzie told her.

"I don't know if I should."

"Why not?"

"Because I don't know what I'm doing. And I don't know if that's fair to you."

"And you think being away from me will help you figure it out? If so – go." Kenzie motioned with her free hand toward the cabins. "Seriously, go and figure it out, because this has been driving me crazy since last night."

"It has?" Lennox realized how much trouble she'd caused.

"Lennox, I thought you were maybe flirting with me, and I had to remind myself that you're straight, and that you were just being nice."

"I *was* being nice. I didn't mean to flirt with you."

"Oh." Kenzie dropped her hand and retreated into herself.

Lennox grunted in frustration; not with Kenzie, but with her own choice of words. She pulled the Velcro apart and leaned in, watching Kenzie move back as she entered the cabana, pulled down the string, and yanked the Velcro back together.

"That's not what I meant," Lennox finally said. "I can't *help* but flirt with you. That's what I meant. It's like, I can't *not* do it."

Kenzie leaned back against the side of the cabana, pulling a pillow into her lap, and Lennox couldn't help but think Kenzie was using that to protect herself from her.

"Have you ever flirted with a girl before?"

"What? No," she answered.

"So, you've never kissed one?"

"No, Kenzie. Not even for a role."

"Oh, I know that."

"You *know* that?" Lennox questioned and leaned against the opposite side.

Kenzie pulled at the fabric on the pillow, staring down at it for a moment.

"I know everything about you. Well, everything that the public knows. I hardly think I know everything about you." Kenzie's fingers moved so quickly as they traced one square in the pattern on the multi-colored pillow, and then, moved to another, and another, and Lennox couldn't help but follow the movement with her eyes. "I'm kind of a fan."

"You're a fan?" Lennox's eyes remained on the fingers, darting from one square to the other.

"You're my lifelong crush, actually. Peyton knows that, which is why she didn't tell me you were coming. Because if she had, I probably wouldn't be here right now." The fingers stopped abruptly, drawing Lennox's attention back up to her eyes.

"I'm your lifelong crush?"

"I was a fan of your show. And I've seen all your movies. I know that's lame, because you're an actress, so saying you're my crush because I've seen all your stuff isn't really fair. I've also seen most of your interviews and read a lot of the print ones. I've always liked you." Kenzie shrugged, and the fingers went back to their movements.

Lennox watched them go with wonder. She considered how they might feel against her skin, and decided she wanted to know that more than anything in that moment.

"Why didn't you tell me before, when I told you *I* was a fan?"

"Because you said you were a fan of the show and my performance in it. That's different."

"Well, I *was* a fan of the show and your performance. But now, I am definitely a fan of *you*." Lennox smiled at her. "I might be your number one fan, actually," she let out, and Kenzie's fingers stopped again. "You're mesmerizing me with that, you know?"

"With what?" Kenzie asked, confused.

"What you're doing with the pillow." Lennox pointed.

"Oh, I didn't even notice I was doing it," Kenzie explained. "Sorry? Should I say sorry?"

"No." Lennox laughed.

"What do you want to do about this?"

"Your fingers?" Lennox asked, and then, felt her cheeks turning red the moment the words slipped out. "I meant–"

"I meant about whatever it is you're feeling." Kenzie smiled and let her off the hook.

"I don't know." Lennox lifted one shoulder and stared at her. "I know I'm attracted to you. I was drawn to you the moment your car pulled into the lot. And I haven't been able to stop thinking about you."

"Can you tell me specifically what you're thinking about?" Kenzie asked.

"Honestly?"

"Yes."

"Your lips," Lennox confessed. "Specifically, what it

would be like to kiss them."

"Oh." Kenzie seemed unprepared for that response.

"And your eyes. Your eyes are perfect."

"Says you, with those blue oceans, over there." Kenzie pointed at Lennox accusingly.

There was a moment of shared laughter, and Lennox liked that sound.

"And now, I'm thinking about that laugh, and how I want to hear it again."

"Say something funny."

"Something funny," Lennox returned rapidly.

Kenzie laughed again and placed the pillow she'd been holding on to next to her instead.

"You got me there." Kenzie placed her hands in her lap.

"Can I sleep in here with you tonight?" Lennox chanced and waited nervously for the reply.

"Just sleep?" Kenzie questioned.

"Just sleep," Lennox answered quickly, and Kenzie bit her lower lip. "But you can't do that anymore." She pointed at her.

"Do what?"

"That lip-biting thing. It's hot."

"It is not." Kenzie laughed out.

"Yeah, it really is. I can't stop thinking about it, so you need to stop doing it." Lennox moved to lie down.

Having not brought her sleeping bag because she didn't want to appear presumptuous, she sat back up, thinking she should go get it but not wanting to leave Kenzie's side because she might change her mind.

"You can just share mine," Kenzie offered. "It unzips all the way. We can use it as a blanket." She unzipped the sleeping bag and held one part up for Lennox to take.

When Lennox did, Kenzie slid down into position, and Lennox hesitated for a moment. In this position, she was next to the woman and also slightly above her. She looked down at Kenzie and flashed to that image she had in her mind from before, where they were pressed to one another and Lennox was kissing her. She gulped at the fantasy and memory combination.

"I should–"

"Don't," Kenzie interrupted. Her hand went to Lennox's cheek and stilled. "Please don't go. Nothing's going to happen. And if you wake up tomorrow and you feel differently, just tell me. But, please don't go right now," she implored.

"Okay," Lennox relented.

She moved to lie beside Kenzie. They both faced the ceiling of the cabana for a long while until Lennox felt Kenzie's hand in her own, and it felt good. It was soft, and warm, and when Lennox went to link their fingers, it felt like it belonged there. She waited, hoping Kenzie would fall asleep first. But they lay in silence even longer before Kenzie's hand pulled away, and she worried she'd done something wrong.

"Do you want to come here?" Kenzie asked softly into the silence, and Lennox watched her lift her arm up. "You don't have to, but–"

"Yeah," Lennox interrupted this time and resisted the urge to smile as she lifted the makeshift blanket enough to slide over into Kenzie's body. Her head went to Kenzie's chest, and Kenzie's arm was around her now. Lennox had nowhere else to place her own arm but over Kenzie's stomach. "I can hear your heartbeat," she whispered after a moment of listening to the constant and fast thud.

"Not fair."

"You can't feel mine?" Lennox asked.

"No."

"And, I'm back to one-word responses again."

They laughed lightly. A few minutes later, Lennox fell asleep to the light touches of Kenzie's fingers in her hair.

CHAPTER 9

KENZIE'S fingers played with the ends of Lennox's hair. She pulled her fingers through to the tips of the silky locks, toyed with them, and then, repeated the motion long after Lennox had fallen asleep. Kenzie was glad she'd gotten that nap in earlier, because the likelihood of her being able to fall asleep, with Lennox on her like this, was next to nil. She still wasn't sure exactly how they'd ended up like this. Lennox Owen was sleeping on her chest. Kenzie could feel her pressed against herself, and Lennox's breathing played against the fabric of her shirt, which was thin and couldn't prevent the goosebumps from appearing on her skin.

After about an hour of staring at the ceiling of the cabana, Kenzie thought about rolling over to get more comfortable, but there was no way she was moving, with Lennox pressed against her like this. She'd rather go the whole night without sleep and live with the consequences than move and chance Lennox pulling away from her again. She stopped the movement of her fingers in Lennox's hair, though, knowing that was contributing to her inability to sleep, and instead, she placed her hand on the small of Lennox's back, gently, so as not to wake her. She didn't accomplish that task, though, because Lennox shifted her head before laying it back down against Kenzie's chest, and her hand – which had been placed on Kenzie's stomach, moved to her left hip and rested there. Kenzie's heartbeat jumped. And that, in combination with her previous movement, was enough to wake Lennox from her slumber.

"Are you okay?" Lennox asked without looking up at her.

"Sorry. Go back to sleep." Kenzie resumed the fingers in Lennox's hair.

Lennox lifted herself up, and her eyes met Kenzie's. She then smiled at her and slid away. For a second, Kenzie closed her eyes in disappointment before she opened them again and gave a fake smile, trying to cover up the fact that she missed Lennox touching her.

"Can't sleep again?" Lennox asked her with tired but kind eyes. "I seem to cause that problem."

"You don't," she lied.

"Yes, I do. But, I'll take it as a compliment." She smirked and lowered her head for a moment before raising it again. "*Should* I take it as a compliment?"

Kenzie rubbed her face with her hands and lowered her arms to her sides. She wasn't sure what to say. She had Lennox Owen lying next to her in a small space. They'd talked earlier about the fact that, for some strange reason, Lennox was attracted to her. Lennox was attracted to the socially awkward, shy, and often aloof Mackenzie, and Kenzie wasn't sure she would ever be able to understand that. And that was especially true because they'd only just met, and they knew very little about each other.

"Yes," she finally admitted. "And just so you don't think that's a one-word response, I'll add to it."

"Okay." Lennox laughed.

"I can't understand it," Kenzie said after another long moment.

"Understand what?"

"Why?" She'd thought about the words but hadn't been able to say them out loud.

"Why I like you?" Lennox's eyes squinted at her.

"Yes."

"You've had girlfriends before, right?"

"Yes."

"Did you doubt their attraction to you?"

"I don't know." Kenzie moved to sit up, causing Lennox to do the same in front of her.

"Yes, you do," Lennox argued back softly. "And I don't mean initially, when you don't know if they like you or not. Once you were dating, and you knew they liked you, did you doubt their feelings?"

Kenzie avoided biting her lower lip, even though this was the exact kind of situation she'd normally do just that.

"I guess not," she expressed. "But this is different."

"Because we just met? Because we're not dating?"

"Because you're you." Kenzie motioned quickly with an open hand in Lennox's direction before putting her hand away in her lap.

"What's different about me? The fact that I've never been attracted to another woman?"

Kenzie lowered her head and shook it from side to side. She kept it down as she tried to figure out what to say next. How could she possibly express what she was thinking, what she was feeling about this strange and foreign situation to Lennox? She couldn't find the words. She was completely inept at situations like this. And she wondered how she'd even been able to get a single date before in her life.

Annabelle had been present, at best, in their relationship. Kenzie had been her first girlfriend, too, after coming out. They had been each other's first in more ways than one. And while Kenzie had felt love for the girl at one time, as she'd gotten older, she determined that it hadn't been love. It was gratitude for Annabelle being there when Kenzie had needed someone to talk to, when she had felt an overwhelming urge to shut down and not express that she was into women. Annabelle had kissed her first and had made every move in their relationship first. That had made it possible for them to even have a relationship, because Kenzie wasn't sure she would have been able to make a move at that time in her life. She had liked Annabelle. She never pressured Kenzie to be more social or to hang out with her friends. She'd seemed comfortable enough with Kenzie's friends in their small apartment and staying over most nights in Kenzie's room, and she had never pushed Kenzie to stay at her place where she had three roommates of her own. When it had ended – it hurt, but not nearly as much as

Kenzie expected it would at the end of a first relationship. And she understood that this likely meant that they weren't meant to be together.

Kelly had been a surprise to Kenzie. Kenzie was always one to show up and work, and then, return to her trailer and wait for them to call her back when they needed her. Kelly had peered in one day to bring her coffee. Kenzie thought it strange, because that was in no way Kelly's responsibility, but she'd stayed, and they'd chatted briefly before Kenzie was called back to set. Kelly did that three times before she had leaned in and kissed Kenzie briefly on the lips. It came as a complete shock, but Kenzie had no time to react, because Kelly had kissed her again and for longer. Then, Kelly had asked her out, and she became Kenzie's second in more ways than one. Kenzie hadn't ever felt the pull toward moving in with Kelly or getting married. She had never considered a future for them beyond what they'd had. And she had known that was wrong and unfair to Kelly because Kelly had obviously wanted more. But, the more they fought about Kenzie's inability to act normally, the more obvious it was to Kenzie that it needed to end. She hated that word, 'normal.' Kelly had used it a few times during their arguments, and Kenzie had let it go each time.

Now, she found herself with another chance to be normal with a woman; and with Lennox Owen, at that. And yet, Kenzie couldn't. She couldn't say what she was feeling. She couldn't express it correctly. And it would likely cost her whatever the hell this was between them. Kenzie's head snapped up at the feeling of Lennox moving. But Lennox wasn't just moving. She was moving into her. Lennox was climbing on top of her, straddling her, while Kenzie's body moved hastily into the back of the cabana.

"Len–"

"Talk to me," Lennox whispered. She placed her hands on Kenzie's shoulders and lowered herself to sit in Kenzie's lap. "Please."

"I'm not good at this." Kenzie gulped.

"You don't have to be good at anything right now. Just talk to me." She smiled.

"That's the part I'm not good at."

"You were fine earlier," Lennox reminded.

"No, I wasn't."

"You talked to me about what's going on between us."

"I was clutching a pillow and thinking about the shapes on it."

Lennox's smile was again, kind, as she looked to her side and grabbed the pillow, placing it between the two of them.

"Here." She then picked up Kenzie's right hand and brought it to the pillow. "Now, talk to me."

"Why do you like me?" Kenzie let out without moving her hand from Lennox's.

"Are you kidding?"

"No," she answered.

Lennox took Kenzie's index finger and placed it on the pillow, encouraging it to move around the square. Kenzie's eyes moved to her own hand, guided by Lennox. Lennox seemed to need a moment to gather her words then, because Kenzie glanced up at her and watched as her eyes looked skyward and then back down at her.

"I can't explain it."

"Welcome to my world," Kenzie said and surprised herself at the joke.

"I was drawn to you," Lennox said as she smiled. "I saw you in the parking lot, and I recognized you. I watched you move, and I watched you hesitate. I couldn't take my eyes off you," she confessed. "You are the most beautiful woman I've ever seen, Kenz. I don't know that I've ever said that before, and I hang out with a lot of beautiful women; most of them are asleep in those cabins right now. But, I don't think I've ever felt the kind of beauty I feel in you," she added. "When I got close to you, it was like I couldn't look away, and I couldn't move away. I just wanted to be next to you. I meant what I said before," she paused.

"You're magnetic to me."

Kenzie gulped and looked back down at her fingers that she was sliding around on the fabric again, trying to focus on anything other than the feeling of Lennox pressed against her body.

"But you don't know me," Kenzie finally said.

"Not yet," Lennox offered a rebuttal. "I'd like to get to know you."

"While we're both at an adult summer camp?" Kenzie was able to look up and meet her eyes.

"We can't help where we met, Kenz." Lennox paused and looked down at Kenzie's fingers that were still moving against the pillow; and now, even faster. Lennox placed her hand on top of Kenzie's and stopped them. "Tell me about where you grew up," she requested.

"What?" Kenzie looked up at her, surprised at the question.

"I told you that I was drawn to you and that you were beautiful," Lennox reminded her. "That is all true, and nothing's going to change that. But, if you doubt what I'm feeling, for whatever reason, because I don't know you well enough yet, then, I want to get to know you."

"I'm boring," Kenzie offered and lowered her hand from the pillow, leaning back against the wall of the cabana.

"You are anything but boring."

"Compared to you, I am *only* boring."

"Is that what this is about? Your crush on me? Or really, your crush on the Lennox Owen you know from interviews and movies?"

"Partly." Kenzie shrugged.

Lennox stared at her for a moment, and Kenzie nearly lost herself in the blue depth of her eyes before she had to look away. Lennox shifted and moved off Kenzie. Kenzie closed her eyes at the realization that she had screwed up, and Lennox was pulling away again.

"I grew up in LA." Lennox started as she sat off to the side, still looking at Kenzie with those deep blue eyes. She ran her hand through the hair Kenzie had been playing with only moments before, and tried to tame it. "I guess I didn't really grow up there, though. I lived there, but I mostly grew up on set," she added. "My parents were both working a lot at the time. I'd be on one set with my mom, and then, go with my dad for his movie for a while. Sometimes, we were in LA. But, most of the time, we moved from city to city, or country to country. By the time I was ten, I had been to at least thirty countries."

"What?" Kenzie questioned.

"Filming and press junkets." Lennox lifted her shoulders and dropped them back down. "You know how it goes. They release the movie in Japan – you go to Japan to be interviewed by the translator." She laughed. "I went to school on the road, mostly. And once I started acting, I had tutors on set. I graduated high school by thirteen, technically. But I kept taking classes with the tutors because it was a nice break from the work when I needed it." She met Kenzie's eyes. "My brother, Will, was my rock," she shared, and Kenzie watched as Lennox thought about how to proceed. "He was the only friend I had when we traveled, and for a few years, there, we did nothing but travel. He was always the more outgoing one of the two of us and tried to make sure I met people my age whenever we could. I assume you know what happened?"

"I heard about it." Kenzie nodded.

"Jamie came along unexpectedly, years after we both started acting ourselves. Once we were on our own, our parents pretty much left us that way. Will and I actually had an apartment together when I was fifteen and he was seventeen. We lived there and worked, and he would drive me to the set when he could. His heart wasn't in it, though. He gave up on acting completely and decided to do the things he really wanted to do, while he could."

"I'm sorry." Kenzie didn't know what else to say.

"When he died, I lost myself for a while," Lennox continued. "Peyton was there for me and helped pull me back in. She's an amazing friend." Lennox lowered her eyes to Kenzie's hands. "You're not doing it anymore." She motioned with her head.

"What?" Kenzie looked down to find that the pillow was no longer in her lap, it was on her side, and her hands were still. "Oh."

"I was there when she met Dani," Lennox started. "I was right next to Peyton, actually." She laughed at the memory. "I'd never seen her like that before. Once they started dating, I thought back to how Peyton had been with the guys I had seen her with. I was there the night she met the guy she dated the longest. She loved him; I have no doubt. But, when I compare that to her reaction at meeting Dani, there is no comparison. She was the happiest I'd ever seen her; and still is to this day."

"They're perfect together." Kenzie smiled at her friends.

"They are. And I asked them about how it felt in the beginning, and what it took for them to take that chance with each other," Lennox paused. "Tonight, I asked them. I guess it was yesterday now. But they were both straight women who had only dated men in the past. Then, they met one another, and everything changed."

"You asked them about it tonight?"

"Peyton told me that if I wasn't sure, I shouldn't tell you, because it wouldn't be fair to you."

"Oh." Kenzie lowered her head again.

"I did tell you, Kenzie. We're talking about it right now." Lennox moved back into her and lifted her chin. "Whatever this is, it feels real to me." She held Kenzie's chin in place. "But you don't trust it yet, and that's okay," she offered. "Just give me a chance?"

"I don't–"

Lennox's lips were on her forehead. Kenzie couldn't move. She couldn't think. She couldn't speak. Her heart was thundering inside her chest at the touch of soft, warm lips on her skin. Lennox's lips were on her cheek, and then, the other cheek. Lennox's lips pressed gently to the tip of her nose, and Kenzie gasped.

"Please," Lennox whispered. "Tell me about where you grew up," she requested again in the smallest of whispers, and her lips moved back to Kenzie's forehead. "I want to know you." Lennox's eyes met Kenzie's, and they were only an inch apart. Kenzie could feel Lennox thinking. She could feel it as much as she felt the hand that now grazed her cheek, and she could feel it as much as when Lennox's lips pressed, or more like gently touched, her lips before pulling away and checking Kenzie's reaction.

"We should get some sleep," Kenzie deflected when Lennox's hand on her cheek slid down to the side of her neck where it remained.

"Now, who's pulling away?" Lennox asked and nodded at the situation she found herself in, pulled her hand away, and sat back against the other wall. "Should I go back to my cabin?"

"I–"

Kenzie could barely breathe. The temperature in the enclosed space had skyrocketed the moment Lennox had touched her, and it hadn't gone back down. Kenzie knew she needed air. Her breathing quickened, she slid forward, opened the screen, and climbed past the hanging canvas to deeply inhale the fresh night air. She stared out at the dark water, lit by the moonlight and lanterns, wrapping her arms around herself. A few moments later, she heard Lennox climb out, but she didn't turn to see her.

"I guess that answers my question," Lennox said after she stood there, apparently waiting for Kenzie to say something. "Sleep well, Mackenzie."

Kenzie heard the footsteps loud at first, and then, slowly fading to nothing at all.

CHAPTER 10

"YOU kissed her?" Peyton whispered to Lennox. They were sitting next to one another on the visitor's bench of the softball field. The game had just started after Peyton had divided everyone into teams. Some didn't want to participate, feeling like softball wasn't really their game, but Peyton had insisted that they needed all of them to form two whole teams. She had even put them into positions based on their lack of interest. Those who wanted nothing to do with it were relegated to the outfield where likely nothing much would happen, given the fact that none of them were exactly professional softball players. The game would be slow-pitch, so the catcher would basically stand behind the plate and pick up the ball after it dropped to the ground, throw it back to the pitcher, and that would be about it. Peyton was the pitcher for their team, and Dani was the pitcher for the home team. Lennox was convinced they had put themselves on opposite teams in an act of foreplay to use later, but she shook that out of her mind because she did not want to think about Peyton and Dani together like that.

"Not like that," Lennox replied.

"You just said you kissed her." Peyton looked over at her friend, clutching her borrowed softball glove in her hand.

"We didn't make out or anything. I just gave her a peck, really, and then, she freaked out and left. So, I left, too."

"You are ridiculous," Peyton groaned audibly and stood.

"Peyton, you're up," Lynn yelled after Cleo struck out.

"Yeah, come on, babe." Dani teased from the pitcher's

mound. "Time for me to strike you out."

Peyton dropped the glove and took the bat from Cleo before heading to the batter's box. Lennox watched on as Dani threw one pitch, and Kenzie, as a catcher, missed it, picked it up, and tossed it back underhand. Lennox couldn't help but laugh at that. She watched Peyton talk to Kenzie about something, and then, Kenzie caught Lennox staring at her and missed the second pitch altogether. It rolled back behind her, and she ran to pick it up. Lennox glared in Peyton's direction, wondering what she'd said to Kenzie to make her look over and decided to bring that up later. Peyton swung and connected. The ball went to third base, where Bobby threw her glove at it to get it to stop rolling. Lennox burst out laughing at the worst-played game of softball in the history of the world, and Peyton applauded herself when she made it to first base safely.

"Come on, Len! Bring me home," she encouraged.

Lennox stood and reluctantly headed to the batter's box to pick up the discarded bat. She picked it up, gave a short glance back at Kenzie, and then, turned to Dani to await her pitch. She didn't swing at the first pitch, which Dani called a strike. She didn't swing at the second pitch, which was also a strike. She knew the last thing she wanted to be doing right now was to play softball, so she let the third pitch go and was promptly yelled at by Peyton for not even trying. She tossed the bat in the direction of the home bench, since they only had the one bat, and headed to pick up her glove. She didn't look back at Kenzie this time.

***

Five innings later, the game was tied. Half of the players in the field were sitting down and tired of playing while the others were barely paying attention at all. Lennox was playing second base, after trying her hand at first base, and left the field already. She had played a few games of pick-up softball over the years but had never taken it seriously. It was hot outside, and the air was sticky. She wanted to eat lunch, and then, spend as much time inside the cabin as possible until the sun went down. Granted, the cabins weren't air-conditioned, but it was better than nothing. A cold shower after lunch would help, too; she decided just as she watched Kenzie take her spot in the batter's box. Kenzie had batted a few times now and had struck out each time. Most of them had struck out repeatedly, though, so no one paid it any mind.

"All right, Kenz. You got this!" Dani encouraged from the bench. "We just need one run, and we kick my girlfriend's ass." She laughed.

"Someone's not getting laid tonight," Jenna said to Lennox from first base.

"Please, like this isn't turning them both on right now," Cleo replied from shortstop, where she appeared to be picking at her nails, with her glove under her arm.

Lennox watched as the pitch went past Kenzie, and it was a ball. Peyton was losing her touch. Another ball went past her, and Lennox had an idea.

"Time out!" she yelled.

"What?" Peyton turned to her. "Why?"

"Just give me a second." Lennox dropped her glove where she was and jogged toward Kenzie, who seemed completely confused.

"What's going on, Lex?" Quinn asked from her position as a catcher.

"Yeah, what's going on?" Dani had moved closer to them.

"I need Kenzie for a sec."

"You do know what a time out is, right?" Dani checked. "It's for your team, not mine."

"Dani, a second." She pointed at Dani, and Dani took a step back.

Quinn didn't seem to care either away and moved toward Dani until she was allowed to move back.

"What's wrong?" Kenzie asked her softly, keeping her

voice down so no one else could hear her.

"There are no outs, and you have two balls."

"What?"

"Don't swing," Lennox told her. "Peyton will walk you."

"So, I get to first base?" she asked.

"Dani is up after you. She'll get a hit because she can't not swing against Peyton. Look at my team." Lennox nodded backward. Kenzie looked beyond her shoulder and could see that half of the players were sitting. Brooke was actually lying down on the right field, attempting to get a tan. "You'll score," she added. "You'll score the winning run."

"You do know I'm not on your team, right?" Kenzie asked.

"I know that." Lennox smiled at her. "Just walk, and when Dani hits it – run like crazy."

"I can do that." Kenzie smiled back. "Thanks."

Lennox backed up and jogged to second base where she picked up her glove.

"Time in?" Peyton asked her.

"Yeah."

Peyton threw one more ball and then a strike. Lennox worried for a moment that she had given Kenzie terrible advice when the second strike crossed the plate. Kenzie looked toward her position for a second, but then, back to Peyton, as the fourth ball crossed the plate, and she jogged to first after dropping the bat for Dani. When she arrived, she exchanged a smile with Lennox, and then, it was Dani's turn. She let one ball go past and trash-talked her girlfriend before the second one connected with her bat and went between Lennox and Jenna. Lennox turned around to watch Brooke – being yelled at by Peyton to get up and retrieve the ball – finally move, jog to it with little effort, and toss it back in the direction of Lennox's glove, but not quite to it. Lennox made slow work of her own movements and picked up the ball just in time to hear the other team cheer loudly.

She turned to see Kenzie running with as much speed as she could muster toward home and score.

"Damn, she's fast," Jenna remarked.

"She was a track star," Lennox stated, and, realizing the game was finally over, she just held on to the ball.

"Cool. I didn't know that," Jenna replied. "It's lunchtime now, right?" And she walked off the field.

Lennox followed behind and watched as Dani held on to Peyton's hips and gave her a puppy-dog face when her girlfriend looked upset at her loss. Lennox smiled at the thought of the surprise Peyton was going to deliver to Dani this week, and the role she, herself, would play in it to make everything go smoothly.

They all made their way – and some of them reluctantly – toward the cabin, where their lunch was already prepared for them. Lennox grabbed a plate for herself and then headed away from the group. She needed some time alone. That was weird for her. She had needed some time alone the day before, and now, again. She wasn't normally someone that needed that much time to think on her own to figure something out, but this situation was the strangest one she had found herself in thus far in her life.

The cabanas were off-limits because they had too many memories now, and because there was a chance Kenzie would want to eat her lunch there today. Lennox made her way down instead, to the boats. They were tied to the dock, and she placed her plate down, untied one, climbed inside, and before she pushed off, she grabbed her plate with the bottle of water and decided she would drift around the lake for a while.

It was peaceful. The water remained calm, and she didn't bother using the oars once she was a fair distance away from the dock. The boathouse was on the other side of the water, and after about thirty minutes and eating everything on her plate, she decided to tie the boat up on that side and explore. The boathouse appeared to be three stories high, which may or not have been the norm; she had no experience with boathouses. Lennox climbed out of the boat and walked along the much shorter but also not as well-kept dock, avoiding the holes and rotted wood in places, to make her way to the ground. She was glad she had decided to wait on that shower, because she was sweating already, and it would have been a waste. She walked all the way around the building, noting the thick woods behind it, and then pulled open the heavy wooden door.

"Oh, hey."

Lennox turned at the sound of another voice – and one that she recognized – to see Kenzie standing there in her running clothes, pulling the headphones from her ears.

"Hi," Lennox replied and couldn't stop her eyes from roaming over Kenzie's body, which was more exposed to her than ever before. Even when they had gone into the bathroom together and had to take showers in adjacent stalls, Kenzie had emerged fully dressed after, with the towel hung over her shoulder. Now, she was in a pair of gym shorts that barely covered her thighs, running shoes – obviously, and no shirt. Kenzie didn't have a shirt on. She was wearing a bright purple sports bra with black dots on it, and her shirt was tucked partly into her shorts and hanging out. "Hi," Lennox repeated and shook herself out of it.

"I went for a run after the game." Kenzie wrapped the headphones around her phone.

"Oh." Lennox's eyes betrayed her again and focused on the light sheen of sweat covering Kenzie's abdomen. "I took the boat," she stated and then, with a lazy finger, pointed at the boat tied to the dock.

"Right." Kenzie held her phone in one hand and lifted that arm, motioning to the boathouse. "Just taking a look?"

"Yeah."

"Cool." Kenzie lowered her arm. She looked down at herself and suddenly reached for her shirt. She pulled it out of her shorts and started trying to put it on. "I'll let you get back to that."

"You're…" Lennox couldn't finish that thought, because she knew if she did, she'd either scare Kenzie away, or she'd say something that would force herself to launch her body at Kenzie's and crash their lips together. She looked at the sky, and then, the water. "You can check it out with me," she said instead and pushed her mind to anything other than Kenzie's body.

"I shouldn't."

"Because you were on the run?" Lennox guessed that wasn't the truth.

"Yes." Kenzie looked to the ground.

"I thought you didn't run anymore," Lennox responded.

"I'm trying something new, I guess." Kenzie looked up at her at that.

"I guess we're both trying something new this week," Lennox risked and rolled her eyes at herself. "I'm going to go inside. Have a good run."

She turned and walked through the door, closing it behind her. She let out a deep breath and then took in the space. It appeared that the first two floors were really one large floor. The boats were stored all around. Some were just lying on the dirt floor while others hung from the rafters. One speedboat was sitting on cinder blocks, and the rest were rowboats of different sizes and colors, mixed with a couple of canoes. There was a staircase to her left, which must have led to the top floor. Inquisitive as always, she climbed them. The loft at the top was used for storage, apparently, and had about a hundred life jackets stacked on both sides of the small space. There was a large, half-moon-shaped window that she walked over to and decided that the view was worth the musty smell of the life jackets and boats. She could see the trees from a higher vantage point and could just make out a smaller lake – or maybe it would be called a pond – beyond them. It might have been a mile from the boathouse, and she considered taking a long walk there tomorrow to check it out, if she could get away again.

"I'm sorry."

Lennox hadn't heard the door open or close, and she hadn't heard the footsteps behind her. Maybe that was what Peyton meant about the woman being invisible when she wanted to be. Now that she was paying attention, though, Lennox could hear them getting closer, and she felt her maybe a few feet behind her.

"For what, Kenzie?" she let out when the footsteps stopped.

"For leaving last night."

"That's all?" Lennox asked and ran her hand through her hair that was damp with sweat.

"I'm not good at this."

"Stop." She turned to Kenzie. "Don't make excuses." She gave a frustrated sigh. "Don't use it as an excuse, Kenz. Just tell me what's going on."

"I don't have the capacity to just express myself like that all the time, Lennox. It's hard for me."

"And you don't think it was hard for me to tell a woman I just met that I can't stop thinking about her, when I've never thought of a woman that way before in my life?" She got it all out in one breath. "Kenzie, I was straight, for all I knew, like, two days ago. Then, last night, I kissed you. And about five minutes ago, I gawked at you because you're sexy in a sports bra. Do you think that's not hard for me to admit?"

"You think I'm sexy?" Kenzie lifted a confused eyebrow.

"No. No more." Lennox waved her off. "I'm not doing this with you anymore. If you want to talk about what I think about you and how I feel, you have to talk to me about you. You have to let me get to know you, like I was trying to do last night before you ran out."

"What if when you get to know me, you don't like me?" Kenzie asked.

Lennox melted at that. She saw the vulnerability in Kenzie's eyes and finally understood what had scared her off last night.

"Kenz, I don't know how I could ever not like you."

"But you're Lennox Owen, and I'm just me." She shrugged.

Lennox walked to her and placed her hands on Kenzie's hips. She was being bold, and she didn't care. Kenzie was hot right now. Her eyes were darker than normal, and her hair was pulled back, so Lennox could see Kenzie's long neck being exposed for the first time. Her shirt was on now, unfortunately, but Lennox would always remember what she looked like in that sports bra.

"You are not *just* you," she said. "You are my longtime crush," she professed to very confused eyes.

"What? That doesn't—"

"Make sense? I know. Tell me about it." Lennox kept her hands in place but took a step toward Kenzie. "I haven't exactly admitted to this to anyone ever, and that includes Peyton."

"Admitted what?"

"That I watched your old show, too." Lennox looked away for a moment. "I've watched you for years. I've seen every episode."

"It was a teen show." Kenzie tried to put pieces together. "And I'm a girl."

Lennox laughed and pulled Kenzie into her. They were hip to hip now, and Lennox's hands migrated to Kenzie's lower back over her shirt.

"I watched you. I watched every scene you were in, and I had no idea why then." She laughed at herself. "It's so stupid, isn't it? I thought I was a fan; you were a great actress, and I was watching you because of that. But, I think there was a little more to it, given the way I've been acting the past couple of days." She met Kenzie's eyes, and as Kenzie's arms wrapped around her neck, she realized something. "I can't kiss you, Kenzie."

"Oh." Kenzie's arms fell immediately to her side, and she took a step back, severing the contact.

"I want to kiss you," Lennox offered to try to soften

the blow. "I want to kiss you like crazy. That little one we shared last night felt like—"

"Electricity?" Kenzie questioned and finished for her. Lennox nodded. "Um, so why can't you kiss me now?"

"Because I told you: I want to know you. I've never done this before. I feel this mysterious connection to you, and it is real. It is very real. But I think Peyton is right: I can't jump into this with you until I get to know you at least a little. And, right now, I know that you're an actress and that you used to run track."

"You know more than just that," Kenzie reminded. "And that's a pretty big part of me, unfortunately."

"Don't say that," Lennox discouraged. "I would never say that it was a bad thing about you, Kenz. Just like I wouldn't say that about my sister." She paused and placed her hand on Kenzie's cheek. "It's a part of who you are. And, honestly, I like it."

"You like that I'm weird?"

"I like that you're you." Lennox tried to explain. "I don't know much about you, but what I do know, I like, Kenz. I more than *like*," she added when Kenzie attempted to look away. "Can we try?"

"Try?" Kenzie looked hopeful.

"Can we, I don't know, take the boat back together and just talk?" She lowered her hand.

"I'd be trapped in that boat," Kenzie acknowledged.

"That was kind of part of the plan." Lennox smiled at her. "But, so would I," she added. "Neither of us could run away this time."

Kenzie looked over Lennox's shoulder out the window and then back to Lennox's eyes.

"Okay."

They made their way back outside and to the boat, where Lennox untied it from the dock after helping Kenzie get inside. She joined her and rowed them into the middle of the lake before lowering the oar onto the floor of the boat. They sat facing one another, occasionally exchanging glances, but mostly staring at their surroundings, pretending the moment wasn't awkward.

"So, should I repeat my question?" Lennox asked after several minutes of floating.

"You want to know about me growing up?" Kenzie remembered.

"Yeah."

"Okay." Kenzie dragged her fingers along the surface of the water back and forth while Lennox watched. "I grew up two hours north of here. We lived in a small, ranch-style house for the first few years," she began.

"Do you have any siblings?"

"No, it was just me. I wasn't exactly planned." Her lips went into a straight line, and she kept skimming her fingers over the water. "My mom was only fifteen when she got pregnant. It was the south, so she was told she should marry my dad. And she did, after I was born. She eventually got her GED, but never went to college. My dad worked in an auto body shop, and before things got bad for us financially, he bought it."

"You don't have an accent," Lennox stated as she realized it.

"I lost it as soon as I could. It took a while, but I stopped saying 'y'all' and lost the drawl." Kenzie paused and stopped her movements. "We moved into a trailer when I was four. My mom stayed at home while my dad tried to get the shop running smoothly. It took him several years, but he finally made it work. She'd left by then and had a new family shortly after. So, it was just my dad and me. We moved into a house again, once the shop was solvent, and things were okay." Kenzie seemed to be speaking at the same time she was remembering. "He died a few years ago in an accident."

"Oh, I'm sorry, Kenz."

"It's okay. He and I weren't close."

"But he was all you had," Lennox reasoned.

"I think my dad was like me." Kenzie met her eye.

"You mean…"

"I think he had the same thing I do. I never asked him. And I don't think he was ever tested or anything, but sometimes, it felt like he had the same problems I do. And we never acknowledged it between the two of us, but he wasn't one to show emotion often," she paused. "I think he loved the shop and his cars more than he loved me."

"Kenz, there's no way."

"He was seventeen when I was born, Lennox. I don't know any seventeen-year-old guy that wants a baby. And then, my mom left, and he had to take care of a young girl. Once he figured out I could make my own meals, that was pretty much the end of our relationship."

"Well, I get that. My parents were kind of the same way, but I'm still sorry."

"I learned how to take care of myself, and that helped later when I went off to school."

"And you got dared to act?" Lennox lifted her lips into a smile.

"I acted a little in high school."

"I didn't know that."

"Why would you?" Kenzie smiled back at her.

"I told you about my unrealized crush and the fact that I watched both of your shows. I've seen interviews, and I've never heard you mention that you acted in high school."

"Because it was small stuff. That's why I'm still confused as to how all this happened to me. I never even got cast as the lead in a high school play. But, somehow, I'm leading TV shows, and I'm in movies." Kenzie tried to grasp. "I only really auditioned back then because I thought it might help me socialize more. Track was an individual sport. I didn't participate in any of the team events, so it was just me and the track. Acting was different. I had to talk to people at rehearsals, and we had to work together."

"How'd it go?"

"Not well. I'm still pretty bad at it," she explained. "I'm not exactly the most social on set."

"Well, I'm not all that social most of the time, either."

"You're not?"

"No. Sometimes I am, but other times – I don't see the point. Not every cast is the one big happy family we tell everyone we are when we do interviews."

"I think they hate me usually, because I don't stick around to talk."

"They don't hate you, Kenzie. They might not understand you, but they don't hate you. It's a job. It's a weird job, but it's a job."

"What do you mean?"

"Just that most people go to work in an office, and they leave at five and go home to be with their families or hang out with their friends. They're not expected to stick around and talk to their co-workers or create lasting friendships. It happens. I have a lot of friends because we worked together. Peyton is one of them, technically. But, it's rare, to find that kind of connection with someone on set. Most of us wave goodbye on the last day of shooting and don't see anyone again until the press tour. After that, maybe we see them at an audition or an event, but it's not like we're all forming these lifelong friendships on every set," she paused. "You should let yourself off the hook a little."

"Maybe."

"Besides, you have enough friends. Who says you need to make more?"

"I do?"

"You're here with a ton of other women, Kenzie, and they're all your friends."

"I barely know most of them," Kenzie argued.

"They're getting to know you, though, and they like you."

"Who told you that?" Kenzie laughed.

"Let's see." Lennox pressed her fingertip to her lips for a moment. "Jenna thought you were crazy fast during softball, earlier, and thought it was cool. Bobby said she thought you were shy, but once you open up, you'd be fun to hang out with. Peyton thinks the world of you, and so does Dani." Lennox met Kenzie's eyes again. "And you already know how I feel about you."

"I have other friends, you know? I'm not a complete loser." Kenzie changed the subject, and Lennox decided she'd allow it, because she was still getting to know Kenzie Smyth.

"You do, huh?"

"Yes, I have two close friends, actually: Kat and Emily. I met them in college. We were roommates."

"Yeah?"

"Emily is somewhere in Africa right now. She joined the Peace Corps last year. She's helping people, and I don't get to talk to her very often, but when she comes back to LA, if I'm in town, we hang out."

"She sounds like a good person."

"She is," Kenzie replied. "Then, there's Kat. Kat and I met freshman year, and she kind of reminds me of Peyton a little. She's outgoing, sarcastic, and funny. She was the one that dared me to audition. She moved to San Diego last year, so I don't get to see her every day. But she comes up to LA once a month or so, and we spend the weekend together."

"And you guys never dated?" Lennox asked and swallowed.

"No, Kat's not gay. She has a boyfriend. Emily's straight, too," Kenzie added. "I've only had two serious girlfriends."

"I've only ever had two serious boyfriends." Lennox realized. "And I'm a lot older than you."

"I'm twenty-six. You're not that much older than me."

"I'm the oldest person here. And it feels like it, sometimes," Lennox returned. "Anyway, tell me about your girlfriends." She then thought about it. "Wait… Don't. I don't know that I want to hear about them."

"Why not?" Kenzie laughed.

"Maybe just not the details."

"Details?" Kenzie looked confused for a moment before she registered it. "Oh, the sex stuff?"

"Yes, Kenzie. The sex stuff. I don't want to hear about you having sex with your ex-girlfriends."

"Okay." Kenzie laughed loudly at that, and her fingers started dancing over the water again.

"And stop doing that." Lennox pointed at her hand. "It's driving me crazy."

"Oh, sorry." Kenzie withdrew her hand.

"No, not like that." Lennox softened when she realized Kenzie had taken her comment the wrong way. "Sometimes, I say things wrong. And I should know better."

"What do you mean?"

"I forget that you might take them the wrong way. It happens with Jamie, sometimes."

"Oh." Kenzie's eyes dropped to the boat bottom.

"No, Kenz. Don't do that." Lennox scooted as close as the boat would allow and still remain balanced. "I'm sorry. I didn't mean that. I just forget that you might have problems picking up on when I'm trying to be funny, or the fact that when I say you drive me crazy when you do that, it's not *that* kind of crazy. It's the *other* kind of crazy." She lifted both of her eyebrows in hopes that that might help her understand.

"*That* kind of crazy?"

"It's your fingers, Kenzie." Lennox felt the blush instantly. "They're really long. And the way they move, makes me think about things. It's the same thing with this." She reached forward and placed her thumb on Kenzie's bottom lip before tugging down slightly. "It's a turn on. That's what I mean."

"You think about my fingers?"

"Yes, I do. It's kind of hard not to, when you move them like that."

"And you've never thought about another woman's fingers like that before?"

"I took piano lessons from the age of thirteen to twenty-one, and I had three teachers. One was a guy, but the other two were women. One of those women was about forty, but the last one was actually a twenty-seven-year-old piano genius that I hired to help me get ready for a role."

"For *Prodigy*?" Kenzie asked about the movie Lennox had filmed in her early twenties.

"Yes, that one. Anyway, she was pretty, smart, and very talented. I literally had to stare at her fingers for two hours, six days a week, for nine months. And never once did I think of her fingers touching me."

Lennox watched Kenzie swallow, and even that turned her on.

"And when you think about me touching you, it makes you want that?"

"It does."

"But you've never wanted that before?"

"No."

Kenzie stared out at the water again before reaching forward and taking one of Lennox's hands in her own.

"What is your favorite color?" she asked Lennox after several minutes.

"Huh?"

"You wanted us to get to know each other, right?" Kenzie slid her own fingers so that they intertwined with Lennox's, and Lennox felt that lightning bolt move from the tips of her fingers to her palm and through her arm, all the way to her heart that pounded like thunder.

"I like orange, I guess."

"Orange?"

"Sunset-orange," she clarified. "Wanna know why?"

"Yes."

"Will and I sometimes forgot where we were. We traveled so much with our parents as kids, and sometimes, we didn't know what city we were in. One day, we were on set somewhere, and we were talking about it. We were sitting in our parents' director chairs while they walked through a scene. I think we were in Texas, maybe. It might have been Arizona. Anyway, it was dusk, and the sun was doing its thing. He said something about the fact that no matter where we were, the sunset always looked the same, and that there was something good about that." She paused at the memory of her fourteen-year-old brother talking to her about the sunset. "We might have mountains or an ocean in the foreground, but the colors the sun makes when it sets are pink, orange, and yellow, and we could always look at them and know we were at least somewhere."

"That's a really good reason."

"Yeah, it is. I haven't watched the sunset in a very long time. You know, just sit there, watch it happen, and see the colors?" Lennox lost herself in the memory for a second and then pulled herself back out. "Anyway, what's your favorite color?"

"It might just be the sunset-orange now." Kenzie shrugged.

"That's a good line, there, smooth talker," Lennox joked and tugged on Kenzie's hand, pulling her a little closer.

"I didn't mean it to be."

"I know." Lennox smiled at her. "What is it really, though?"

"I can't tell you now."

"What? Why not?" Lennox tugged on that hand lightly again.

"Because you'll think it's a line again."

"Oh, yeah? Now, you *have* to tell me."

"Blue."

"Why would I think that's a line?" Lennox laughed lightly.

"Because my favorite blue is staring back at me." She met Lennox's eyes.

"Oh, wow!" Lennox laughed louder. "Really? How are you still single with lines like that?"

"I told you," Kenzie defended. "It wasn't a line. It's the truth. I've always loved blue."

"And that specific blue?"

"Yes," Kenzie answered. "Can I ask you a question?"
"Sure," Lennox allowed.

"When you're acting, would you say you're putting a part of yourself into the role?"

"What do you mean?"

"I mean, when you're in a scene where you have to be sad, or angry, or happy, is that you? At least, in part?"

"Oh. I guess so, yeah. I think it's that way for most actors."

"Then, that kind of blue. The dark blue of your eyes has been my favorite blue for a long time."

"What?" Lennox was confused at the change back to the favorite color.

"Lennox, if what you just said is true, and you put yourself into the roles you're playing and the emotions that come along with them, I've seen those eyes when they were sad and crying, and happy and laughing. I've seen them when they were frustrated or upset and angry. I watched them flare when you threw a vase at Jason Reid, when he played your cheating boyfriend. And I've loved them in every shade and variation. I've always loved that blue."

Lennox's jaw dropped slightly, and she only hoped Kenzie wouldn't take it the wrong way this time. Her mouth went dry, and she sensed the sincerity in those words and the vulnerability in those dark-green eyes.

"That was beautiful," she remarked a moment later.

"It's just the truth."

"Kenz, you've got to stop saying that. It's not *just* anything. You're not *just* anything. What you said might be the nicest thing anyone's ever said to me. It's definitely the most romantic."

"I didn't mean it romantically. It's a fact. Well, it's a fact about my opinion that your eyes are the best color I've ever seen in whatever shade they're in."

Lennox bit the inside of her mouth, trying to hide her nervousness at this revelation and how Kenzie continued to not grasp what she'd just said and what it meant.

"You know the one part of my job I have to fake, though, because I could never put that part of myself out there?"

"No."

"When I do love scenes, I can't fake that. I mean, I have to, you know, fake it." Lennox laughed softly. "We all have to do that when we're pretending to have sex with another actor. But, when I'm in those scenes, I try my best, I really do, but I just can't give myself over to it. I can't give the other actor that piece of me; the piece I reserve for someone I'm with for real," she paused. "So, there's one way you haven't seen my eyes yet."

"I bet they're even more beautiful," Kenzie let out, and then her own eyes grew three sizes.

"You *are* a smooth talker. I'm serious, how do you not have a girlfriend?"

"I haven't had a girlfriend in a long time."

"I just don't get how, though."

"Why don't you have a boyfriend?"

"Because I just broke up with Aaron?"

"And before him?"

"I had two relationships that were worth mentioning."

"Noah Mason and Lucas Benjamin."

"Yes." Lennox chuckled and reminded herself that Kenzie likely knew her history, or at least, the parts that were public. "I met Noah when I was nineteen. We were friends for a couple of years before we started dating. It lasted until Will died."

"What happened?"

"He wasn't there when I needed him," she replied. "Peyton was there. She helped Jamie and I get through those first few months. But my boyfriend of three years had no idea what to do, so he just didn't do anything." She looked around as she heard a bird start singing. "He went to film in Australia almost right after it happened and then took another job in New York. I was devastated when he ended it over the phone because he couldn't deal with the *new* me. I wasn't even sure what that meant, but I had to get over losing Will, and then losing him, too." She looked at Kenzie's face and saw it flash with anger. "What?"

"I worked with him. He guest-starred on my show. I was nice to him."

"You *can* be nice to him, Kenz."

"I want to kill him right now."

"It's okay. It sucked back then, but it's okay."

Kenzie considered her next words carefully. Lennox could read it on her face and in that nervous lip bite.

"Did you love him?"

"Yes," she replied. "I loved him."

"And Lucas?"

"Lucas and I were never the best match," Lennox admitted. "He was what I thought I needed after Noah and after I lost Will. I was ready for a little adventure in my life and thought Lucas was the right person to provide it."

"Adventure?"

"Yeah – clubs, bars, getting out and having fun, meeting new people. And Lucas was the guy. He knows almost everyone in the business and everyone who supplies to everyone in the business; if you know what I mean."

"Drugs?"

"Cocaine was his favorite. And he drank, too. He hid it from me well for the first year. And then, when I found out, I put up with it for a while, but it got bad, and he went to rehab in Hawaii."

"But you stayed with him?"

"Because I thought I needed that kind of life, and I guess I did for a while. But then, I moved past that. I never really loved him, to answer your question."

"Did you ever do drugs?"

"No, drugs are not for me. I drink, but rarely. And I hate smoking; it's gross. I tried weed once, when I was seventeen, because Will's friend passed it to me, and I didn't know what to do. I inhaled it too deeply, coughed, and that put me off all drugs forever."

Kenzie laughed and brought her other hand to their joined ones.

"I hate smoking, too. I don't do drugs because I don't want to, but also because they might react with my heightened nervous system. And I drink sometimes, but that's usually to appear to be more social. I cut myself off at a beer or one glass of wine."

"We have that in common, then," Lennox attested. "And that's important, because I hate kissing smokers."

Kenzie's eyes got big again, and that made Lennox laugh.

"You did that on purpose?" Kenzie fired.

"I did, yeah. And it was worth it." Lennox placed her free hand on top of the three joined ones. "I have a question for you now."

"Okay."

"Earlier, did you hear that I said you hadn't seen my eyes like that *yet*?" she risked.

"Yes." Kenzie gulped.

"And you understood what I meant by that?"

"Yes."

"How do you feel?"

Kenzie sighed and turned to look at the shore for several long moments, and Lennox thought maybe she'd gone too far.

"It's a battle," she returned softly.

"A battle?"

"I'm not great at expressing stuff like this unless I have a script, okay?" Kenzie turned to face Lennox.

"Okay."

"So, I'll try to get this out right." She took both of her hands and pulled them back before she leaned forward and wrapped them around Lennox's neck. "I find you incredibly sexy all the time," she released. "I always have. But now, you're here in person, and I think you are the most beautiful woman on the planet. I want to respect the fact that you've never been with another woman, and that this is new to you.

And I want to take things as slowly as you need to; if you still like me after all this getting to know me stuff. But, my brain is fighting with other parts of me that want to tear your clothes off and lie you down in that cabana tonight." She closed her eyes as if to scold herself, while Lennox watched on and felt her own body react to the words. "I want to kiss you, Lennox. I want to touch you. I want you. I want to know everything about you. I want to keep talking to you like this because it's important, and I wish we could sit out here on the water all day and do that. It's hard for me to make the first move. And I think, with you, I might have to, because you've never done this before. But I don't want to do anything you're not ready for, or that I'm not ready for. And I don't know what to do with all that, because that's the first time I've ever felt all that at once."

"You think I'm sexy all the time?" Lennox lifted an eyebrow.

"That's what you took away from that?" Kenzie pulled back, but Lennox stopped her with hands on her forearms to keep them in place. "Lennox, I am very attracted to you. Why do you think I went running yesterday and today?"

"What? Why?" Lennox asked and ran her hands up and down Kenzie's arms.

"You know why."

"You had to run it off?"

"Yes, I had to *try* to run it off. I've not been successful. I can't stop thinking about you."

"I can't stop thinking about you, either," Lennox returned. "I think I've gotten about three hours of sleep since I got here."

Kenzie pulled her arms away at that and picked up one of the oars. She moved so quickly, Lennox worried she'd done something wrong, until she remembered – Kenzie always moved that quickly.

"We should head back. It's been a while. And I told Davica, Quinn, and Jack I'd play cards with them when I get back from my run."

"Can I ask you a very personal question?"

"The other questions haven't been personal?" Kenzie shot back and began rowing them toward the shore.

"Are you fast at everything?"

"I don't follow. I told you about–"

"I know," Lennox interrupted. "I'm asking about sex," she confessed. "Your–"

"Orgasms?" Kenzie let out a little louder than she'd planned and promptly blushed, which caused Lennox to laugh wildly and grab the other oar.

"Yes, that's what I meant."

"You want to know if I…"

"Fast? Yes. You don't have to answer."

"Oh, it's been a while." Kenzie was nervous, and it was adorable.

"How long is a while?" Lennox wanted to know. Kenzie gave her a look that said that she didn't want to answer. "Aaron and I never slept together," she offered up, realizing that the look on Kenzie's face was embarrassment. "We dated for two months, if you could call it that, but we were in separate states for most of that. We had four actual dates."

"But you didn't have sex?"

"I told him I wasn't ready after the first two, he didn't ask after the second two, and then, we didn't have another." She rowed alongside Kenzie as they slowly crept toward the shore. "Lucas was the last guy I was with," she admitted and then watched realization appear on Kenzie's face. "Yeah, it's been a long time."

"You didn't with anyone else?"

"I don't just have sex, Kenzie. I've been with two guys my whole life," Lennox added. "Noah and Lucas. And I still kind of regret Lucas, but I've gotten to a place where I'm okay with it," she paused. "Not exactly what you expected?"

"No," Kenzie shared. "But, I like it."

"When this whole thing is over, we should go out," Lennox suggested as the boat slid nearer to the dock. "I'll be working a lot, so it might be hard to make it happen. I know you're busy, too."

"We don't have to wait, Lennox," Kenzie replied. "We can go out here."

"Here?" Lennox grabbed the rope and dropped it over the post on the dock, to hold the boat in place.

"We can sneak away again." Kenzie placed her oar back in the bottom of the boat. "I'd like to sneak away again, if you would like to do that."

Kenzie was nervous again, and Lennox wasn't sure if she wanted to kiss her more when she looked sexy and sweaty, like she had earlier, or in the moments like this – when Kenzie was nervous and didn't know what to say.

"I'll sneak away with you."

"It's a date then." Kenzie smiled back.

CHAPTER 11

KENZIE could not believe the afternoon she'd had. Kenzie couldn't believe the last three days she'd had. She'd met Lennox in person that first night and spent every moment since thinking about her. She never considered Lennox Owen would be interested in women, and definitely never considered she would be interested in her, specifically. And yet, here Lennox was – staring at her from across the picnic table while Kenzie played cards with Quinn, Davica, and Jack. Lennox was talking but not *really* talking to Lynn and Jenna. Bobby and Mandy were preparing to build a fire for the night. They wouldn't light it yet; the sun was still up. They'd all eat dinner and then light the fire for the nightly s'mores and music playing session.

Tomorrow was the 4th of July, and the whole day was planned by Peyton and Dani. They had an agenda that they had already delivered to the group, and everyone was excited. They seemed particularly glad when Dani listed off the events, and she hadn't mentioned another softball game. Kenzie wouldn't have a problem playing softball again. She had been a hero today, and that was mainly because of Lennox. After the game, Kenzie had planned on retreating immediately into a run, but some of the girls wanted to talk to her, and she had spent a few minutes enjoying getting to know them before she was ready for a break and a run to try to get Lennox off her mind. Kenzie had no idea Lennox had taken a break herself and that they'd run into each other at the boathouse. Thank God she had, though. That time they had shared in the boat was quite possibly the best hour or so of her life. She thought about that as she played her next card. That first night in the cabana had been the best time of her life. And then, last night, when they'd talked before she'd fled, had been the best time of her life. And today was now at the top of that list. Lennox Owen had been a part of the top three moments in her life, and she had only known her for as many days.

She felt eyes on her again and glanced in Lennox's direction to find her staring at her. When Lennox had been found out, she smiled, and Kenzie smiled back before returning to her card game. She wasn't sure what they should be doing based on their conversation earlier. She knew this wasn't something Lennox was ready to let everyone here know, so they shouldn't spend all their time together or the others might get suspicious. She also knew that none of them knew she was gay, either, so maybe they wouldn't get suspicious of them in that way, but they would likely want to know why both of them kept running off together or kept sitting next to each other and whispering to one another. No, this was better. Separating and talking to other people was better for them for now.

"Ladies, it's dinner time. But, before we go, it's time to talk about the cabin switch," Peyton announced.

"Come on, Peyton. Do we have to change? My stuff is already out," Lynn objected.

"Yes, Lynn," she returned.

"You and Dani aren't changing. How are you two supposed to bond with us if you're all cuddled up alone?" Bobby asked.

"Yeah," April concurred. "You two should join in."

"Dani and I are the ones that brought you all here. We know all of you enough," Peyton pointed out. "So, in cabin one, we have Sarah, Jack, and Carlie." She scrolled through her phone. "In two, we have Kenzie, Lennox, Cleo, and

Maddox. In three, it's April, Tiana, and Brooke. Four, is Lynn, Jenna, and Bobby. And five, is Quinn, Mandy, and Davica." Peyton put her phone back in her pocket. "Let's grab some food and then report back to the fire pit for some dessert."

"S'mores," Quinn muttered to Kenzie. "I'm ready for something other than s'mores."

"You know she'll have something off the charts good for tomorrow. She goes crazy with the holiday food prep," Davica announced.

"Tomorrow is going to be fun," Quinn added and nudged Kenzie's shoulder. "This is your first *fourth* with us. You ready for this?" She laughed.

"I guess," Kenzie replied.

"You'll have a blast. Just don't drink too much before noon. You won't last," Davica advised and stood.

***

Dinner was great. Kenzie ate nearly everything on her plate before she took a look around at the other women still eating. She had always been a fast eater, finishing before everyone else around her practically all the time. She had gotten used to it and sat back, checking the other table for Lennox's progress every few minutes. When she noticed Lennox had finished, she dropped her own plate off and grabbed a couple of bottles of water, shoving them into the pockets of the sweats she'd put on after her shower, and headed in the direction of her new cabin. She'd already moved her stuff over to it but hadn't yet unpacked. She pulled out one of the unused plastic bags she had brought with her to separate her dirty clothes from her clean ones and went back to the cafeteria cabin. She snuck inside through the front door, while everyone else was out back, and grabbed a couple of apples, granola bars, and individually wrapped brownies, along with a few other things she thought Lennox might like. She then carried her bag outside, dropped it off before she got to the tables so no one else could see, and approached Lennox at her table. She placed a hand on her shoulder and earned a glance with a smile.

"Can I borrow you?" she asked.

"Sure." Lennox understood her meaning and stood. "Let me just drop this off."

Lennox made her way inside to drop off her dirty dishes and then returned outside, where Kenzie was waiting with the bag she had moved the water bottles into along with the two beers she had grabbed inside just in case.

"Where are we off to?" Lennox asked when she saw Kenzie was prepared.

"I know a place," Kenzie offered, and they walked past the group in silence.

Kenzie caught Peyton's curious glance and a smile. She smiled back and blushed before walking on.

"So, this is our date, right?" Lennox asked when they were beyond the fire pit, heading toward cabin three. "And we're in cabin two tonight."

"I know. We're not going to the cabin." Kenzie pointed beyond it. "I found a place when I was running. I thought we could go there."

"Can I pick up something before we go, though?" Lennox asked.

"Yeah, sure." Kenzie stopped when Lennox placed a hand on her arm only for a second before running off toward cabin two.

Lennox returned, carrying two sweatshirts and a blanket. She held out one sweatshirt to Kenzie, and Kenzie took it with her free hand.

"It's supposed to get a little chilly later," Lennox commented. "Just in case."

"Thank you."

"Lead the way." Lennox motioned with an open hand.

Kenzie placed the sweatshirt under her left arm and moved the bag she was carrying to that hand. She took a chance and extended her right hand, once they were beyond the view of the others, and watched as Lennox looked down at it, smiled, and took it. They walked along the trail for the next few minutes in relative silence, until they emerged on the other side of the thick row of trees into a patch of high grass. Kenzie pulled on Lennox's hand, and they walked through it.

"Watch out for snakes," Kenzie warned.

"What? Snakes!" Lennox practically squealed and jumped back toward the trail, dropping Kenzie's hand.

Kenzie laughed and walked back to take her hand again.

"Come on. I'll protect you," she offered.

"How can you protect me from snakes?" Lennox asked.

"You are such a city girl!" Kenzie exclaimed and pulled a reluctant Lennox back into the tall grass. She watched as Lennox's eyes darted around, checking for the creatures. "Any other fears I should know about?"

"Depends on where you're taking me," Lennox replied, still looking at the ground. "Are we going to a house filled with spiders?"

"No." Kenzie chuckled. "But that boathouse probably had a least a hundred of them."

"Don't tell me that," Lennox returned, and when they made it through the grass, she let out a grateful breath.

Kenzie intertwined their fingers and walked them through a small grouping of trees, and then, turned them to the left to move around another patch of that tall grass she knew she'd never get Lennox through. After they got through another tree grouping, Kenzie stopped and looked over at Lennox, who had realized they'd arrived all on her own.

"You found this on your run?"

"Yeah. And then, I noticed you looking at it through the window of the boathouse. I thought we could sneak away to here," she answered.

They were standing in front of a much smaller lake than the one next to their campsite. It was the size of maybe half a football field. And just on the other side was a small hill, covered in brightly-colored purple and orange flowers. It also happened to have the best view of the sun that was just about to set for the night.

"I wanted to check this out tomorrow," Lennox said.

"Sorry," Kenzie replied, thinking she had ruined Lennox's plans.

"No, that's not what I meant." Lennox squeezed her hand and turned to face her.

"Oh." Kenzie looked away.

"Kenzie, I'm happy you brought me here. You somehow read my mind earlier."

"I did?"

"Yes, I wanted to come here. You figured that out and brought me. You read me," she confirmed. "That's pretty amazing."

"Because of who I am?" Kenzie asked.

"No, because no one reads me," Lennox returned. "Peyton can, sometimes, but that's because we've been friends forever. Jamie struggles, and she's my sister."

"She's like me, though." Kenzie squinted at Lennox, trying to understand.

"No, no one is like you, Mackenzie." Lennox ran her hand through Kenzie's hair and slid it gracefully behind her ear. "And, trust me, I keep a lot of things to myself, normally. I don't tell a lot of people what I think or how I feel. You may not believe that, given this experience and how I can't seem to stop telling *you* how I feel, but Peyton can attest to it later, if you want to verify." She smiled. "I usually show up to work, do my job, put in some face time with the people I need to do that with, and go home to an empty house, now that Jamie's gone."

"Why don't you tell people what you think?"

"I don't know. I guess there wasn't much of a point to it." Lennox turned to face the water. "Can we sit?"

"Yes," Kenzie answered and watched Lennox spread the blanket she'd brought on the grass about ten feet in front of the water. "Why wasn't there a point?" Kenzie questioned and set the bag down next to the blanket.

"What?"

"Why don't you tell people what you think or how you feel? Why is there no point?"

Lennox sat on the blanket and looked up at her. Kenzie remained standing, as if to tell Lennox that if she answered the question, she'd sit down.

"I'm an actor, Kenz. You know how that goes. You show up, say the lines, and go. No one really wants to hear what you have to say."

"I do." Kenzie sat next to her but didn't face the water.

"Kenz, I don't want to talk about that stuff now." She turned her face to the water.

Kenzie caught her profile and thought her even more stunning than she'd considered possible.

"You're beautiful," she said.

Lennox turned back to offer her a shy smile. Kenzie took the opportunity to slide over behind her. She watched as Lennox watched her and clearly wondered what she was doing. Kenzie spread her legs and rested her palms on her own knees. Without saying a word, she met Lennox's eyes, and Lennox's shy smile grew wider. Lennox turned to face the water, and Kenzie moved closer. Lennox lifted up her arms so that Kenzie's could slide in and she could wrap herself around her waist. It took a few minutes, but Lennox finally relaxed back into her, and Kenzie relaxed the arms on the taut abdomen, resting her own head on Lennox's shoulder.

"Sunset-orange," Lennox remarked.

"I thought this would be the best view for you to see it," Kenzie replied.

"Thank you. This is perfect."

"It is," Kenzie agreed. "Lennox?"

"Yeah?"

"I want to know what you think."

"Right now?"

"No, you said no one cares, and you were talking about work."

"Kenzie…"

"What?"

"This is a date. This is our first date. I'm enjoying myself and the view. Let's just–"

"Tell me," Kenzie insisted.

"Why?" Lennox tensed.

"Because you've made me feel so comfortable, Lennox. You seem to understand what I need and get me to tell you things I don't tell anyone." She stopped herself and started to pull back.

"You want me to do the same." Lennox held her arms in place. "Stay," she requested.

"Okay." Kenzie relented, not wanting to stop touching Lennox anyway.

"I have ideas sometimes, for the script or a scene. It started with my first show, and it happens nearly every movie I work on."

"You have script ideas?"

"Yeah, just little things, sometimes. It'll be a line change or maybe a thought about how I should say something. I'll read a scene and not think my character or even another character would do whatever it is they do in the scene. Sometimes, I'll have ideas of my own for shows I'm not even on." She rested her hands on top of Kenzie's and relaxed again. "Like your show."

"Old show or a new show?"

"Both." Lennox laughed lightly, and Kenzie felt it all over her body. "But, the new one, mostly."

"You have ideas for my show?"

"Just, like, little things."

"Like what?" Kenzie giggled at the thought.

"It's a zombie show."

"I know. I'm on it, Lennox."

Lennox turned around in her arms. Her eyes were so bright, Kenzie nearly gasped at the sight. Lennox was smiling, and her hand was on Kenzie's knee, like it was the most natural thing in the world for her to be touching her there.

"Okay... So, in the first season, you guys were fleeing the zombie swarm, and you made your way to the desert where you got stuck for, like, five episodes."

"Yeah, that was a pain in the ass to film. It's over a hundred degrees during the day and about forty at night." Kenzie recalled that painful shoot.

"I had this idea for season two that, since you and your family are making your way back to the city, you could end up on a college campus. It's been saved from the zombies, and there's a group of students that have a section blocked off. There are probably some professors there, too, but I haven't worked that part out yet. Anyway, I thought there would be a med student that had a hard life or something, and she was kind of the de facto leader of the bunch. I don't know the exact number of people yet, but I was thinking no more than twenty. You guys would pitch in there and move into an old dorm. I thought your mom would have her own room, and you would share with your sister for a while, and then–" Lennox stopped herself. "Holy crap!" She covered her mouth with her free hand.

"What?" Kenzie laughed. This was by far the most expressive she'd seen Lennox since they'd met. "What, Lennox?" she asked again and poked Lennox in the side.

"I am so stupid." Lennox lowered her hand. "I had this whole thing scripted in my head. You, or your character, technically, you're only eighteen, and you were about to graduate high school when the outbreak happened."

"Yes."

"You had a boyfriend that died, and I thought it would be interesting if you struck up a friendship with the med student I mentioned. She's, like, twenty-five in my mind, but she's gay." Lennox lifted an eyebrow. "I thought you'd get closer to her throughout the season and that you would..."

Kenzie burst out laughing and had to pull herself back a little. She flopped back on the blanket, grateful that Lennox's sweatshirt was behind her head.

"You turned my character gay?" She continued to laugh.

"I know. It's ridiculous. Forget I said anything." Lennox moved the hand that had been on Kenzie's knee.

"No, Lennox. Now, you're misunderstanding me." Kenzie pulled on Lennox's hand and put it back on her knee. "I'm not laughing because it's a bad idea. I'm laughing because I am gay. I'm gay in real life, and somehow, you made my character gay, too."

"I was actually thinking about the fact that I had pictured you with a girl in these scenes in my head."

"You did?" Kenzie lifted her head.

"Yeah." Lennox looked down at her. "And that girl looked a lot like me."

Kenzie's mouth went dry as Lennox stared down at her. The look in those blue eyes had Kenzie wondering if her green ones matched the intensity.

"Now, I can see my favorite color," Kenzie said.

Lennox gave her a surprised smile, and Kenzie acted before she lost the courage. She tugged on the front of Lennox's T-shirt, pulling her down until Lennox hovered just above her. "Is this okay?"

"Yes," Lennox whispered, and her eyes went to Kenzie's lips.

"I think you're a writer, Lennox Owen," Kenzie shared.

She ran her hand through Lennox's hair and slid it behind the woman's ear, while her other hand still held on to Lennox's shirt.

"What?" Lennox was taken aback by that comment.

"You're a writer. That's why it bothers you so much when they don't listen." Kenzie lifted her head slightly. "I'm going to kiss you now." Her lips were millimeters away from Lennox's.

"Okay," Lennox whispered back and licked her lips.

Kenzie lifted her head the rest of the way and connected their lips. It was brief, that first connection, and Lennox pulled back slightly after to meet her eyes. Then, she leaned down and captured Kenzie's lips with her own. It was slow and paced, at first. Kenzie moved the hand that had been on Lennox's shirt a little under it to feel the skin beneath, while the other went to the back of Lennox's neck to hold her close. Lennox moved into her. She lay down and hovered over Kenzie, with her hands on either side of Kenzie's head.

Kenzie wondered when Lennox would stop it. The kiss became heated, and Kenzie's hand slid around to Lennox's back, still under the shirt. She moaned at the touch, and Lennox seemed to be moved at that sound, because her lips started moving faster, and Kenzie could barely keep up. That had never happened before. Kenzie had no problem keeping up. She was faster than almost anyone at anything. But Lennox Owen was kissing her with a pace and passion she had never felt before.

This was the part of her nervous system disorder she hadn't shared with anyone else, and that included her parents or the doctors that diagnosed her. Of course, they'd told her about the symptoms and what she might have to deal with, but she had never confirmed that she had this one. At first, it was because she had no frame of reference. But, as she grew up, started dating, and, therefore, became more physical with people, she knew it had to be true. For Kenzie, light touches were not just light touches. She could feel everything. When she was hot, she was on fire. When she was cold, she froze. And when someone like Lennox Owen kissed her like this, it was as if every one of her cells resonated with pleasure. When Lennox lowered herself even farther down into her body, Kenzie's eyes shot open, because she knew what would happen if they didn't stop.

"Lennox?" she asked when Lennox's lips moved to her jaw, and then, her neck. "Oh." She managed when the touch of Lennox's tongue met her skin.

"Yeah?"

"We should–" Kenzie's hand slid up Lennox's back, and her nails dragged back down. "We have to stop." She kept her hand frozen at Lennox's back.

"I thought that would be my line." Lennox pulled up to meet Kenzie's eyes and smiled down at her. "Hi," she said from above, with swollen lips and dark eyes, and it was the most adorable thing Kenzie had ever seen.

"Hi," she said back.

"That was nice." Lennox ran a hand through Kenzie's hair. "Are you okay?" she asked when she noticed Kenzie look away.

"You're just a really good kisser," she breathed out.

"So are you." Lennox kissed her gently on the lips. "You want to stop?" she asked and applied a soft kiss to Kenzie's collarbone.

"No, I don't," Kenzie admitted. "But we should."

"We don't have to."

"I should tell you something." Kenzie met the blue eyes above her.

"Okay?" Lennox moved to sit up and straddled her, keeping her hands on Kenzie's stomach.

"Sometimes, when it's been a long time – and it has been a long time for me – I have a little adjustment issue," she tried.

"Adjustment issue?"

"The nervous system thing," Kenzie said and then realized she needed to provide more information. "I feel things differently than other people."

"Oh… Bad different?"

"Intense different," she offered. "Never this intense, though," she added.

"Should I stop touching you right now?"

"No, please, don't." Kenzie placed her hands on top of Lennox's. "It's never been like this for me, okay? When I touch things, it's heightened. I feel more than the average person. Like, when you touch a peach, you might feel the fuzz on the outside, but I not only feel it, I see it through the touch; if that makes any sense. It's like it's a foot tall, and I'm running my fingers through it."

"That's why you're always running your fingers along things."

"It calms me down," Kenzie supplied. "It doesn't happen with everything – or, at least, not to that degree." She slowed her speech down, wanting to make sure she explained this correctly. "I've kissed a lot of people in my life." She watched Lennox's eyebrow lift. "For work; I've kissed most of them for work. I've maybe kissed eight people as me, though; for real. And it's never done that to me."

"What did it do?" Lennox questioned, and when she appeared to notice that Kenzie was having an issue expressing it, she took Kenzie's hands in her own, brought them to her stomach, and placed them there, under her shirt. "Describe it to me."

"I can't, when you're doing that." Kenzie watched as Lennox encouraged her to run her fingers along her stomach. "Jesus, are you always in the gym?" she exclaimed.

Lennox laughed and placed her own hands back on the ground, hovering above Kenzie once again.

"I'm in the gym sometimes, yes, but not always. Tell me, Kenzie." Lennox smiled down at her, met Kenzie's eyes, and then flitted down to Kenzie's lips. "I'll tell you, okay?"

"What?" Kenzie asked, focusing on the feeling of Lennox's skin on her fingertips, which were the parts of her that were touching Lennox.

"I'll tell you what it feels like to touch you first." She paused and leaned down.

Kenzie could feel her breath against her own lips as Lennox's were right above them. Lennox pressed lightly into them before pulling away and gliding her lips over Kenzie's skin to her cheek.

"When I first touched your hand, to help you with

your bag, I thought it was static electricity. But I'm starting to doubt that." She kissed Kenzie's cheek.

Kenzie gasped and removed her own hands from under Lennox's shirt. She couldn't be touching her and listening to this while she felt every touch. Kenzie wanted to focus on the touches being delivered to her skin.

"You felt that?" she breathed more than said.

"I more than felt it. I *knew* it," Lennox revealed. "I had to keep my cool, and I also had to try to sort out what I thought about it." She pressed her lips to the spot just behind Kenzie's ear, and Kenzie shivered. "I know that, too."

"Know?"

"Know that I'm supposed to be here with you right now. I know that I'm supposed to be touching you like this. It's the one thing I know for sure." Lennox met Kenzie's eyes again. "Tell me," she whispered the request against Kenzie's lips.

"My body tingles," she managed. "It makes me shake, sometimes; tremble," she added. "It's never been this bad." Kenzie exhaled against Lennox's mouth.

"Or this good?" Lennox questioned.

"Yeah, that."

Lennox laughed silently, but the smile on her face was wide, and Kenzie never wanted to stop looking at it. She never wanted to stop looking at her.

"Do you want to stop?" Lennox asked, and Kenzie tried to discern the expression on her face.

"Do *you* want to stop?"

Lennox lifted up and looked down at her with a smile. She took the hands that Kenzie had, again, placed in fists at her sides, and put them on her waist. She moved her own hands to Kenzie's hips, slid them under her shirt ever so slightly, and stilled them.

"What do you think?" she asked. "Do you think I want to stop?"

"You've never done this, so I–"

"Kenz, what am I doing right now?" Lennox asked

and ran her hands up and down Kenzie's sides.

"Driving me crazy," Kenzie replied and received a wild laugh in response. "You don't want to stop." She guessed the moment Lennox's laughter stopped.

"No, I'd be perfectly content being here with you all night, watching the sunset, and occasionally, maybe, making out." She lifted a sexy eyebrow. "But if you need us to slow down, we can."

Kenzie slid her hands under Lennox's shirt and used her fingertips to graze the soft skin she found. Lennox's eyes closed. And, for a moment, Kenzie just watched her. She resonated with the heightened sensation that came with her touching Lennox's skin, but she was able to tune at least part of the intensity out, because Lennox was beautiful. She recognized Lennox's fingers on her own skin, moving slowly up and down, and then inside, resting her palms on Kenzie's stomach before repeating the motion. When Lennox opened her eyes, Kenzie was still staring, and she lowered her eyes.

"I–"

"Don't" Lennox moved her right hand higher up under Kenzie's shirt and rested it over her heart. "Don't look away, Kenzie. It's me." Lennox lowered herself back down. "Kiss me. It's okay."

Kenzie gulped and felt Lennox's hand drag back down and rest again at her side, this time, over Kenzie's shirt. Lennox's other hand moved to hold herself above Kenzie. Kenzie took both of her hands away from Lennox's body and lifted her head up to meet Lennox's request. She kissed her slowly, and Lennox slowed the kiss even more. Kenzie's lips shook at the continued contact.

"Sorry," she managed out between soft kisses.

"Why?" Lennox kissed her again.

Kenzie turned her head away and tried to move. Lennox took the hint and climbed off her, sitting to her side.

"I should be better at this. Why are you so good at it?" she questioned.

"What?" Lennox was confused by the abrupt shift. That, Kenzie could tell. "Good at what? Kissing? Trust me; you are very good at kissing."

"I'm gay, Lennox. I'm the gay one. You're not, and you're so much better at this than I am. You've never kissed a girl before, but it's so easy for you," she returned.

"Hey, calm down. It's fine." Lennox placed a hand on top of Kenzie's on the blanket.

"Is it?" she asked.

"Kenzie, I wanted to kiss you, so I kissed you. And I want to keep kissing you. It's that simple. I don't know what it means yet, but I know that's what I want."

"It's hard, Lennox," Kenzie shared and slid her hand out from under Lennox's.

"I know," Lennox said softly.

Kenzie looked up and noticed Lennox was staring out at the water and the setting sun beyond it. Again, she was caught by the woman's beauty, and how no sunset could ever compare. Lennox brushed her hair behind her ear and turned back to face her with a smile. "So, I'll ask again, then. Do you want to stop?"

Kenzie realized what Lennox was asking. She wasn't referring to the kisses they'd just shared, or the fact that they'd been close to moving beyond them for a moment. She was asking if Kenzie wanted to stop all of it. She was giving Kenzie an out for the whole thing: for the impromptu date they were on; for the fact that they were obviously attracted to one another; and for anything that might come out of that, after this week at the summer camp.

"It feels different," Kenzie offered instead of an answer to the question.

"I know." Lennox nodded.

"No, not the girl thing."

"That's not what I'm talking about, either," Lennox replied. "That is different for me, yes. But, Kenzie, that's not the part that's most different. Is that how to say that?" She laughed lightly. "Most different?"

"Yes," Kenzie answered.

"I told you that I've only been in love once, and that's true. I've dated, and I've had two relationships, but I've only been in love one time." Lennox turned back to the setting sun and took a moment to appreciate the remainder of the now dark-orange, mixed with greens and pinks. "I can be as patient as you need me to be, Kenzie. We can slow things all the way down. We can go back to hand-holding or passing notes during study hall that ask, *'Do you like me? Check yes or no.'* " She took another moment to observe and then flopped down on the blanket, using the sweatshirt as a pillow. "Whatever you need." She turned her head to Kenzie. "I just know that this is right. And I think you feel that, too; along with everything else you feel. And that's scary."

"You're not scared?" Kenzie asked.

"Of course, I am," Lennox supplied. "I'm terrified, Kenzie." She placed her hand back on top of Kenzie's. "I've never done this before. It's not like I planned to come to this thing and find someone I could fall–" Lennox stopped herself, and her eyes lowered away from Kenzie's. "This was the last thing I expected."

"I never did that," Kenzie said.

"Did what?"

Kenzie moved to lie down next to her, disconnecting her hand from Lennox's but lying close, because she had to be close to her right now.

"I never got a note in school that said, *'Do you like me? Check yes or no.'* "

Lennox smiled and rolled on her side, matching Kenzie's position.

"I would have sent you that note."

"No, you wouldn't have." Kenzie laughed at the thought of a young Lennox Owen sending her a note like that.

"If I would have gone to a normal school, and you were there, I would have."

"You would have been several years older than me

then, too, and wouldn't have given me the time of day," Kenzie rebutted.

"Fine. Let's assume we were in school, and we were the same age; in the same class. I would have noticed you, and I would have given you all the times in the day." She slid her hand over Kenzie's cheek. "All the times. You could have 3 p.m., and 1 p.m., and 10 a.m., and even 6 a.m., and even 6 p.m., and–"

Kenzie cut off the ramble with her lips. Lennox hadn't been prepared for the kiss, and it took her a second to stop laughing and respond. Kenzie felt the laughter deep in her body. It resonated in her bones and vibrated. Her nerves were on fire, and it was the good kind of fire. She slid on top of Lennox for the first time, and when her body pressed down into Lennox's, she knew this was right. They fit. They strangely fit. She had never truly fit with anyone, and that had been especially true with the women she had dated.

Lennox seemed to be holding back. Her hands were at her sides, and she wasn't pushing Kenzie for more than she could offer. Kenzie was holding herself up, and while she wanted to touch Lennox's body again, because it was perfect, Kenzie knew she needed to keep her hands off her now. The more she touched her, the more intense it got. And that scared her, because, if she got used to that feeling, she'd crave it. If she got used to the feeling of Lennox's skin against her fingertips, she would need it forever. No one else would be able to compare. And if Lennox changed her mind, if she reconsidered what was happening between them, Kenzie would be devastated.

"I want you," Kenzie gasped out as she pulled her lips away.

"I want you, too," Lennox replied, and Kenzie watched her squeeze her hands into tight fists.

"You're holding back because of me," Kenzie stated and knew the answer.

"I'm holding back because of me," Lennox returned.

"Don't lie."

"Kenzie, you have no idea what you do to me. And, right now, all I want is to take your shirt off. I want to take my shirt off. I want your sweats off, and I want my shorts off. I want all of it off," she commented.

"You do?" Kenzie could only laugh and sat up, still straddling Lennox's hips.

"Yes, I do. But I'm not ready for that, and you, kissing me how you kiss me, makes me want that. So, I'm drawing blood on my palms, squeezing them into fists, to try to keep from touching you, because, once I do, I don't think I can stop. And I don't think you're ready for that, either."

"You are so beautiful," Kenzie expressed and picked up both of Lennox's hands at the same time. Lennox relaxed them, and Kenzie took both of them to her lips and pressed sweet kisses on her palms. "Can we sit here for a little while longer?"

"We can sit here all night," Lennox returned and watched Kenzie kiss her fingers one by one.

"Will you tell me more about your ideas for the show?"

"I told you all of it." Lennox lowered her hands and placed them on Kenzie's hips instead.

"Don't lie," Kenzie repeated and gave her the softest expression she could.

Lennox thought about what to say next. Kenzie could sense her brain wheels moving inside that head, and she climbed off her, moving to Lennox's side and reaching inside the plastic bag to grab the two beers she'd brought along with some of the snacks.

"I wrote some of it down." Lennox finally admitted after the second sip of her beer.

"And?"

"It doesn't matter. Nothing's going to come out of it. It's not like the producers of your show are going to read it."

"Then, why did you write it?" Kenzie fired back with a lifted eyebrow.

"I don't know."

"Yes, you do. Why did you bother writing it down if you didn't think anything would happen with it?"

"You know, I think I liked you better when you just gave me one-word responses."

"I'm more comfortable with you now. We're beyond that," Kenzie returned.

"I'd hope so. You just had your tongue down my throat." Lennox took another drink of her beer, and Kenzie laughed.

CHAPTER 12

Lennox had just kissed, and kissed, and kissed a girl. No, she hadn't kissed a girl. She had kissed a woman. She had kissed a gorgeous, complex, smart, and funny – even though Kenzie, herself, had no idea she was funny – woman. Lennox had kissed Mackenzie Smyth, the woman she had watched on a supernatural TV show for four seasons, making sure never to miss an episode even when she was shooting one herself. Lennox had downloaded them on her phone and recorded them to watch on her DVR. She had even bought all the seasons to stream whenever she wanted. And, as she stared at Kenzie, who was biting into an apple, she realized that the only reason she had watched that show religiously, and the only reason she watched her new show, was because Kenzie was on it. Lennox had felt a connection to her from moment one in person, but she'd be lying to herself if she didn't admit to feeling one even before that.

She'd never thought about the possibility of being bisexual or gay. She had dated guys, and that was just how it was for her. She still wasn't sure how to identify herself, now that she'd made out with the creature with dark-green eyes that had little flecks of gold – or maybe it was more brass than gold – in them. Kenzie seemed comfortable in the silence between them since they had wrapped their conversation about the show and Lennox's ideas. Lennox thought back to when she had dated Noah and Lucas, but particularly Noah, whom she had loved. She'd mentioned ideas for her own show and had some thoughts on his films as well, when she'd helped him read his lines or even select which movie to do. He had never seemed all that interested in what she had to say. He'd listen, of course. He would nod and mutter a few words here and there, but he never took it further than that, and he had never suggested she take it further, either. Lucas had been the same, but Lennox had chalked that more up to his lifestyle and addictions than his actual opinions of her ideas.

Kenzie had listened thoughtfully, as she'd walked her through her entire outline of the next season and how it would impact each character, and her character, specifically. In the first season of the show, Lennox thought Kenzie's abilities had been wasted and under-utilized. Kenzie had been relegated to the background of most episodes, only getting a few to really shine and show her stuff. Now that Lennox knew her and knew more about her, she found her raw ability even more astounding. Kenzie could go from tears to laughter in a scene in an instant, and from fiery anger to joy just as quickly. And Lennox had no idea how someone, who struggled with emotion regularly and had a hard time expressing herself or socializing with others as Kenzie did, could accomplish so much.

"Do you like it?" Kenzie asked while Lennox remained staring at her.

"Like what?" Lennox turned her head to watch a squirrel scurry up a tree next to them.

"Acting."

"Oh." When Lennox turned back to her, Kenzie was watching her, and she gave her a shy smile, like she'd just been caught. "Yeah, I like it enough."

"Enough?" Kenzie took another bite of her apple.

"It's what I've done my whole life. I guess you could say I was born for it, with my parents."

"But your brother and sister didn't do it forever." Kenzie risked, and Lennox recognized the concern on her face.

"You can talk about him. It's okay," she encouraged. "And, no, they didn't. Will tried, but he wasn't a fan. And Jamie didn't have it in her, but part of that was–"

"The Asperger's?" Kenzie finished.

"No, I don't think so," Lennox corrected. "She was a lot younger than us when Will died, and my parents didn't know what to do after the accident. Jamie had gone to school on set like me for a few years, but that wasn't working. So, they tried to stay in one place. They stayed in LA for over a year when she was about ten, and sent her to a real school. She got some focused help from teachers that understood her, and then, my parents couldn't stay." She paused at the recollection. "It was like they got bored or something. My dad got offered the director on a film that shot in New Zealand and would take at least six months, with the promise of a sequel or trilogy if it performed. And my mom went with him, because she took something shooting in South Africa for a few months. Jamie had to tag along. She spent four months in New Zealand with no one that understood her, and then, a couple in South Africa before they returned to LA. When they got back, I could tell she had regressed back to her old, quiet self. She had no friends or even kids her age. And while I could deal with it because I had Will, or maybe because I had better coping skills, she couldn't." Lennox grabbed the apple from Kenzie's hand and took a bite. "She struggled after that. And once Will died, my parents ditched us again, and I took Jamie in. She lived with me until she graduated from a real high school, with the best teachers I could find, and she went to therapy for a few years to teach her coping skills and how to deal with the emotional stuff she struggled with. She moved out when she went to college, and she actually did well in the dorm room. Now, she's in the army, and she's learning to be an engineer. She's happy, and it's amazing." Lennox took another bite.

"You are amazing," Kenzie returned.

"How'd you get that from everything I just said?" Lennox tried to laugh off the compliment.

"Because you took in your little sister and gave her a life when she was struggling. Not everyone would have done that, Lennox."

"Why do you still call me Lennox?" She changed the subject. "I told you to call me Len or Lex. Everyone calls me Len or Lex."

"I like your name. Why would I shorten it? It's beautiful."

"It's not beautiful. It's basically a boy's name. I think my parents were hoping for another boy."

"The name Lennox is a Gaelic name. In Gaelic, the meaning of the name Lennox is: 'Lives near the place abounding in elm trees. People with this name tend to be creative and excellent at expressing themselves. They are drawn to the arts, and often enjoy life immensely. They are often the center of attention and enjoy careers that put them in the limelight. They tend to become involved in many different activities, and are sometimes reckless with both their energies and with money,'" Kenzie rattled off, and Lennox just stared at her.

"Where did you get all that?"

Kenzie lowered her head on Lennox's shoulder, and Lennox didn't move. She feared if she moved an inch, if she breathed, it would make Kenzie move. She held on to the breath she had been about to let out and waited for her reply.

"I memorized it from the internet," the woman finally stated. "I told you, I think your name is beautiful. A few years ago, I looked it up, and I memorized the description. I thought maybe one day, if I had a daughter, maybe I'd name her Lennox," Kenzie admitted.

Lennox relaxed a little and placed her hand on the small of Kenzie's back, rubbing it up and down. When Kenzie didn't move her head, Lennox continued the movement and passed Kenzie back the apple with her other hand.

"Well, I don't think I could name my daughter after myself. That seems a little egotistical," she replied.

"You want a daughter?" Kenzie asked.

Lennox watched as Kenzie's fingertip slid up and down her thigh, stopping at the hem of Lennox's shorts, and then, going down to her knee before Kenzie repeated the action. Lennox felt the touch on the skin, but she felt it elsewhere, too. It was in her heart. It was in her mind and her soul; the feel of Kenzie's fingers on her skin. She closed her eyes to try to focus on answering the question.

"I don't know. Maybe. I am in my thirties. I guess I should figure that out soon," she answered. "You?"

"No," Kenzie replied.

"But you said you might name a–"

"It was just in my head. I like the name, but I don't think I would want kids if–" Kenzie stopped, and the movements on Lennox's leg stopped at the same time.

"If they're like you?" Lennox completed Kenzie's thought.

"Yes."

"God, why not?" Lennox asked, and Kenzie's head lifted to look at her. "You're beautiful, Kenzie. And you're remarkable. I would have no problem if I had a daughter that was like you."

"I always thought that if I ended up with someone that wanted kids, she could have them. Then, they wouldn't have to have my genetics," Kenzie paused. "It's just that my dad was like this – or, at least, I think he was – and I'm like this."

Lennox pressed her lips to Kenzie's and pulled back, placing her hand on Kenzie's cheek to keep her from looking away.

"And you're perfect," she complimented. "God, Kenz, you're perfect."

Kenzie smiled at her, and it seemed to Lennox that it met her eyes, and Kenzie actually believed her. She believed that Lennox thought she was perfect. Lennox hadn't finished that thought out loud, though. She had held a part of the sentence back, just in case it was too much too soon. She had just almost told Kenzie that she was perfect for *her*.

✧✧✧

They stayed out by the pond until after ten before they walked back in the dark, with only a flashlight to guide their way. They nearly toppled over fallen branches, holes in the ground, and each other more times than they could count, but they'd laughed and caught each other every time until they were back by the cabins. Lennox held on tightly to Kenzie's hand; not wanting to let it go until they stood in front of their new home for the night.

"I'd say we could sleep in the cabana again, but I heard Jenna, Davica, and Brooke say they were taking one each tonight." Lennox kissed Kenzie's hand. "So, we'll have to share our room with Maddox and Cleo."

She dropped the blanket and sweatshirts to the ground. They'd already disposed of their trash.

"Right," Kenzie commented as they approached the cabin. "It's quiet," she added.

"They're all in bed early tonight. Tomorrow is the big holiday blow out, so I'm sure they want to be rested and up early. They'll start drinking by ten," Lennox explained.

"Oh, wow. I don't think I can do that."

"Then, don't. Just hang with me. I'm basically a chaperone, anyway."

Kenzie stopped walking and turned to her.

"I don't know how to handle tomorrow," she confessed. "I don't go to parties like that. I avoid most events that I can for work, too, when they're like that. But then, there's you, and I don't know what to do with that, either."

"What about me?"

"Do we talk to each other when other people are around? Should we pretend like we don't know one another that well? They don't know I'm gay, obviously, but I don't think I care if they do now. I trust most of them, and I don't think Peyton would have invited them if she didn't trust them. They all know about her and Dani and haven't said anything. But, even if I wanted to hold your hand like this, you're still figuring this whole thing out, and I don't want to make a mistake tomorrow. So, can you tell me what I should do?"

"Oh, baby, you're so cute, sometimes." Lennox leaned in and kissed her.

Her hands went around Kenzie's neck, and she pulled her in. Kenzie reacted to the unexpected touch by tensing for a moment before she kissed Lennox back and did so slowly and deliberately. Her hands went around Lennox's waist and tugged her closer. Lennox allowed her tongue entrance and played with Kenzie's, wondering how it felt to Kenzie to have their tongues connect like this. To Lennox, it was soft and smooth, and when she took Kenzie's bottom lip between her teeth and heard Kenzie gasp, she did her best not to smirk. She pulled the bottom lip she'd been adoring between her own lips and sucked. This earned the hands on her back as Kenzie rubbed up and down before they slid a little farther down and didn't cup Lennox's ass but just rested there instead, as if awaiting either permission or rejection. Lennox took one of her hands and placed it over Kenzie's, encouraging her to do whatever she wanted, and then, placed her hand on Kenzie's hip while their mouths continued to revel in the feeling of completeness.

That was what it was to Lennox. It was the sense of being whole for the first time in her life; and that was just with the kiss. She lifted the hem of Kenzie's shirt slightly and slid her hand under it. Kenzie didn't stop kissing her. And when her hands on Lennox's ass squeezed, it caused a moan to escape from Lennox, and then, Lennox's hand moved on its own to cover Kenzie's right breast. She grasped it lightly and found her legs growing weak with the combination of the kiss and this new touch; this new exploration. She was turned on, and her body was reacting to these touches in ways it never had to the touches from her previous relationships. She was wet, and she wanted Kenzie. She wanted to touch her everywhere and have Kenzie soothe the pleasant yet torturous ache between her legs. Kenzie's hands were at the waistband of her shorts now. Her lips had moved to Lennox's neck, and her tongue slid out and up from Lennox's collarbone to her earlobe, which Kenzie sucked into her mouth before letting it go.

"You are perfect," she whispered into Lennox's ear, and her hands were inside Lennox's shorts now, grasping her ass.

They were standing thirty feet from the cabin they'd be sharing with two other women tonight, and they were making out at a fevered pace. Kenzie had her hands inside Lennox's underwear, but she wasn't moving them around. She wasn't searching. She held them in place, and Lennox wondered if that was more for her benefit than Lennox's. Lennox's hands were on the move, too, and she found she enjoyed putting them in the pockets of Kenzie's adorable, baggy sweatpants, using that position to pull the woman closer and rub the side of Kenzie's thighs. Lennox wanted her lips on skin, and she moved them to Kenzie's throat, sucking and licking and kissing until Kenzie's gasps grew louder, and her hands slid still inside Lennox's underwear to her sides. If she moved them another few inches, they'd connect with Lennox in a way that neither of them wanted while they were in public like this and definitely didn't want it like this for the first time; for Lennox's first time with another woman.

"Um…" There was a throat clearing. "Hi, guys."

Kenzie and Lennox stopped instantly and separated their bodies, with Kenzie pulling her hands out of Lennox's pants, and Lennox removing her hands from Kenzie's sweats.

"Mad." Lennox straightened her shirt before turning to Maddox and then back to Kenzie. "What are you doing out here?"

"Definitely not what you two were doing," Maddox replied. "Mackenzie," she greeted.

Lennox watched Kenzie as she straightened her shirt and then stared at the ground, probably in embarrassment.

"Hi," Kenzie replied, but so softly, Lennox barely heard it.

"I was just going to the bathroom," Maddox explained. "I figured you guys were in a cabana or something."

"Those are occupied tonight," Lennox offered in explanation.

"I think you can probably convince some of them to bunk together if you want some privacy," she suggested. "Or, better yet, let me do something. Hold on." She went back inside the cabin, and Lennox had no clue what she was doing.

"You okay?" She turned immediately to Kenzie. "Kenzie, it's okay. Mad won't tell anyone. I know her."

"I'm okay." Kenzie looked up at her. "It's not about her," she replied.

"You're not upset?"

"When you touch me, it's—"

"Hey." Maddox came back outside, interrupting Kenzie's sentence.

"Cleo and I are going to the cabanas tonight. She's grabbing her stuff. You two, take the cabin."

"What? No. We're—"

"Obviously in the middle of something." Maddox pointed back and forth between the two of them. "I suspected something was up with you two. You keep running off together."

Cleo emerged from the cabin with sleeping bags and handed one to Maddox before she rubbed her sleepy eyes.

"Cabanas?" she asked.

"We'll share one and make the others squeeze together. It'll be fun. I actually wanted to stay out there at least one night, anyway."

Maddox winked at Lennox and pulled Cleo along.

"Thanks, Mad." Lennox offered a light touch on Maddox's forearm as she passed.

"Have fun, you two." She looked at Kenzie, who actually met her eye and smiled back.

They watched the two of them walk in the direction of the cabanas before Lennox turned back to Kenzie.

"Are you okay with this? I can ask them to come back."

"When you touch me, it's an avalanche, Lennox. It's all I can do to contain myself. I want to never stop and have to stop at the same time; because it's too much, but not enough. I don't know how to make sense of that."

Lennox ran her hand through Kenzie's long dark hair and made sure to connect their eyes and then their hands.

"You come inside with me, and we get ready for bed," she started. "We squeeze into one of these twin beds together, and we hold each other all night. You start getting used to the feeling of my skin, and I can hold on to you, and I won't let go, Kenzie," she continued. "I won't let go, okay?"

"Okay."

CHAPTER 13

"WELL, you two have some explaining to do." Peyton's voice woke Kenzie, and her eyes opened to see the tall blonde standing at the end of her bed.

No, it wasn't her bed. It was their bed. She was in bed with Lennox. Lennox was half on top of her, in fact, and she was still asleep.

"Peyton?" she asked with surprise.

"Yeah, why is my best friend on top of you there, Kenz?"

"Because she wants to be," Lennox answered instead and lifted her head slightly. "Why is that your business, Peyton Gloss?"

"Because, as far as I know, you've never woken up on top of a woman before," she retorted.

Lennox leaned up, looked down at Kenzie, smiled at her, and then kissed her gently and sweetly on the lips.

"And you've never done that before, either," Peyton added.

"I have done that before recently; a lot, actually. Why are you in here?" Lennox sat up all the way, which forced Kenzie to slide over a little to accommodate her.

What Kenzie noticed though, was the fact that Lennox hadn't hidden anything about this from Maddox the night before or Peyton now. She had kissed her in front of Peyton. She could have denied it. She could have said they had fallen asleep talking or something. Peyton might not have believed that, but Lennox could have said it. Lennox placed a hand on Kenzie's thigh while staring at her best friend with accusing eyes. And Kenzie watched her, with her messy morning hair and tired eyes that were still so beautiful. She ran her hand through that hair because she couldn't not do it. She had to be touching her.

"Are you two a thing now?" Peyton asked, sitting on the end of the bed. "Did you guys…"

"No, we didn't." Lennox completed Peyton's sentence. "And when we do, that will be none of your business." She had said *when* not *if*. "And we're figuring things out; right, Kenz?" Lennox turned, probably noticed the look of immense shock on Kenzie's face, smirked at it, and squeezed Kenzie's thigh.

"Right," Kenzie replied with a nod.

"And what about the rest of this week? Do you want the others to know, or are you going to hide it? I won't say anything if you don't want me to."

"I don't care if anyone knows," Lennox answered immediately. "I really don't. I like those girls out there. But, Peyton, you and Dani are my family. If any of them have a problem with me liking Kenzie, they can go screw themselves."

"None of them will have a problem with it. They couldn't care less who you date, and I mean that in a good way." She looked at Kenzie. "Kenz?"

"Yeah?"

"You're not out with these people. Do you want to be?"

"Yeah," she repeated the word but stated it this time.

"Yeah?" Lennox asked her.

"Yeah," Kenzie stated again.

"Can either of you say something other than *yeah*?" Peyton mocked.

"Yeah," they both said at the same time and promptly laughed.

"I love this." Peyton softened. "You guys, I love this." She pointed at them with two fingers. "I knew this would happen, by the way."

"You what?" Lennox guffawed. "No, you didn't."

"Yes, I did. I am an excellent matchmaker. Ask Dani."

"Why did you think that?" Kenzie asked and leaned forward, suddenly more interested in this conversation than she had been, and that was saying something.

"I've met both of you, and you just seemed like you might understand each other weirdly. I don't know… It made sense to me." Peyton stood. "Lennox wouldn't shut up about your show and you in it the last three times she and I talked. She wouldn't stop talking about how talented you were. And then, you, Kenzie Smyth, have had a major crush on this one forever," Peyton referenced. "You kept staring at that Glamour cover she did where she had that vest and tie combination, and it was pretty obvious where your eyes were going. You're not that great of an actress; it turns out."

"Where were your eyes going?" Lennox turned back to her with a cocky smile.

"Nowhere." Kenzie swung her head rapidly from side to side.

"Yeah, right," Peyton rejected. "I'm going outside. You two, stop making out long enough to meet us. It's already ten. You missed breakfast, so grab something quick and then meet us at the lake. We're taking the boats out first."

"We'll be out in a minute," Lennox answered for both of them.

"I'll come back in here in ten minutes if I don't see you out there. And if you're naked in here, I'm going to be pissed, because I don't want to see that," Peyton said all that as she pushed open the screen door with a flourish and made her way outside. "And these cabins are made of screens. Screens, guys. You can see through them."

Lennox and Kenzie shared a laugh at the sometimes dramatic Peyton Gloss. Then, Lennox turned to Kenzie and moved rapidly until she had Kenzie lying down and was hovering over her.

"Really?" she asked, and Kenzie knew what Lennox was referring to.

"It's okay. I don't care if they know." She ran her hands up and down Lennox's back, finding that their night of physical closeness made the touches come easier to her. And, while still intense in the best way, it was less scary, and she could touch more. "I guess I'm surprised that you don't care if they know."

"Why would I care if they know?"

"Because you're not gay. This is new. I haven't told anyone outside of a few people that I know really well, and I'm definitely not out in the public. I've known I was gay for sure since I was sixteen. I came out to my parents in college. You're just…"

Kenzie wasn't sure how to say the next part. She didn't want to define Lennox's sexuality for her; that wasn't her place. But she also didn't know exactly what was going on between them, either.

"Completely into you," Lennox finished. "I don't know what that makes me, but I don't care. If they ask, I'll tell them that. That's the truth."

"Okay."

"Is it?" Lennox reached for her cheek. "Is that okay for now? That I don't know?"

"Of course, it is," Kenzie assured and moved her arms around Lennox's neck. "I don't care what you are or how you define yourself," she revealed. "I just like you. And if you like me, that's all I care about."

Lennox leaned down and captured Kenzie's lips for a kiss they knew wouldn't go anywhere, since Peyton would keep her word and return if they didn't make their way outside soon. Kenzie's sensations were still heightened at every touch, and she knew, somehow, that even if she got used to touching Lennox, the intensity of their connection would never fade. She, again, recognized the fear and terror that came with letting someone in like this, and she did her best to push it out of her mind as Lennox kissed her forehead once, stood, and pulled Kenzie up with her to begin their day.

***

"Hey there, ladies," Maddox greeted with a cocky smile as they approached the picnic tables around the embers of the fire from last night.

"Mad," Lennox returned with a smile and a shake of her head.

Maddox was applying a healthy layer of sunscreen to her shoulders and neck, while Brooke and Lynn were finishing up their coffee at the table across from the fire pit, and Dani was leaving the bathroom with Davica, Jenna, Quinn, and Bobby.

"So, did you two enjoy your privacy last night?" the woman asked and put the cap back on the sunscreen.

"Yes. Thank you," Lennox answered. "You guys didn't have to leave, though. We didn't do anything," she added.

"What? We left so you *could* do something." Maddox winked at Kenzie. "Anything you two care to tell the rest of the class, by the way? I was able to get away with not telling Cleo last night because she was on her way to a fun morning hangover."

"I don't think we're making an announcement on the loudspeaker; if that's what you're getting at," Lennox offered.

"I'm gay," Kenzie admitted.

Lennox turned to her and gave her a shocked and confused expression.

"Well, it's not a loudspeaker, but okay." Maddox laughed lightly.

"I just–" Kenzie stopped herself and thought about how to say what she wanted to say. "I don't say that out loud very often."

"And how did it feel?" Lennox asked her and took Kenzie's hand.

"Good." Kenzie smiled at her and squeezed the hand she now held. "It felt good."

"You guys know I'm gay, too, right?" Maddox questioned.

"What? No." Lennox turned to face her.

"Yeah, have been my whole life." Maddox shrugged her shoulders and smiled at them. "I just assumed you guys knew."

"How did I not know?" Lennox asked.

"I'm not exactly out in public, but that's just because most people don't care about who a photographer dates, regardless of who her famous friends are. I don't flaunt it, but, yeah, I have a girlfriend. She's in Toronto right now, on a shoot."

"She's a photographer?" Lennox questioned.

"She's a model." Maddox lifted an eyebrow and turned to Kenzie. "Congrats, by the way."

"For being gay?" Kenzie replied.

"For snagging this one." She pointed at Lennox. "She's a catch, from what I hear."

"What do you hear?" Lennox wanted to know.

"Peyton is always talking about how awesome her best friend is, and how she wants you to find the right person and settle down. I didn't know about your interest in girls, though. If I had known that, I would have asked you out when we met for the first time."

"Hey," Kenzie proclaimed and promptly looked at the ground in embarrassment.

Lennox laughed at her outburst and squeezed her hand again before returning her attention to Maddox.

"Sorry, Mad. I wasn't interested back then." She glanced at Kenzie. "It's different with this one." She nodded toward Kenzie. "She's special."

"No worries. I've got my hot model girlfriend, and I'm very happy." She walked in the direction of the lake. "I'll see you guys over there. Apparently, there's a competition."

Lennox dropped Kenzie's hand and headed to the sunscreen bottle on the picnic table. She opened it, squirted some into her hand, and nodded toward Kenzie.

"Sit down. I don't want you to get burned."

"Maddox is gay?" Kenzie wasn't focused on Lennox's *polite* command, but she walked over to the table anyway and sat down on the top of it. "I had no idea. Peyton never said anything."

"Peyton wouldn't tell you if someone else was gay, unless they specifically told her it was okay to. You know that." Lennox sat down next to her.

At first, Kenzie was shocked by the coolness of the sunscreen on her skin, and then, by the soft hand rubbing up and down her arm. She was mesmerized as she sat and Lennox applied SPF to both of her arms, the back of her neck, and then, gave her a glance that made Kenzie lift an eyebrow at her.

"What?"

"We're going to be in a boat, in our bathing suits." She motioned with the bottle toward Kenzie's stomach and stood. "I mean, you should put sunscreen there."

Lennox was nervous. Maybe it was flummoxed but, for some reason, the idea of applying sunscreen to the rest of Kenzie's body had her off her game, and Kenzie could only smile at the adorableness.

"You don't want to put it on for me?" she teased.

"I do," Lennox returned almost immediately. "I just don't want it to be too much for you; the touching part."

Kenzie swallowed and lifted her shirt, revealing the bikini top she'd put on prior to leaving the cabin. That had been interesting. The cabin was one big room, and the two of them had to dress for a day on the water without peaking. It had turned into a bit of a game, with Lennox dressing in one corner and tossing her shirt over in Kenzie's direction with a laugh, and then, Kenzie upped the ante by tossing her shirt and sweats at Lennox. They had managed to laugh through it, and Kenzie had emerged wearing another T-shirt and a pair of board shorts she'd bought specifically for this trip. Beneath her shirt and shorts, she had on a dark-green and white-striped bikini, and the top was currently being stared at by Lennox.

"I can handle it," Kenzie returned and allowed Lennox to stare with dark heat in her eyes for a moment longer before she tugged on Lennox's hand, pulling her closer to the table and spreading her legs so Lennox could settle between them. "And when you're done, I get to do you," she added and pressed her hand to Lennox's stomach under her shirt. "I still haven't seen your bathing suit."

"Did you buy that one because it matches your eyes?" Lennox asked as she finally looked away from Kenzie's chest and abdomen back up to her eyes.

"No, I didn't buy it, actually," Kenzie replied.

"Oh, shit!" Lennox smacked her forehead in realization. "You wore that on the cover of Sports Illustrated back in March." She looked back down at the bikini. "Gift after the shoot?"

"You remember what I wore for a random cover shoot?"

"How did I not know?" Lennox squeezed sunscreen into her palm and appeared to be asking *herself* that question. "You did Vanity Fair with the TOP-30 under 30 last year and wore that black and white pantsuit; and Entertainment Weekly had you in that rugged, backpacker kind of stuff for the show."

"You know my magazine covers, Lennox?" Kenzie teased and allowed Lennox to cover her throat and chest with sunscreen before lying back on the table with her head on the shirt she had just taken off.

Lennox stood between Kenzie's legs and stared down at her before she began applying lotion to her stomach. She seemed to be enjoying herself, taking her time, and staring at Kenzie's eyes as she moved. Kenzie guessed she was waiting for her to freak out or pull back at the touches and their intensity, but Kenzie focused on the sensation of having Lennox half on top of her all night. She recalled the feeling of Lennox's skin against her own and what it had been like to rub her back and play with her hair, running it through her fingertips while Lennox slept.

"I guess I do," Lennox answered her question. "I've always thought you were beautiful." She smiled at Kenzie as she continued to rub the lotion that was already well-rubbed-in into Kenzie's skin. "Sit up so that I can get your back," she remarked and then pressed both hands into Kenzie's stomach. "Wait. Don't yet."

"What? Why?" Kenzie asked.

Lennox leaned down in response and placed her hands on either side of Kenzie's head, hovering over her in a position Kenzie was starting to become accustomed to and loved. Lennox stared down at her with those deep blue eyes and didn't move for several movements.

"Tonight, can we try to find somewhere to be alone again?" she asked, and her eyes flitted to Kenzie's lips and then lower. "I'll do the whole group hang thing today for Peyton, but I want time with you later."

"You mean like another date, or tonight-tonight? Sleeping, I mean." Kenzie tried to make sense but worried she hadn't until Lennox smiled.

"Both," she answered and lowered her lips to Kenzie's.

It was short and not meant to go anywhere, but it was nice to feel Lennox that way before they would join the entire group at the lake. Lennox pulled herself back up and then lifted Kenzie's arms so that she was sitting atop the table. She moved to slide behind her, placing her legs on either side of Kenzie, and started rubbing the lotion on her back.

"Did I just watch you two make out?" Bobby approached them and asked.

"I'm pretty sure we just saw you two make out," Davica repeated.

"We did not make out," Kenzie stated, tired of having Lennox lead in these conversations, because she shouldn't have to handle all social situations for them. "We kissed briefly."

"You kissed briefly?" Jenna joined in. "When did that start happening? I didn't know you two were dating. Did I know they were dating?" She turned to Bobby.

"I didn't know they were dating," Bobby replied. "I didn't know Lennox swung that way. She never told me."

"Me neither," Davica said.

"All right, I get it." Lennox rested her head on Kenzie's shoulder. "Kenzie and I only met when she got here. We're exploring things," she answered vaguely.

"You were on top of her exploring *something* a minute ago."

"Yeah, like her tonsils," Jenna backed her up.

"I didn't–" Lennox let out a low growl that Kenzie felt against her entire body.

It rocked her, and she closed her eyes to try to focus on something else, but the sound that came from Lennox reverberated, and Kenzie shook for a second. Lennox must have felt her physical reaction, because her hands went to Kenzie's hips and then around her body, pulling her back into her. She opened her eyes and found three sets staring back at her.

"Damn, girl." Davica's eyes got big. "You liked that, huh?" She laughed.

"Are you okay?" Lennox whispered into her ear and held her tightly.

"I think she's more than okay," Bobby answered for her.

"Bobby, shut up," Lennox fired back. "We'll meet you guys at the lake, okay?"

"Fine. Fine. I hope I'm not in your boat," Bobby retorted. "You two obviously haven't had sex yet; since Lennox, here, seems a little tense."

"Bobby, stop!" Kenzie worked up enough courage to half-yell at her. She leaned back into Lennox's body, needing her presence for this. "This isn't something you just mock. So, back off, okay?"

Bobby's demeanor completely changed when she realized she had overstepped with her joke.

"I'm sorry. Too far; I got it."

"We'll see you guys down at the water," Kenzie returned with a nod and an acceptance of Bobby's apology.

"For what it's worth, I think this is nice," Jenna supplied and smiled. "You two look really good together. It's actually sick how hot you are together, and I mean that in a good way."

"Thanks, I guess," Lennox said.

The three women walked off, leaving them alone at the picnic tables, while everyone else made their way to the water for whatever boat competition Peyton had planned for them. Kenzie didn't move. She relaxed back into Lennox's body, allowing the woman to hold on to her and keep her in place. When she recognized that they'd been sitting that way in silence for several minutes, she shifted out of Lennox's grasp and stood.

"I should do you."

"You should, huh?" Lennox laughed and offered a sexy eyebrow. "I think I'd like that." She paused, and her face changed. "Oh, sorry. I shouldn't joke about that," she added.

"About sex?" Kenzie smiled at her and reached for the hem of Lennox's T-shirt.

"Bobby did, and–"

"Bobby shouldn't joke about it. *You* can joke about it. It's actually funny when you joke about it."

"It is?"

"Yeah, you do this sexy thing with your eyebrow that I like," Kenzie admitted and watched Lennox's arms lift over her head so she could pull her shirt off and place it next to her instead.

"Do you like it?" Lennox asked when Kenzie's eyes immediately went to her chest.

"You can't wear that out there." Kenzie's eyes shot back up to meet Lennox's.

"What? Why not?"

"It barely covers anything!" Kenzie grabbed at Lennox's shirt and shoved it against her chest, all while Lennox laughed.

"Do you recognize it?" She lightened her laughter to wait for a response.

"It's from the movie."

"Which movie?" Lennox pressed, took the shirt, and placed it back down on the table.

"*Counterstrike.*" Kenzie licked her lips.

She glanced back down at the black and white bikini that barely covered full breasts, and she could picture what the bottoms looked like; and they didn't come close to covering Lennox's ass. She knew because she'd seen this exact bathing suit in a film where Lennox had played an undercover agent that needed to use her God-given attributes to convince the criminal to give her what she needed. In the movie, Lennox had walked slowly out of the water toward him, wearing this exact suit.

"Do you like it?" Lennox placed her hands on Kenzie's hips.

"Yes."

"But I can't wear it today?" Lennox lifted the corner of her mouth.

"They'll see pretty much everything."

"And you don't want anyone else to see me?"

"No," Kenzie returned with a glare. "I'm sorry. You can wear whatever you want. I shouldn't have said that."

"Do you want to be the only person who gets to see me wear this, Kenzie?"

"Anyone who saw that movie has seen you wear that."

"Not up close," Lennox returned. "And not like this." She pulled Kenzie's hands to her body and placed them over her breasts.

"Lennox!" Kenzie exclaimed, and her head was instantly on a swivel, swinging around to check for anyone who might be around; but they were indeed alone.

Lennox let out another one of her wild laughs and let

go of Kenzie's hands so they could drop to her sides.

"So, you're not a boob girl? Got it." She smirked.

"Hilarious," Kenzie returned with a bit of sarcasm, and she thought about that for a moment.

Kenzie wasn't sarcastic. She had a hard time understanding it most of the time when other people were sarcastic. She had a hard time understanding many social cues that other people seemed to have no problem with. But, with Lennox – it was different, and she smiled at the thought.

"What?" Lennox asked and lifted one of Kenzie's hands to her lips.

"Nothing," Kenzie lied, not wanting to admit that she'd noticed something about herself.

Lennox pressed her lips to the tip of Kenzie's index finger.

"What happened before? When I was holding you? Were you okay?" Lennox kissed the next finger, her eyes not leaving Kenzie's green ones.

Kenzie trembled at the third kiss to her finger and gripped the sunscreen bottle with her free hand, squeezing it and not realizing that it was open. Sunscreen squirted from the top, causing Lennox to crack up again and Kenzie to blush before she squeezed again, but this time – in the direction of Lennox's stomach.

"That's what you get for laughing," she replied and began rubbing Lennox's skin. "And I just wasn't expecting it before. You make me shake," she revealed. "It hasn't happened before. I'm still getting used to it."

"I make you shake?" Lennox leaned back on her elbows, allowing Kenzie to run her hands all over her.

"You make me tremble." Kenzie gulped after the words.

Lennox stared up at her with darkened eyes and an expression that told Kenzie she needed to find a way to be alone with this woman later tonight, if it was the last thing she did.

CHAPTER 14

LENNOX laughed as Peyton tried to row their boat away from the shore but managed to trap them against a rock instead.

"Len, help me! We're losing," she insisted.

"Why? This is funny." Lennox laughed more and held her oar still. "Come on, Pey, get us to the finish line," she encouraged.

"Your girlfriend is beating us." Peyton tried pushing the oar against the rock to get the small boat to move back into the water and the path she had laid out for the competition.

"She's fast," Lennox commented as she watched Kenzie and Quinn in a different boat about twenty feet ahead of them, moving quickly toward the invisible finish line.

"At everything, apparently." Peyton jested. She finally managed to get the boat out of the trap and began rowing wildly while Lennox pretended to row along with her.

"I assume that's a commentary on something other than her rowing skills." She didn't take her eyes off Kenzie's bare arms as the woman rowed with vigor. Her muscles were defined just enough to be visible and sexy to Lennox, who watched on. "And we didn't do anything, by the way."

"You kissed her."

"We kissed each other," Lennox returned. "And you said we'd be good together."

"I think you *are* good together." Peyton slowed her rowing slightly, apparently giving up, once Kenzie and Quinn crossed the finish line they'd determined was a tree on the far shore. "I thought you liked her before you even met her."

"Yeah, you'll have to explain that one to me, because I didn't see this coming at all." Lennox placed the oar in her lap.

"Did you honestly not think you could be with a woman, Len?"

"I never thought about it before, no."

"Neither did I."

"And then you met Dani. I know."

"And then you met Kenzie." Peyton winked. "It happens."

"But how did you know it would happen with me?"

Peyton placed her own oar in her lap and allowed the other boats with Jenna, Lynn, Carlie, and Cleo to pass them.

"There's something about Kenzie, isn't there? She's different."

"She's amazing," Lennox let out in a breath.

"I know that. I love that girl. I'm just saying there's something different about her that people don't seem to get. And I was one of them, at first. But when I took the time to get to know her, I liked her. She's great. But not everyone is patient like that."

"So, you knew I'd be patient enough to get to know her?"

"Yes, I did."

"But that just means I'd be a good friend to her. How exactly did you see me falling–" Lennox smacked her palm into her mouth.

"Shit, Len!" Peyton shouted. "You're falling in love with her?" She leaned in and whispered, "For real?"

"Well, it's not for fake, Peyton."

"Jesus, Len. I thought you two might hit it off, and maybe you'd go on a date after all this or something. I didn't expect you to fall for her after, like, four days." She moved her head back and forth, as if considering something. "Then again, I didn't expect you to spend every free moment you had with her this week, either. I've hardly had five minutes alone with you."

"You were the one that told me to make sure she was comfortable."

"I guess you did that and then some," Peyton mocked. "How is it, by the way?"

"I told you, we didn't do anything."

"I'm not asking about sex, Len."

"What? Kissing?"

"Lennox Owen, I'm asking how is it to finally be falling in love with someone that is worthy of that love?"

"Peyton, you can't say anything to her about that, okay? I don't want to scare her off. We just met, and I'm not even sure I know."

"You're sure you like her, right?"

"Yes, I know that. I'm crazy about her. I can barely stop looking at her." She turned her head in that moment to find that Kenzie was looking at her, and she was smiling. Lennox winked at her and offered a smile before Kenzie rowed and laughed at something Quinn had said. "I don't know what to do, though, Peyton."

"About what?"

"Tell me how you knew." Lennox changed the subject. "Tell me how you knew I liked her before I met her."

"Remember that time I borrowed your phone?"

"I remember when you *stole* my phone to change all my contact names to Penis McScrotum. That was not funny, by the way." She glared back at Peyton.

"That was Dani's idea. And you fell asleep first last year. Your fault."

"Sometimes, I wonder why I'm friends with you."

"You love me." Peyton winked. "Anyway, while I was changing your contacts and trying not to laugh because you'd wake up, I noticed you had some episodes of a certain TV show downloaded. And then, I noticed you had a few bookmarks set up."

"You mean you went snooping through my phone?"

"Yes." Peyton smiled back. "Three bookmarks, Len. Really?"

"What were they?" Lennox tried to think back to their holiday gathering the previous summer and what she could have had bookmarked on her phone. "Oh!" It dawned on her.

"Yeah, *that* gif," Peyton confirmed. "She had to kiss that female co-star because the network was doing that lame sweeps thing. Kenzie hated having to do that, by the way," she added. "You had a gif of that very moment bookmarked on your phone, along with her IMDB page and a photo spread with an interview she'd done around that time about the new show." Peyton wagged an accusing finger at her. "She was only half-clothed, Len. You should be ashamed of yourself."

"Yeah, yeah." Lennox lowered her eyes in shame.

"And, you kept talking about her randomly. You'd somehow find a way to bring up Mackenzie Smyth even when what we were talking about had nothing to do with her." Peyton laughed and began rowing them back toward the shore. "I should have introduced you two sooner. I would have, but you guys were always in different cities. Actually, how is that going to work? You're always on set, and she's on a different set in another city. Have you thought about that?"

"I haven't thought about anything beyond this week. I was too afraid to consider the future."

"That's not like you. Why?"

"What do you mean?" Lennox asked and decided to help with the rowing because that would get her to the shore faster.

"You had no problem thinking about a future with Noah or Lucas. I know Aaron was a bust, but with your big relationships, you never worried."

"Yes, I did. I just didn't tell you back then. Look, with Noah, it was different. He and I knew each other for a long time before we started dating, so I wasn't really worried about the future with him. We'd set that friendship foundation, you know?"

"And Lucas?"

"I didn't want to worry. I didn't want to stop back then. I just needed something different after Will died and Noah gave up on us. I jumped in headfirst, and look how that went."

"Well, as far as I know, Mackenzie is not an addict or adrenaline junkie," Peyton argued.

"But she's also different than both of them. She's different than anyone I've ever dated or had feelings for, Peyton. I can't explain it. She's just…"

"Right?" Peyton guessed and turned her head toward her girlfriend, who was climbing out of her boat and headed for dry land.

"I told her she was magnetic," Lennox told Peyton a little reluctantly.

"Magnetic? Damn, that's good. I need to use that with Dani."

"You and Dani are already together. You don't have to woo her anymore with your words." Lennox laughed.

"I will *always* woo that girl with my words," Peyton acknowledged. "She's the best part of me, Len. All the love songs are about her."

"That's because all the love songs you write are actually about her, Pey."

"No, not just mine." Peyton turned back to Lennox. "All the love songs." She smiled and shook her head from side to side. "Every last one is about that woman to me." She connected her eyes with Lennox's. "Are all the love songs about Kenzie for you?"

Lennox thought about that question and turned her head to see Kenzie getting out of the water, wearing her bikini top and board shorts, and looking like the sexiest thing Lennox had ever seen when Kenzie shook the wind and water out of her hair. Then, she watched her hug Quinn, apparently in a victory celebration. When Quinn turned away to chat with April and Tiana, Kenzie wrapped her arms around her body, not knowing what to do next. She looked vulnerable then, and Lennox just wanted to wrap her arms around her and pull her in. Kenzie looked to the ground for a moment and appeared to gather herself before taking three steps and joining the conversation with the other girls. She was brave. She was beautiful, she was funny, and she was brave.

"Oh," Lennox uttered.

"Yeah, I thought so," Peyton said after a moment.

***

After the boat races – of which there were three and a water gun fight that Lennox more observed than participated in, followed by capture the flag – where Kenzie had been placed on the other team by Peyton specifically to drive Lennox crazy, the group was more than ready for lunch, which was sandwiches and hot dogs by the water. Some lay out while they ate, taking in more of the sun, while others played a game of volleyball off to the side with the old net the campground had up already. The drinking had started much earlier, and Bobby and Mandy were well on their way to drunk and tossing a Frisbee back and forth with little success.

"Hey there." Kenzie stood in front of the cabana, where Lennox had stationed herself out of the sun.

"Long time no see." Lennox smiled at her and then leaned forward to tug on her T-shirt. "You've been a social butterfly today. What brought that on?"

Kenzie had spent much of her time that day bouncing from group to group, trying to get to know the other girls. Lennox had maybe had five minutes with her all day, and she'd missed their time together like crazy.

"I just decided to try." Kenzie shrugged.

"Join me?" Lennox gave another light tug.

"In there?" Kenzie nodded to the cabana.

"Yes, in here, Kenzie." Lennox laughed. "You're starting to burn a little, and it's out of the sun," she commented and ran her hands up and down Kenzie's forearms.

"I am not starting to burn," Kenzie objected.

"Okay, I lied. I just want you in here with me."

Kenzie laughed, and Lennox moved back to allow her to enter the space. The cabana swung a little as she did, catching her off guard and launching her into Lennox's lap.

"Get a room, you two!" It came from Sarah.

"We are," Lennox retorted and pulled Kenzie into her.

"I guess so." Jack was standing next to Sarah and giggling.

"Jack, can you close the thing?"

"Gladly," Jack interjected, reached for the string, and pulled down the canvas, covering them.

"Hi," Kenzie said from her position, straddling Lennox.

"Hi, back." Lennox ran her hands over Kenzie's back under the T-shirt she'd donned after the water activities. "I've missed you."

"I missed you, too." Kenzie leaned down and connected their lips.

Lennox was glad she wasted no time, because while everyone seemed to know about them now, and no one cared, they hadn't had a moment where they could do this part all day, and they likely wouldn't for the next several hours, if Peyton's schedule had anything to say about it. The kiss was slow. Kenzie's hands were in Lennox's hair, while Lennox's hands were slowly lifting up Kenzie's shirt, and then, there was a moment where Lennox pulled it up and disconnected their lips so that she could pull it off, leaving Kenzie in only her bikini top.

"I'm going to kiss you here, okay?" Lennox placed a fingertip on Kenzie's collarbone.

"Okay," Kenzie more or less whispered.

Lennox's lips hovered over her skin and then connected gently at first, pressing an open-mouth kiss there.

She felt Kenzie tremble slightly, and she held her in place. She moved her lips, grazing the skin as she did, and kissed Kenzie again before she couldn't go at that pace anymore. Her hands grasped Kenzie's back and slid down to her ass to cup it, while Kenzie slid into her body, and they both went back a little into the back of the cabana, which swung as a result. Lennox's hands moved up to the two connected strings holding Kenzie's bikini top together at her back, and she played with the hanging ends of them as she slid her tongue along the top of Kenzie's breasts and felt Kenzie's hips twitch once, and then again, when she repeated the motion.

"Okay?" Lennox said against her skin.

"Can you take your shirt off?" Kenzie asked into her ear.

"You can take it off for me," Lennox whispered back, knowing they needed to keep it down, since there were about fifteen other women drinking, yelling, and playing just outside.

Kenzie pulled back slightly, lifting Lennox's shirt and tossing it to the side, before going back in and connecting their lips. Lennox felt Kenzie's hands on her neck, cradling her in place, while their tongues danced, and their lips drowned together.

"Lie down," Kenzie requested.

Lennox complied and moved so that she was able to lie flat, with a pillow under her head.

"I'm going to kiss you here, okay?" Kenzie matched her earlier words and pointed at the spot between Lennox's breasts.

"Whatever you want." Lennox granted and closed her eyes when Kenzie laid herself on top of her and took what she wanted from her body.

She kissed the spot once, and then again, before sliding over to the left and grasping Lennox's right breast in her hand. Her tongue was sliding down over her bikini top to the nipple that had grown hard quickly, and she closed her hot mouth around it over the fabric. Lennox's hips lifted when Kenzie breathed over the nipple and squeezed the other breast.

"We can't do this here." Kenzie's hand moved from Lennox's breast to her thigh, where she held it there and balled it up.

"I know."

"But I want to," Kenzie finished.

She flattened that hand and then lowered herself so that she could kiss Lennox's stomach, moving her lips left and then right, and then dancing with her tongue around the belly button, earning a surprised gasp from Lennox.

"Me too," Lennox replied, and her hands moved to Kenzie's long, wavy hair.

"Yeah?" Kenzie's lips made their way to the spot above the button of Lennox's jean shorts and kissed the skin there.

"Yes," Lennox gasped out.

"Jesus!" Kenzie exclaimed in a whisper.

She leaned back down and stole another kiss from Lennox's skin, and the hand that had been stilled on her thigh, slid down to her calf instead, silently requesting that Lennox lift that leg into an upside-down "V". Lennox complied and was rewarded with kisses from Kenzie, who was now between her legs, gliding her lips up and down the inside of Lennox's thigh and running her hand along her calf.

"Kenz, I'm–" Lennox's hips lifted, and Kenzie turned and stared down at them, as if in complete surprise.

"You're…"

"We should stop." Lennox snapped her head back and tried to regain her composure. "They're out there," she added more to remind herself that their friends were only feet away.

"I know." Kenzie kissed her thigh again and made her way back to her stomach. "I just can't seem to stop. You feel so good." She slid her tongue from Lennox's belly button up to the spot between her breasts, and then, resumed again on her throat. "I've never wanted someone like this, Lennox," she whispered into Lennox's ear before nibbling on her earlobe.

"What happened to it being too intense?" Lennox laughed lightly to try to stop herself from getting even more turned on by the fact that Kenzie's hips were now right where her own hips were; and with her legs spread, Kenzie had settled between them and was rocking down into her.

"Do you know what I did all last night?" Kenzie asked.

"What?" Lennox snapped herself out of the revelry that was Kenzie's hips rolling down into her center. "What are you talking about?"

"While you slept, I held you."

"Oh, yeah. I know."

"No, you don't," Kenzie argued and kissed her jaw. "I didn't fall asleep until the sun came up, Lennox," she added in explanation. "I spent all night running my fingers up and down your body, feeling your skin, and memorizing it." She leaned up and kissed Lennox's lips. "Like this spot." She pointed to the pulse point on Lennox's neck. "I felt your pulse there, and it became mine. I heard your heart beating in time with mine, and I could feel the little hairs on your skin when I slid my fingers across your back." She kissed Lennox's forehead. "I pressed my lips here a few times. Whenever you shifted, I could get another touch." Kenzie leaned up and hovered over her, stopping her hips entirely. "I could spend forever memorizing you."

"God, Kenz." It was all Lennox could express.

She had no idea how this woman above her was still single. How had someone not snatched her up when she could say things like that and make them feel like they were the only people in the world; make them feel like all the love songs were written about them?

"I spent all night touching you so that I could touch you more and not get overloaded. All I want to do is touch you, Lennox."

"That's all I want, too." Lennox kissed her, and she kissed her hard, pulling Kenzie down into herself further. "Which is why we should stop now," she let out regretfully after a moment. She then grunted low, and Kenzie crashed down into her, her head on Lennox's shoulder. "Baby, you okay?" she asked and placed a hand on Kenzie's back and the back of her head.

"You keep making those sounds, and I won't be," Kenzie mumbled against her neck. Lennox laughed and squeezed her tightly. "That's the second time you've called me *baby*."

"Sorry? It just kind of slips out." Lennox ran her hands soothingly up and down her back.

"No one's ever called me that before."

"What? What did your ex-girlfriends call you? Wait. Do I want to know?" she asked.

"Nothing. Kenzie or Kenz, I guess." Kenzie lifted up and looked down at her.

Lennox brushed the hair behind her ears and leaned up to kiss her lips one more time.

"We should go," she said reluctantly. "I think I need to change."

"We're supposed to go tubing after lunch. You should keep your bathing suit."

"I'm going to change bathing suits." She moved to sit up and watched Kenzie's expression change to confusion. "Kenzie, we just did… stuff."

"Oh!" Kenzie got it. "You're wet?" she whispered and placed her hands on Lennox's bare hips. "Really?"

"Yes, really. Now, get off me so I can go change before I combust." Lennox laughed, and Kenzie rolled off to allow her to sit up. "Wait. Did you not… Did you not get turned on?"

"What?" Kenzie sat all the way up. "No, I absolutely got turned on. Are you kidding?"

"Come change with me?"

"No way," Kenzie objected. "If I go back to that cabin

with you, where we could actually be alone, we wouldn't leave. You go. I'll change when you come back. I think I need to jump in the water to cool myself off, anyway."

Lennox laughed and climbed out of the cabana, turning to help Kenzie out, and then, she stood there, taking in the beauty in front of her.

"All the love songs," she muttered.

"What?" Kenzie questioned softly.

"Hey, tubing starts in five minutes. Dani's got the keys to the speedboat, and she is driving… So, prepare to be tossed," Jack offered them as she walked past with Jenna and April in tow.

CHAPTER 15

KENZIE took a sip of Lennox's beer, since she didn't have one of her own and didn't feel like going to the cooler they had about ten feet away to grab one. She was sitting on the ground, with Lennox between her legs, leaning back into her, and she had no plans to move unless Lennox did.

"So, what's going on with you two, exactly?" Bobby asked. "And I'm not trying to be an ass. I really want to know." She motioned with her beer bottle toward the two of them as Kenzie passed her bottle back to Lennox.

"We are having fun, enjoying this holiday celebration with our friends," Lennox gave a non-committal answer.

Kenzie understood why she said that. They hadn't talked about what they were to one another nor what would happen after the week ended and they all went back to their regularly-scheduled lives. Kenzie didn't want to think about that part. She'd been able to avoid it most of the time, but thinking about not lying next to Lennox or not seeing her for several days, weeks, or months, when they both went back to work, made her heart ache. She knew it was fast, what had happened between them, and that they had a lot to talk about, but she knew this wasn't just fun for her, and she was pretty sure Lennox felt the same way. If Kenzie brought it up, though, and Lennox didn't feel that way, then it would be over. And she wasn't ready for that.

"Now, who's being an ass there, Lex?" Bobby chided.

"I like Lennox," Kenzie decided to offer the group that had gathered around them. "She likes me," she said and then whispered into Lennox's ear, "Right?"

"Yes." Lennox laughed and placed her hand on Kenzie's cheek without turning around.

"That's what we know so far," Kenzie finished and let out a deep breath.

Lennox squeezed the hand that was over her stomach in encouragement.

"And you're gay?" April checked.

"Yes."

"And Lennox?" Tiana sat next to April and joined in.

"I don't know. I just realized that I've been crushing on this one, here, for much longer than I even knew. And then I met her in person, and that was it."

"That was it?" Mandy questioned from her position on a blanket next to Bobby.

"Yeah." Lennox leaned back into Kenzie, who squeezed her tighter and supported her when Lennox's head went to her shoulder. "She was it."

They'd all had a chance to ride on an inner tube as Dani, Peyton, or one of the other girls drove the speedboat Peyton had rented for the day. Lennox had been thrown at least twenty feet in the air on her ride, and it scared Kenzie to death as she rode in the boat and looked on. She nearly jumped from the boat into the water when Lennox didn't pop up right away. Her heart raced like crazy, and she made it to the side of the boat just as Lennox appeared and smiled, waving her arms in the air. After the boat, they'd all sat by the water on blankets or towels to dry off, drink, and have some snacks. So far, Kenzie hadn't notice anyone getting too drunk, but it was only five o'clock in the afternoon. There was a lot of time left in the day for that.

"So, Kenzie, why didn't any of us know?" April asked and looked a little sad.

Kenzie and April had met only twice, so Kenzie was a little surprised at her reaction. They'd spent very little time alone together; only getting ready at Peyton's for an event they were all attending. They'd gotten along well and had exchanged some texts after that, but they hadn't seen one another in two months, at least.

"No one really knows." Kenzie shrugged. "Peyton and Dani know, obviously. But, outside of them, only a few of my friends from college, my agent, manager, publicist, and lawyer know."

"Let me guess: they told you not to say anything publicly?" April assumed.

"Yeah, but that was a while ago. I haven't brought it up with them since."

"Why not?" Bobby asked.

"Because there wasn't any reason," Kenzie returned.

"Ah, you weren't dating anyone," Tiana guessed.

"Yeah. No one that mattered." Kenzie started running her finger along Lennox's hand and arm, focusing on the sensation of the short blonde hairs against her fingertip.

"Can you imagine yourself coming out with Lennox Owen on your arm, though? You'd be the hottest couple in the world," Mandy suggested. "Since it doesn't look like those two are planning on coming out anytime soon." She nodded toward Peyton and Dani, who were sitting next to each other, staring out at the water and enjoying some private time.

"Guys, let's not, okay?" Lennox requested as she sat up, turned around, and faced Kenzie. "You okay?" she whispered and placed her hand on Kenzie's neck, running her thumb across her skin.

"Why?"

Lennox lowered her eyes to Kenzie's right hand, which was in the grass next to their blanket, running back and forth. She hadn't even realized she had been doing that.

"Kenz?" Lennox checked. "Baby?"

"I think I need a break," Kenzie admitted.

"Okay. Break from what? Me? Them? Do you need some time to yourself?"

"You guys ready for our hike?" Peyton and Dani had joined the group and stood, facing them.

"I think I'll pass." Lennox turned to deliver and then

turned back to Kenzie.

"You should go," Kenzie encouraged. "You don't have to worry about me."

"I *am* worried about you," Lennox leaned in and delivered. "Do you need time alone?"

"I don't want to need time alone," Kenzie returned and placed a hand on Lennox's thigh. "I don't want to need it," she repeated.

"Baby, it's okay. Everyone needs a minute to themselves sometimes."

"But I need it more," Kenzie professed. "And I don't like that about myself."

Lennox kissed her then and placed her arms around her neck.

"I'll go on this hike thing Peyton wants, and you go back to the cabin and just relax, okay? I'll make sure everyone stays out of your hair. Listen to music or read or something."

"I don't want to miss out on any time with you. We only have two more days." Kenzie felt herself getting emotional, which happened rarely. She lowered her eyes so Lennox wouldn't see the tears that were building. She was grateful when she heard Peyton gather the troops away from them to go on the hike through the woods before dinner that she'd planned. The two of them sat on the blanket now and were relatively alone. "Day five and day six, and then you're gone," she muttered. "Day five and day six, and then you're gone," she repeated under her breath.

"Repetition?" Lennox lifted her head to make Kenzie look at her. "How many times?"

"Three." Kenzie wiped her eyes and couldn't believe Lennox understood.

"Say it again," Lennox encouraged and held her chin so she'd keep looking at her. "It's okay."

"Day five and day six, and then you're gone," Kenzie stated with more volume this time.

"Better?"

"How did you know?" she asked. "Your sister?"

"She doesn't do that, but I've read enough to know that some people do. How often does that happen?" Lennox questioned.

"Not that often anymore. It's just when I'm really anxious."

"And you have to repeat it three times?"

"Yes."

"You think I'll be gone? That this will be over when this week ends?"

"I don't know, and that scares me." Kenzie was honest.

"I'll skip the hike, and we'll talk, " she offered.

"No, it's okay. I'm okay. I need some time to myself right now."

"Kenz, don't talk yourself out of this, okay? I'm not going anywhere." Lennox sounded sincere, and Kenzie nodded.

She stood and waited for Lennox to stand before she kissed her cheek and headed toward the cabin to spend some time on her own for the first time in a while – and that was very strange for Kenzie.

***

Lennox stood and watched Kenzie walk away. It took everything in her not to follow the woman and continue the conversation they needed to have. But she had to let her go, because it was what Kenzie needed.

"Everything okay?" Peyton had returned.

"Yeah," she lied.

"How are you an actress? You are a terrible liar," Peyton reasoned. "What happened? Did someone give you two a hard time or something?"

"No," Lennox answered. "She's just worried about what happens after this week, and… I don't know. I guess I'm starting to worry, too."

"You guys have a lot to figure out. You don't have to go on the hike if you need to be with her."

"She needs to be alone right now."

"Did you piss her off or something?"

"No, she's–" Lennox started and stopped. "She's been around people for a few days now without much of a break. She just needs to decompress, I think."

"Well, I can see that. She's spent all that time with you, and you're a pain in the ass," Peyton joked and slugged Lennox's shoulder, trying to lighten the mood. "Come on. Dani picked out the trail, and you and I can bring up the rear and talk about later."

"Sounds good," Lennox told her best friend, and they made their way toward where the rest of their group was, waiting at the trailhead.

***

"Hey, you didn't go on the hike, either?" Maddox entered the cabin.

Kenzie was sitting on the bed she'd shared with Lennox the night before, with her headphones in her ear. She pulled them out when she was surprised by Maddox.

"Sorry, I didn't know you'd be in here," she gave back.

"I kind of hurt my ankle earlier, when I smacked into the water, thanks to Dani's terrible boat-driving. I opted to sit that out and get the stuff ready for dinner. I just came in here to get a sweatshirt. You okay?" Maddox sat on the side of the bed next to the one Kenzie occupied.

"I was just looking for some alone time," she admitted.

"Oh, sorry. I'll head back out and leave you alone."

"You don't have to go," Kenzie told her. "Just, sometimes, I need some time to myself; and there's been a lot of activity this week."

"Yeah, it can get to you. Gets to me, too." She leaned in as if she was sharing a secret. "Between you and me, I didn't hurt my ankle. I just didn't want to go on the hike."

Kenzie laughed and realized she'd left her music playing on her phone. She turned it off and wrapped up her headphones.

"Peyton can be a drill sergeant," she offered in reply.

"That's true." Maddox looked at her. "Are you really okay?"

Kenzie bit her lower lip in response before deciding that Maddox had been a good friend to her so far. She could trust her.

"Can I ask you a question?"

"Sure." Maddox leaned back, waiting.

"You and your girlfriend, how long have you two been together?"

"Oh, I guess about nine months. I've known her for a little over a year, though."

"And she's a model, so she travels a lot?"

"Yeah, we both do," Maddox returned.

"How does that work?"

"You mean the distance thing?" she perceived.

"Yes."

"Well, it's not easy," she admitted and settled in. "I love her, though, so we make it work. It just takes a lot of effort. Sometimes, she's on the other side of the world, and it's morning for her and night for me. I can't go to sleep if I don't see her face." Maddox smiled at the thought. "She'll FaceTime me, and we'll talk. It's not the same as being together, but she's at that point in her career where she's getting all these opportunities, and I don't want to take that away from her. I'm doing my thing, too, and it's important to me. We know that what we have is worth the work and that things will settle down for us. Like, in a month, we're taking a three-week vacation and going to relax and do nothing – but do that together on a beach in the middle of nowhere. I can't wait."

"That sounds nice."

"Are you worried about you and Lennox?" Maddox checked.

"It's new," Kenzie said, suddenly uncomfortable with the change in the conversation.

"And it seems pretty great from what I can see."

"It is," she returned. "I really like her."

"I heard you had a little crush on her before you guys met."

"Big crush," she admitted with a blush.

"And you actually like her for real now?" Maddox questioned. "Do you know how rare that is, Kenzie? You actually met someone famous, and they turned out to be better than you imagined; better than that crush you had. I'm right, aren't I?"

"She is better in reality than anything I could ever imagine," Kenzie revealed. "She understands me; and I thought no one understood me."

"Do you think she wants this to end after this week?"

"She said no."

"So, you're more worried about making it work with the busy careers?"

"She's not gay," Kenzie reminded her.

"Is that important to you? How she labels herself?"

"She's Lennox Owen!" Kenzie let out. "She's Lennox freaking Owen! Do you have any idea how many people want to be with her? How many guys would–" Kenzie stopped herself and drew shapes on her dark-blue sleeping bag that was under her. "She could have anyone. Why would she want me? Here – it's one thing. But out there – it's different."

"Kenzie, Lennox could have anyone. You're right. She's beautiful, smart, funny, and – let's be honest – she's got a lot of fame and money. People are attracted to that. But she's not someone that's going to lead you on. Has she ever been with another woman before?"

"No."

"And she's been with you now."

"Not like that," Kenzie corrected. "We haven't done that yet."

"But you've done stuff?"

"Yes."

"And has she been repulsed by you or done anything that would indicate that she doesn't want to do the other stuff someday?"

"No."

"So, she's into you and has enjoyed the physical stuff you've done so far?"

"I think so."

"Kenzie, the girl's been all over you today. And I saw you two last night. I swear, I thought you had your hands moving in a very specific direction, and she did not at all seem like she was about to pull away." Maddox laughed. "She wants you; and I don't just mean she likes you and enjoys spending time with you. That girl has major hots for you."

"Maybe."

"Maybe?" Maddox laughed again. "Kenzie, she's spent the entire day staring at you with those hot as fuck eyes of hers, and they weren't cute, puppy-dog eyes, either. Ask anyone. We all noticed. When you were in that bikini, I thought she was about to tear it off you with her eyes."

Kenzie laughed at that remark.

"Okay. I get it," she said after she calmed her own laughter.

"Don't go crazy, okay? Just talk to her when she gets back. You two will figure something out. Just remember – she seems crazy about you. And I think you're pretty crazy about her, too."

Kenzie nodded, and Maddox patted her knee before she stood, grabbed her sweatshirt, and left her alone in the cabin.

CHAPTER 16

"SHE thinks I'm a writer," Lennox explained as she and Peyton followed about ten feet behind the rest of the group along the trail.

"A writer?" Peyton looked at her in disbelief. "Where'd that come from?"

"I told her I had this idea for the next season of her show, and she thought it was a good idea. She got me to admit that I'd actually written them down and that I liked it."

"You've written down an idea for her show?"

"Yeah."

"Like, for real?"

"Yes, Peyton. Why is that so hard to believe?"

"Because you've never mentioned it to me. I've known you forever, and I don't think you've ever told me you liked writing."

"I'm an actress. I'm the actress that shows up, runs her lines, and that's it. That's what they expect from me, so that's what I do."

"But, I'm not them, Len." Peyton stopped walking. "I'm your best friend. And, in case you forgot, I'm also a writer. Different format, but same concept."

"When people tell you not to think about it every day for most of your life, you start to think there's no point, and you don't bother talking about it with anyone, Pey." Lennox stopped alongside her.

"But, that's what I'm saying, Len – I'm not just anyone. You're like my big sister. I tell you everything. I tell you more than I tell my actual siblings. I told you about my feelings for Dani before anyone else. You read my lyrics before they're even all together and I can barely make sense out of them."

"I tell you everything, too, Peyton. This isn't a big deal." She pressed on and motioned that they should join the group.

"Lennox, you told Kenzie after, like, a day; and you never told me."

"I'm sure there's stuff Dani knows about you that I don't know."

"Dani's my girlfriend of two-plus years, Len. You just met Kenzie. And, don't get me wrong – I'm glad you did, and I'm happy for you two, but I'm just a little disappointed, I guess, that you felt you couldn't talk to me about this."

"It's not like that, Peyton. I didn't see the point in talking about it. It wasn't going anywhere. It still isn't. It's not like I'm making a career change from an actress to a writer or anything. You just asked about what we talked about, and that was one of the things."

"Do you like writing, though?" Peyton questioned and snapped a leaf off a branch they walked under.

"I guess, yeah."

"You guess?"

"I get these ideas sometimes," Lennox sighed. "I'll be sitting at home, doing nothing, or in my trailer, reading lines, and I get an idea in my head, and the only thing I can do to get it out is to write it down," she paused. "Sometimes, I just make notes on my phone of random things like characters or whole scenes, and other times, I get out my computer and open Final Draft."

"You have Final Draft?"

"Yeah," Lennox replied.

"And you do what then?"

"I write," she answered like that was the stupidest question she'd ever gotten. "I try to piece the scenes together into something, but it never amounts to much. I think I have the beginning of three movies and the ending of one. And then, I wrote some of the season two stuff for Kenzie's show."

"Len..." She stopped Lennox with a hand on her arm.

"Do you remember when I was working on my second album, and the record company didn't believe in the songs? They wanted a different sound and thought the lyrics didn't work?"

"Yeah."

"And what did you tell me?"

"I don't know. That was a long time ago, Peyton."

"You told me that my vision was important. That my words, my music mattered, and that I should fight for what I thought was right."

"Okay. Why–"

"Lennox, if people are telling you your words don't matter, or that they don't want to hear your ideas – you don't stop having the ideas or stop writing your words, using your voice. You find better people to surround yourself with." She nodded. "And it sounds like Kenzie might be one of them."

Lennox smiled at the mention of Kenzie's name.

"She's worried about what happens next."

"I know."

"I just want to be with her, Peyton. I don't know what that means or how we do that. She'll be in London in a couple of weeks, and I won't."

"It's not that big of a deal. Dani and I manage distance when we have to, and we make it work."

"But when you two first started dating, you were both in the same city. You were writing the album, so you were in New York, and she's based there. You had, like, five months before your travel started. We don't have that luxury."

"What's your next project?"

"I'm in LA. I've got the re-shoots for *Fireflies* and then, ADR for Express after that."

"And the next movie you're working on?"

"I'm reading scripts when I get back. Tom wants me in at least two next year, and maybe three if it works out schedule-wise. He thinks we'll get some award buzz for

Fireflies and wants to capitalize on it with some gritty, independent stuff, and then, a big Hollywood one after, if we can swing it." She rattled on the details from the last conversation she'd had with her agent the week before her arrival.

"You sound like you hate all of that."

"What? I don't."

"Len, do you even want to shoot three movies in the next year?"

"I don't have much of a choice, Peyton."

"Of course, you do. Look, I have a record contract. I have to do two more albums in the next two years. I'm obligated to deliver. You have your re-shoots and your ADR you have to fulfill, and then whatever your press obligations are for those movies, but you haven't signed up for anything else yet, Len. Don't. Take a damn break. As far as I know, these once a year things I do are the only real vacations you take."

"I take time off. It's not like I don't take breaks."

"No, you don't. You may not be shooting, but Tom always has you reading a script or auditioning for something or appearing on a talk show. You're in every magazine every single month, I swear. All of that takes time and energy, and you should just take a break."

"I don't need career advice, Peyton. I wanted advice about Kenzie."

"It's kind of the same thing there, Len. Think about it." Peyton kicked at a rock. "Okay. So, can we talk about my kind of really big thing now?"

Lennox laughed at the ability Peyton had to change the subject so instantly.

"Sure."

***

Lennox stood inside her cabin and ran her hand through her hair, trying to figure out where Kenzie had gone, since the woman wasn't in the one-room building.

Everyone had gone into their cabins to change out of their hiking boots or change into sweatshirts, since the night air had cooled, and then, they would report to dinner. Lennox couldn't find Kenzie and had already gone to the cafeteria cabin to check. She exited the cabin and waved at some of the girls she passed on her way to the cabanas. She searched all three of them and found them empty. She turned to face the water to try to find another idea as to where Kenzie might be and saw a small light about a hundred yards away down the shore of the lake through a small grouping of trees. She couldn't make out much else in the light of the late setting sun. She headed in that direction, wrapping her arms around herself and regretting not grabbing a sweatshirt of her own. She realized it was a lantern the closer she got. As she made her way through the trees, she discovered Kenzie lying flat on her back on a blanket, with her eyes closed and with her headphones in her ears. Lennox looked around and noticed that Kenzie had managed to find a flat patch of short grass amongst a group of trees and brush that gave her some privacy. Lennox stared at her with a smile on her face and considered approaching in silence, but – given their surroundings – she thought that might be a bad idea.

"Kenz?" she said with just above-normal volume. "Kenzie?"

Kenzie's eyes shot open in surprise, and she lifted only her head to see Lennox standing there. She went to move, and Lennox held up a hand.

"Don't." She walked up to the blanket and knelt in front of her. "Just stay like that."

"Okay." Kenzie pulled the headphones out of her ears and turned the music off on her phone, sliding it to the side. "How was your hike?"

Lennox didn't answer. She slid on top of Kenzie and looked down at her.

"How was your alone time?"

"Fine." Kenzie gulped.

"Are you done with it now?"

"Yes," she replied.

"Good." Lennox captured her lips without asking permission this time and reveled in their feel.

It had been too long since she'd kissed this girl, and she needed to have her lips on her. She needed her hands on Kenzie's body, and she had never needed that before. She had never needed someone like she'd needed Kenzie since the moment they'd met.

"I missed you," she shared and kissed Kenzie's neck.

"I missed you," Kenzie returned and ran her hands under Lennox's shirt. "I'm sorry about earlier; about needing some time."

"Don't be." Lennox kissed her cheek and then her forehead. "Don't be sorry about that, okay? I understand."

"You understand me, don't you?" Kenzie asked, and that surprised Lennox.

"I think so, yeah." Lennox kissed her lips. "And you understand me."

"I don't know that."

"You called me a writer."

"Because you are a writer. You just don't want to admit it, for some reason."

Lennox could see the light from the lantern flicker in Kenzie's eyes, and she just watched it for a moment.

"Because everyone before you told me not to."

"You should be yourself, Lennox. You're captivating," Kenzie replied with a smirk, using the word Lennox had used before to describe her.

"When you go to London, I have to stay in LA."

"Yes." Kenzie's smile disappeared from her face instantly.

"I have to wrap up some stuff for two movies I've already finished."

"I know. I get it. We don't have to talk about this now."

"Yes, we do," Lennox told her. "We have to talk about it now, because – if you're ready, Kenzie – I'm ready."

"Ready for..." Kenzie looked hopeful and ran her hands around to Lennox's chest, where she left them there. "It?"

"Yes, Mackenzie." Lennox smiled at her from above. "I am ready to have sex with you, and I would like to do that. But I also don't just have sex with someone I'm not dating; and we are not technically dating."

"Oh, right."

"So, I would like to talk to you about something." Lennox leaned down and kissed Kenzie's neck. "I think we'll have to figure out this long-distance thing while I have to wrap up those jobs." She kissed Kenzie's collarbone. "And then, I was thinking I could come to London until you wrap there." She kissed the other side of Kenzie's neck. "And, after that, you'll be in New York, and I just happen to own a place in New York. I could maybe be there, and you could maybe be there." Lennox lifted herself and met Kenzie's surprised yet happy eyes. "And then, we can go from there?" she chanced.

"What about work? I thought you had scripts to read."

"I do, but I can do that anywhere. I can figure out my schedule after you wrap. If this works, and we're still together, we can maybe try to work near each other; or, at least, we'll know how to navigate the distance part better."

"You want to be with me?"

"Mackenzie Smyth, I want everything with you." She leaned down and captured Kenzie's lips again, but then, she was promptly turned over onto her back.

Kenzie's lips attacked Lennox's already greedy ones. She moved them to Lennox's neck and then down her chest, pulling her shirt down slightly as she went. Her hands found purchase on either side of Lennox's head, and Lennox wasted no time in trying to pull off Kenzie's shirt.

"Wait." Kenzie shot up quickly, straddling Lennox's waist. "Are you sure? Lennox, are you sure? Because it's okay if you want to wait. We don't have to do anything until you're ready."

"I'm sure," Lennox confirmed. "But, *fuck*, you're cute when you're trying to be all noble," she admitted with a chuckle.

Kenzie reached for her shirt and pulled it over her head, revealing a pink bra underneath. She went to lower herself back down but decided to change that plan at the last second and instead, grabbed at Lennox's hands, pulling her up. She lifted Lennox's shirt up and over her head and looked down at the bikini top she still wore.

"I'm the only one that gets to see it like this," Kenzie remarked and bit her lower lip, and Lennox nearly came right then. She gulped as Kenzie reached around her back and untied it, letting the strings fall down Lennox's back before reaching for the tie at her neck. Kenzie slid the two strings apart and watched, transfixed, as the suit fell away, and Lennox sat in front of her, naked from the waist up. "Beautiful," she whispered out.

Lennox had never believed someone more about anything in her life. The way Kenzie looked at her, the way she touched her, and how she said things like that, made her feel like, to Kenzie, she was the most beautiful person in the world.

"Kenz, can you…" Lennox suddenly felt exposed and nervous – but the good kind of nervous, that came before important events happened in her life.

Kenzie reached behind her back and unclasped her own bra, letting it fall, and then tossing it onto the blanket. Lennox stared at Kenzie's chest, a mere foot away and right in front of her eyes. She had never seen breasts this up close before, and while she had never had the desire to before, she wanted to touch them now. She wanted to taste them. She leaned forward and pulled Kenzie in by the waist, pressing her lips between them and running her hands for the first time up and down Kenzie's naked back. Kenzie's breathing grew ragged, and Lennox recognized that she might need to slow down a little. But, just as she went to pull her lips back, Kenzie surprised her again and pushed her down lightly, resting herself over her. Their breasts pressed together for the first time, and they both gasped in unison. Kenzie kissed her then, and she seemed to enjoy the fast pace of their kisses before she slid down Lennox's body and met her nipple with her tongue, while applying subtle pressure to Lennox's other one with her finger and thumb.

"You have to tell me to stop if you want to stop," Kenzie said when she looked up at her.

"Why would I want you to stop?" Lennox's hips lifted and lowered on their own when Kenzie's lips pulled her nipple into her mouth firmly and sucked.

She wasn't sure what that felt like to someone with Kenzie's condition, but it felt like nothing before in Lennox's sexual experience. Kenzie's lips were soft, and hot and pliant, and they moved to the exact spot Lennox seemed to want them. Just as Lennox's body registered that it needed to be touched somewhere, Kenzie's lips were there, applying pressure or wet kisses, and releasing some of the tension that had Lennox coiled up into a tight, metaphorical ball since the moment their hands touched that roller bag. Kenzie's hand went to the button of the shorts Lennox had thrown on after the hike and stopped.

"Okay?"

"I should tell you something." Lennox breathed out as Kenzie's lips met the spot just above that button. "I don't always–" She gasped when Kenzie's tongue slid just under the button and then back out and up to her belly button.

"Sorry, what were you saying?" Kenzie looked up and met Lennox's eyes.

Lennox was certain she'd never seen a sexier sight than Kenzie in that position, looking up at her with near-black eyes and her mouth open with wet lips, waiting to touch her skin once more.

"Nothing," Lennox replied.

Kenzie waited another moment and gave her a confused expression, as if to check that Lennox was okay. Lennox pressed her hand softly to the back of Kenzie's head in encouragement, and Kenzie lowered her lips to the skin before her hand undid the button of Lennox's shorts and, after, slid down the zipper. Lennox watched Kenzie sit up and slide the shorts down her legs before her eyes met Lennox's center. She still wore her bathing suit bottoms from earlier, and Kenzie's eyes seemed to darken even more, or maybe it was just the lack of light from the sky.

What Lennox had almost admitted, was that she often had a difficult time achieving orgasm. This was true whether she was with a lover or even just touching herself. Noah had complained a couple of times with grunts of frustration, and then, he'd stated his concerns out loud toward the end of their relationship that her inability to come when they had sex, made him feel like he wasn't good enough. Lennox had ended up consoling him and making it about her body and not his inability to please her. While that was partially true, she also knew Noah didn't excite her toward the end of their relationship where sex was concerned, and to help his seemingly fragile male ego, she'd begun to fake it.

With Lucas, it had been less difficult in the beginning because it was new. But, even then, her orgasms never seemed to just happen or happen quickly. The difference between Noah and Lucas, though, was that Noah cared. He was frustrated at times, but he also cared about her and wanted her to feel good. So, when he couldn't make that happen, it hurt him as well. Lucas likely cared in the beginning. But sex for him was really about him more than her, and once his addiction took over, they'd essentially stopped having sex.

Outside of the two people she'd been with, though, her body didn't even seem to like her own touches, and that made her wonder if she even knew herself and her own wants and needs in that department. She also wondered often what all the fuss was about, because she'd never had one of those explosive orgasms she'd heard so much about. And, God, she wanted one. Even if it was just once in her life, she wanted to know what it felt like to explode like that.

Kenzie's mouth was back on her own, and her hand, that was not holding her up, was moving up and down Lennox's stomach and then lightly toying with a nipple. Lennox knew Kenzie was holding back. She could tell that Kenzie was more than ready to move this along as her hips were beginning to rock into Lennox's. And Lennox was wet. She was hot, and wet, and she wanted Kenzie's hands on her. She stopped Kenzie's hand with her own and lowered it down to cover her sex. Her hips shot up when Kenzie cupped her between her legs.

"Lennox," she whispered.

"Take them off," Lennox instructed.

Kenzie wasted no time. Her hands moved swiftly and smoothly to pull at the bathing suit. Lennox lifted her hips and her legs when needed to allow Kenzie to tear them from her body and toss them aside. Before Lennox could request it, Kenzie knelt back, undid her own shorts, and slid them off her legs, standing as she did. Once gone, Lennox saw those eyes meet her own, and they stared for a moment before Kenzie lowered her hands to her matching pink panties, gulped silently, and then pulled them down her legs. She knelt immediately in front of Lennox, and Lennox could tell Kenzie was intentionally looking at her eyes and not the now exposed parts of her body. Lennox didn't coax or encourage. She waited.

She knew this was one of those moments Kenzie needed for herself; to gather herself after what they'd already done and before what they were about to do. Kenzie's eyes lowered slowly; almost painfully slowly, because Lennox wanted her to touch her. She wanted Kenzie back on top of her, she wanted to feel the press of her, and move against her. She would allow Kenzie this time, though. She knew that while this was a big moment for herself, this was also a big moment for Kenzie. Lennox had a moment where she thought about how Kenzie might have fantasized about this before. Kenzie had told her that she was her lifelong crush. It was entirely possible and maybe even likely that she'd thought about this moment, and Lennox worried that she might not measure up to whatever Kenzie had envisioned, so she lowered her own eyes and turned her head to the side.

"Hey, where'd you go?" Kenzie questioned and was back on top of Lennox.

"Nowhere. Sorry," she replied, turned back, and wrapped her arms around Kenzie's neck, trying to pull her closer.

"Lennox, tell me," Kenzie requested and pressed her forehead to Lennox's. Lennox swallowed, and Kenzie lowered her lips to her throat to kiss her there. "Please."

"Have you thought about this before?" Lennox asked and realized she did want to know the answer.

Kenzie met her eyes and seemed to think before answering.

"Thought about having sex with you?" she reasoned and ran her hand over Lennox's cheek.

"Yes."

"That's embarrassing." Kenzie laughed and lowered her head to Lennox's shoulder, where she pressed her forehead to it.

"So, that's a yes?" Lennox resisted laughing at how cute Kenzie was being.

"Yes," she admitted. "You are someone I've thought about doing this with before." Kenzie hesitated then. "Not just this though."

"What do you mean?" Lennox ran her fingertips over Kenzie's bare back.

"It wasn't just sex, Lennox." Kenzie lifted herself up and confidently stared down at her. "I wanted everything with you. I pictured us together, but I never thought it would happen for real," she paused. "I never thought this would happen. You are so beautiful." Kenzie kissed her gently and added, "And I cannot believe you want this with me."

Lennox considered how to respond to that. She

thought about telling Kenzie she might not come, because she had always had a hard time. She thought about telling her that she wanted whatever she'd pictured; that she was crazy to think Lennox wouldn't want her. Instead, she kissed her. She pulled Kenzie down into her, and Kenzie ended up on her elbows, trying to hold herself up. But Lennox wasn't paying attention to that. She registered the feel of Kenzie against her and ran her hands down Kenzie's back, gripping her ass and pressing her ever closer. She wanted her inside her skin. She wanted Kenzie's hands everywhere at once and for her lips to follow suit. She wanted to beg Kenzie to touch her and release her from the tension, the want, and the need she'd only just discovered upon meeting the dark-haired beauty above her.

Kenzie's hips were on the move, and they weren't rocking into her. They were rolling down and somehow swirling around between Lennox's legs. It was Kenzie and her way of moving her body – whether it be due to the nervous system condition or just Kenzie knowing how to move against a woman, Lennox wasn't entirely sure, but she also didn't care in the slightest. Kenzie's hand slid between them, and Lennox's eyes shot open at the first touch. She wanted to watch Kenzie's reaction. She needed to see it, and she did. She first noticed that Kenzie's eyes closed tightly, as if she needed to take a second to absorb the event, and then, they relaxed but remained closed as her mouth formed a small 'O' shape, and Lennox felt the hot breath as she exhaled against her mouth.

"Are you–" Lennox started, but Kenzie opened her eyes and closed her mouth, causing her to stop.

"You feel so good," Kenzie answered the unanswered question. Her fingers slid between Lennox's wet folds, and she gasped before Lennox had the chance to do that herself. "You're hot, and it's slick." Kenzie pressed her forehead against Lennox's. "I could drown in you, Lennox," she remarked and began stroking. "I want to drown in you," she added in a growl of a tone.

Lennox registered the two fingers sliding back and forth over her sensitive clit. But she was even more aware of Kenzie's free hand, which was beside her, because as she turned her head slightly, Lennox could see it was balled into a fist, clutching at the thin blanket separating them from the grass and dirt.

"Don't hold back," she instructed. "Don't." She kept her eyes on Kenzie's hand and watched as she relaxed it.

"I'm afraid."

"Don't be afraid." Lennox placed her hand on the one currently stroking slowly between her legs. "Just let go."

Kenzie's eyes flickered in the lantern light, and it was as if they were on fire; on actual fire. Her chest rose and fell rapidly, as if there was something buried inside her, trying to get out. Lennox had never been more turned on in her entire life. And as Kenzie entered her and pushed farther inside, Lennox gripped the blanket with balled fists of her own and resonated with the sensation of being completely whole in this way for the first time. Kenzie was done being shy or afraid, and Lennox thought she was the sexiest thing she'd ever seen when Kenzie leaned back over her and used her hips along with her fingers to push inside and pull back out slowly for only a few strokes before she sped up, and Lennox thought she'd come undone just watching her. Kenzie's pace became fevered, and Lennox spread her legs wider and lifted them both so that her knees were in the air while Kenzie rocked hard against and inside her.

"Lennox," Kenzie whispered again with closed eyes from above her.

"Yes, baby," she encouraged. "Yes, don't stop." She could only let go of the blanket with one hand, because she needed the other to keep her somehow glued to the ground, and she used her now free one to grasp the back of Kenzie's head and pull her lips to her. "Kiss me," she ordered, and Kenzie did until Lennox's gasps and her rugged breathing prevented their mouths from remaining connected.

Kenzie's eyes met Lennox's, and that fire in them had

not diminished in the slightest as her thumb flicked Lennox's clit and her two fingers curled and straightened, causing Lennox's hips to rock up, down, and back up again. Lennox heard herself grunt and heard Kenzie moan before she felt it. She gasped; not at the actual sensation of a building orgasm but at the fact that she was about to have one at all. She tried not to get her hopes up. This had happened before. She'd get close but not go over entirely, and she'd be left unsatisfied. She tried to figure out how to explain that to Kenzie; how to ensure Kenzie knew it had nothing to do with her. But then, she wouldn't have to do that, because she was coming; and she was coming hard.

"There?" Kenzie asked, but Lennox didn't register the question.

"Yes!" she screamed, but it wasn't a response. It was a sound, a word she could not contain inside her. "Yes! God!"

Both of her hands were in fists again, pulling and tugging at the relenting blanket that would not hold her in place as she tumbled and exploded over the cliff of her orgasm. Tingles turned to bursts and fireworks. Her body actually shifted almost onto its side, and she would have rolled over completely had it not been for Kenzie holding her in place.

"Kenz!" she gasped out as she was still feeling the high not coming down yet.

Kenzie's thrusts hadn't slowed at all, and Lennox worried that if Kenzie didn't start to slow down, she might come again. And she wasn't sure her body could handle another orgasm of that intensity. But then, Kenzie was moving, sliding down Lennox's body. Within seconds, Kenzie had her mouth covering her sex, and she was sucking, tasting, and moaning against it. Lennox flashed black behind her eyes, but it wasn't black – it was the deep dark-green of Kenzie's intense eyes. Lennox spread wider for her as Kenzie took what she wanted and feasted on Lennox just as Lennox had started to come down.

Lennox's hand went to Kenzie's head, and she gripped

her hair, pulling harder than she knew she should, but she had no choice. As Kenzie moaned and nibbled lightly with her teeth before sucking hard and fast, Lennox needed to hold on to something. Kenzie's fingers were still inside her, but they had slowed as she'd changed her focus. When Lennox gripped her hair particularly hard, Kenzie must have noticed she was about to come unglued again, and her strokes inside returned to the fevered pace that Lennox wasn't sure how she had been able to keep up to.

Kenzie's eyes lifted up to watch Lennox watching her, as her head shook rapidly from side to side, and Lennox growled at the sensation paired with the one she was experiencing inside. Kenzie's eyes on her and her free hand, tweaking a nipple, was what shoved Lennox forcefully into the abyss of another welcomed and intense orgasm. She wondered how the earth wasn't shaking beneath her, because that was how it felt; it was earth-shattering, and she waited for the ground to open up and suck her into it. When she had told Kenzie to take what she'd wanted, she had no idea it would lead her to this.

Kenzie waited for another several minutes, delivering slower and slower strokes with her tongue and her fingers, before she kissed the inside of Lennox's thighs, her stomach, her breasts – having to combat the heaving chest Lennox couldn't quite calm – and then, Lennox's throat and her lips, while her hands went into Lennox's hair and at her neck.

Kenzie felt Lennox's pulse, and Lennox knew she was enjoying that; knowing she had done that to her. So, she closed her eyes and let Kenzie revel in it; in her and in what they'd just shared. She allowed Kenzie to slow her touches to grazes and skims and to breathe out the feel of her in short gasps.

"Lennox?"

"Yeah, baby?" Lennox ran her fingertips over Kenzie's back.

"Are we okay?"

Lennox squinted her eyes and grabbed Kenzie's face, pulling her up so she could look at her.

"What? Why would you ask me that?" she wondered with concern.

"I didn't want to hurt you or go too fast."

"Kenzie, you just gave me the best two orgasms of my life." Lennox laughed out. "I cannot believe I just did that; that you just did that to me." She laughed more when she saw Kenzie smile shyly. "I shouldn't be surprised, though, given what you've done to me so far. God, Kenz, you are…" She placed her hands on Kenzie's cheeks. "You're a gift."

"I go too fast, sometimes. I can't control myself. But with you, it was worse," she said. "I mean that in a good way," she elaborated when Lennox undoubtedly gave her a questioning stare. "I just wanted all of you at once, and I couldn't stop myself."

"You can do that to me again anytime you want." Lennox ran her hands down Kenzie's chest, leaving one hand over her heart to feel it beating wildly. "Are you okay?"

"Yes."

"It wasn't too intense?"

"It was the most intense experience of my life," Kenzie returned and placed her hand over Lennox's. "And I want you again," she added, and the fire returned to her eyes.

"Oh, no!" Lennox laughed. "Your turn." She lifted herself up while still being straddled by Kenzie.

"You don't have to do anything to me."

"What are you talking about? I've been dreaming of this for days. And if Peyton is to be believed, I've been dreaming about this for a lot longer than that."

Kenzie looked down at her and kissed her lips gently before pulling her closer and pressing Lennox to her chest.

"I already came once," she said to the top of Lennox's head.

"What?" Lennox snapped her head back to look up at

the now shy expression on Kenzie's face.

"When I was touching you." Kenzie bit her lower lip. "I came. I come fast most of the time. It's because of my condition. Normally, it's just when I'm…" Kenzie faded instead of stopping entirely this time. She then took a deep breath in and appeared to gather some courage. "Touching myself. When I touch myself, it doesn't take long. With others, it's normally not that fast. But when I was inside you, I couldn't stop it."

"I didn't hear you."

"I'm not great at that part."

"What part?"

Kenzie gulped, and Lennox admired how unbelievably beautiful she was in that moment, and how brave she was to share this much of herself with Lennox.

"Being expressive. I'm not good at that."

"Oh, baby." Lennox kissed between her breasts. "I want to touch you. If you can't handle it, that's okay; we don't have to. But I want to touch you, Kenzie." Lennox paused and closed her eyes. "Can you come again?"

"Not usually right away."

"Wait… You came just from touching me? With nothing touching you?" Lennox returned her mind to what Kenzie had just told her.

"I told you; I could drown in you, Lennox Owen."

"And I am in love with you, Mackenzie Smyth." She breathed against Kenzie's chest the most honest sentence she'd ever uttered and felt the shaking of Kenzie's body as she clutched Lennox closer still.

Kenzie didn't say anything back, and Lennox hadn't expected her to. She also hadn't expected to tell someone she had known for four days that she was in love with them. But it was the truth, and it was better for her to admit it now than to hold it back. Of that, she was sure.

CHAPTER 17

KENZIE'S heart was racing, and she knew Lennox could feel it against her skin and would likely draw conclusions about what that rapid beat meant. She worried that Lennox would be concerned about having expressed those words, that sentiment to Kenzie. And Kenzie knew she should say it back. She should tell Lennox how she felt about her; that, in her twenty-six years on this planet, she had never felt for anyone what she felt for Lennox Owen; she had never had a connection to anyone like this, and all she wanted was to spend her life telling and showing what that meant to her. She couldn't, though. She couldn't say it, and she wasn't sure why. But she didn't want to lose Lennox because she wasn't ready yet. She didn't have the words to describe it yet.

"Kenz, baby?" Lennox had waited patiently long enough, and Kenzie knew what would happen next. "Lie down," Lennox whispered against Kenzie's chest and let go of her back.

"I don't—"

"Lie down," Lennox said a little louder and gave a light push to Kenzie's stomach. "I want to touch you. I'm going crazy not touching you," she informed.

Kenzie hadn't expected that. She'd thought Lennox would want words from her, and if she didn't deliver those words, Lennox would want to leave. Kelly had done that. She'd told Kenzie she loved her three times, and Kenzie hadn't been able to just say the words back. Now, as Kenzie lay back and gave into the intoxicating scent of Lennox's arousal, that she could lick off her own lips, and the press of Lennox's body to her own, she knew she'd never experienced love before this; and that had been why she'd never been able to express it back then.

"I might not be able to… again," she offered. "But that's not you. I can usually come only once, and then my body has to settle down. It's a process. It happens so fast, and then I have to recover. It's not you, though, okay?"

"Baby, I just want to touch you, okay? You don't have to feel pressured to do anything or make anything happen. If you can't come, it's okay. If you come right away, that's fine. And if it takes a while, that's okay, too." Lennox leaned down and pressed her lips gently to Kenzie's forehead. "I want to be inside you." Lennox rolled her hips into Kenzie's and kissed her eyebrow. "And I want to move against you like this." She repeated the movement. "And slide my fingers around to feel how wet you are." She kissed Kenzie's eyelid and then moved to the other side to do the same. "I want to taste you." She pressed her lips to Kenzie's nose. "Now, tell me what you want." She kissed Kenzie's lips, and Kenzie wondered if she could taste herself on them.

"I don't know," she gasped out against Lennox's lips.

Lennox rolled down into her, and she thought she might combust. Her fingers dug into Lennox's back, and she worried she might be hurting her, but Lennox didn't flinch or show any kind of discomfort.

"Kenz, you can tell me."

"It's always fast," she admitted. "I hate that it's always fast," she followed.

"Oh," Lennox surmised and stopped rolling her hips.

"No, don't. I don't want you to stop. It's just something I hate that I wish I could change."

"And you've tried?"

"I can't do it myself. It starts, and I can't stop it; even if I stop touching myself." She tried not to be embarrassed at the admission and reminded herself that she was talking to Lennox. It was okay with Lennox. "No one else ever tried," she offered of her ex-girlfriends.

Lennox nodded and looked down Kenzie's body.

"I can't blame them for wanting to go crazy with you, Kenz. You're so sexy, it's hard to keep my hands off you all the time."

"You can do what you were doing again." Kenzie gave her a small smile and earned one in return.

"I have a better idea," Lennox replied.

She pressed her lips to Kenzie's neck but lifted her body as she did, holding herself above her, completely unattached from Kenzie's body. Kenzie missed the heat and the pressure immediately, but she took in the tight muscles on Lennox's well-defined arms, as she carried her body weight, and she didn't mind that visual at all.

Lennox sucked Kenzie's pulse point for several moments, taking short breaks and returning to the motion, before licking, sucking, and kissing Kenzie's sensitive skin. When Kenzie's hips rose, Lennox stopped for a second and waited for them to lower before she moved to a different spot and a different type of touch. She lowered herself to Kenzie's chest and used a hand and her mouth to, again, apply gentle and sometimes firmer touches. But, the moment Kenzie's breath grew ragged, or her hips lifted on their own, she'd stop and shift to another position and offer a different type of touch. Lennox grazed Kenzie's stomach with cool fingertips and then applied hot lips to the spot. Kenzie had never been touched like this before. Her skin was on fire, and her fists were at her sides, but she was enjoying every single touch applied to her body.

Lennox touched her like this for what felt like forever, but was likely only five minutes or so, before she lowered her lips to Kenzie's nipple and gently kissed it. Kenzie's skin broke out into goosebumps, and she watched Lennox smirk when she noticed. Lennox still held herself completely above Kenzie, and Kenzie wondered how much longer she'd be able to keep her body up like that. Her lips engulfed her nipple, and Kenzie's hips shot up instantly.

"Hold on, baby," Lennox mumbled before she kissed the spot. "Hold on for me," she encouraged and sucked again.

Kenzie held her breath while Lennox sucked and then changed nipples, offering a squeeze to the breast she'd just left.

"I don't know if I can."

"I do." Lennox licked between her breasts. "I know you are capable of much more than you give yourself credit for." She offered the other nipple the same attention and then lowered herself more. "I love your skin." She ran a hand along Kenzie's side. "It's so soft," she added and kissed it.

She continued moving along Kenzie's stomach lower, and then higher, and then to the left, and to the right. Kenzie could barely stand it, but she was trying. She wanted to hold on. She wanted to know what it felt like to have all this before she let go. Lennox lowered still, and after several minutes of kissing Kenzie's stomach, her lips moved to her thighs as her fingers lightly spread Kenzie's legs.

"I might come," she breathed out when Lennox's lips were dangerously close.

"Don't," Lennox ordered quietly and moved away from the spot. "Please, let me touch you." She kissed her hip and then licked it, sliding her tongue to Kenzie's belly button.

"Come up here," Kenzie managed. Lennox complied and made her way back up to Kenzie, kissing her mouth immediately. Kenzie moved her hands to Lennox's ass, pressing her down into her. "Touch me."

"You're ready?"

"Yes, touch me," Kenzie repeated.

Lennox lowered her hips and her lips, but she did so at a slow pace. Kenzie wanted fast, though. She was ready for fast. She tried to speed up the pace of the kiss, hoping

Lennox would take the hint, but Lennox only smiled into her mouth.

"Baby, slow," she offered.

Kenzie knew what she was doing, so she tried to change her own focus. She tried to slow her body down. But the touches Lennox was providing, made that very difficult, and she felt her orgasm begin to take hold. Lennox hadn't even touched her yet, and Kenzie didn't want to disappoint her. She wanted to feel her there, too. She wanted Lennox's hand between her legs. And then, it was there; Lennox was touching her. Her fingers were dancing in Kenzie's wetness and gliding through it slowly.

"Oh!"

"Wow," Lennox muttered into her mouth. "That's for me?" she asked with a shallow gasp.

"Yes," Kenzie let out, and Lennox smiled against her lips again.

"I love it," Lennox said, and Kenzie wasn't sure if she was referring to how wet she was or just the part about having sex with another woman. But, either way, she didn't care.

Lennox's fingers were on either side of her clit. Their strokes were slow but sure, and Kenzie's body was one stroke away from overload; one second away from having to stop because it was too much. Lennox stopped. She met Kenzie's eyes and her fingers stilled. She knew. She could tell that Kenzie needed a break, or she wouldn't be able to continue, and Lennox gave that to her.

"Thank you," Kenzie remarked and felt tears well up in her eyes.

Lennox didn't say anything. She smiled and slid herself back down Kenzie's body, carefully removing her fingers as she did. When she ended up between Kenzie's legs, she pulled them apart farther still and rested herself between them.

"Tell me," she asked and removed every part of her body from Kenzie's.

Kenzie closed her eyes and registered the lack of stimuli, calming herself with her fingers dragging along the thin blanket, and sensing the grass blades beneath and the small rocks and the ground under that. She repeated the words silently to herself, 'I'm ready. I'm ready. I'm ready.' Then, she said them out loud.

"I'm ready," she confirmed.

Lennox moved to her center and licked from Kenzie's entrance to the tip of her clit before she took her into her mouth fully and sucked. Her hands went around Kenzie's legs and on her hips as she pulled her face closer, burying it between Kenzie's legs entirely as she licked and flicked with her tongue where she'd, somehow, known Kenzie needed her.

"Yes!" Kenzie uttered and surprised herself, because she never said anything like that during sex. She normally came silently and had to tell her lovers to stop. But she shouted again, "Lennox!"

She came hard in Lennox's mouth, and it was anything but fast. The orgasm lasted longer than usual, and that was in part because Lennox slid a tentative finger inside her just as she'd shouted her name. Another finger joined in, and Lennox pumped slowly inside, matching the movement to the pace of her tongue, still wreaking miraculous havoc on Kenzie's sensitive nervous system.

When Kenzie finally came down, it was with Lennox still inside her but lying next to her, soothing her with soft kisses and whispers in her ear. Kenzie had never experienced anything like that before in her life, and the tears appeared again in her eyes.

"Are you okay?" Lennox asked.

"I think I'm supposed to be asking you that," she returned and wiped at the tears in her eyes.

"I am more than okay," Lennox returned.

"Yeah?"

"Yeah." She moved a strand of hair from Kenzie's face. "Will you do something for me?"

"Anything." Kenzie turned her head to her.

"Can I be your girlfriend?" Lennox had this look on her face that told Kenzie she was actually nervous about her answer.

"You want to be my girlfriend?" Kenzie asked with a shy smile back.

"Yes."

"I want to be your girlfriend," Kenzie replied.

Lennox smiled and looked down at her hand, which was still between Kenzie's legs.

"I should move those."

"Yeah." Kenzie let out a laugh. "Just go easy. I'm still a little wound up."

"Yeah?" Lennox's eyebrow lifted.

"No way!" Kenzie replied and kissed Lennox's lips. "Besides, we've been out here for a while. Peyton is likely going to send a search party."

"Oh, shit! Peyton!" Lennox lifted up slightly and withdrew her fingers slowly.

"What's wrong?"

"She has a thing planned for tonight," she recalled. "We should get back."

"Can we spare maybe another five minutes?" Kenzie shrugged.

"What did you have in mind?" Lennox smiled back at her and grazed her lips over Kenzie's.

"I just want to hold you," Kenzie returned. "I need another minute before I'm calmed down all the way, and holding you makes me calm."

Lennox nodded and fell back into her arms, resting her head on Kenzie's chest. Kenzie placed an arm over the one Lennox had on her stomach, linking their fingers together and sinking into completeness she'd never thought possible.

CHAPTER 18

AFTER enjoying another ten minutes together, with Kenzie holding on to her and them sharing soft kisses every now and then, they finally stood, dressed, and walked out of the woods hand in hand. Lennox couldn't stop smiling. She squeezed Kenzie's hand when they made it back to the cabin before going inside. They'd managed to make their way past the group of women without being noticed so they could return to their bags, grab fresh clothes, and change before the rest of the night's festivities. They'd missed dinner, but Lennox didn't feel hungry. She felt oddly sated in every way, despite the fact that she hadn't eaten since lunch, and even then – she hadn't eaten much. When they got inside, they were alone, and she spun Kenzie in her arms before the girl knew what was happening.

"Hi," Kenzie said when her arms went around Lennox's neck and Lennox's went to her waist.

"Hi." Lennox wiggled her eyebrows at her. "Where should we sleep tonight?" she asked and walked Kenzie backward toward the bed they had shared the night before. "I doubt we'll be able to wrangle this whole place away from Maddox and Cleo again."

"I already talked to Peyton about that, actually," Kenzie revealed.

"You did?"

"Yes," Kenzie returned with a smile. "I told her I wanted to have the night to be alone with you. I didn't have anything planned, though." Her eyes grew big.

"I know." Lennox laughed.

"I just wanted to hold you again. And – I don't know, I can't do that with the others around. It feels strange."

"I get it." Lennox met Kenzie's forehead with her own. "So, where are we sleeping tonight?"

"Peyton and Dani are giving us their cabin."

"What?" Lennox pulled back. "They are? That's surprising."

"Why?"

"Peyton's doing this thing…" Lennox stopped herself when she realized she was about to reveal her best friend's secret. "I'm just surprised she'd do that tonight."

"You know something I don't, don't you?" Kenzie ascertained and pulled Lennox back into her.

"Yes, but I'm not allowed to tell anyone." Lennox kissed her neck.

"Not even your girlfriend?" Kenzie asked.

Lennox pulled back and smiled.

"I have a girlfriend," she commented mostly to herself. "That's different."

"Different good?" Kenzie asked with concern in her eyes.

"Oh, baby, yes. Different *very* good." Lennox leaned back in and kissed her. "We both need to take a shower. We should go while everyone is out there and occupied. Make it quick, so we don't miss any more of the fun."

"Lennox, are you really okay with everything that happened tonight?"

"I am very okay with it, Kenz. And if you're lucky, I might even let you do it again in the shower."

Kenzie's eyes grew three sizes, and Lennox nearly cackled at the sight.

***

Lennox had changed into a pair of jeans, tennis shoes, a dark-blue T-shirt, and a black zip-up hoodie, while Kenzie had opted for another pair of adorable sweatpants that were light-gray, with a light-purple tank top, and the other zip-up hoodie Lennox had brought with her, claiming it smelled like her and she wanted to wear it. It was a light-pink one, and with a purple tank top and light-gray sweats, Lennox told her she looked like Easter in human form. But Kenzie was not swayed, and she was absolutely adorable. Her green eyes were light; possibly lighter than Lennox had ever seen them. And Lennox tried her best not to think about how dark and fiery they'd been earlier, because that only made her want Kenzie again, and they were walking to meet their friends, so that would have to wait until later.

"There they are. Where'd you two run off to?" Cleo asked when they approached the shore.

"Just hanging out in the woods and then in the cabin," Lennox replied for them and squeezed Kenzie's hand to get her to go along with it.

"I needed some time alone," Kenzie added. "And then, she came to find me." She looked over at Lennox.

"Speaking of which, I have to go find Peyton now. I'll be right back." Lennox kissed her cheek and ran off in the direction of Peyton's cabin.

When she arrived, Peyton was inside, sitting on the edge of the bed and staring down at something in her hands. Lennox stood just inside the screen door for another minute before she said anything.

"You okay?" she asked.

"What if she says no?" Peyton mumbled.

"What?" Lennox walked over to the bed and sat on the side next to her. "What are you talking about, Pey?"

"What if she says no, Len? We said we weren't going to do this. We're not out. And if we get engaged – if she wears this ring ever in public, people will know."

"That's kind of the point, right? That's why you're asking her."

"But, last night, we were talking about you and Kenzie, and how hard that's going to be for the two of you to go public if and when you decide to." Peyton stopped herself and looked up at Lennox. "Sorry... I guess we both just assumed you two would last beyond this week and that you'd have to figure out that part."

"It's okay. I hope we do." Lennox shrugged.

"She said something that had me re-thinking this." Peyton held up the small, black box in her hand.

"Peyton, she loves you. Hell, Dani adores you. She'll say yes."

"This is a big deal, Len."

"I know that. It's marriage."

"I'm worried she might say no because she's not ready."

"Then, you guys will talk about that. But, Peyton, you know Dani better than anyone, and probably better than she knows herself. You've been together for over two years. You live together. You travel together. You have two cats and a dog together."

"No one knows that."

"The important people in your life do," Lennox retorted. "Her family knows. Your family knows. I know. All your friends are here tonight. You and Dani are forever, Peyton. And if you're finally ready to make that commitment and tell the world that you're forever, I think that's amazing. And I think Dani will, too."

"I think I am." Peyton opened the box and revealed a massive round-cut diamond ring. "I want her to wear this, and I want people to know she belongs to me."

"I think that's perfect."

"It's going to be hard. We'll have to admit to the fact that we lied to everyone."

"You will, yeah." Lennox considered. "Or you don't. You can just get engaged to the woman you love, marry her, and live happily ever after and not tell any of them anything about the past or how you two got here. *They* don't matter, Peyton. You and Dani matter." Lennox stood. "Now, I set it all up for you before I came in. Go grab your girl. I'll keep the natives from getting restless," she pronounced, kissed Peyton on the top of her head, and left the cabin.

She walked back toward the lake where she saw Dani

talking to April and Sarah. She winked at Kenzie as she walked past her, brushing Kenzie's arm with her fingertips as she did for good measure and also because she just wanted to touch her again.

"Dani, Peyton needs you at the cabin," she told Dani as she approached the group.

"Why? The show's about to start," Dani replied. "She should be down here. Where's my girlfriend?" She looked around, and Lennox stifled her laughter.

"In your cabin. Go get her."

"I heard it's *your* cabin tonight," Dani returned and grabbed her elbow gently. "And you know Peyton is going to want details tomorrow." She lifted both eyebrows into arches. "I kind of do, too, especially since we're sleeping in a cabin on the other side of the campground so you two could have some space."

Lennox laughed and looked back at Kenzie, who was in conversation with Bobby and Jack.

"I'll ask her before I go and share anything with you two." She nodded toward Kenzie.

"Whipped already?" Bobby teased.

"Absolutely," Lennox returned. "Go," she gave Dani another order.

"Okay. Make sure everyone waits for us, though. I don't know why she's not down here." Dani talked as she walked back to the cabin to find Peyton.

Lennox didn't want to interrupt Kenzie's conversation and enjoyed the fact that she seemed to be making so many friends here, so she chatted with Bobby, and then Tiana and Jenna joined in, until she felt arms wrap around her from behind and Kenzie's head on her shoulder.

"Hey, baby," she greeted and covered Kenzie's arms.

"Where's Peyton?" Kenzie kissed Lennox's neck.

"That's a greeting," Lennox joked.

"You know something. Peyton isn't here; and she hates to miss when everyone's together."

"I do know something," Lennox replied, and was met

with a poke to her stomach, which caused her to laugh and turn around. "Hey, you'll know soon enough. The show's about to start. Let's find a spot to watch."

"It can't start without Peyton," Kenzie said.

"She can see it from where she is," Lennox explained. "Come on. You want to watch from the dock with me?" she asked and turned in Kenzie's arms.

Kenzie looked out at the dock over Lennox's shoulder and then to the group of women gathering on blankets and towels and in folding chairs near the shore.

"It's kind of in front of everyone."

"Good point," Lennox cut her off and kissed her. "We can't make out if we're in front."

Kenzie smiled at her. Lennox knew Kenzie wasn't thinking about kissing her in front of the others. She just didn't want to be in front. It would put her more or less on display and would make her uncomfortable. Given Kenzie's chosen career, it was probably odd to most people, but not to Lennox. To do what Kenzie did at work – stand in front of a hundred people and express emotion – took a lot of energy out of her. And, on her days off, all Kenzie wanted was her invisibility.

"Cabana?" Kenzie lifted her eyebrows hopefully. "We can lift the canvasses and see."

"Deal." Lennox kissed her again.

They walked back to the closest cabana, which was unoccupied, as they all were. The other women had decided to sit near the water, which was fine by Lennox, who was looking forward to more alone time with her girlfriend. That would take some getting used to for Lennox. In her entire life, she'd never thought she would have a girlfriend. She'd also never thought she'd kiss another woman, unless it was for a role; and she'd known she'd never sleep with one. But, as she sat back in the cabana and welcomed Kenzie between her legs, wrapping her arms around her and kissing her neck gently, as fireworks took over the sky – bouncing and flashing their bright greens, reds, and yellows – she knew she'd been wrong to believe that. She thought back to the bookmarks on her phone and the fact that she'd followed Kenzie's entire career and loved looking at pictures of her and reading her comments in interviews. She thought back to the words she had expressed earlier that Kenzie hadn't returned or commented on; and she wasn't worried. She knew how Kenzie felt about her. She felt it in her soul that this woman, that she was holding, was falling for her the same way Lennox was falling for Kenzie. She had no problem waiting for Kenzie to be ready to say it, and that was especially true if they had more nights like this.

"It's beautiful," Kenzie said after a few minutes of watching the fireworks Peyton had orchestrated through the screens of their cabana.

"It is," Lennox agreed and kissed Kenzie's neck. "You are, too." She ran her hand up to the zipper of Kenzie's hoodie and pulled it down, exposing more of Kenzie's neck in the process.

"What are you doing?" Kenzie giggled.

"How do you expect me to keep my hands off you after what we just did out there?" Lennox replied; her hand moved under Kenzie's T-shirt, and her nails dragged across her stomach.

"Lennox!" Kenzie gasped out.

"What?" Lennox knew she had a wide smirk on her face. "Problem?"

"Babe, we can't do this here. Our friends are out there, and it's open." Kenzie referred to the cabana, but Lennox hadn't heard that part.

"You just called me *babe*." She pressed a kiss behind Kenzie's earlobe.

"I guess I did."

"Have you called anyone else *babe* before?" Lennox ran her tongue along the outside of her ear.

"No," Kenzie breathed out.

"And do you like calling me that?"

"Yes."

"Will you call me that when I'm touching you later?" Lennox pressed, and her hands moved to Kenzie's breasts to cup them.

"You have to stop. I'm–"

"You're what?" Lennox's tongue went back down to her neck, and she slid it to Kenzie's shoulder before letting her teeth gently nibble the spot. She used one hand to squeeze Kenzie's breast while her other one moved down to cup Kenzie over her sweats. "You're what?"

"You know you can't do that, because…" Kenzie let out a slow, steady breath, and Lennox saw her hands were back in fists.

"Because you'll come?" she whispered in her ear.

"Yes."

"Do it," Lennox ordered softly. "It's okay."

The fireworks burst and crashed around them. Their friends were turned away from them, laughing and talking while they drank and enjoyed the show. Lennox had no idea where this courage had come from. She hadn't planned this, but holding Kenzie and breathing her in after what they'd just shared, made Lennox insatiable, and she was lucky to have a girlfriend that could, apparently, come with only the slightest touch.

"I can't."

"Yes, you can," Lennox encouraged, using one finger to apply pressure to Kenzie's clit over her sweats. She wanted to touch her. She wanted to slide her hand down Kenzie's pants, but she worried that might be too much. "Fuck it," she said to herself more than Kenzie. "I want you," she added.

Just as Kenzie started to gasp from her touch, she removed her hand and slid it beneath the waistband of Kenzie's sweats and the blue underwear she'd watched her put on after their separate showers, which Kenzie had insisted on and Lennox was now getting her back for.

"You feel good." She touched Kenzie's clit with one stroke and then another, feeling her shudder. Lennox worried she might be going too far, but Kenzie didn't stop her. She leaned back into her instead, allowing Lennox more access. "Yeah?" Lennox checked.

"Yes," Kenzie whispered back, and Lennox watched her take a pillow from beside them and place it in front of them instead, to cover up what they were doing in case someone turned around and caught them. "I've never done anything like this before," she got out in between ragged breaths.

"Neither have I. But I can't resist you, Kenzie," she expressed and felt Kenzie grow wetter as her strokes grew more confident and rapid.

"I'm going to..." Kenzie placed a hand around Lennox's neck and pulled her ever closer. "I'm coming," she whispered, and it was almost unheard, because just as she had said it, the finale of the fireworks show began with a triumphant and loud boom, resulting in a massive red, white, and blue burst, and the applause of their friends, who had no idea Lennox was behind them, touching Kenzie like this and experiencing the sensation of her trembling against her as Kenzie came down.

"You're beautiful, Kenzie. I'm so crazy about you; I just got you off in front of our friends because I can't help myself." She kissed Kenzie's temple as Kenzie relaxed back into her. "Don't ever doubt that, okay?"

"Okay," Kenzie confirmed.

"There you guys are." Davica pointed at Dani and Peyton, who approached from the left walking hand in hand. "You missed the whole thing!" she exclaimed.

Lennox kissed Kenzie on the cheek again and slid her hand out as Kenzie gripped the pillow closer to cover them more fully. When they were in the clear, Lennox gave Kenzie a light push so they could get out of the cabana.

"Am I about to find out your secret?" Kenzie asked.

"I think so." Lennox followed Kenzie out and helped her straighten her clothing since it was her fault it was messy.

She turned to see Dani and Peyton were close enough now that, in the dark, she could see the glint of a diamond on Dani's finger and the hint of tears in her eyes.

"We saw it from the other side," Dani said and used her left hand to wipe a tear off Peyton's face, and it was then that Lennox noticed that Peyton had been crying, too.

She smiled and grasped Kenzie's hand before pulling her back into her body and wrapping both arms around her waist from behind.

"Look at Dani's hand," she whispered.

"We have some news," Peyton announced.

"Peyton asked me to marry her, and I said yes!" Dani yelled it and held up her hand, showing off her new piece of jewelry and, hopefully, one she'd wear forever.

Instantly, every single member of their group stood – if they weren't standing already, and rushed to the two of them to offer hugs and take their first look at that giant ring. Lennox opted to hang back with Kenzie, to give Peyton and Dani a chance to get through the rest of the group's congratulations and hugs before she'd offer one of her own.

"You knew?" Kenzie asked.

"I did. I would have told you, but Peyton asked me to keep it a secret."

"You know those rules don't apply to the girlfriend, though, right?" Kenzie said over her shoulder.

"She doesn't know you're my girlfriend yet. I figured tonight should be about them. I'll tell her about us tomorrow." She kissed Kenzie's temple.

"And what exactly will you tell them?" Kenzie turned in her arms and met her eyes. There was a flash of something there Lennox couldn't make out. "You're beautiful in the moonlight. I can see light blues in your eyes," she revealed. "How are you this beautiful?" she asked a seemingly rhetorical question. "It shouldn't be allowed."

"How do you go from being all shy and adorable to saying things like that to me in a matter of minutes? *That* shouldn't be allowed."

"I think you bring it out in me. You bring a lot of good things out in me, Lennox."

"I think you make me who I'm supposed to be," Lennox offered back. "I feel better since I met you."

"Me too." Kenzie leaned in and pressed her lips gently to Lennox's. "Go, congratulate your best friend," she encouraged. "I'll be right behind you."

Lennox kissed her quickly and headed over to Peyton and Dani, who had a little space between them and the retreating huggers.

"Congrats, you two," she offered.

"Thank you," Dani said first. "And thank you for helping set the whole thing up. You two are dangerous with your secrets sometimes," she returned.

"What did you help set up?" Kenzie asked from behind her.

Lennox hugged Dani first and then Peyton while Kenzie did the opposite.

"Your girlfriend here, helped set up a picnic for me on that side of the lake. We were on the shore and watched the fireworks," Peyton offered.

"She proposed right when the finale began, and I said yes." Dani squeezed Peyton's hand. "Now, I get to go buy her that ring." She pointed to Lennox.

"What?" Peyton gave Lennox a quizzical expression.

"Dani and I went to lunch one day, and she wanted to check out rings for you. We saw one, and she picked it out. She just needs to go buy it now," Lennox offered.

"You knew?" Peyton shoved at her shoulder.

"Ow!" Lennox exclaimed and took a step back, nearly toppling over a rock that caught her left foot, but Kenzie was there.

"I've got you." She caught Lennox at the hips and steadied her.

"Shit. Sorry, Len," Peyton apologized. "Wait a minute. No, I'm not. You knew she was going to say *yes*, and you didn't tell me?"

"What the hell do you think that pep talk was earlier?"

"You told her I'd say yes?" Dani questioned. "I told you to keep the whole thing a secret."

"And I did," Lennox defended. "Jesus, you two. I kept your secret, and I kept your secret." She pointed to each of them in turn. "I've been a great best friend. I even kept it from her, and I hated doing that. So, I should get a damn prize or something." She referenced Kenzie, who still had her hands on Lennox's hips.

"You called me her *girlfriend* earlier," Kenzie told Peyton. "I thought you said you hadn't told them," she said to Lennox.

"I haven't," Lennox reminded.

"I think I've let that slip a couple of times today. I just assumed. You two have been all over each other, and then Lennox wouldn't stop talking about you and the future on our hike, so…" Peyton faded out.

"Are you guys a couple? Official?" Dani asked.

"Yeah, we are," Lennox replied. "I just wanted tonight to be about you two, though."

"You definitely deserve a prize," Dani stated and patted her shoulder.

"I think Kenzie will take care of that for us, fiancée." Peyton turned to Dani and wrapped her arms around her neck.

"Why didn't you two do it here?" Jack approached and asked. "We could have been a part of the whole thing."

"Yeah, flash-mob-style," Davica added from just behind her.

"Because our entire lives are in front of people," Peyton answered without taking her eyes off Dani's. "Every time we leave the house, people snap pictures and post stories about us. They want to know every detail of our lives, and there are some things that should just be between two people. I didn't want it in front of anyone, including you guys or even our families. I wanted it to just be us, and I knew Dani would want that, too." Peyton leaned in and pressed her forehead to Dani's.

Lennox watched Dani close her eyes and let another tear fall down her cheeks.

"Well, that's fine, as long as we are invited to the wedding," Davica returned.

"And now, the drinking and partying will commence!" Mandy yelled and then promptly ran down the dock and jumped into the water fully clothed.

"We have cabin fourteen on the other side of the parking lot." Peyton pulled away from Dani but kept hold of her hand to tell Lennox. "It's a solo cabin. I was already planning on staying there tonight just so she and I could celebrate. You guys have our cabin, and if you want it for the other nights – take it."

"I thought you wanted us to socialize and make new friends," Lennox teased.

"I want you to be happy, Len." Peyton placed a hand on her cheek and turned to Kenzie. "And I've never seen you this happy."

CHAPTER 19

KENZIE took in what Peyton had just said, and knew she was saying it to Lennox but telling both of them. She watched as Peyton hugged Lennox with one arm, still not letting go of Dani's hand, and then, the two went down to the water to mingle with the rest of the crowd and probably allow more of them to get a close-up of the giant ring she'd just placed on Dani's finger.

"I think Peyton just gave us an excuse to ditch the group and spend the rest of the night alone. You interested?" Lennox gripped her hips.

Kenzie knew her response instantly. She wanted nothing more than to spend the rest of the night alone with Lennox in a cabin they now had all to themselves. But she also knew that she liked these women, and the week was already getting away from her. They had three more nights, technically, but only two more days, and she wanted to at least spend a little more time celebrating with them, since she'd already missed much of the day.

"Can we stay out here for another hour or so?" she chanced and witnessed Lennox's surprised expression.

"Really? I thought you'd want to flee as soon as we could."

"I do," Kenzie admitted. "That's why I think I should stay." She looked at the group of women standing around laughing and drinking. "I don't do this."

"I'm glad you want to try." Lennox leaned in, kissed her nose, and met her eyes.

"Is it okay?"

"You'll just have to find a way to make it up to me." Lennox winked and gave a more than suggestive stare.

"All night, if you want," Kenzie said it and realized she'd meant it. "I will stay up all night with you."

"Baby, you're going to have to, because I can't stop touching you." Lennox pulled Kenzie in and, instead of kissing her again, she wrapped her arms around her waist and hugged her.

Kenzie took a moment before she moved her arms to Lennox's neck and rested her head on her shoulder, breathing her in. Lennox smelled of pine and salt, likely from sweat and the sticky night air, and she had a hint of some kind of citrus, probably from her shampoo or body lotion.

"You smell nice," Kenzie shared and ran her hands up Lennox's back over her shirt.

"So do you," Lennox replied and kissed Kenzie's neck lightly once and then again. "You're shaking," she said when Kenzie's body trembled.

"You, touching me, still does things," she explained.

"I like that I do things to you. Lennox chuckled against Kenzie's neck. "And I'll do more things to you later, but go on and be social." She pulled back.

Kenzie pecked her lips gently and ran off toward the water, knowing Lennox would be following behind. She chatted with Mandy, who had a towel around her body and wet hair from her jump in the water. Mandy tried to convince her to do the same, but Kenzie had already showered and wasn't planning on doing so again. Bobby and Cleo were in one of the rowboats while Quinn and Sarah were taking another out to join them. April, Jenna, Davica, and Lynn were all on the speedboat that had been docked for the night. There was music playing from its speakers, and they sat along its cushioned benches, talking and laughing while clinking their bottles together. Dani and Peyton were sitting with Brooke, Tiana, and Jack, and all five of them had wide grins. Dani had her arms around Peyton's waist and kept kissing different parts of her neck and face. Kenzie smiled as she watched on.

"Hey there." Maddox moved to stand next to her. "I

noticed that you and Lennox disappeared after the hike. Everything seems okay, so I assume you guys talked?"

Kenzie's eyes got big. They had technically talked, sure, but that talking had led to more, and then, that other activity had taken the rest of their time together.

"We did. Everything is great, yeah," she returned.

"I'm glad." Maddox took a long drink of her beer. "You guys are going to figure things out for after?"

"She's going to take some time off, I think, and join me on set," Kenzie replied and turned to see Lennox joining the others on the speedboat, taking a drink of an offered beer.

"That's great." Maddox smiled.

"She's great," Kenzie stared at Lennox while she replied.

"Not exactly what I said, but… sure." Maddox laughed.

"Sorry." Kenzie turned to her, realizing she was, perhaps, being rude. "I can't seem to not look at her."

"Can't blame you there. She's on Maxim's Hot 100 for a reason. I think she was number one two years in a row."

"Three," Kenzie corrected.

Maddox laughed again and lifted her beer in acknowledgement before walking off. Kenzie moved over to where Peyton and Dani were in conversation, and stood off to the side while she took a deep breath and then joined the conversation.

"Where are you guys thinking about having it?" Brooke asked.

"I just said yes, Brooke," Dani argued.

"I know. But Peyton, over here, is the hyper planner, so I know you two have talked about this."

"We hadn't, actually," Dani began. "I mean, we'd talked about maybe getting married one day, but it was always so far off into the future that the details didn't seem to matter."

"And now?" Kenzie questioned.

"Now, I can't wait to marry her." Dani smiled at Kenzie. "I know we have a lot to figure out. For starters, everyone on the planet can see this ring from wherever I am, and I don't want to take it off." She kissed Peyton's neck again. "I want to wear it and my wedding band for the rest of my life, so that means we have to tell people or that they'll at least find out. I don't know what we'll do about all that yet, but I can honestly say now, that none of that matters to me."

"Yeah?" Jenna asked.

"I used to worry so much about how people would respond to us being a couple," Peyton answered instead. "I have this image out there, and a lot of my fans come from red states and may not approve of me being in love with a woman."

"You have a lot of fans that wouldn't have a problem with it, too, though," Kenzie argued.

"I know. And they've been so supportive."

"They assume you two are together anyway. Look at how you are together. I mean, come on." Tiana pointed between them.

"Give the people what they want." Dani laughed.

"We spent the first year of our relationship really, just trying to figure out how it had happened," Peyton continued. "I had never experienced the kind of connection I'd experienced with Dani, but I'd had close friends that were girls, too. So, the beginning was about trying to determine if that time she touched my hand was as a friend or as something more. Then, we kissed for the first time, and I had to figure out if I could even do this. She had to do the same." Peyton squeezed Dani's arms around her waist. "But, it came down to the fact that I can't *not* be with her." Peyton leaned her head back. "She's the best thing that has ever happened to me. I could ignore that, or I could embrace it; and, the reality was – I didn't really have a choice. I couldn't ignore this."

"That's so cute." Tiana wiped a fake tear from her eye.

"That's how I feel right now."

The words were whispered into Kenzie's ear from behind. After the initial startled feeling of someone sneaking up behind her, she resonated with the hypnotic sound of Lennox's whisper and shivered.

"I couldn't ignore this." Lennox wrapped her arms around Kenzie's waist. "I can't take my eyes off you," she added another whisper. "I've been trying to. I climbed on that boat and had a beer, I talked to Bobby about her next tour, and I talked Jenna out of skinny-dipping while drunk. And, the whole time, all I wanted to do, was get over here and feel you." She laughed lightly. "Do I sound like a horny teenage boy right now?"

Kenzie turned around in her arms and wrapped her own around Lennox's neck.

"Yes." She smirked. "But I like it."

"I like you," Lennox returned.

"I like you, too." Kenzie leaned into her body, pressing her hips against Lennox's. "Take me to the cabin."

Lennox pulled back to check on what she'd just heard.

"I thought you wanted to hang out. It's only been about a half-hour."

"I want you," Kenzie whispered into Lennox's ear this time and felt the woman shake at the sound. "Underneath me, above me, inside me." She kissed Lennox's ear. "And I want to touch you, be inside you, taste you again. I miss you."

Lennox gulped, and Kenzie felt it, withholding her smirk for later. She let go of Lennox and turned to see that the group had disbanded, but Dani and Peyton were still standing there, watching them.

"Do we need to throw you two in that icy-cold water out there?" Peyton lifted an eyebrow.

"No, we're going to take care of it in a different way," Lennox delivered, and Kenzie felt the pull on her hand. "See you tomorrow," she added as they rushed off. "Late," she said. "Like, do not disturb us, we'll find you, kind of late. Like, the curtains will be pulled over the screens, and no one should enter, kind of late."

Dani and Peyton laughed, and Kenzie tried not to be embarrassed at the fact that most of the others now knew what the two of them would be doing all night. Then again, she recalled what Peyton had said earlier, and decided that none of that mattered. She couldn't ignore this even if she tried.

***

"Twin beds," Lennox stated as the two of them stared at the two twins Peyton and Dani had pulled together so they could sleep. "Did they really have sex on this?" she asked.

"I don't want to have sex where they had sex," Kenzie stated and shook her head rapidly from side to side.

"So cute," Lennox expressed as she took in the movement. "There are two other beds," she pointed. "We could move them together."

Kenzie took a look around the room. They'd already lowered the curtains – that were really just canvas, much like the ones on the cabanas and one on the screen door – so that no one would be able to invade their privacy for the night.

"I've got a better idea." Kenzie moved to one of the two beds Dani and Peyton had shared.

She slid one mattress off the bed frame and onto the floor before moving rapidly to the other. She lined them up next to each other on the floor and turned to Lennox.

"I thought you didn't want to… where they did."

"Grab the other ones," Kenzie instructed and pointed to the other two thin mattresses, watching as Lennox moved one and then another one on top of the other two, used by Dani and Peyton.

Kenzie grabbed a blanket Lennox had packed and their sleeping bags. She unzipped both sleeping bags all the way and covered the mattresses with them while Lennox let the blanket out and shook it into the air before placing it on top of the sleeping bags and pulling it back slightly for them to climb under.

"You are very creative." Lennox laid back on the mattresses as Kenzie brought over their pillows, quickly placing one under Lennox's head before it could hit the mattress.

Kenzie slid under the blanket next to Lennox, and she was glad they'd decided to change into some sleep clothes prior to figuring out the bed situation. Lennox had changed into just an oversized T-shirt and her underwear, and Kenzie had put on a pair of old cheer shorts she'd stolen from Kat and never returned, along with the same tank top she had on earlier. Lennox rolled on her side and faced her while Kenzie placed a hand on her cheek and stared into her tired eyes.

"You're so pretty," Lennox said, and her eyes closed for a moment before opening again.

"And you are so tired, aren't you?" Kenzie asked when she noticed the look of exhaustion on Lennox's face she'd missed before.

"What? No." Lennox pulled Kenzie into her. "I am not."

Kenzie laughed and slid her hand down Lennox's side to around her back.

"Yes, you are," she argued.

"I don't want to sleep. I want to not sleep." Lennox pressed her lips to Kenzie's with little enthusiasm.

"Why don't we just talk for now and see if your body agrees?" Kenzie suggested.

"I like talking to you," Lennox replied in a near whisper, causing goosebumps to cover Kenzie's flesh, because it was both adorable and sexy, and she wasn't sure how Lennox managed to accomplish that.

"I like talking to you, too," she said.

"But I don't want to talk, either. I want to touch you." Lennox ran her hand along Kenzie's throat. "We only have three more nights, and then, I likely won't see you for a while."

"What do you mean?"

"I'm back in LA for a couple of weeks, and then, I'm in New York and LA for the reshoots. You're off to London."

"I know. But we can still see each other, right?"

"I guess, but it's going to be hard." Lennox rolled onto her back and faced the wooden rafters in the ceiling. "Once I'm done, though, I'll come to London. So, we just have to get through the first month or so."

"Yeah." Kenzie moved closer to her and rested her head on Lennox's shoulder. "I'm going to miss you," she confessed.

"I don't want to lose this, Kenz."

"Lose what? Me?"

"This," Lennox said but offered no real explanation.

"I don't know what—"

Lennox turned her head to face her.

"This feeling I have when I'm with you, like everything is finally good. I'm where I'm supposed to be. When you're not around, it's like I'm missing something now; and I've always felt that in a way. I've always felt like I was missing something. But now that I know you, now that I have you, I can't be without you again." Lennox paused, and her tired eyes closed. "I've known you for four days."

"I know." Kenzie ran her hand along her cheek, down her chest between her breasts, and stilled on her stomach.

"And this place is special. It's just us here. The real world is out there, and I don't know what's going to happen when we leave here. You'll go to work, and we'll do long-distance for a little, but people are going to start with the rumors once they see us out in public together; and I've never hidden my relationships from the public."

"And I'm not out yet," Kenzie added.

"No, but I'm not going to pressure you to be, either." Lennox yawned a reluctant yawn. "If you don't want them to know, I don't care."

"But you've never hidden your relationships."

"No, and I hope I won't have to hide this one forever, but I won't pressure you to be out, either. I don't even know what I am yet, and people will start asking once they know we're together. It's going to be questions about how we met, when we met, how long we've been together, how we realized we had these feelings, and whether or not I'm gay or if you have a problem with me being bisexual or not using a label," she rambled. "It's just going to be different than it is here, and I don't want that to get in the way of us; of what we feel for each other." Lennox's eyes were vulnerable and wanting, and Kenzie knew she was waiting for her to respond.

"Okay." She smiled softly and knew her answer was lacking, but everything Lennox said had her worried.

She tried her best to stare into the blue eyes examining her face and not think about the fact that, once they left here, she'd be carted off to London to shoot a movie, and Lennox would be busy with her own work. They'd be eight hours apart and have to figure out how to talk to each other around their busy schedules until Lennox could join her in London. Then what would happen? The press there is crazy, and once they see them leaving a building together, people will start to make assumptions; or, at least, the stories of their new friendship would start. Everyone, once a member of Peyton's so-called *squad*, had gone through this part, including Kenzie. The questions in the interviews became more about Peyton and what it was like hanging out with her or being a member of this exclusive group. And once two members of that group started hanging out, the stories intensified. Kenzie closed her eyes temporarily before opening them to find Lennox still staring back.

"Will we be okay?" she asked.

Kenzie wasn't sure what the answer was to that question. She flashed back to when Annabelle left for Sacramento at the end of their relationship. She had driven her to the airport and hugged her after unloading her luggage from her car. Annabelle had asked if they would be okay, and she had lied. She had told her yes, and she'd known that wouldn't be the case. She couldn't lie to Lennox, and she wanted more than anything to be able to guarantee her that they would be okay. Instead of saying anything, she kissed her lips gently and lowered her hand to Lennox's center, feeling Lennox's body tense as she slid her hand back up, and then under her panties, where she stroked her. Lennox's face turned toward the ceiling, and Kenzie leaned in, whispering into her ear.

"You've made me so happy," she spoke the truth and kissed Lennox's earlobe as she continued to stroke her softly between her legs.

Lennox's body was still tightly wound, but it began to loosen as Kenzie's fingers slid through her wetness and dove inside briefly. Kenzie watched her hips lift and drop and repeated the motion before returning her focus to Lennox's clit.

"I might not be able to come," Lennox gasped out as her hand sought purchase on the side of Kenzie's head. "I have a problem sometimes." She was clearly trying to explain something, but she wasn't able to get it out.

"Tell me." Kenzie leaned up, holding her head up with her hand and continuing her strokes.

"I have a hard time coming every time." Lennox's hand was gripping the sleeping bag beneath her.

Kenzie watched her own hand move beneath the blanket and found herself getting incredibly turned on, but she tossed water on her internal fire so that she could focus on Lennox.

"Did you not, earlier?" she asked and hoped.

"I did." Lennox's hips lifted and stayed for a long moment while Kenzie sped up. "Oh, God!" she exclaimed and lowered. "What are you doing to me?" she asked, but Kenzie knew it was rhetorical.

She dipped inside again, noting the coating of arousal on her fingers as she pulled them back out, and moved three fingers in hard circles over Lennox's clit as she watched

Lennox shift, lift up, then lower, and let out a hollow scream as she came. Kenzie slowed but didn't stop, until Lennox placed a hand on top of her own. Kenzie remained there, touching her hot, wet skin, until she saw Lennox's eyes close and remain closed for several minutes. When Lennox's breathing evened out, Kenzie knew the woman was asleep. She slid out slowly and watched her sleep until she, herself, rolled onto her back, stared up at the ceiling, and let sleep take her.

CHAPTER 20

LENNOX woke up to the sounds of someone breathing next to her. It took a moment for her to register where she was, and then, she opened her eyes with a smile. She turned her head to see Kenzie on top of the blanket, likely because of the heat, and on her stomach, with her face toward Lennox. It was relaxed and beautiful, and Lennox fell a little more in love with her then. It amazed her how quickly her feelings for this woman had blossomed and then intensified. She knew that this was right. She could only imagine ever staring into those dark-green eyes in the way that one does with someone they love ever again. Mackenzie was what and who she wanted, and Lennox knew it, likely, in the same way Peyton knew Dani was the one for her. She thought back to the previous night, where they'd had grand plans to stay up all night making love and adoring each other but had instead given themselves over to sleep because, since coming here, neither of them had gotten much. She remembered Kenzie touching her and how it felt, and she remembered coming against Kenzie's hand and registering the shock that this woman had been able to bring her to orgasm three times with relative ease.

Thinking of that only made Lennox want more. She wanted to take advantage of this time in the cabin, where they had privacy. She then thought back to touching Kenzie in the cabana, only a few feet away from their friends, and that had her unable to resist touching Kenzie now. She brushed Kenzie's hair out of her face and slid on top of her. She had known that would wake Kenzie up, given her condition. When Kenzie stirred and smiled from below, Lennox straddled her ass and lifted her shirt to kiss the skin of her back.

"Good morning," she greeted between kisses.

"Morning," Kenzie returned. "What exactly are you doing up there?"

"I was thinking about touching you, and I realized you were next to me, so I didn't have to think about it."

Kenzie's eyes drifted to Lennox's phone, which was on the side of their makeshift bed. She pressed the home button, and the clock appeared.

"It's nine-thirty," she offered.

"And?" Lennox licked up to her neck as her hands slid into Kenzie's shorts and underwear, cupping her ass.

Kenzie gasped and tensed as Lennox rolled her own hips down into her.

"We should probably get dressed and go outside."

"No way." Lennox's hand drifted around and cupped Kenzie's sex.

"Lennox," Kenzie whispered into her pillow.

"I'm going to make you come fast, and then, I'm going to make you come slow. Then, maybe we can talk about getting dressed and going outside." Lennox ran her fingers up and then down, and her hips rolled again.

"And what about me?"

"I'm pretty sure I just told you."

"No, what about me?" Kenzie went to turn over, but Lennox held her position. "What if I want to touch you?"

"Let me do this, and then we can come together." She leaned up and, with one arm, pulled her shirt up and off, tossing it aside before she became more insistent with her fingers and pressed her breasts into Kenzie's back. "I love how fast you can come," Lennox commented and applied more pressure. "But I love how you looked last night, when I made you wait," Lennox added and stroked, listening to Kenzie's breathing intensify. "Will you do that for me again?"

"Will you let me touch you during?"

"Can you handle that?" she asked.

"I don't know." Kenzie gripped the corners of the mattresses with her hands.

Lennox almost came at the sight of the woman beneath her, with the perfect muscles in her back, tense with need, and her hands hanging on to the one thing that could hold her in place, while Lennox moved faster and felt her own underwear grow wet as she drove down into her.

Kenzie came seconds later and wasted no time in turning them over, yanking off Lennox's underwear, allowing Lennox to pull off her own clothes right after, and then sliding on top of her, moving insistent fingers deep inside her, and watching Lennox while she pumped them. When Lennox was almost there and barely hanging on, Kenzie moved Lennox's hand to her own center, and Lennox cupped her as she rode Lennox's thigh. Lennox watched as Kenzie moved slowly and managed a fevered pace inside her at the same time. Her clit was hard and swollen, and she knew it was begging to be touched. She wanted Kenzie to touch her there. But if Kenzie did, she'd likely come. So, instead, she watched Kenzie's internal struggle unfold above her. Her eyes were closed, and the hand that wasn't currently working inside Lennox, was in a fist at her side. Lennox could only imagine the amount of focus it was taking this woman to both touch Lennox and keep herself from coming. She watched Kenzie's breasts bounce and wanted to touch them, but she knew she shouldn't. Instead, she moved her free hand between her own legs and touched herself. Her clit was more than ready, and Lennox knew that, with a few short strokes, she would likely go over. She watched Kenzie sense her movement, open her eyes, and look down at what she was doing to herself. Lennox nearly apologized, but then, Kenzie came. She rocked harder and faster on Lennox's thigh and hand as she watched Lennox stroke herself.

"God!" Kenzie yelled out. "Yes, Lennox!" she yelled

even louder, and Lennox went over then.

When Lennox came down all the way, Kenzie was already on top of her, pressing into her, with her fingers still inside. Lennox could feel Kenzie's hard breathing against her chest as she took the hand she'd just used on her own body and ran it soothingly over Kenzie's back.

"That was sexy," Lennox said after a moment, when she could finally form words.

"I think they could hear me out there," Kenzie mumbled into Lennox's skin.

"Good. They'd know you liked it." Lennox laughed and watched Kenzie lean up and glare at her. "What?" She laughed more. Kenzie's glare turned to a vulnerable stare. "What?" Lennox stopped laughing.

"Last night, you said you have a hard time coming."

"Oh, yeah." Lennox exhaled a deep breath. "Always have."

"I don't want you to fake anything with me, Lennox."

"I'm not." Lennox sat up a little and gripped Kenzie's hips. "Baby, I don't have to fake anything with you." She sat up more and kissed between Kenzie's breasts. "I promise you."

"Okay." Kenzie pushed her back against the mattress. "Then, I'll be right back." She slid backward a little, spread Lennox's legs, and shifted her head between them.

***

It was around noon when the two women finally emerged from the cabin and made their way to the bathroom to shower. This time, they knew they'd have at least ten minutes alone, since everyone else was likely either at the water or at some other activity and wouldn't be reporting back until lunch at one, so they showered together. They kissed and helped one another wash their hair and body, but they stopped at that, afraid that – even though they'd suspected they'd be alone, someone might come in. Once finished, they sat across from each other at one of the tables outside the cafeteria cabin and tried their hand at a game of Scrabble, mainly to take their mind off things they'd rather be doing – because they, unfortunately, couldn't spend their entire day having sex.

"No way, Lennox. That is not a word."

"Yes, it is," Lennox defended.

"Qat? Really?" Kenzie stared down at the board in disbelief. "Fine. What does it mean?" She wiggled her eyebrows at her.

"What does what mean?" Maddox joined them along with Quinn, who sat next to Lennox.

"Qat. Lennox, my adorably mistaken girlfriend, here, thinks that's a word," Kenzie said.

Lennox loved that comment, despite the fact that they were in a heated Scrabble battle. Kenzie had called her *adorable* and her *girlfriend*, and, most importantly, she'd done so with ease and in front of others.

"Never heard of it," Quinn offered the group as she took a sip of her water.

"It's a plant." Lennox's eyes dared Kenzie's.

"A plant?" Kenzie offered back.

"It's a flowering plant, native to East Africa and the Arabian Peninsula," Maddox spoke up, staring at her phone. "I just looked it up."

Kenzie's eyes were playful in their disbelief, but they were also sexy, and Lennox couldn't help but think about how they'd looked earlier in the shower, when she'd gently grazed the inside of Kenzie's thigh teasingly.

"Told you."

"Not fair," Kenzie argued. "How did you even know that?"

"*Counterstrike*, my dear," Lennox returned and grabbed more letters from the bag.

"What?" Kenzie laughed.

"When I prepped for the movie, I had to learn about stuff. We traveled to Saudi Arabia, remember? Well, we traveled to a desert in California and shot the rest on a sound stage, but one of the characters had to chew the leaves because they're used as a narcotic. He got shot."

"There goes *Slumdog Millionaire* over there." Peyton sat on the other side of Lennox.

"What?" Kenzie questioned.

"Peyton, really?" Lennox turned to her friend.

"She hasn't told you we call her *Slumdog*?"

"No." Kenzie met Lennox's eyes.

"It's stupid."

"No, it's not," Peyton argued. "You've seen that movie, right? I mean, I know Lennox, here, wasn't in it, but you do watch movies she's *not* in, too, don't you?" she jested.

"Yes, and you're an ass," Kenzie said with a smile.

"I don't think I've ever been more attracted to you than I am right now," Lennox tossed to her with a smile.

"Yeah, yeah." Peyton shoved at Lennox's shoulder for that remark. "Anyway, Lennox, here, has been in the biz so long and traveled the world before that, she basically has a story for everything. You can ask her something or, apparently, play a game with her where she has to pull out random words, and she'll have a story about how she knows it."

"I do not. It's not like that," Lennox told Kenzie.

"Why is that bad?" Kenzie asked her. "I think that's pretty cool," she gave Lennox a smile, "that you've been everywhere, and you know so much."

"Yeah, if you're ever in the Arabian Peninsula and get shot or stabbed, Lennox knows how to find the plant you need to chew to dull the pain," Quinn joined in.

"You can also drink it," Lennox offered without thinking.

"Slumdog!" Peyton sang out and stood. "Lunch is in twenty. And then, we're taking our chances at archery."

"Lord, you with an arrow? I think I'll pass," Lennox chided.

"I'm actually pretty good at archery," Kenzie stated, and all eyes went to her.

"You are?" Maddox asked.

"Yeah, I had to learn it for the show. She has a crossbow," Kenzie referenced her character.

And, because Lennox had seen every episode of it, where Kenzie's character fights off zombies with a crossbow, she knew it was likely true that Kenzie was good with a bow.

"Slumdog two?" Maddox shrugged in Peyton's direction.

"Katniss." Peyton pointed to Kenzie. "She will represent district twelve. Who else among you will represent your home with Katniss to–" She started in a booming voice as the others started appearing at the tables and forming around them to watch Peyton's display.

"I volunteer as tribute," Lennox interjected and stared directly into Kenzie's eyes.

"Good Lord, someone get cold water for those two," Bobby stated and pointed at both of them. "Their happiness is making me depressed," she joked.

"I think it's sweet," Lynn added and smiled at both of them.

"As long as they don't get engaged this week, too, I think I'll be okay." Bobby winked at Lennox, and Lennox smiled back before she returned her glance to Kenzie, who looked slightly terrified.

They ate lunch, with everyone sitting across from one another as they'd done during their game, which Lennox had won. When everyone began walking to the archery field to try their hands at something different and break up some of the camp monotony, Lennox took Kenzie's hand in her own and squeezed it.

"Are you okay?" she asked after a few more steps.

"Do you want that?" Kenzie wasn't looking at her.

"Want what?"

"What Peyton and Dani are doing?"

"Walking to the field?" Lennox watched her two friends heading in that direction in a small group in front of them.

"Getting married."

Lennox stopped, and Kenzie stopped when Lennox's hand pulled her back a little.

"You want to talk about that now?" Lennox gave her a look of disbelief.

"Sorry, I blurted that out. I shouldn't have." Kenzie appeared nervous or anxious, and Lennox wondered what had turned her back into that.

"Baby, what's wrong?" She grabbed for Kenzie's shoulders and placed her hands on the sides of her neck, running her thumbs over Kenzie's skin. "I can feel your pulse right now. It's crazy."

"They brought stuff up in there, and it made me think. And when I think a lot, sometimes, it's bad," Kenzie replied and closed her eyes briefly before opening them again. "I can't stop once it starts."

"And you're thinking about that? Engagement? Marriage?" Lennox paused and risked the next part, "With me?"

"No," Kenzie answered.

"Oh." Lennox found herself disappointed with that response. Not that she was ready for anything close to those steps with anyone, but hearing Kenzie just say no like that, took her back. "Do you not want those things eventually?" She added reluctantly, "With anyone?"

"I shouldn't have said it. I've upset you," Kenzie recognized. "I'm stupid. I'm sorry."

"You are anything but stupid." Lennox pulled her closer to her, allowing others to move farther ahead of them. "We can talk about anything you want at any time, okay? If you want to talk about this, we can. But don't let some random comment throw you off or upset you, or even make you think I want something that I may not."

"So, you don't?"

"Kenzie, I don't know." Lennox laughed and took a

step back from her. "Honestly, I haven't thought about anything like that in the longest time."

"Noah," Kenzie said under her breath.

"Yes, Noah and I talked about it a few times. But we were young and figured we'd wait a while. Then, Will died, and he left. I never even considered that with Lucas. And there's been no one else serious until you."

"I'm serious?"

"Kenzie, what part of me coming to London for you or telling you I'm falling in love with you doesn't sound serious to you?" Lennox stepped back into her. "I *am* in love with you," she confirmed. "I'm not falling anymore. I'm already there, and I don't expect you to be. I know this is crazy and probably a lot for you to manage emotionally." She hoped Kenzie wouldn't be offended by that comment. "I want you, Kenzie. And I don't need you to change or want something because you think I do. That's not how this will work."

"Okay."

"Please don't just say *okay*," Lennox requested. "Not if it's not okay."

"Sometimes, I let comments like that get to me, because it's a normal thing people do and talk about. They want those things and think about it, plan it and talk about it with their friends and the person they're with."

"And you worry that you're not normal because you don't?"

"I'm not normal, Lennox." Kenzie shrugged. "I don't understand some things that other people do or say, or it takes me longer to grasp it. I have to try, when everyone else is just okay with it."

"Kenz, you're not normal." Lennox shrugged right back. "You're not. You're completely and totally not normal because you're more than that. You're amazing. You're awkward sometimes and beautiful all the time. You're funny when you don't know it, you're sweet, and you've been careful with me; you're smart, and you make me feel like I can maybe change things in my life if I want to because you're not normal." She let out a sigh. "You are you. And I don't want *normal*. I want you."

"What if that wears off?"

"I don't think that's likely."

"But you don't know that," Kenzie countered.

"How do you know you won't get sick of me, Kenz?"

"I'd never get sick of you." Kenzie grew even more serious. "You're the only person I've ever–" She looked down at the ground, and Lennox watched her fingers as they moved against her jeans at her sides, trying to touch the fabric to calm herself.

Lennox stepped closer and offered her hands to Kenzie. She placed them palms-up in front of her, and Kenzie stared for a moment before she took them and ran her thumbs along Lennox's skin.

"That same way you know you want to be with me, is the same thing I know about you."

"I never thought I'd meet someone, Lennox." She stared down at their joined hands. "It wasn't possible for me. You get that, right?"

"No, I don't, actually. Because I've met you."

Kenzie looked up and offered a small smile.

"I couldn't ever be myself," she explained. "With Annabelle, I tried to be like everyone else in college. I told myself I had to talk to the other students in the class and try to be social, even when I didn't want to be; and she liked me. When I dated Kelly, she wanted me to be those things; and I couldn't, because I was working then, and acting takes everything out of me. I like it, I do. I never thought I would, and I never thought I'd be good enough to do it like this, but I enjoy it. It just drains me. So, at the end of the day, or even the end of the season, I can't be that person. And Kelly didn't like that I needed to be alone, or that I didn't want to go to that party." Kenzie took a step closer to Lennox this time. "You let me be me." Her eyes were welling up with tears. "You like me for me, and you don't expect me to be anything different."

"I don't want you to be different."

"You're the first person," Kenzie said. "I love Peyton, but even Peyton wants me to be different sometimes."

"Peyton's just Peyton."

"I know. I get it. I do, and I don't mind it, because she's Peyton and basically the most giving person on the planet." Kenzie lowered their still joined hands and gave them a squeeze before detaching them and placing her arms around Lennox's neck, pulling her forehead against her own. "I've never dated someone where it was like this. And we just met, but it feels so real to me, Lennox. It feels so right that I thought we needed to talk about those things because that's what other people do. I never thought I'd meet someone I would even consider taking those steps with. And now, it's like a different world has opened up to me, and, one day, I might have those things that other people have."

"Earlier, you said you weren't thinking about it, though," Lennox pressed.

"Because I wasn't, up until meeting you," Kenzie replied. "I shouldn't have brought it up just because Bobby made a comment," she added. "I get that now. I'll try not to let stuff like that get to me."

"Just talk to me, okay? That's all you need to do."

"I will. I know I can. And, Lennox?"

"Yeah?"

"You're the only one I've ever felt that way about."

Lennox leaned in and kissed her gently at first, but then allowed it to grow deeper. It remained slow, and they kept it that way until it ended naturally. She stared into Kenzie's green eyes for a moment, kissed her forehead, and then took her hand to walk them down to where the rest of the group was likely already shooting arrows at targets.

"Come on, Katniss. Let's see what you've got."

CHAPTER 21

KENZIE marveled at Lennox's ability to not just understand her but also calm her and make her feel not only safe but wanted. She was wanted by someone and not just physically, like a lot of her fans seemed to want her – or, at least, made comments about wanting to do things to her because she was hot. There were the ones that said they wanted to marry her, but they didn't know her. They only knew her characters or saw a few pictures. Lennox knew her, and she still wanted her. She wanted to be with Kenzie and come to London with her.

Kenzie tried to clear her mind of the fact that Lennox was currently staring at her with her sexy blue eyes and long blonde hair, pulled back in a messy ponytail, while Kenzie held the bow in the proper form, aiming her arrow at the target. Knowing Lennox's eyes were on her wasn't helping her aim, but she focused on the red dot about twenty feet away, took a deep breath, and let go.

"Damn, Katniss," Jenna commented from behind her. "District twelve is going to win. Should have chosen Kenzie for your team, April." She pointed at April, who had her team of two others behind her.

Peyton had divided their group of eighteen into six teams of three. They'd each take four shots at the target twenty feet away and add up their team total. Then, it would come down to the top two teams and their top shooters. They'd shoot four arrows, and whoever had the highest score would win bragging rights for their team and would have drinks brought to them by any of the losers for the rest of the day. Peyton had selected six captains, and Kenzie had been chosen first by Quinn. Apparently, Quinn had paid attention during their Scrabble conversation, and she had also chosen Jenna. Peyton ended up with April and Davica, while Lennox was selected by Dani and joined by Tiana later.

Lennox had already gone for her team and had scored three hits to the target. One earned her five points, the other earned her seven, and another one earned her only three, while the other scraped the edge of the target and slid along the short brown grass behind until it came to a stop. Kenzie had resisted laughing. The rest of the women had shot in much the same manner, and Peyton kept score on her phone, noting that Kenzie's team was in third place prior to her shooting. She needed a total score of twenty-three to move them into second place and then the next round of the impromptu tournament. Her first shot had earned her a seven, and Kenzie was disappointed because she knew she could do better than that. She lined up her next arrow and did not glance in Lennox's direction. She calmed herself again and released, earning her team an eight.

"Len, you're salivating," Dani commented and laughed. "Down, girl," she added and shoved Lennox, who shoved her back.

"I'm not ashamed," Lennox said. "I am completely turned on right now and plan to let her have her way with me later," she added.

Kenzie glared at her in disbelief, since nearly everyone heard that and laughed. Lennox wiggled her eyebrows at her, and Kenzie promptly missed her third shot, earning only a two. Lennox laughed, and Kenzie knew then that she'd only said those things to mess up her concentration. Quickly, she pulled the last arrow out of the container on the ground, lined up the shot, and let go without hesitation.

"Shit!" Maddox exclaimed.

"Yes! We're moving on!" Quinn clapped, and Jenna gave her a high-five. "We choose Kenzie," she added, regarding the next round.

"Kenzie versus who? Bobby, who from your team?" Peyton asked Bobby, whose team had come in first place, thanks to their combined score. Unfortunately for Kenzie, Quinn and Jenna both missed two shots each, so they'd only managed second place. "Mandy scored the highest," Peyton reminded.

"Mandy's up." Bobby pushed her bandmate toward the firing line.

Kenzie heard all of this but didn't pay attention. She was still staring at Lennox, who was staring back with a look that told Kenzie if they weren't surrounded by these women right now, Lennox would be all over her. Kenzie picked up the next arrow, pulled back, not even waiting for Peyton to tell her to start, and shot once and then the second time. She paused only for a second before firing her third shot, and then, she pulled back for the fourth time, looking at Lennox as she did, now completely familiar with the form of the bow and the wind's speed and its direction as it hit her skin. She fired without looking at the target and then passed the bow to Mandy without checking her results. She walked the ten steps to Lennox, grabbed the back of her head, and kissed her hard. Her tongue pushed its way inside, and Lennox met it with her own, wrapping her arms around Kenzie's body and pulling her into herself even closer.

"I guess game over?" Mandy questioned.

"She hit four tens." Kenzie heard someone say. "I think she almost split this arrow. Holy Fuck!" Whoever said it, added.

Kenzie couldn't give enough of her focus to figuring out who, though, because she was running her fingertips through silky locks and playing with a hot tongue with her own. After she resonated that a throat, or rather two or three throats were clearing behind them, she reluctantly pulled back with a few short pecks to Lennox's welcoming lips.

"Congratulations?" Lennox chuckled. "Somehow, I think *I* just won."

"I'm in love with you, Lennox," she said so that only Lennox could hear.

Lennox's expression was awe and amazement, and surprise mixed with joy, and maybe concern, too.

"You don't–"

"Stop." Kenzie pressed her fingertips to her lips. "I am. I'm not just saying it. I am," she repeated.

"Kenzie, you shot four tens. How much practice did you get for your show? I mean, damn," Bobby approached them and asked.

"I might have forgotten to mention that after I learned it for the show, I liked it and joined an archery club. I go shooting once a week in LA, when I'm home, and there's an Olympian archer that goes there, too. She's taught me a few things."

"She?" Lennox lifted both eyebrows, and Kenzie laughed, pulling her in for a hug.

"She is married, with two kids, and is about fifty-two," Kenzie told her. "You have nothing to worry about," she whispered to her.

"Well, con-artist Katniss, here, is the winner, which means Jenna, Quinn, and Kenzie get the full bottle service experience tonight by the rest of us losers," Peyton supplied. "And now I need to join an archery club because I suck at this."

"Finally, something you're bad at," Lennox joked, still hugging Kenzie.

"I don't want the whole bottle service thing," Kenzie pulled back and said to Lennox. "Unless you're interested in bottle service in bed?" she asked suggestively.

"Yes," Lennox replied instantly, earning a laugh from Kenzie.

***

Lennox sat on the ground with Kenzie in front of her between her legs as they enjoyed the rest of the afternoon with the group before they'd head back for dinner. She'd watched nearly all the others take archery lessons from her girlfriend for over an hour and decided she'd wanted one of her own. When she'd stood there with Kenzie behind her though, whispering seductively in her ear the instructions for making a good shot, the result was worse than when she'd tried it on her own, so she gave up.

She ran her hands up Kenzie's back and squeezed her shoulders before deciding she could use a shoulder massage. She dug into those tense muscles, allowing Kenzie to relax into the touch while they sat in the grass and listened to nature around them along with their friends, who were talking about their upcoming projects, tours, albums, and everything else.

"Kenzie, you've got a movie coming up, right?" Lynn asked.

"I'm shooting in London after this and then in New York," she explained while Lennox continued her massage.

"And, Lennox, you're doing what next? I heard you were thinking TV, maybe."

"No, I have some scripts to read, but nothing for TV."

"What about that Paul Simmons show? He's a major director. I thought they were hoping to line you up for that? It's supposed to be huge; based on that book series, and on HBO. You know that's going to go for, like, six seasons, at least, and will win all the awards," Lynn kept on.

Lennox stopped rubbing Kenzie's shoulders and rested her hands on Kenzie's knees instead.

"I got the call, yeah," she replied.

"And? That's huge, Len," Peyton added. "You didn't tell me about that."

"I have to think about it," Lennox said and kissed Kenzie's shoulder.

Peyton met her eye and seemed to understand what she was saying and decided to help her out by changing the subject.

"Anyone want to take the boat out again? I'm thinking a few runs around the lake and then dinner." She stood, pulling Dani up with her.

"I'm in."

Lennox continued her massage, but Kenzie didn't relax back into her this time.

***

"I believe I am obligated by law to provide bedroom bottle service to you now." Lennox stood from the dinner table and held out her hand for Kenzie to take.

"I was kidding," Kenzie returned and set her water bottle down on the table.

"I'm not," Lennox replied. She withdrew her hand. "Go to the cabin, and I'll be there in a minute, with everything we need to stay inside all night and not come out until tomorrow."

"Gross, you two," Mandy commented and stood.

"I didn't say anything gross, Mandy. So that's on you," Lennox told her.

"I was going to go on a run," Kenzie told her.

"You want to do that now? It's getting dark." Lennox sat back down next to her.

"Yeah, I didn't run today. And – I don't know – I think I'm back into it. I didn't realize how much I missed it."

"Okay," Lennox agreed. "I could come with you. I don't know about you being out there in the dark like that."

"I have a headlamp," Kenzie supplied and mocked putting it on.

"Why do you have a headlamp?" Lennox laughed.

"I was going camping. I didn't know what to bring. Peyton said there might be hiking. I brought a headlamp and a whistle."

"What do you need a whistle for, Kenz?" She laughed harder.

"You're supposed to have a whistle in case you get hurt. You can blow it, and someone will find you," Kenzie answered.

"I heart you." Lennox laughed at her cuteness and kissed her forehead. "Do you want any company?"

"No, I like running alone."

"Okay. How about an hour? Is that long enough? If you're not back, we'll go looking."

"I'll bring my whistle." She kissed Lennox, stood, and headed toward the cabin.

Lennox watched her as she left, enjoying the look of her ass in those jeans, when Peyton flopped down next to her.

"Hey, why didn't you tell me about the call for the show? I knew you wanted to drop it before, but Kenzie's gone. Wanna explain?"

"We're not supposed to take work calls here, right?" Lennox turned to her. "I need immunity from punishment."

"Fine. Immunity granted for this one call," Peyton gifted.

"My agent called late last night. Kenzie was asleep, and my phone buzzed. It woke me up, and I noticed who it was, so I stepped outside to take it," she paused. "I only took it because I noticed I'd missed three calls already and had a text saying it was time-sensitive, I promise."

"Immunity has been granted already, Lennox."

"They don't even want me to read for it. They just offered it outright, and it's a done deal if I agree."

"Len, that's awesome. Why don't you seem to think that's awesome?"

"Peyton, it starts shooting next month. They fast-tracked it to get it out by next April. It's twelve episodes, and it shoots in New Zealand."

"New Zealand?"

"It's a period show and epic. I haven't read the books but, from what I've been told, it's a big deal. It's a four-year contract, Pey."

"They haven't even shot a pilot yet."

"They don't do that for these kinds of shows," she explained. "It has a huge fan base because of the books, and they're shooting season one, airing it, and then shooting season two as soon as the press tour for season one is done."

"So, you'd potentially be in New Zealand for years then and, basically, coming home for a visit every now and then?"

"It's eight months a year, and then, at least a month each year for press. That only leaves three months to do something else or…" Lennox faded out as she saw Kenzie emerge from the cabin, wearing a pair of running shorts and a tank top, with her headphones in.

"Or not seeing your brand-new girlfriend?"

"I said I had to think about it. I have to tell them by the end of the week. They have to start looking elsewhere and need to know fast."

"Do you want it? I thought you were doing more movies. Three in the next year or something. Wasn't that the plan?"

"It was, but they'd been dancing around this for about a month now. I made a comment in some magazine or show recently, that I was interested in doing TV, and the offers started pouring in. This one was at the top of my list, but I hadn't heard anything definitive before I came here. And now, I have, and I'm with Kenzie, and I don't know what to do."

"Babe, I'm going to go with Maddox to take some pics, okay?" Dani leaned down and kissed Peyton's cheek.

"Sure. Have fun." Peyton returned her glance to Lennox as Dani and Maddox walked off to, likely, grab Maddox's camera. "Dani's been getting into photography recently. She's pretty good. Maddox has been teaching her when she's around," she paused. "And now, back to you."

"No, let's talk about this other thing so I don't have to think about my thing."

"Does Kenzie know?"

"No, I went back to sleep, and she was so out, she didn't even wake up."

"And when you two were missing for several hours this morning, you didn't fill her in? Or were you too busy doing other things with your mouths?"

"You're the worst; you know that?"

"I am not." Peyton laughed.

"This place has been magical for us, Peyton." She looked at Peyton sincerely. "Honestly, I'll never be able to repay you for this. It's been fun to see everyone, but it's changed my life so completely."

"Because you finally met Mackenzie Smyth, your girl-crush turned girlfriend?"

"Yes." Lennox laughed. "I love her, Peyton. It's crazy, and unplanned, and so unexpected, but I love her."

"And have you told her?"

"I told her I'm *in* love with her."

"And she said what?"

"Nothing the first time."

"There's been more than one time?"

"Yes. And today, she said she was in love with me, too."

"That's great, Len. I'm so happy for you; for both of you. You guys seem great together."

"We are, and I don't want to ruin that by taking a job in another country."

"But you want the job?"

"I don't know. I did. I wanted it before. And now, I don't know. I told her I had some stuff to finish in LA, and then, I'd meet her in London and come back to New York with her when her work moves there. If I take this, I have to fulfill all my obligations and then rush off to New Zealand for the next eight months. When would I even see her? Christmas? Or a few random weekends when we're both so tired from flights and work that all we do is fall asleep next to each other?"

"Say what you want about that but, God, I love falling asleep next to Dani," Peyton thought out loud. "There's just something about falling asleep next to the person you love most in the world and waking up next to them the next morning. And I think that's especially true when you have to spend time apart because of work," she surmised. "But look, I went on tour for eight months after Dani and I got together, and we made it work. I was in Asia for a month, Australia and New Zealand after that, and then most of Europe, and she came along when she could, but she had Fashion Weeks and photo shoots, and rarely did they happen to be in the same country as my shows. We made it work, Lennox, because we love each other and because we knew it was only temporary."

"Four years isn't temporary."

"Yes, it is," Peyton told her. "Four years isn't forever. It's a job, and it's eight months of those years, and then it's over. Even if it goes for two more, it is still temporary. If you and Kenzie are forever, then this is only a small piece of the life you'll have together. If you really want the part, you need to think of it like that, and also understand that while it will hurt to be apart and it will hurt Kenzie if you tell her you can't go to London with her, she does do this for a living, too, Len. She gets how this all works. At least, you have that." Peyton stood. "I'm going to go find my fiancée and that famous photographer to see if maybe she'll take some candids of us we can show the family later, since we got engaged here and everything. You okay?"

"Yeah, I'm good." It was a partial lie, but she didn't want to keep Peyton from enjoying her time here.

"We can talk about this anytime, okay?"

"I know. Thanks, Pey."

"Of course. I love you; you know that?"

"I know. I love you, too," Lennox returned and looked in the direction of the trail she knew Kenzie had taken, hoping somehow that the path would illuminate the answer to her newest life problem.

CHAPTER 22

Kenzie ran and listened to the music pumping from her phone through her headphones. She wished it could drown out the thoughts and worries she'd become plagued with. No matter how reassuring Lennox had tried to be, Kenzie had these raw nerves that she did not have the coping skills to battle. She had never had so much to lose before. The scariest moment in her life had been before that first audition, when she had held those sides in her hands and tried not to think about the fact that she had enjoyed acting in high school. She had tried not to consider that maybe this was the best way for her to spend her future and not go to law school or graduate school to delay the inevitable. She had done her best to not think about the fact that she wanted it. She had wanted something different than the life she'd thought she wanted. She'd needed something different. After the audition, she'd tried to talk herself out of wanting it. She'd stared at her ceiling and listed all the reasons why she should not try acting even if she didn't get this part. The long hours would create a problem for her. She had no problem working long days, but the energy required to be around all those people and work with them might just be too much. Plus, she'd already put three years into school and only had one year left. She'd continued those thoughts until she'd heard back that she'd gotten the part, and then she knew that was it. This was what Kenzie wanted to do, even though it would require her to adapt and make a new life plan.

She rounded the last section of the trail that would lead her back to the field where she would find the cabins, and narrowly avoided tripping over a long branch on the path. She gripped her headlamp and held it in place the rest of the way just to be safe. The moment she emerged, she stopped running, took out her headphones, bent over, and tried to catch her breath. It was after nine, and she'd been running for a long time. She wasn't sure how far she'd gone. She could check her phone later, but she knew she'd pushed herself too far. She had only been running a few times, and before that, it had been months since she'd even attempted it. Her muscles already ached, and her body was covered in sweat. Insects buzzed around her, attracted to the salt. Kenzie pulled off the headlamp and knelt in the grass. She wanted to go farther. She wanted to keep running because, if she kept running, she wouldn't have to worry about anything else. It was just her against herself, and that she could handle.

"You okay?" Maddox asked as she approached. "Did you hurt yourself?" She held out her phone with the flashlight on it aimed near Kenzie.

"No, I'm fine. I just overdid it," she returned and looked up with squinted eyes.

"You ran in the dark?"

"Yeah, I had my lamp." Kenzie held out the headlamp and stood, feeling her muscles tighten in anger.

"Lennox was looking for you. Did you tell her you were going for a run?"

"Yeah, I was just gone longer than I expected. I'll find her," she replied.

"Couldn't you have called her? Reception is surprisingly good here. I just got off the phone with my lady." Maddox smiled.

Kenzie stared down at her phone for a moment and realized something that caused her to laugh.

"I don't have her number," she let out and continued laughing.

"You don't have your girlfriend's phone number?"

"Didn't need it." Kenzie wiped the sweat off her forehead. "I guess we should probably do that before we leave here."

"Probably." Maddox laughed. "She's crazy about you, you know? I can tell."

Kenzie stopped laughing and met Maddox's eyes.

"Thanks." She inhaled and exhaled, calming her heart back down. "I should go shower."

"Go, find your girlfriend, Kenzie. She really has been looking for you. Peyton convinced her not to go far, but she's tried out a couple of trails she thought you might be on."

"I'll find her," she assured and watched Maddox walk back toward her cabin.

Kenzie took a look around. Through the dark, she couldn't see much. The tall street-like lamps illuminated only a little, so she walked back to their cabin first, and when Lennox wasn't there, she grabbed her stuff and went to the bathroom, where she ran into Lynn and April. She climbed into the shower and allowed the steam and heat from the water to soothe her muscles. She could have stayed in there for hours, but she knew she needed to find Lennox. She hoped Lennox would be back in their cabin by the time she'd returned from the shower, but she wasn't. So, with the lantern in one hand and her headlamp in the other, Kenzie set out to find her wayward girlfriend, regretting that she'd been gone for so long, Lennox had to go find her.

She went back down the start of the few trails she'd run on previously and didn't see Lennox. She'd known that Lennox told Peyton she wouldn't go far, but she also knew that Lennox would look for her until she found her. So, she chanced a trip around the lake to the boathouse, but after the long walk around, her trip had proven fruitless. Then, she had another idea and headed farther from camp.

"Lennox?" she said when she spotted her.

"There you are," Lennox replied and jogged toward her, carrying a flashlight she had been aiming at trees to try to find Kenzie, and water. She wrapped her arms around Kenzie and pulled her in. "I was worried. You were gone too long."

"I know. I'm sorry. I lost track of time." Kenzie gave the explanation and did her best to wrap her arms around Lennox while holding on to her light. "You came here?"

"I tried the boathouse and the trails you'd taken the other day, and I couldn't find you. This was the last resort before I told everyone we all had to go looking for you. It's so late, baby. You shouldn't be running this late." Lennox pulled back and looked at her. "Did you shower?" She seemed to realize.

"I went back to the camp and cleaned up. You weren't at the cabin, so I came looking for you. I didn't think you'd be all the way out here, though." Kenzie looked out at the pond they'd shared snacks and a first date at only a couple of days before. "You had to walk through the tall grass at night to get here."

"I did," Lennox confirmed. "Though, I more like ran quickly and darted from side to side than walked."

"You risked the snakes for me?" Kenzie smiled at her.

"Of course, I risked the snakes for you."

"We should go. It's a long walk back, and it's late." Kenzie smiled and turned her head back toward the camp.

"Or, we could sit out here for a while. It's not going to get any darker," Lennox suggested and gripped her hips. "We could sit by the water and make out." She wiggled those sexy eyebrows.

"We should get back. You know Peyton will send security after us if we don't."

"You're no fun." Lennox offered a puppy-dog pout, and Kenzie wanted nothing more than to kiss it off her face and replace it with a smile.

"I guess not, but I would like to keep you safe," Kenzie offered. "It's my fault you're out here. And, even though we have the camp to ourselves, there could still be people out here or animals."

"Animals like snakes?" Lennox seemed to remember.

"I was thinking more like coyotes and wolves, but sure." Kenzie turned off her headlamp and slid it into the pocket of the sweatshirt she had again borrowed from Lennox's stuff, and held out her hand for her to take. "Come on."

"How was your run? Long?" Lennox asked.

"I was in the zone, I guess," Kenzie deflected as they started walking toward the cabin.

"In the zone or avoiding something?" Lennox pressed.

"What? No," she lied. "I just started running again, and I guess I forgot how much I loved it."

"Okay," Lennox said, but Kenzie heard the sigh more than the word and knew it wasn't okay.

Lennox could see into her now. She had always understood her, and that would only continue to grow as they spent more time together. She would likely never be able to lie to Lennox without Lennox knowing. And while that was a good thing, because it would encourage her to always be honest, it was also inconvenient in moments when Kenzie wasn't ready to be totally honest.

They arrived back at the camp, and Lennox dropped her at their cabin before going to the bathroom and letting Peyton and the others still sitting around the fire know that they'd gotten back safely. Kenzie sat still on their makeshift bed and stared blankly at the wall. When Lennox returned, she was freshly showered and wearing a pair of dark-green shorts and a white T-shirt with a logo and a number on it. Her hair was still wet and down around her face, and she smiled the moment she saw Kenzie. Kenzie couldn't help but smile in return. Lennox dropped her stuff off and climbed on top of Kenzie, straddling her hips. Kenzie's arms wrapped around her, and she pulled her into her, breathing in her scent.

"Are you too tired?" Lennox questioned.

"No." Kenzie really was too tired.

Her body ached from her run, and her mind was restless. She knew she should fall asleep and begin again tomorrow, but the scent of Lennox and the touch of her skin pressed against her, mixed with the water droplets still falling from her hair, made it nearly impossible to say no to her. Then, there was the thought that after this trip, they'd be apart for a while, and she didn't want to miss any more chances to be with Lennox like this.

Lennox's lips found hers, and she lifted her own shirt over her head between their deep, slow kisses. Kenzie held on to her and allowed Lennox to remove her shirt after several moments. Then, she was on her back, and Lennox was on top of her. Lennox removed her shorts and her underwear, before removing her own, and settled between her legs.

***

Kenzie woke to the sound of something vibrating. She hadn't been completely asleep. She'd been watching Lennox sleep for about an hour before she had finally been able to close her own eyes, but she hadn't fallen all the way when the sound snapped her out of it entirely. She thought it was her phone at first, so she reached around, searching for it on the floor. But when she touched it, it wasn't the culprit, so she left it there and lifted her head slightly to see that it was Lennox's phone, which was charging on her side of the bed. The vibrating stopped by the time Kenzie figured it out, and she went to lie back down when it vibrated again, this time, shorter. She figured the person had left Lennox a voicemail. Then, came another vibration. This one was longer than the previous one, so Kenzie lifted her head again, assuming the person was calling back. On the screen, she saw a text message. It gave her pause as she read it, but then, another one came in right after, and it was quickly followed by a third, and Kenzie knew she'd be getting no sleep tonight.

***

She pretended to wake up when Lennox teased her nipple with her fingers and opened her inquisitive eyes when Lennox's mouth sucked on it. Kenzie's hips lifted, and Lennox wasted no time sliding her hand between her legs, finding the right spot to touch her, and giving Kenzie the release. Kenzie rolled them over and brought Lennox the same kind of release with her mouth before she slid back on top of her, kissed her deeply, and rolled off to lie next to her.

"You okay?" Lennox asked after a long moment of shared silence.

"Yeah," Kenzie returned.

Lennox's hand went to her cheek, and she turned Kenzie's head to her.

"Baby, what's wrong? You didn't?"

"No, I did," she interrupted. "I always do."

"Must be nice." Lennox laughed.

"You didn't?" Kenzie shot up and turned back to Lennox, who was lying gloriously naked next to her.

"I did." Lennox ran her hands along her back to try to calm her. "I meant, in general. I told you, I had a hard time with that."

"But not with me?"

"No, not with you." Lennox smiled at her. "You just know what to do, apparently." She leaned up and kissed Kenzie back. "Lie back down with me. Let's just stay in here until lunch, go out there to eat, and then come back. We can spend the rest of the day in here together like this," she suggested.

"It's the last day," Kenzie stated. "Full day," she added. "I'm leaving at ten tomorrow. I have to return the rental car, and my flight is at noon."

"I know. That's why I want to spend today with you."

"We shouldn't ignore everyone else, Lennox," Kenzie fired back.

"Okay, you're mad at me about something." She leaned all the way up and kissed Kenzie's shoulder blades. "Is it that we're leaving tomorrow?"

"When will I see you after that?"

"I don't know." Lennox wrapped her arms around

Kenzie's waist. "Let's go grab some food and hit the bathroom. We can come back here, eat, and compare schedules, okay?"

"I'm flying back to LA tomorrow."

"I know. I am, too. Why don't we try to change my flight, and I can go back to LAX with you? I have a dinner with a few people tomorrow night, but I can come to your place after, or you can stay at mine if you want. I have to fly to New York the day after and meet with some studio people, but I'll be back in LA a couple of days after that. When do you leave for London?"

Kenzie's head was swimming with the logistics of this new relationship. The only experience she'd had dating someone in the business had been with Kelly, and they'd worked on the same show. They'd never had to navigate distance, and Kenzie hadn't felt anything like this for Kelly.

"I have tomorrow night, and then I'm on a plane. Things got moved up on me, and I have an early flight."

"So, we have tomorrow night." Lennox tried to be optimistic. "It's strange to me that you haven't seen my place, and I haven't seen your place." She kissed Kenzie again. "Why don't I do my dinner thing, and then I'll pick you up? We can go back to my place and spend the rest of the night together. I have a hot tub." She kissed Kenzie again, and her hands cupped Kenzie's breasts. "I'm in the hills, and no one can see if we're naked and touching each other," Lennox said in a higher voice.

"Sure." Kenzie stood and grabbed for the clothes she'd tossed the night before. "I'm going to the bathroom."

"Kenzie, don't. What's going on? I told you, I'm coming to London. We just have to get through this month, and I'll see if I can fly there in between; maybe do a weekend or something."

"Why? What's the point?" Kenzie threw on her shorts and shirt. "What's the point, Lennox?"

"What are you talking about?" Lennox moved to the edge of the bed. "Why are you getting so upset right now?

We knew this was coming."

"Obviously, I wasn't totally informed."

"Informed? About what, Kenzie?" Lennox reached for her own T-shirt and threw it on.

"Nothing," Kenzie grunted. "Just let me go." She turned to open the door to the cabin.

"Let you go? What? Outside? You're not even wearing shoes, and your underwear's on the floor." Lennox stood and grabbed at her shorts, which she slid over her legs. "Or did you mean *let you go*, let you go? Kenzie that's not happening." Lennox moved toward her. "I won't let you go." She placed her hands on Kenzie's cheeks. "I can't. Don't push me away because you're scared of being apart."

"Apart for how long?" Kenzie whispered.

"We talked about this."

"We didn't talk about the part you're taking," Kenzie let out, and Lennox lowered her hands.

"What part?"

"The show." Kenzie took a step back and gripped the handle of the door. "I can't do this if you're going to be gone so long, Lennox. What would we have? You'd be across the world for eight months, and I have a show here that I'm committed to for the next two years, at least. We'd have, at most, a month or two a year, and some weekends and holidays thrown in until it's over."

"Kenzie, I haven't taken that part yet."

"Yet?" Kenzie's eyes were filled with tears. She tried to breathe to push them back but failed, and a tear slipped out. "I'm not angry. I understand. It's your career, and it's a great part. I just can't, Lennox." Another few tears grazed her cheeks as they fell. "I can't be with you but not be with you for that long."

"Kenzie, I just found out they want me. I haven't even had the chance to think about what I want yet."

"You'd be stupid not to take it," Kenzie said and opened the door. "You're a star, Lennox." She walked through the door and let it close behind her.

She gathered herself as best she could and jogged in the direction of Peyton's cabin across the street past two security guys, who seemed confused at her appearance. She threw the door open and was met with a gasp from Dani, who was sitting on the edge of the bed, putting her shoes on, and big eyes from Peyton, who was brushing her hair.

"Hey there, Kenzie. Everything okay?" Peyton questioned.

"I need to get out of here," Kenzie breathed out.

"Are you crying?" Dani stood and approached her. "Peyton, she's crying."

"I'm fine. I just need to get out of here. I can't be here anymore."

"You just got here." Peyton dropped the brush on the bed.

"Dani, please." Kenzie looked at Dani.

"She needs to leave the camp, Peyton," Dani surmised. "What's wrong, sweetie?" She placed a hand on Kenzie's shoulder.

"Where's Lennox?" Peyton asked and sat on the bed.

"I need one of you to go to the cabin and get my stuff. I can't."

"Kenz, what the hell?" Peyton stood almost as quickly as she'd sat down.

"Please, Peyton," she begged. "Please, just get my stuff so I can go."

"Go where? Where is your girlfriend, Kenzie?"

"Babe, come on." Dani turned to Peyton. "Just do as she says. I'll talk to her."

"Fine, but I'm getting Lennox, too." Peyton started to leave.

"No, Peyton. I can't see her."

"Can't see her?" Peyton stood next to Dani now. "Did something happen? Did she do or say something?"

"No, she didn't do anything. I just need to go." Kenzie wiped at her cheeks. "I need my phone. I left it there. I need to book a flight for today, and then I have to get home."

"Okay. Okay," Dani started. "You can use my phone. Peyton will get your stuff, and you can book a new flight."

"Dani."

"Babe, she needs you to do this, okay?" Dani gave a sympathetic glance in Kenzie's direction before meeting Peyton's eyes. "I've got her."

"Fine." Peyton left the cabin, and Dani moved Kenzie over to the bed, where she sat her down.

"Do you want to talk about it?" Dani asked after sitting down next to her.

"I can't breathe, Dani." She felt her chest tightening and clutched at it.

"Okay, okay. Lie back." Dani moved Kenzie to lie on the bed and stood. "I'll grab you some water, okay? You're having a panic attack, I think. Just stay there."

"I love her," Kenzie breathed out. "I love her," she said again.

"Okay, Kenz. Let Peyton get her for you, then. Maybe she can help right now."

"She's leaving," Kenzie managed through short breaths. "And I can't be mad at her."

"Leaving? Why can't you be mad?" Dani opened a bottle of water and walked back over.

"It's her work." Kenzie's breath came in even shorter bursts, and her tears fell more regularly.

"Sweetie, drink this. And let's get you calmed down." Dani tried to hand her the water, but Kenzie didn't take it.

She ran her fingers along the blanket, trying to feel something that could calm her down, but realizing now that the only thing that could calm her was the touch of Lennox's skin. She closed her eyes and tried to remember what that felt like. She had only touched Lennox a few moments ago, and she was already starting to forget.

CHAPTER 23

LENNOX slid on her shoes quickly and ran out of the cabin, trying to locate her girlfriend. She looked around and felt the sun streaming down on her. It was brighter than usual, she thought as she noticed nearly every other woman at this camp other than Kenzie. Lennox turned and found Peyton walking briskly toward her.

"What the hell happened between you and Kenzie?"

"Where is she?" Lennox looked around Peyton to see if Kenzie was behind her. "Where is she, Peyton?"

"She's in my cabin, freaking out. Dani's with her. What the hell happened?" Peyton asked her, and Lennox started moving immediately. "No, stop." Peyton pulled on her shirt and brought her back. "She doesn't want to see you."

"She's my girlfriend, Peyton," Lennox argued.

"I know that. She begged me to get her stuff and not you, so I'm trying to respect her wishes. And Dani wants me to just listen to her. Let's go inside, and you can tell me what happened."

"I want to see her. She's just scared, Peyton. She's pushing me away because she's scared. I need to help her calm down." Lennox stopped herself and ran both hands through her tousled hair. "I love her, Peyton. I love her, and she doesn't want to see me because she's scared, but I love her." Lennox tried not to let the tears fall from her eyes.

"I know, Len. I know." Peyton ran her hands up and down Lennox's arms. "Let's just go inside, I'll get her stuff, and I'll go back to the cabin and try to get her to talk to you."

"She saw my phone this morning. That's the only thing I can think."

"What was on your phone? Something from Aaron?"

"No, my fucking agent won't leave me alone about this stupid part. He texted while I was asleep. She must have seen it, or maybe she just freaked out after the conversation yesterday about it. She ran off last night for a while, and I know she was avoiding me, but last night we–"

"I think I know." Peyton squeezed her shoulders.

"And then, this morning we…"

"Again?" Peyton lifted an eyebrow.

"And then, she pulled away. And, Peyton, I just found her."

"I know. Come on."

Peyton pulled her back inside the cabin, where Lennox watched her gather Kenzie's things. She noticed that Peyton mistakenly grabbed one of her sweatshirts and tossed it into Kenzie's suitcase, but she didn't say anything. She knew Kenzie liked wearing it. She lowered her head because it was too hard to watch Peyton pack Kenzie's things. After a few minutes, she heard the sound of a zipper on the bag, and it felt like a stake to her heart.

"Peyton, I can't lose her."

"You won't." Peyton opened the door, holding on to the roller bag. "I'll talk to her, and it'll be fine. But you should think about that part thing. You need to figure out if you want it or not. Whatever you decide, it's not just about you now; you have this other person who cares about you. And if you want the part, you need to figure out how she fits into that, and be prepared if she doesn't want to fit into it. If you don't want it, then tell her that, and everything will just move on. But, be sure, Len. If you're not sure, don't tell her. Because, if you change your mind later, you might lose her." Peyton left the cabin, and Lennox closed her eyes.

***

"What the fuck, Dani?" Lennox yelled as she watched Kenzie's rental car drive off and Dani waving at her as she went. "What the actual fuck?" she yelled and tried to run after Kenzie's car. "Kenzie!" she yelled.

"Lennox, come on." Dani ran after her just as Lennox stopped her fruitless running.

"She left? Where's Peyton? How could you just let her leave?" She turned to Dani.

"Peyton is on the phone with the airline, moving up her flight. And we can't keep her here if she doesn't want to stay, Lennox. She wanted to go."

"Peyton said she was going to get her to talk to me."

"She didn't want to. I'm sorry." Dani offered a hand on Lennox's shoulder.

"Fuck sorry." Lennox ran back toward her cabin and tossed her things into her bag before running back outside toward the parking lot.

"Lennox, stop." Peyton was outside by her car.

"What flight did you put her on?" she asked and used the remote to unlock the rental.

"Len, she asked me to tell you that she needs some time, okay?"

"Time? She's going to London in two days."

"I changed her flight, Len," Peyton stated and grabbed Lennox's hand. "She asked me to do it."

"Tell me the flight number so that I can go catch her."

"She's taking my plane, Len. She's taking it to London."

"What?"

"I'm sorry," she apologized and squeezed Lennox's hand. "I didn't want to, and I tried to talk her out of it, but she said she didn't want to go home. She just wanted to get there and get to work and try to take her mind off everything."

"Take her mind off me?"

"She's never done this before, Len. I don't think she's ever been in love."

"I know that," she interrupted. "You don't think I know that, Peyton?" Lennox grew frustrated. "I know more about her than you do. I know this is new for her, and I know she's never been in love. I know this is fast and scary, because I'm scared, too. I've been scared since I met her. I thought I was having a heart attack because it wouldn't stop racing inside my chest." She pounded her fist against her chest. "I know she has trouble dealing with stuff, because I know her. I understand her, Peyton, and I love her. That's why I didn't run. That's why I didn't let the fact that I'm terrified of finally finding the person I'm supposed to spend my life with, get to me. I'm still here." Her tears fell freely as she collapsed to the ground. "I've watched everyone around me find someone, Peyton. You and Dani found each other. Jamie has a boyfriend, who asked my permission to ask her to marry him. He asked *me* because my father is shooting a movie in some country on the other side of the planet and can't be bothered. Susan, who did makeup for my last movie? I introduced her to her girlfriend. They're already living together and got a dog a few weeks ago. It turns out, Maddox is also all but settled down. And I'm so happy for everyone, but I've never had that." Lennox wiped her tears. "I have never felt what I feel for her, and she just ran away."

"I know." Peyton sat next to her on the white gravel and rubbed her back.

"What are you supposed to do after you meet them and they leave?" Lennox managed between heavy sobs. "If she won't talk to me, if she doesn't want me, what am I supposed to do, Peyton?" She hung her head. "I know what it's like to have her now."

"It'll be okay."

"No, I don't think it will."

***

"What am I supposed to do, Dani? She's just sitting in the car."

"Get her to come out here and eat, Peyton. I don't

think she's eaten anything all day. I don't even know if she's had water." She motioned to Lennox, who was sitting inside her car. "It's also really hot, and she's just sitting there."

"I tried. She won't leave. I think she wants to go, but she doesn't know where."

"Because you sent Kenzie to London," Dani argued.

"I didn't send Kenzie to London. Kenzie ran away to London."

"Babe, I love you." Dani wrapped her arms around Peyton's neck. "I love you like crazy. I love you so much, I'm going to marry you. But, Lennox and Kenzie needed to talk it out, and you just put her on a plane. You gave her a way to run, babe."

"Dani, you saw her. What was I supposed to do?"

"I know you were in a bad situation, honey. I'm just trying to figure out how to put our friends back together. And I don't think having one roasting in her car, while the other one flies to the UK, is really the best way to do that."

"I don't even have her phone number," Lennox muttered.

"Len?" Peyton turned to see Lennox standing there.

"I've been staring at my phone for the past hour, but I don't have her phone number." Lennox's eyes were bloodshot. She'd seen them in the rearview mirror of her car. "I never got her number."

"Len, come on. Let's get you something to eat," Peyton tried.

"I'm not hungry," she replied. "Can you give me my girlfriend's phone number?" she asked.

"Sure, Len. It's in my phone. I left it in the cabin. Why don't you go with Dani to the tables, and I'll go get it?" She motioned for Dani to take Lennox.

"She's probably already in the air, isn't she?" Lennox asked as Dani took her arm.

"I don't know, sweetie. Maybe."

For the next three hours, Lennox lay in her cabin, staring at the ceiling between moments where she stared at her phone, hoping for some response. She'd called Kenzie three times and sent her twice as many text messages. On her fourth attempted call, she was sent straight to voicemail and recognized that Kenzie had probably turned her phone off. She didn't leave a message and, instead, rolled over on her side and cried. Peyton and Dani brought her dinner that she didn't eat, and then, they returned her bag, which she'd left in her car when she'd discovered she had nowhere to go. Kenzie was in the air, heading to another country. Lennox didn't want to go home because Kenzie wouldn't be there. She fell asleep with tears still in her eyes and woke up the following morning to the sounds of people outside.

Lennox grabbed her bag, leaving the plate of food on the ground, and walked outside. She made no attempt at goodbyes and dropped her bag in her car. She then turned before climbing inside, to see Peyton offering her a pity glance. Lennox just rolled her eyes and drove off, leaving the place she'd once thought of as *magical* behind forever.

***

Lennox made it home by four in the afternoon, and her first thought, when she entered her house, was that it no longer felt like home to her. She had loved the house when she had first laid eyes on it and spent a lot of her time working on decorating and furnishing it. But now, it all just felt like stuff. It didn't matter and had no real worth. She threw her bag down, showered quickly, and dressed for dinner with her agent.

"Len, this is huge," Tom told her the moment she'd sat down. "They're offering you what you'd make on three blockbusters, for the first season."

Lennox looked around the restaurant at the tables of people staring at her. She'd grown used to that a long time ago, but being in the middle of nowhere for a week had almost made her forget what it was like to never be anonymous in public. She took a long drink of her water and met

Tom's brown eyes as they looked up for a moment from his phone.

"Tom, I don't know."

"What do you mean, you don't know?" He set the phone down. "Lennox, this is the next step in your career."

"What about the movie plan you had, like, a week ago?" she asked.

"That was the plan, yeah, but then this rolled in." He motioned with his hand in that annoying way people do toward their waiter. "Lennox, you were looking for that next thing. And this is it. This is Emmy territory for sure. You'll win at least two, if not more, and you'll get the Globes to go with them. In between seasons, we'll get you into a short indie film, so you'll still be in the movies."

"I don't know, Tom. That's a lot. I was kind of hoping to take some time off."

"Off? Why? You're in the prime of your career, Len. It only goes down from there."

The waiter approached, and Lennox watched Tom order for both of them.

"I've been working since I was a kid. I haven't had more than a month off in my life; and that wasn't really a vacation, because you had me reading every other day."

"For parts you wanted, Len."

"Well, right now, I don't know what I want," Lennox admitted. "And I'm not hungry. So, can we just make this quick?"

"What do you mean? I just ordered." He motioned toward the kitchen with his hand and then picked up his phone again when it buzzed.

"I gotta get out of here." Lennox stood abruptly. "I don't know, Tom. I don't know about any of it. Just let me think about it, okay?"

"They need an answer by the end of the week at the latest, Lennox."

"I know. I remember." She grabbed her purse and walked past the onlookers, who stared and took pictures, until she was outside in the parking lot of the LA restaurant, passing the photographers yelling at her to smile or answer questions.

The car was luckily parked close, so she could climb in and drive off, avoiding running over the more aggressive members of the paparazzi, and join LA traffic. She sat at a stop light, with white knuckles gripping her steering wheel, and let the tears fall down her cheeks until she made it home, climbed into bed, and picked up her phone.

"Kenzie, please call me," she said in between sobs she wasn't even trying to hide. "Baby, please. I need to hear your voice. I need to know that you're okay and that you're safe. I know you're scared; I get it. And I'm sorry I didn't tell you that my agent was annoying me about taking this part, but I need to talk to you. Please, call me back." She hung up and did her best to stay up just in case Kenzie was awake or would hear the phone while asleep and call her back.

CHAPTER 24

KENZIE was trying to enjoy work. The script had impressed her enough that she had taken the job without even negotiating. She had been on set for a week now, and she'd tried to be more social this time. She had learned everyone's names and tried to learn things about them that she could recall later if she needed small talk topics. She'd spent her days in her trailer either reading lines or listening to music. She spent the nights she wasn't working in the hotel and had even made plans to go for dinner with a few people from the cast the following week.

She'd also spent much of her time listening to her voicemails from Lennox; repeatedly. She noted how sad Lennox was in each one, and she suspected and hoped that, as time went on, she would sound less sad. But, each day, Kenzie had woken up to a new message from Lennox, and instead of sounding like she was getting better or moving past the whole thing, Lennox sounded worse; and Kenzie hated herself. The last thing she had ever wanted to do was to hurt Lennox. She was in love with her, and she didn't think that would ever change, but the thought of losing Lennox was too much for her to handle.

She'd lost her mother, and then, she'd lost her father. She'd lost Annabelle and Kelly, because she'd been unable to be what they needed. And now, she had lost Lennox, because she couldn't deal with the fact that Lennox would leave for work. She could go off and make a movie, or in this case – a show, and they could do long-distance because they had no other choice. They fit. They were right together. If Kenzie could only face the fear of possibly losing Lennox, they could be together now.

Of course, she'd lost her already, really. She'd chosen to run because, if she lost her now, it wouldn't be as bad as if she'd lost her later, after they'd had months and maybe years together. It was easier this way, and Lennox would move on. She would do her work in LA and New York and then go to New Zealand for the next eight months. She'd probably find some guy there, with a nice accent, they'd go out a few times, and Lennox would forget all about Kenzie and what they'd shared at some lame summer camp.

"Kenzie, Lennox isn't doing well," Peyton's voicemail told her. "Please, just call her. You don't have to talk about the future or anything. She just needs to know you're okay. She's worried about you, and so am I. Please, just call someone, okay? Call Dani if you want to, or Maddox. We love you, okay?"

By week three of filming, Kenzie had stopped listening to Lennox's messages, but she had texted Peyton and Dani both that she was okay. She was at work, and she was okay. She wasn't okay, though. She missed Lennox. She missed her eyes, the way Lennox's skin felt when she touched it, the way she smelled when Kenzie held her close. She missed everything about her.

"Hey, Kenz, we're hitting up *Stonehenge* tonight. You in?" Mary Matthews, her co-star, asked as Kenzie sat at the lunch table outside, trying to appear open to conversations with others but really hoping no one would talk to her, because all she wanted to think about was how Lennox looked at her the first time she'd said she was in love with her.

"You're going tonight? Is it even open in the dark?" she asked.

Mary laughed just as Nora Eads approached and slid her arm into Mary's.

"Not the monument. It's a club," Nora corrected her.

"Oh."

"Yeah, it's supposedly okay with celebrities. They have a VIP room, where we can party and not be hounded."

Mary and Nora were newly famous, as Kenzie defined it. Nora had starred in a superhero movie that past summer, and the sequel would be filmed after she wrapped this film.

Mary had her own show that was about to go into its second season and was working on her first film. They were both in their late twenties and, apparently, were enjoying their new lives. Kenzie, however, wasn't sure she had ever felt worse.

"No, I think I'll pass," she said.

"Come on. You never go out with us." Nora sat across from her. "We're starting to take offense." She crossed her arms over her chest and gave Kenzie a playful stare.

"I just got the best news!" Marco Charles, the male lead and Kenzie's character love interest, appeared at Mary's side.

"What's up?" Mary asked.

"I got the part," he announced.

"We know, Marco. We're in the middle of filming," Nora teased him.

"No, on the show. I show up in episode three. So, as soon as I wrap here, I'm on my way to New Zealand." He jumped slightly off the ground, and his longer than average blonde hair lifted slightly as he did. "I'm not a regular this season, but they said I will be, most likely, in season two. I have six episodes in season one. How cool is that?"

"New Zealand?" Kenzie perked up at the mention of the country where there couldn't be that many TV shows filming.

"Yeah, *Phoenix Rising*. You heard of it?" Marco asked and sat down next to her. "It's based on the books."

"Yeah, I've heard of it," Kenzie replied and forked her macaroni.

"Isn't Lennox Owen starring in that?" Nora asked. "I saw it in the trades that she'd signed on."

Kenzie gulped and closed her eyes, realizing that she'd been avoiding this very subject for weeks now. She had not read anything online about Lennox for fear that she'd hear this very news. Her girlfriend, and probably her ex-girlfriend, thanks to her own cowardice, would be in New Zealand for the next eight months. It was a good thing. Lennox would be good in the role, according to everyone, and she would move on with her life.

"I'm due in makeup." She stood and threw her uneaten food into the trash can.

"Come on. *Stonehenge*, tonight? We'll grab you from the hotel at eight," Mary pressed.

"I'll think about it," Kenzie lied.

She wasn't due in makeup. She had an hour before she had to sit in the chair, but she didn't want to hear any more about *Phoenix Rising* or Lennox Owen. She fell onto the bed in her trailer and stared at the ceiling until she did have to go put on a brave face followed by the face of her character, who was getting dumped by Marco's character. The scene was a short one, and she and Marco were professionals. They nailed it in a few takes and were sent home for the day by seven, which was a minor miracle and one she had planned on taking advantage of. She wanted to go for a run and get in some reading time on the book she'd just started before she fell asleep, pretending she wasn't horribly upset and unable to eat any more than a few bites of food; and that was merely to sustain herself.

Kenzie changed into her running gear, including a hat that would offer her some protection against identification, and grabbed her phone, preparing her running playlist, when there was a knock on the door. She checked the time and noted that it was five after eight. She left the phone on the table next to the bed and headed to the door, trying to figure out how best to turn down Mary and Nora for at least the fifth time since they'd started shooting.

"Guys, I was just about to–" She stopped instantly when she saw Lennox Owen standing just outside her door.

Lennox had her hair down, and it framed her beautiful face perfectly. Her eyes brightened when she saw Kenzie, and her smile appeared before it disappeared again. She wore a dark-green sundress with short heels. She looked perfect.

"Hey, Kenz," she greeted with clenched fists at her

sides that unfurled when Kenzie looked down at them.

"What are you doing here?"

"Do you really have to ask me that?"

"Lennox–"

"Stop." Lennox took a step closer to her, and her hands were on Kenzie's hips now. "Just listen."

"I didn't–"

"You ran," Lennox stated and pulled Kenzie into her. "You ran, and I let you because everyone told me you needed to run. You needed time, and I gave that to you. But it has been the longest three-plus weeks of my life, Kenzie."

"Hey, Kenz. You ready?" Mary and Nora appeared to their left. "Oh, shit! Lennox Owen?"

Lennox pulled her hands back, and Kenzie stood staring at the two women who'd interrupted Lennox's speech.

"Hi." Lennox turned and put on a smile Kenzie recognized as fake. "Lennox." She held out her hand to Mary.

"Yeah, we know." Mary shook her hand, and then Nora did the same.

"You two know each other?" Nora asked and pointed between them.

"Yeah, we met a while ago," Lennox replied and wrapped her arms around herself. "She's friends with one of my friends. I was in town for the night and thought I'd stop by to say hi." She glanced back at Kenzie. "Right, Kenz?"

"Right."

"Cool. You should come out with us. We're going to a place called *Stonehenge*."

"At this hour?" Lennox asked, and Kenzie stopped the smile on her face at the question.

"It's a club," Mary explained. "You should come. Kenzie, you should change, though." She pointed to the hat.

"I was going for a run."

"You've been avoiding hanging out with us, but no more. We're holding you hostage, and Lennox is in. Right,

Lennox?" Nora prodded.

Lennox looked back at Kenzie, and Kenzie looked down at the patterned hotel carpet.

"Yeah, I'm in," she answered.

"Awesome. Kenzie, you need like... ten minutes? We'll take Lennox down to the lobby. We're meeting Marco and Benny down there." She pulled at Lennox's arm.

Lennox gave her a stare that said she was both sorry and, somehow, also not sorry, and trotted down the hall with Mary and Nora while Kenzie was left shocked and alone in her hotel room. She sat on the edge of her bed for at least five minutes before her phone buzzed, and she picked it up. Lennox had texted and asked her not to run again. Her words caught in Kenzie's throat, and she stood, removed her hat, and started to change into some jeans and a light-blue scoop-neck shirt. She threw a light, black jacket over it and replaced her running shoes with some black flats. Her hair was pulled back and was a lost cause, since it would take her too much time to try to do something with it, and she wore no makeup but threw on some quick powder and mascara before she grabbed her purse, tossed her phone in it, and headed to the elevators. When she emerged in the lobby, she watched Lennox seemingly easily navigate introductions with Marco, Benny, and Benny's friend, Julian, who was on the crew of another movie shooting in London. Lennox smiled and shook hands while Kenzie stood back, considering running back up to her room and hiding out. But she didn't, because Lennox's text still stuck in her mind.

"Damn, girl, you dress up nice." Mary saw her and gave her a wink.

"We ready?" Benny asked and gave Kenzie a once-over. "I was thinking you and I might share a dance tonight, Kenz." He approached her and gave her a noble bow in jest. "Care to take my arm, Madame?" He held out his arm for her to slide her own into, and Kenzie met Lennox's eyes.

"Sure," she replied, and they headed toward the revolving doors.

They took two cars to the club since they couldn't fit in one, and Lennox had ended up with Nora and Marco, while Kenzie was with Benny, Julian, and Mary. Kenzie sat between Mary and Benny, and noticed as Julian and Benny flirted back and forth with one another. That would make things easier. Benny was gay and, therefore, would only want to dance with Kenzie as a friend. She could do that.

"Hey, you okay?" Mary placed a hand on her thigh and asked. "You look like you've seen a ghost."

"I'm fine." Kenzie swallowed.

"Why didn't you tell us you knew Lennox Owen?" Mary removed her hand.

"I guess I didn't know it mattered."

"Are you kidding me? Of course, it matters." She laughed and turned to stare out the window. "Marco and I both have a major crush on her."

"What?" Kenzie snapped her head around to look at her.

"Yeah, when he saw she was coming with us, he about flipped out," she replied without turning toward Kenzie. "She's so fucking hot in person." Mary turned back at that. "Marco has the advantage, though, obviously. As far as everyone knows, she's totally into guys. But, there were some rumors that maybe she and Peyton Gloss were more than just friends."

"They're like sisters," Kenzie defended.

"Well, they're obviously not together now, since Peyton and Dani Wilder have come out and gotten engaged. I got to say, I didn't see that one coming. But, maybe she and Peyton were together before and just stayed friends."

"They were never a couple." Kenzie fisted her hands. "They're best friends."

"Okay." Mary shrugged. "So, no chance for me then. That sucks."

"I didn't know you were gay," Kenzie admitted.

"It's pretty hush-hush right now. My manager wants me to wait until after this movie is released to come out, but

I might wait longer. We'll see."

"Why would you wait longer?"

"It's a timing thing. When it makes the most sense for my career, I'll tell people. Of course, if Lennox Owen *is* interested, and she and I go and get engaged, like Dani and Peyton, I'll happily tell the world."

Kenzie didn't say anything else the entire drive to the club, and when she climbed out of the car, she watched as Marco offered his hand to help Lennox out of the car. She hung her head when she watched Lennox smile at him and then walk into the club next to him. Mary and Nora met Kenzie at the car and ushered her inside, with Benny and Julian taking up the rear. When they entered, the music was loud, and Kenzie wanted to cover her ears to prevent the electronic beat from entering her mind. She hated it, and she didn't want to be here. She made her way to the VIP room and sat down immediately on the plush sofa, while the rest of the group seemed to be more interested in ordering drinks from one of the waitresses. Kenzie closed her eyes and laid her head against the back of the sofa.

"Hey, use my hand." Lennox must have sat next to her.

Kenzie opened her eyes and turned her head to see that Lennox was holding out her hand.

"What?"

"The music is loud. You're…" She faded but looked down to where Kenzie was gliding her fingertips along the red velvet fabric. "Use my hand instead."

"Lennox, what do you want?" Marco asked, and Lennox turned her head to him. "Just water for me."

"What? Come on, we're going to have a good time." Mary sat on the other side of Lennox. "Let me get you something. Martini sound good?"

"Water sounds good," Lennox returned and then looked at Kenzie. "Water?"

"Yes," Kenzie answered.

"Can you get us both water?" she asked Mary.

"Sure, I guess." Mary stood reluctantly, and then Kenzie watched as Marco sat down in her place.

"So, how do you two know each other?" he asked and pointed at the two of them.

"They're both friends with Peyton Gloss," Nora answered for them and sat in a matching chair next to the sofa.

"Yeah? I heard she's nice." He took a sip of whatever he was drinking.

"She is," Lennox answered politely.

"Here's your water." Mary handed Lennox a glass and then handed the second one to Kenzie before she sat on the chair opposite Nora's and looked upset that she'd been usurped by Marco.

"Do you maybe want to dance when you finish that?" Marco asked Lennox and referred to the water she had yet to take a drink of.

"I think she'd rather dance with the girls tonight; right, Lennox? Kenzie, Nora, let's go. The music's perfect." Mary stood and placed her drink on the table between them all.

"I don't–" Lennox started, but then she was being pulled up by Mary's hands and turned her head back to Kenzie, who sat completely still.

"Come on, dance with me," Mary continued. "Nora, you, Kenzie, and Marco talk. We'll be right back." She pulled Lennox's hand, and they neared the room's exit.

Kenzie watched Lennox turn around to her, silently pleading for her to save her from the dance with Mary, but Kenzie didn't stop them. She just sat on the sofa and ran her fingers along the fabric, trying to figure out how she'd gotten into this situation.

"So, is she single?" Marco asked the second the two women were out of the room.

"Huh?"

"Lennox. I haven't heard about her dating anyone. She's gorgeous. I can't believe you didn't tell me you knew her."

"What famous friends have you not told us about,

Kenzie?" Nora asked.

"Hey, losers! Julian and I are going to hit the dance floor. We'll be back in, like, an hour," Benny explained and was happily pulled out of the room by Julian's hand.

Kenzie tried to focus on the feel of the fabric beneath her fingers, but she could only think about Lennox out there, dancing with Mary, and Mary's hands all over Lennox's body. Marco continued to talk about how hot Lennox was, how she'd laughed at his joke earlier, and he wanted to kill Mary for trying to pick her up, too, just to mess with him. Kenzie stood abruptly, nearly knocking over the drinks on the table.

"Kenzie?" Nora checked.

Kenzie didn't say anything. She left the room and moved quickly and smoothly into the wide expanse of the two-story club, where she saw a dance floor filled with people – and *too many* people for her liking. She swallowed, took in a deep breath before letting it back out, and drew her path through the crowd in her mind. She made her way to the dance floor, but as she turned around quickly, she couldn't see Mary or Lennox. Her heart was racing faster than the music, and she wanted to leave. She needed to leave. Kenzie needed to be back in the hotel room alone, staring at her ceiling until she fell asleep.

"Baby, it's okay." Lennox's whisper caught her off guard, but the arms around her waist caught her off guard even more. "I'm here," she whispered into her ear from behind.

"Where's Mary?" Kenzie asked and wondered if Lennox could even hear her over the music.

"I sent her to the bar. Come here, please." She pulled Kenzie even closer.

"Lennox, we're–"

"In public, I know. Do you really care?" she asked. "Dance with me?"

Lennox smelled of citrus and possibly lavender, and Kenzie tried to focus on the question and not the memories returning to her because of Lennox's intoxicating scent.

"I can't dance," Kenzie muttered when Lennox's hands slid from around her waist to her hips and turned her around. "I've never had a role where I had to learn," she added and looked at Lennox's eyes, which were beautiful.

Lennox didn't say anything. She took Kenzie's arms and wrapped them around her neck before wrapping her own around Kenzie's waist and pulling her into her body.

"I've missed how you feel," Lennox said into her ear. "I've missed how you smell," she added. "I've missed everything about you, Kenz."

"Lennox, we tried, and it didn't work," Kenzie replied but linked her hands around Lennox's neck and pulled her into her.

"What are you talking about? Of course, it worked. You got scared, and you ran, Kenz."

"Because it was easier to lose you now than lose you later." Kenzie pulled back to look at her.

"Why would you lose me at all?" Lennox asked with a tilted head and ran her fingers along Kenzie's cheek.

"I got your drink." Mary had, apparently, returned, and with the music blaring, they had failed to notice. "But I guess you don't need it." She noted their closeness. "So, I guess I don't have a chance after all." She lifted an eyebrow.

"What?" Lennox asked her, confused.

"Nothing. I'm a little embarrassed, so I'm going to leave you two alone and try to find some other hot girl to pick up tonight." She walked off and took the drink Kenzie assumed Lennox didn't really want, with her.

Kenzie turned Lennox's face back to her and met her lips with her own. Lennox took only a second to respond. Then, Lennox's mouth was greedy, and it was attacking Kenzie's mouth. Kenzie's hands were on Lennox's back, pulling her closer, while the deep bass of the music continued beating around them, along with the rest of the people on the dance floor. Lennox's tongue slid between Kenzie's lips, and Kenzie moaned when Lennox explored and dove deeper into her mouth. When Kenzie's overstimulation started to take over her senses, she pulled back slightly, and Lennox's now dark eyes met her green ones.

"I can't be here," she remarked and watched the recognition on Lennox's face.

"Hotel?"

"Yes."

They pulled apart to find Marco, Benny, Julian, and Nora staring at them with wide eyes and shocked expressions.

"We're going to go," Lennox said and took Kenzie's hand.

"I guess Mary was right," Marco uttered.

"Marco, shut up," Kenzie said.

She pulled Lennox outside the club, and they were met immediately by cameras and questions from the paparazzi that hadn't been there when they'd arrived only moments earlier. Kenzie stood in shock, still holding Lennox's hand. She dropped it at the first flash and couldn't move.

"Kenz, come on." Lennox wrapped her arm around her waist from the side. "Babe, come on," she repeated when Kenzie didn't move.

"Babe? Lennox, are you and Mackenzie a couple?"

"How long have you two been together?"

"Why didn't we know you were gay?"

The questions came in rapid succession, and it took a pull from Lennox down the sidewalk where she waved and waved until the third taxi that passed finally stopped for them. Lennox ushered Kenzie into the cab and climbed in beside her. She slammed the door closed and then turned to Kenzie, who was staring straight ahead. She told the cab driver the address of Kenzie's hotel, and as they drove off, she wrapped her arm around Kenzie's shoulders.

"Hey, it's okay. We're okay," she said.

"No, we're not," Kenzie disagreed. "They know, Lennox."

CHAPTER 25

LENNOX stared at Kenzie the entire ride back to the hotel before she paid the cab driver, helped her out of the taxi, and had to follow her rapid steps into the elevator. She had been silent for the rest of the ride, knowing Kenzie needed it to try to calm down. But, as they made their ascent to the tenth floor, she couldn't stay silent anymore.

"Kenz?"

"What?" she asked gruffly.

The elevator dinged on the eighth floor, and the doors opened to reveal an elderly man, who stared at them either in confusion or recognition of who they were.

"We're going up," Lennox explained, and he looked at the elevator button he'd pressed likely incorrectly as the doors closed. "Baby, talk to me."

"Why are you here, Lennox?" Kenzie asked as the doors opened to the tenth floor, and she didn't wait for an answer before she fled and headed down the hall toward her room.

"Are you going to wait for an answer?" Lennox followed rapidly behind her.

"Can we just get inside, please?" Kenzie held her card to the lock, and it beeped.

She opened the door and went inside, with Lennox following her again and allowing the door to close and lock behind them.

"Why are you angry with me? *You* kissed me. *You* pulled me out of there by the hand."

"Why are you here?" Kenzie tossed her purse on the desk by the window of the modest room. "Why are you here, Lennox?"

"Because I love you," she stated loudly and stood ten

feet away from her. "I love you, Kenzie. And I've spent the past three weeks trying to talk to you, but you won't return my calls. You won't talk to Peyton or anyone else, and you just disappeared. You ran away."

"Yes, I ran away. I left. Why did you follow me?" Kenzie ran her fingers along the zipper of her jacket.

Lennox took the necessary steps toward her so that there was only a foot of distance between them, but she didn't touch her.

"Tell me to go," she managed to mumble, even though it was the last sentence she wanted to say. "Tell me you honestly want me to leave, and I will make sure you never see me again, Kenzie. I will tell Peyton not to invite us to the same things because I was so unbelievably wrong about us, that you can't even stand to be in the same room with me. Tell me that. Tell me to go so I can go and try to put my life back together, because I am miserable. I have been miserable without you. I am walking through my days like a zombie on your damn show. I'm getting yelled at while I work because my heart's not in it, and I can't get my lines right. I cannot stop thinking about you being here and not talking to me. So, if you would please just tell me to stop thinking about you, stop wanting to be with you, I would really fucking appreciate it," Lennox finished and exhaled the breath she had been holding.

"I can't," Kenzie whispered and reached for Lennox's hand. "I want to, but I can't."

"You want to tell me to go?" Lennox took her own hand back. "Jesus, Kenzie!"

"I want to not need you," Kenzie corrected, and Lennox looked into her eyes again.

"Keep going," she encouraged.

"I can't, Lennox. I'm not good–"

"Bullshit." Lennox took her hand again. "You are good at it with me." She had tears in her eyes now, and she closed them to try to get the tears to go away. "With me, Kenzie."

Kenzie reached for her waist and pulled her toward herself.

"I know," she admitted. "I'm better with you."

"Then, why can't you just be with me?" Lennox allowed a tear to fall when she opened her eyes.

"I am. I'm sorry. I'm here." Kenzie pressed her forehead to Lennox's. "I'm sorry." She kissed her nose. "I'm sorry, Lennox." She pressed her lips to Lennox's mouth, and, after a moment, Lennox responded.

Slowly – and even more than slowly, Kenzie's everything took over Lennox's senses. She smelled her, tasted her, felt Kenzie's skin when she reached for her face to pull her in closer. Kenzie was there. She was in front of Lennox, and they were together. She basked in the feel of her as she slid the black jacket off Kenzie's shoulders and let it drop to the floor.

"Let me make love to you," Lennox breathed out against Kenzie's mouth.

Kenzie didn't say anything. She just reached for the zipper on Lennox's dress, that she'd worn specifically for Kenzie tonight, and slid it agonizingly slowly down her back. She moved her fingers to Lennox's shoulders and slid the thin straps down off them before she watched it fall to the floor.

"Me first," Kenzie finally said, and her eyes raked over Lennox's body and the underwear she'd, again, specifically chosen for this night. "Green again?" Kenzie seemed to say to herself.

"The only color I've been able to see these days." Lennox shrugged. "You're all I see, Kenz." She pulled up on Kenzie's shirt and tossed it before reaching for the black bra Kenzie had chosen, and unclasped it to allow it to join their discarded clothes.

A phone buzzed in Kenzie's purse followed by Lennox's on the ground in her own purse, but Lennox didn't care. She kissed Kenzie and walked them to the bed, where she laid Kenzie down and moved on top of her. The phones continued to buzz as Lennox kissed down the side of Kenzie's neck while Kenzie's hands pushed down on her dark-green bikinis to get them down her legs. Lennox lifted up to oblige, and when they were gone, she moved her own hand to Kenzie's jeans, which she unbuttoned and unzipped while Kenzie attacked her neck with her lips. Before she could finish, Kenzie had them turned over and stood. She stared at Lennox, naked in her bed, and there was a look of reverence on her face that Lennox wanted to memorize while Kenzie kicked her own jeans and underwear off and pulled Lennox's legs off the bed. Kenzie spread them wide as one of their phones buzzed again, and she kissed up Lennox's thigh while Lennox lifted her head to watch. One of Kenzie's hands moved to Lennox's breast, while her other one opened her and then moved to the other breast as Kenzie's tongue grazed her clit delicately.

"Oh," Lennox let out with slight embarrassment, because – despite the intense emotion of the night, she'd been turned on since the moment she'd seen Kenzie dressed in her running outfit. "God." She moved a hand to the back of Kenzie's head.

Kenzie's tongue was slow and deliberate, and her hands on Lennox's breasts were light. She was torturing Lennox and knew what she was doing would drive Lennox crazy. Her lips pulled Lennox's clit into her mouth, and she sucked as she continued to apply light pressure with her fingers and thumbs to Lennox's nipples.

"I love touching you," Kenzie said before she pulled Lennox back into her mouth.

"Baby, say it. Please," Lennox let out. "I need to hear you say it if you feel it." She looked down as Kenzie lifted up and met her eyes with dark and eager green ones.

She watched Kenzie as she seemed to work through several thoughts, all at once; then, she watched as Kenzie kissed her thigh, and Lennox thought that might be the end. Kenzie couldn't say it; either because she didn't feel it, or because she wasn't capable; and if the latter was the case,

Lennox didn't know what she would do.

"I love you, Lennox Owen." Kenzie kissed her thigh again, met Lennox's still watery eyes, and then moved her lips back to Lennox's clit, making the woman come twice before she finally stopped and slid back on top of her.

***

"How long can you stay?" Kenzie asked at nine o'clock the next morning as she ran her fingers between Lennox's breasts.

"I have a flight later today."

"What?" Kenzie shot up and stopped touching her. "You just got here."

"I know, but I have to be back at work tomorrow. This was the first weekend I could get away. I know it's not long, but I had to see you. I had to know if you still wanted this the way I do."

"And when can you come back?" Kenzie asked as she stood and reached for her clothes they'd thrown all over the night before.

"Hey, we have time. I don't have to leave for a few hours. Come back to bed," Lennox requested and held out her hand for Kenzie to take. "There are still things I want to do to you that we didn't get to last night." She smirked.

"My phone died," Kenzie remarked as she pulled it out of her purse.

"Kenz, come on. You're freaking out again." Lennox sat up, letting the sheet fall away from her body.

"I'm not freaking out, Lennox."

Kenzie plugged her phone into the charger on the bedside table and pulled a T-shirt over her body.

"Okay. So, come back here and talk to me. Or, we don't have to talk."

"You're leaving in a few hours, Lennox." Kenzie sat on the side of the bed, facing the phone she seemed to be staring at until it re-initialized.

"Yes, so I have time. I'll need to stop by my room to grab my stuff, but it's not like I unpacked anything. Then, I'm good to go." Lennox placed her hand on Kenzie's back and rubbed gently. "Kenz?"

"Everyone knows, Lennox," she said after a long silent moment. "They all know."

"Is it really that big of a deal, Kenzie? Dani and Peyton are out now."

"And they've been followed like crazy," she returned without turning to Lennox. "I've been trying not to pay attention, because it scares me but also because Peyton and Dani just remind me of you. But I know they announced their engagement, and then every single person with a camera or a question showed up at their place. They've been locked away ever since, just waiting for it to die down so they can leave to get a damn cup of coffee in peace."

"That was their choice, Kenz. They knew it would happen. Trust me; they were prepared. And as annoying as it is – I talked to Peyton yesterday, and they're fine. Honestly, they've been enjoying it."

"How?" Kenzie snapped and turned her head.

"Because they actually have uninterrupted time together for the first time in years." Lennox laughed lightly and kissed Kenzie's back through the shirt she had thrown on haphazardly. "I can imagine what they've been up to in there."

"It's not funny, Lennox." Kenzie stood.

"Okay. It's not. I'm sorry, but I guess I just don't care about that right now, Kenz." Lennox slid out of bed and found her dress, which was the only article of clothing she had in the room. "I was enjoying the afterglow of the all-night sex-a-thon with my girlfriend that I haven't seen in over three weeks and missed like crazy. And now, all she wants to do is run again." She grabbed at the bra and the panties.

"Lennox, I'm not running."

"You couldn't get your clothes on fast enough once

you found out I had to leave today." Lennox slid on her underwear and then clasped her bra behind her back.

"I shouldn't have kissed you last night," Kenzie stated as she watched Lennox dress.

Lennox gaped at her. She stared at Kenzie's tousled hair and her gorgeous green eyes. Lennox's eyes lowered to the shirt the woman had thrown on and then the nothing she had on below it. They lowered farther to the dress she, herself, had chosen because she'd thought Kenzie would like it, and she slid her legs through it, not bothering to try to zip it.

"You're probably right." Lennox felt her heart tighten with the comment. "We should have talked first. I shouldn't have let that happen."

"I kissed you, Lennox."

"Because I was touching you on the dance floor."

"You don't own my actions, Lennox Owen. I may be awkward and not have a lot of coping skills, but I own what I do. You don't get to own that, too."

"What do I own then, Kenzie? If you own your actions, and if I shouldn't feel responsible for them, then explain what happened a few weeks ago – when you ran away, and then again – when you wouldn't return my calls or my texts. I'd especially like to know about the messages you heard where I cried my eyes out, because I didn't know if you were okay or if I'd ever see you again. Tell me about your actions then, Kenzie. Tell me why you couldn't pick up the phone, or why you couldn't just tell me you were scared. Tell me that, because – if I'm not responsible for you running off, or you kissing me last night, or how you're acting right now – then I deserve a damn explanation."

"I couldn't," Kenzie replied.

"That's you accepting responsibility for your actions? You saying you couldn't?"

"I was terrible to you," Kenzie finally said and sat back down on the bed, this time facing Lennox. "I was terrible, Lennox. I didn't know what to say to you."

Lennox sat on the other side of the bed, facing Kenzie, and hung her head for a moment before she lifted it to see that Kenzie had tears in her eyes.

"You just had to talk to me. I didn't need anything more than that," Lennox offered and slid more onto the bed.

"We should have talked more last night," Kenzie stated and wiped at a tear.

"Before we jumped back into bed? Yeah, probably." She turned and matched Kenzie's posture.

"I'm sorry."

"Me too," Lennox said.

"What do you have to be sorry for?"

"For not telling you about the offer as soon as I heard about it." Lennox placed a hand on Kenzie's bare thigh. "Things happened so quickly between us, Kenzie. And – I don't know – I guess I wanted to figure you and me out before I tried to figure out what was next for me."

"Lennox, I've lost most people I care about in my life." Kenzie turned to Lennox and wiped another tear that Lennox hated causing. "My mom left and started a whole other family with kids that weren't her own. I thought I might hear from her once I started making money and getting recognized, but she didn't even reach out to me then. She was so disappointed in me, in the fact that I wasn't what she'd imagined I would be, that she didn't even try to get money out of me." Kenzie paused and met Lennox's eyes. "My dad might have been physically there, but he was never mentally there. And then, he wasn't there at all. I didn't have a lot of friends and no other family. When I went to college, I made some, and I still don't know how, exactly. But Kat has at least tried to keep in touch with me after we both moved on in our lives. The only relationships I had didn't end well, and they both ended because I wasn't what they needed. I've never been enough, Lennox." She wiped two more tears. "I've never been enough for someone to want to keep around forever. And you had this opportunity to take this part… and I understand, I do. It's a big deal for your career, and it will open even more doors for you. But it was too much. Falling for you so quickly and then losing you, even if it was only to a long-distance relationship, when I'd only just found you, made me think I would really just lose you, period. You'd put in the effort at first, and so would I, but the time difference and the work would get in the way. Nightly calls would turn into weekly ones, and then we'd be too tired to take the long flight to see each other on the days we did have off."

"Kenzie, we could have talked about this."

"I know. But I wouldn't have believed you."

"What?"

"You would have tried to convince me that we could make it work, and I wouldn't have believed you, Lennox." Kenzie gathered her thoughts. "People always tell me they'll stay, and they go anyway. I caught my mom trying to leave us once when I was young. She had packed a bag and planned to leave in the middle of the night, but she didn't expect me to hear her and get out of bed. She lied about what she was doing and told me to go back to sleep; that she was going back to bed, too. I asked her if she would leave. I somehow knew what she was doing. I asked her, and she promised me she would never leave me."

"Then, she did…"

"Annabelle told me we'd make the distance work, but then we didn't. I wasn't enough to make her want to try."

"Kenzie, did you ever stop to think that it has nothing to do with you not being enough for them?"

"What?" She turned to Lennox.

Lennox moved her hand to Kenzie's cheek and offered a small smile.

"Baby, they weren't enough for you," she said. "And I don't know if *I* am. I can't make promises like everything is always going to be okay. But I know how I feel about you, and I know that you're enough for me."

"You can't really know that. What happens when you

get to New Zealand, and we aren't able to see each other for a few months? It's been so hard being away from you for three weeks, Lennox."

"Well, that's mainly because you wouldn't talk to me. If we're talking, it won't be as bad. It'll still be hard, but it won't be as bad, Kenz."

"You'll be working fourteen-hour days on one side of the earth, and I'll be doing the same on the other. When will we even be able to talk? Is today the last time we'll see each other until one of us is on hiatus?"

Lennox leaned in, pressing her forehead to Kenzie's and kissing the tip of her nose.

"You'll see me next weekend." Lennox kissed her gently. "And for the next month after that here, Kenz."

Kenzie pulled back with shock in her eyes.

"What are you talking about?"

"I didn't take the part, Kenzie," she revealed. "You haven't been keeping up with the trades at all, have you?"

"No, I didn't want to hear…" Kenzie stopped herself. "Marco said you'd signed on."

"Marco doesn't know what he's talking about." Lennox laughed. "My agent hasn't made it known yet, because he's still hoping I'll change my mind. But, considering I'd have to be there next week, I don't think that's happening." She met Kenzie's eyes again. "I'm sorry. I should have told you all this last night, but we just fell back into things, and then we didn't talk, and I didn't want to talk about anything that might–"

"Make me run again?"

"Yeah. I only came this weekend because I wanted to make sure you still wanted me. I called you to tell you I was coming, but I stopped leaving voicemails a while ago. And I thought about sending a text…"

"But you were scared I'd tell you not to come?"

"Yes," Lennox returned and sighed. "I'm flying back next Saturday, Kenzie. I'm staying at Peyton and Dani's place in London. And I want you to stay there with me."

She squeezed Kenzie's hand.

"You gave up the part for me?"

"I gave up the part for me. I didn't want it. The thought of working that hard for the next four years, with no break, made me realize that my heart's not in it right now. I need some time off, and I want to spend that time with you."

"Are you sure? This was a huge–"

"Opportunity?" Lennox laughed. "No, it wasn't. I mean, yeah, it is. But it's for someone else. Kenz, I don't exactly need opportunities like that. I get offers all the time, and I can spend my break looking through some scripts and finding one I really want to do, or maybe I won't. I don't know. I just know I have more than enough money, and I don't need an opportunity like this. Let it be someone's big breakout role while I'm taking a vacation and spending time with the woman I love."

"Will you end up resenting me if whoever gets it ends up winning all the awards?" Kenzie lifted a concerned eyebrow.

Lennox laughed and stood. She slid the dress she hadn't bothered to zip off her body and stood at the side of the bed, dressed in only her underwear.

"Mackenzie, I couldn't care less about the awards; winning them or losing them. I don't think I ever have. I just want to spend the rest of the time I have today with you, in this room, talking about anything and everything before I have to leave. And then, I want to call you when I get home, and every morning and night until I can come back." She slid under the blanket. "So, if you don't care if I ever win an Emmy or another Golden Globe, then I'd like you to slide back in here with me and ignore that phone, order some breakfast, and catch up with me on what we missed."

Kenzie smiled, though seemingly reluctantly at first, before it took over her entire face, and she stood.

"Let me at least get you something else to wear first. Not that I don't love you in underwear and nothing at all, but if we're just going to talk – you need to cover up. And I don't think that dress is going to do it."

Lennox laughed as she sat up and watched Kenzie move to the drawer to pull out a shirt and a pair of her shorts, tossing them to Lennox, and then grab the room service menu.

"Okay, we're ordering food, because I didn't eat at all yesterday. And then, you're telling me about your apparent lesbian co-star and if I need to crowbar her kneecaps or something."

"What?" Kenzie chuckled and opened the black binder to find the menu page.

"Has she hit on you?"

"Lennox, she spent last night hitting on you," Kenzie explained. "And don't think I didn't want to smack the shit out of her for it."

Lennox laughed and pulled the shirt over her head before standing to slide the shorts over her legs.

"Babe, you're missing something." She pointed at Kenzie's bare lower half.

"Oh!" Kenzie seemed to realize she'd yet to put on pants or underwear.

She shook her head and stood back up, leaving the menu on the bed for Lennox to look over.

CHAPTER 26

It took everything in Kenzie to have to say goodbye to Lennox when it was time for her to leave for the airport. Every ounce of energy she had in reserve, Kenzie used it in their last long kiss before she watched Lennox head out the back door of the hotel's restaurant to avoid the press and fans that had gathered out front since the pictures and the story of their affair had been released. Lennox had no tears in her eyes, but Kenzie sensed they would likely emerge, and she hated that she continued to, somehow, be responsible for Lennox's tears. But they smiled in the end, because they knew they'd be seeing each other in only a week; and they could do a week apart.

Lennox had been right. Things would be better this time because they had each other. Kenzie wouldn't retreat into herself this time, and she wouldn't run away. Lennox had not only come after her; she had given up something everyone else had told her to take at least in part because of Kenzie and their new relationship. Kenzie would make it through this week, and then, they would be together. They would be in the same city, in the same building, and they would be together. That was all that mattered.

"Kenzie! Kenzie!" She'd never heard her name yelled so much in her life.

Every day she left the hotel, the press was there, and they wanted answers. They shouted questions about the movie every now and then, but most of the questions they yelled were about Lennox. Kenzie had yet to comment, which was only causing them to yell louder and scream Lennox's name as often as they could to try to get some kind of reaction out of her. Kenzie had heard Dani and Peyton's names mixed in there, too, but she slid into the black SUV the production team picked her up in each day, without a word.

Kenzie's publicist told her not to say anything until she had a chance to come up with a strategy for how to deal with this. She also admonished Kenzie for not telling her about Lennox to begin with, and then – for being so stupid and getting caught. Kenzie thought about firing her at the comments but decided she at least needed her to get her through this. Then, she'd reevaluate everyone she paid based on how they treated this situation and how they treated Lennox when the time came.

"Kenzie?" Mary knocked on the door of Kenzie's trailer as Kenzie sat reading a story that claimed she and Lennox had known one another for years and had been dating the whole time.

It was the second story she'd seen like that. Then, there was one that claimed Lennox was pregnant with their child. Another story had them living together already, and one suggested that their relationship was the reason Peyton and Dani finally had the courage to come out themselves. The one Kenzie hated the most, though, called Lennox a liar because she'd used Noah and Lucas – and, likely, countless other men – as a cover for her apparent lifelong love of women. Some of the comments on that story made Kenzie want to throw her computer at the wall, because none of that was true, and Lennox had made no comment about their current relationship or any of her past relationships since the story broke. Kenzie was starting to believe the "no comment" idea wasn't a good one.

"Come in." Kenzie closed the computer as Mary entered the trailer.

Things had been tense between them for the past several days, ever since Mary had practically thrown herself at Lennox, and Kenzie ended up making out with her girlfriend in public.

"I know you probably hate me... I get that I'm not your favorite person right now." She stood in front of the table that was both Kenzie's desk space and meal location in her small on-set trailer.

"I don't hate you," Kenzie replied. "You can sit down."

"Are you sure? I tried to make out with your girlfriend the other night."

"Wait. You what?" Kenzie's eyes widened.

"She didn't tell you I tried to kiss her, did she? I just let that slip, and now you hate me more."

"You tried to kiss Lennox? You knew her for three seconds."

"It was stupid. I sort of pre-gamed before we left for the club. Nora and I had a few drinks, and I was already tipsy when we got there. She said she'd dance with me, and I got a little ahead of myself and tried to kiss her. We weren't even on the dance floor yet. We were still off to the side. No one saw anything – thank God, because she pushed me away immediately, and I mean *immediately*. She saw me leaning in and practically jumped back into a wall and shoved my shoulders. I took the hint. But then, she must have seen you, because she turned her head and noticed something, and she smiled for a second before I offered to grab her a drink so that I could get away from the embarrassment. And then, I was even more mortified when I saw the two of you on the dance floor. Well, you know what happened next."

"Yeah."

"I just assumed she'd told you."

"She probably didn't want to embarrass you or get me

angry with you or something."

"She's too kind, then."

"She is," Kenzie agreed. "She actually asked me if you'd hit on me at all. I guess that makes sense now, considering you tried to shove your tongue down *her* throat after about thirty seconds. She probably thought you had tried the same with me."

"I would have, had I known." Mary laughed. "I'm kidding," she began. "Look, I didn't know about you two. I would not have done it, had I known. I think the alcohol and finally seeing Lennox Owen in person, after Marco and I had that whole thing, just got the better of me. I'm sorry. I honestly didn't know you *or* Lennox were gay, though."

"I am. Lennox isn't," Kenzie corrected. "Or, at least, she hasn't said she is. She's undefined at the moment."

"Got it." Mary nodded. "I just wanted to apologize to you. And, if I ever see her again, I will do the same. If you could maybe pass that along in the meantime, though, I'd appreciate it."

"I'll let her know," Kenzie offered.

"How long have you two been together? How have you kept her a secret there, Kenzie? She's Lennox Owen. Every person on earth would love to have her on their arm."

"I know," Kenzie admitted. "I still can't believe she's with me."

"Why not? You're gorgeous, too, and you're talented and smart. You're a catch, Kenzie Smyth."

"Thanks?" Kenzie wasn't sure how to reply. "We met about a month ago."

"Really? Only a month?"

"Yeah, at that July 4th thing Peyton invited us to."

"I still cannot believe Peyton Gloss and Dani Wilder are a couple. I mean, I knew about the rumors, but I never imagined either of them actually played for my team."

"They met, and that was it," Kenzie told her without revealing too much, since it wasn't her story to tell. "They fell in love with each other right away."

"And was that how it was with you and Miss Lennox?" Mary gave her shoulder a light shove, and Kenzie blushed.

"I guess it was, yeah." Kenzie smiled, because she couldn't not smile. "I had a crush on her for the longest time. I mean, I was a fan, like everyone else, and I thought she was so beautiful and funny in her interviews, and she seemed kind. I never thought I'd meet her. Then, I met Peyton, and I knew they were good friends, and Peyton invited me to this thing for the first time… and there she was. Lennox Owen was helping me with my bag and then finding me when I ran off because I'm not great at socializing with so many new people. And, suddenly, I was confessing my secrets and falling in love with her when she did the same. I thought it was just me. 'Lennox is straight,' I told myself. 'You have to stop thinking about her like that.' But then, there was something happening," Kenzie continued. "Something was really happening. And it wasn't only me; she felt it, too. And, by the end of it, we were together."

"And have been ever since," Mary stated as she smiled back at Kenzie.

Kenzie didn't know how to respond to that, so she just nodded and picked up the script she'd been avoiding reading.

"I should probably get back to this," she said instead.

"Sure. Sorry, I just interrupted you like that." Mary stood. "I'm happy for you two, Kenzie. You're cute together."

"Thanks."

"Oh, I heard she turned down *Phoenix Rising*. Marco was, obviously, very disappointed, but I assume that was because of you."

"She just didn't want to do it, I think. I guess I played a part in the decision, but it wasn't all about me."

"I'd wager it was mostly about you, the way she was kissing you the other night."

Kenzie's blush returned, and she looked back down at her script. Mary took the hint and left the trailer, closing the door behind her. Kenzie's phone buzzed, and she lowered the script to see a text message from Lennox. She shouldn't even be awake back in the States, but Kenzie picked up the phone, went to the message, and smiled.

"Hey," she greeted after dialing Lennox's number. "You should be asleep."

"I get to see you tomorrow. How am I supposed to sleep knowing that? I would've called, but I wasn't sure if you were on set."

"I'm waiting for lighting," Kenzie shared. "I've probably got another hour until they're ready for me."

"And… are you alone?" Lennox's tone had shifted, and Kenzie recognized it.

"Lennox!"

"What?"

"I am not having phone sex with you in my trailer. You'll be here tomorrow. We can have real sex."

"What if an orgasm will help me sleep?" Lennox teased.

"Then, give yourself one." Kenzie laughed back.

"You know I can't do that as easily as you can. But I might be able to, if you join me," Lennox pressed.

"Have you always been this dirty?" Kenzie joked.

"No, you bring it out in me, I guess. But, I'm just kidding. I love you, but I don't even think your voice could get me there tonight."

"What's wrong?" Kenzie leaned back.

"Nothing," Lennox lied.

"You're a terrible liar. Now I know why you lost that Oscar." Kenzie smirked.

"Hey, that's mean!" Lennox fired back, but playfully. "I'm fine. I'm just tired. It's been crazy here, and I miss you."

"I'm sorry about all this; the stories and stupid people who don't know you or us."

"I know. It's not your fault."

"I kissed you in public."

"And I kissed you back. It's not like I pushed you away and told you to save it for later, Kenz. I wanted to kiss you."

"Speaking of that night… I heard from Mary that there was something you left out."

"Oh, shit. She told you she tried to mount me in the club?"

"Mount you? No!" Kenzie laughed at the word choice. "The word she used was 'kiss,' Lennox."

"Well, it felt like a lot more than that when I pushed her back. She told you that part, right? That I pushed her back?"

"Yes. She was here to apologize, and she told me to tell you she's sorry, too."

"She should be. I just met her, and she's launching herself at me."

"She said she was tipsy and blamed the alcohol."

"Excuses, excuses." Lennox breathed deeply. "I saw you right after I pushed her, you know?"

"She said she thought you saw something, and she figured out later it might have been me."

"Oh, it was you," Lennox started. "I saw that hair pulled back and then that jacket. Where did you get that jacket? You look hot in it." She laughed and appeared not to require an answer before continuing. "I saw you, and the room went blurry."

"Were you drugged?" Kenzie teased.

"No. I'm just tired right now, so I'm not using the right word."

"And I thought you were a writer," Kenzie continued joking.

"You seem to think I am, anyway," Lennox replied. "Fine. Let me try again. I think I loved you from the moment I first laid eyes on you, Mackenzie Smyth. I'm talking about the first time I saw you, and not the first time I met you."

"Lennox."

"It was a picture in a magazine, and that was all I

needed. I just didn't know it yet. Then, I met you, and I did. I knew it, and it was perfect. You ran, and I was lost. I couldn't eat or sleep. My house didn't feel like home anymore, and I thought I'd never feel that perfection with you again. And then, last weekend, I'm in that club, and Mary tried to kiss me. I pushed her back, and there you were. You're taller than most, so I could see you. But, Kenzie, I can always see you. I would always be able to find you, to see you – to *really* see you. And you were so beautiful. You looked like you were on a mission, and I followed you with my eyes as the whole room left, and it was only you. I saw you, and you were anxious, and I had to go to you. I wrapped my arms around you, and I finally felt it."

"Felt what?" Kenzie whispered and wondered where her voice had gone.

"Home," Lennox replied. "It felt like home."

"I love you," Kenzie offered back, wishing she could deliver a speech to Lennox like the one she'd just received, that brought tears to her eyes.

"I love you," Lennox said back. "All the love songs," she said.

"What?" Kenzie laughed.

"Nothing." Lennox laughed it off, but Kenzie remembered her saying something like that to her before.

"Lennox?"

"Yeah?"

"You're my home, too."

Lennox didn't say anything, but Kenzie was certain she could feel her smile through the phone.

***

"When does she land?" Peyton asked Kenzie as Kenzie sat in her hotel room, wishing she could pick Lennox up at the airport, but the press outside the hotel that followed her everywhere she went, including to set, where security had to keep them back, made that impossible.

"She already landed. She should be here soon. I just wish she was here already."

"You two are so cute." Peyton laughed. "She's been so damn anxious all week, trying to make the week go faster so she could get to you."

"She's been dealing with a lot," Kenzie replied.

"Yeah, like missing her girlfriend."

"And the press."

"Yeah, they're a pain the ass."

"How are you and Dani doing with it?" Kenzie changed the subject after checking the time again.

"We're good. We planned for this, though. I told everyone on my team I was proposing, so they had the whole statement ready for release and a strategy plan. Now, we just have to wait them out. They'll get bored, eventually."

"But, you guys are fine just staying inside all the time?"

"Kenzie, Dani and I are more than fine. She's been thinking about taking some time off anyway, and she is considering going to school for photography. She's working on putting together a portfolio, and I'm writing. I'm just sitting around the house, with my gorgeous and talented fiancée, writing love songs about her and using the recording studio I had built in when we bought the place to lay down the tracks. It's like a perfect vacation for us."

"Love songs, huh?" Kenzie smiled.

"Yeah, all my love songs are about her. You know that."

Kenzie looked off at the wall of horrible-patterned hotel wallpaper, that clashed with both the pattern and the color of the carpet, and realized what Lennox had been saying all along.

"All the love songs?" she mumbled to herself.

"Did Lennox tell you about that?"

"Huh?" Kenzie snapped back to attention.

"I knew I was right about you two. All the loves songs are about you to *her*, and all the love songs are about her to *you*; aren't they?"

***

"God, I missed you like crazy," Lennox announced the moment Kenzie opened the door to her hotel room and immediately pulled Kenzie into her.

"I missed you, too." Kenzie breathed her in and ran her hands under the back of Lennox's shirt, needing to feel her skin.

"I swear, it took me forever to get here. The traffic is horrible right now." Lennox pulled back and stared into Kenzie's eyes. "Hi."

"Hi," Kenzie greeted back and leaned in, applying a gentle kiss to her lips.

"Do that again." Lennox pulled her back in and kissed her more deeply. "Worth the wait," she commented when they pulled apart. "So many things I want to do right now… I don't know where to start."

"Like what?" Kenzie chuckled and asked.

"You want the list?" Lennox smiled at her.

"How can I help you do them if I don't have the list?" Kenzie pulled Lennox farther into the room and then reached for the large bag she'd left in the hallway. "Is this all you brought?"

"I had some stuff shipped to the house already. This is just the stuff I didn't want to ship." Lennox sat on the bed and watched Kenzie as she rolled the bag toward the desk. "Ready for the list?"

"Sure." Kenzie laughed.

"Okay. I am starving – I am not built for plane food, even when it's a private jet my best friend lets me borrow; and I haven't eaten since yesterday, I think."

"We can order room service."

"And I am exhausted and feel like I need to sleep for a week."

"You're sitting on a bed." Kenzie pointed out from her standing position.

"And I want to get you in it with me and tear off those

clothes." Lennox tugged on the T-shirt Kenzie was wearing and yanked her closer to her. "I think I just decided what I want first."

Kenzie smiled as she moved to straddle Lennox on the end of the bed and wrapped her arms around her neck.

"Is that the whole list?"

"Not the whole list, but the top three." Lennox ran her hands up and down Kenzie's back under the shirt, and Kenzie realized she was trying to take off her bra.

"You looking for something there, Lennox?"

"Yeah, your boobs. Take this off." She lowered her hands to the hem of Kenzie's shirt and lifted it.

Kenzie laughed wildly and climbed off her to straighten her shirt.

"We should wait to do that until we're at the house. I'm all packed and ready to go, so you need to decide. Room service here first, or pick up something on our way to the house? I have a car waiting outside."

"Front or back?" Lennox asked, and Kenzie knew what she meant.

"Out back. The hotel knows we'll be making our escape. And I think they're both glad to see me go, and probably a little upset, too, since their hotel is getting all sorts of press right now."

"Yeah." Lennox's mood seemed to change at the mention of the press. "They caught me at the airport, so prepare for more. They know I'm here. One of them followed the car and almost rear-ended us, according to the driver."

"What?" Kenzie sat down next to her on the bed and took her hand. "Babe, are you okay?"

"I like when you call me that." Lennox's smile returned, and she placed her head on Kenzie's shoulder.

"I know."

"And yes, I'm okay now. I would like to try to avoid them if we can. I don't think anyone knows we're planning on staying at Peyton's place, so we might have a few days of privacy before they figure that part out."

"Well, I have a few days off, so the timing is good. It won't raise suspicion that I'm not leaving the hotel each morning. Once they get ahold of the call sheet with my name on it, though, and I don't leave here in the morning, they're going to figure something's up."

"Then, let's enjoy the time we have before that happens." Lennox lifted her head and kissed Kenzie's neck. "Let's get out of here. We can pick something up on the way."

"And when we get there, you'll give me the rest of your list?" Kenzie requested.

"I'll think about it. But, first, I want hours in bed with you. I don't care if we're clothed or naked. I want to relax with you. We've never been able to just relax together."

"I seem to recall us having several days of supposed relaxation."

"With drill sergeant Peyton on our backs to participate and eat meals with the rest of the group instead of lying around all day? Yeah, love that girl, but I want me and my girl to have a whole day where we do nothing."

"Nothing?" Kenzie lifted her eyebrows.

"Eat." Lennox kissed Kenzie's lips. "Sleep." She kissed her again. "Sex." She kissed Kenzie once more. "That's my list." Lennox stood and pulled Kenzie up with her. "Now, let's get out of here."

Kenzie grabbed her large roller, Lennox grabbed her own, and they left the room together to proceed to the elevator. They resisted touching since there were cameras in the high-class hotel elevators that would catch them, and they both knew it would take no time at all for that video to be released online. It was difficult for Kenzie, to stand next to Lennox and not touch her. Lennox's hair was pulled back and slightly wind-blown, and she'd worn no makeup, which was how Kenzie preferred her. Her lips were red and full, and Kenzie knew how soft they were. Her neck was long, and her V-neck shirt gave Kenzie a glimpse of the cleavage beneath. Kenzie gulped silently and continued to stare.

"You see something you like there, Kenz?" Lennox mocked without turning to face her.

"All the love songs," Kenzie uttered, and that earned her a surprised expression from Lennox before the elevator opened on the basement floor, where they were met by two members of hotel security.

The smile that had appeared on Lennox's face disappeared instantly when she saw them, and she took Kenzie's hand. The security guards helped with their bags while they made their way toward the exit and into the waiting car. Their bags were loaded into the trunk, and Kenzie watched as Lennox glared around to see if they'd been noticed before they were finally able to pull away and head toward the house.

CHAPTER 27

LENNOX made her way into Peyton's London townhouse, and Kenzie followed behind with her bag. Lennox closed the door behind them both and held up the bag of takeout they'd had the driver stop for on the way.

"Late lunch and then sleep?" Lennox proposed.

"Whatever you want." Kenzie smiled at her and looked around at the expansive foyer.

"You've never been here, have you?" she asked.

"No." Kenzie shrugged.

"Let's take this to the kitchen and eat, and then, I'll give you the tour before sleep." Lennox held out her hand for Kenzie to take, which she did. "I almost bought a place in London last year."

"Yeah?"

"Yeah. I looked, but I didn't see anything I was crazy about before I got busy with work again." Lennox looked down at three boxes on the white marble floor as they headed out of the foyer, past the staircase, and toward the kitchen. "The caretaker must have brought my stuff in."

"Caretaker?" Kenzie asked.

"Whenever Peyton's not at one of her properties, she hires someone to take care of it."

"So, someone's going to be here when we're here?"

"No, they won't come while we're here. It's a service she uses. She's already told them to leave this place alone for the next month." Lennox glanced sideways at Kenzie as she pulled her into the kitchen. "What about you? Ever thought about investing in other properties?"

"I guess, but I haven't looked seriously yet. I just have my place in LA," Kenzie said.

"Have a seat." Lennox motioned to one of the four

stools at the long kitchen island. "She redid this whole place when she bought it. She and Dani had just met, and she started spending a lot of time with other models. A lot of them are British. She wanted a place where they could all hang out in private and have fun, so she remodeled the kitchen to make it bigger, and even added another bedroom among other things." Lennox set the bag of food on the island and looked around. "It's nice. Peyton always has had good taste."

The kitchen was massive. Along with the island that could easily fit more than the four stools, there was a long kitchen table with bench-style seating made of dark weathered wood. The cabinets were lighter, to offset the darkness, and the countertops were a darker shade of marble than the floor. The appliances were all brand new and stainless steel. The refrigerator reminded Lennox of a restaurant-style fridge as it was see-through, with double doors and filled with food of all kinds.

"Lennox?" Kenzie brought her out of her stare.

"Sorry. I guess I'm more tired than I thought."

"Or hungrier than you thought. You're staring at the fridge." Kenzie turned her head toward it and then back at her.

"I was just thinking that Peyton must have done that for us to make sure there was food here when we arrived. She's just amazing sometimes." Lennox smiled and placed a hand on Kenzie's cheek. "Let's eat, and I'll give you the tour."

She sat next to Kenzie, and they used the plastic cutlery that came with their grilled chicken salads, and ate in relative silence for several minutes before Lennox's phone buzzed in her pocket. Assuming it was Peyton, calling her to make sure she'd arrived safely, Lennox pulled it out and was surprised to see her publicist's name on the screen.

"You can get that," Kenzie told her.

"It's just my publicist. I'll get back to her later." She ignored the call and put the phone on silent.

"Everything okay over there?" Kenzie asked. "I mean, with me here, and you being there… You had to deal with a lot of it on your own."

"It's fine. I've dealt with this stuff before." Lennox let out a deep breath and refocused on finishing her salad. "So, if you could buy a house anywhere, where would it be?" She turned to Kenzie with a smile.

"Where are you in this hypothetical?" Kenzie gave her a shy smile.

"Hopefully, right next to you," she replied honestly.

***

"Okay, so the living room and the den, that Peyton mainly uses as a writing room and an office, are on the first floor," Lennox informed as they walked briskly past the rooms.

She was really just giving Kenzie an overview so that the woman could easily navigate the place and they could get upstairs to relax.

"This floor has two guest bedrooms and one guest bath, along with a game room." Lennox pointed out as they continued past that floor and up the stairs. "The third floor has two more guest rooms, two guest baths, and another office, that can also be a guest room if they need it. And this floor has the master bedroom with a bath and a separate staircase that leads to the rooftop pool, that Peyton was smart enough to cover up with, essentially, another roof and the walls so the paps couldn't sneak a peek when they decide to swim," she explained. "Come on."

She pulled Kenzie's hand as they headed into the master bedroom. She'd already brought their bags up the small elevator, that only fit two people in, at most, and was mainly used to get stuff from one floor to the other, while Kenzie had cleaned up from their meal.

"Here's where we'll be sleeping for the rest of our time in London," Lennox introduced and watched as Kenzie took in the space.

Peyton had a thing for white linen, and the bed, Lennox knew, had high thread count soft white sheets, a white duvet over them, and several white pillows adorning the bed. The walls, though, were pale green with white crown molding. She had guessed once that the green had been Dani's choice, and Peyton had confirmed it. Next to the king bed, there were two end tables made of dark wood, and a large flat-screen TV hung on the wall above the dresser the two shared. There were two comfortable recliners off to the left, and the master bathroom was off to the right.

"It's beautiful," Kenzie remarked and squeezed Lennox's hand. "I was fine at the hotel, but this is a lot better."

"Come on." Lennox pulled her toward the bathroom, where she showed Kenzie the steam shower with three showerheads, a large Jacuzzi bathtub, and a large walk-in closet that was relatively empty, since Peyton and Dani didn't usually stay here more than a few times a year. "All our stuff will fit."

"I didn't bring that much with me," Kenzie shared and wrapped her arms around Lennox's waist from behind as they looked into the closet. "I have one bag. I'm working, so they dress me."

Lennox turned in her arms and met her eyes.

"And I get to undress you." She kissed Kenzie's lips.

"You said you wanted to sleep."

"I do," Lennox relented, and just the mention of the word *sleep* had her holding back a yawn. "I'm thinking about maybe taking a bath first, though. I think it will help me relax."

"I'm not helping?" Kenzie asked and placed her hands on Lennox's hips.

"You are more than helping. But, with work, everything else, and missing you, it's just been a rough month, and I feel like this is the first chance I've had to unwind."

"Bath first, then," Kenzie agreed and moved toward the tub where she closed the drain and turned on the water.

"I don't know, maybe Peyton has some bubble bath, or some candles or something around here." She looked around as if assessing where they would likely be stored.

"I prefer the jets to the bubbles, and we can dim the lights, but I want you in there with me," Lennox told her. "Maximum relaxation can only be achieved if you're holding me." She meant it, too.

Lennox felt as if the only time she'd ever been fully relaxed, calm, and also completely herself, had been every moment she'd spent with Kenzie since they'd met.

"I'll grab towels. You get the stuff you need out of your bag, and we'll take a bath," Kenzie offered and kissed Lennox before moving to the closet to locate the towels.

Lennox headed into the bedroom, unzipped her luggage, and reached for her toiletry bag and a pair of soft pants, new underwear, and a white tank top, which she stared at for a minute.

"Lennox?" Kenzie's questioning voice asked, and Lennox turned to see she was standing in the doorway to the bathroom. "Everything okay?"

"I was wearing this the day we met." Lennox held up the shirt.

"Trust me, I remember," Kenzie replied.

"I remember Peyton packing your things that last day," she started and stared down at the shirt in her hand. "I couldn't fully process what was happening. I just watched her shove clothes into that bag." She pointed at Kenzie's roller.

"Lennox, I'm so sorry." Kenzie moved toward her.

"I don't know why I thought of that just now," she said. "Sorry, I guess I just went back there for a second."

Kenzie was in front of her, taking the shirt and other articles out of her hand to toss onto the bed. She lifted Lennox's shirt up and off her body before undoing her jeans and helping her out of them. Lennox let her unclasp her bra and slide her panties off, too, while she stood there, not moving. She was so tired.

"I am so sorry I did that to you," Kenzie said after a moment.

"Do you have my sweatshirt? I saw Peyton pack it, and I remember thinking I'd rather you have it because at least then you'd still have a piece of me. It would be with you, and maybe you'd call me to try to return it or something."

"I have it. I brought it with me." Kenzie lifted her own shirt off her body before moving to her bag, unzipping it, and reaching for the sweatshirt, which she removed and held out to Lennox. "I haven't even washed it. I haven't worn it either. I sleep with it sometimes. It still smells like you. It's been fading, but there's still a little there."

"I like that." Lennox smiled at her and took the sweatshirt from Kenzie's hand. She threw it onto the bed and walked the few steps toward her girlfriend, taking off her bra, her pants, and underwear, leaving her naked in front of Kenzie. "I'll wear it later for you."

"Okay," Kenzie agreed with a smile. "Bath?"

"Yes."

They sank into the large tub together. Kenzie sat behind her – legs spread and arms wrapped around Lennox, pulling her tightly to her own body and offering the safety and comfort that Lennox had craved for weeks, but especially in the past week, when she'd been swarmed by press and amateurs who wanted a shot of her leaving somewhere. They wanted to know about Kenzie and their relationship, and accused her of lying about who she was or how long they had been together. One of Noah's big fans had even thrown a rock through her car window. Luckily, Lennox hadn't been in it at the time, but the woman had filmed the whole thing and posted it online. Lennox thought about pressing charges but decided it would only make things worse. The window was repaired, and Noah even called her when he'd heard the news about her dating a woman to ask her if she was gay.

They hadn't spoken in years and, out of the blue, he wanted to know if she had been gay the whole time and if that was the reason it hadn't worked between them. Lennox had to remind him that the reason it hadn't worked out was because he ran off when she'd needed him, and they'd ended their conversation. She hadn't heard from Lucas, but she hadn't expected to, since their relationship – though long-term – had never been the forever kind. And Aaron had called her to ask the same question Noah had. Lennox had explained how it all went down and apologized, because the press had been on him as well, due to the story of her relationship with Kenzie breaking at around the same time the world found out Aaron and Lennox were no longer casually dating.

It had been a whirlwind. Lennox had gotten used to the press and cameras and people staring at her, whispering as she walked past, long before this; but it was different this time. People had always been supportive of her before. She was America's sweetheart for the longest time. And, suddenly, they were all against her; calling her a liar and a cheater, and some even said she was going to hell because she loved a woman. It had been more intense than she'd anticipated, and it was starting to weigh on her.

As Kenzie slowly lathered her skin with her favored soap, Lennox closed her eyes and let the lavender scent move over her while Kenzie hummed softly into her ear, soothing her to sleep. When she woke, it was because Kenzie was trying to shift beneath her, and Lennox snapped to attention, realizing she was still in the water and that the water was now cold.

"How long was I out?" she asked as she sat up, allowing Kenzie to do the same.

"Only about an hour," Kenzie replied. "I think. There's no clock in here." She sat up as well. "I wanted to run the water to make it hotter, but I couldn't reach the handle without moving you, and I didn't want to wake you."

"You let me sleep on you for an hour in lukewarm water?" Lennox turned in the wide tub to face her.

"Yes," Kenzie answered plainly, as if it was nothing.

"And what did you do the whole time I was out?"

"Counted."

"Counted what?" Lennox laughed.

"First, the tiles on the wall behind us." Kenzie nodded toward the wall with white and light-green tiles. "I did the white ones first and then the green. I counted the lines in the wallpaper after that. There are two hundred and fourteen." Kenzie pointed to the thin stripes of gray on the wallpaper opposite them. "And then, I had to get creative," she laughed.

"How so?" Lennox let the drain plug up to allow the cold water to escape.

"I didn't have much else to count, and I wanted to touch you to pass the time, but I thought I might wake you. So, I counted the flecks of silver that sometimes show in your eyes. I had to do it from memory. There are four in each eye that show up regularly when the light hits them a certain way, but I've seen more, too. So, I counted them, and that made me think of the last time I had seen them below me." Kenzie began to blush.

"And?" Lennox pulled her closer after she plugged the drain again and started the hot water back up.

"And I..."

"You?" Lennox ran her hands up the inside of Kenzie's thighs.

"You know what happened. I couldn't control it. I thought of you and I, and the last time we were together, and you were here, pressed against me, and–"

"And you came?" Lennox exclaimed a little louder than she intended. "While I was asleep on top of you, not touching anything?"

"Yes."

"Silently?"

"Yes. But you were touching me, technically. You shifted once, and your butt kind of ended up against me, and–"

Lennox interrupted her explanation with loud, wild

laughter, and Kenzie's blush spread across her face as she lowered her head.

"No, baby. Don't be embarrassed." Lennox wrapped her arms around her neck and pulled her closer. "I love that you can do that. I can't believe that you *can* do that, but I love it." She kissed Kenzie gently. "I wish I could do that."

"It's not as good now," Kenzie said.

"What do you mean?" Lennox asked and shut off the hot water.

"Now that I know what it can be like, it's not as good."

"Keep going," Lennox encouraged, knowing Kenzie was thinking something that she couldn't verbalize easily.

"It's different with you." Kenzie wrapped her legs around Lennox, which forced Lennox to straighten her own legs, and allowed Kenzie to straddle her. "What you make me feel when you touch me – I don't feel that on my own. I never have. And so, even though I *can* do that, it's not as good as when you touch me." She leaned down and kissed Lennox, wrapping her arms around her neck. "And I have missed you touching me."

"I've missed that, too." Lennox let out and kissed between Kenzie's breasts. "I've missed that like crazy."

"Can we finish this up and go do that out there?" Kenzie asked as Lennox took a nipple into her mouth.

"Why wait?" Lennox's hand slipped between Kenzie's legs, and Kenzie's hips bucked at the contact. "One in here, and then we go out there." She didn't ask.

Twenty minutes later, they were lying in bed, with Kenzie on top of her, stroking Lennox softly while kissing her neck. Lennox came the moment she slid inside, and then Kenzie made her come again before she slid off to lie on her side. Lennox rested her head on Kenzie's shoulder and felt Kenzie's fingertips on her bare back as the touches, again, pulled her to sleep.

CHAPTER 28

KENZIE left the bedroom shortly after she woke up from her short nap, and she allowed Lennox more time to sleep before she would wake her up so that Lennox could get adjusted to the time difference and sleep through the night. Kenzie threw on a pair of shorts and a shirt and then made her way through the house. She almost went up to see the pool but decided she wanted Lennox to show her that part of the house later and, instead, she headed downstairs and explored the other guest rooms. She noted Peyton's consistent decorating style, and then made her way to the first floor, where she took in Peyton's office – that was more like a sofa with instruments all around, including the grand piano in the corner. There was sheet music on the stand next to it, and Kenzie approached to see that it was one of Peyton's songs. For a moment, she wished that she had Peyton's way with words. Peyton could take the simplest moment of her life and turn it into a powerful summer anthem, or a shared moment with Dani about ice cream – and make it into a long song that everyone sings along with at her shows.

Kenzie made her way to the kitchen to grab a snack and something for when Lennox woke up. She knew Lennox liked apples, and, luckily, Peyton had seen to it that the bowl on the island was filled with fruit. Kenzie picked out two green ones and then noticed Lennox's phone light up without a sound. Her eyes naturally went to the source of light. And when she recognized that it was Lennox's phone, she pulled her eyes away. She wouldn't make the same mistake twice. But then, she heard her own phone buzz across the counter. She moved to see who was calling, assuming it was Peyton, checking in, but discovering it was Carson, her agent, instead. Kenzie didn't want to ruin the perfect day that had been Lennox's return, but with Lennox asleep and nothing else for her to do at the moment, she figured she would take the call, tell him to leave her alone for the next few days, and return to Lennox's side to wake her.

"Hey, Carson."

"How did they get it?"

"What? Slow down." Kenzie sat on the stool at the end of the island. "How did who get what?"

"They're quoting a source close to Kenzie Smyth," he said as if she understood. *"Kenzie and Lennox met only a short month ago but fell in love at first sight and have been together ever since. Kenzie had hidden her sexuality from her fans and defines herself as gay, while she was quoted as saying Lennox is undefined and has chosen not to label herself. Lennox made the trip to visit her girlfriend last week and was caught in a passionate kiss on the dance floor. After which, they had to leave the club immediately or, our source says, they might have combusted, it was so hot. Lennox has since returned to London to spend the next month with her love while Kenzie wraps up filming there. Our source also says that they have left the hotel Kenzie had been staying in to stay at a friend's house in London. It's believed that the house belongs to Peyton Gloss, who recently got engaged to Dani Wilder."* He stopped, and Kenzie heard him throwing paper. "I don't give a shit about that part. Kenzie, did you give them this? How did they get this?"

"I didn't give anybody anything," she replied and felt the heat in her cheeks. "Carson, I haven't spoken to anyone about Lennox. I've been avoiding the press and not saying a word."

"Could it have been someone in that camp you went to? Maybe one of Peyton's friends, or even Lennox?"

"No, Lennox wouldn't have told anyone anything. She's been avoiding it, just like me." Kenzie stood and let out a deep sigh before shaking her head and walking toward the front door. Without moving the closed curtain, she peeked out the window to the right of the door and noticed three press vans and an already gathering small swarm of people with cameras and microphones. "They're here, Carson."

"What? Where?"

"The press found us. We're at Peyton's house in London."

"How the fuck did they find you?"

"I don't know. No one at the camp would have said anything. I trust them."

"Then, how?"

"Shit!" Kenzie exclaimed in realization. "Mary."

"Mary?"

"Marry fucking Matthews," she repeated in anger.

"Your co-star?"

"She met Lennox last week, and she tried to kiss her. She didn't know we were together. And yesterday, she apologized to me. She asked me questions, and I didn't think anything of them."

"Kenzie, you know better than that."

"She's an actress, and she's gay, too. We're in the middle of shooting a movie together."

"Well, it's out there now. It's not terrible. We just weren't prepared for it."

"What do we do now?"

"Ignore it. It's everywhere today, but tomorrow, people will move on to something else. Maybe you can talk your friend Peyton into leaving her house or something. That'll change the narrative."

"I'm not doing that."

"I'm joking. I'll call Lennox's publicist, and we'll talk about how to handle it. I'll get back to you. But you should leave the house. I can get a new hotel room booked for you now. I'll use your alias."

"I have to talk to Lennox first."

"Talk to her, and I'll go ahead and book it. I don't want you at the same hotel as the rest of the cast, especially if your fucking co-star is their source. Just keep your phone on you. I'll text you the hotel and send a car for you."

"I don't know yet, Carson. Let me talk to her." Kenzie made her way up the stairs. "She may still want to stay here."

"She can stay there, if she wants. You're in a hotel under an alias for the rest of the shoot."

"You don't get to decide where I live. I'll talk to Lennox, and I'll call you back." Kenzie hung up the phone and made her way back to the master bedroom, where she saw Lennox lying on her stomach, dead to the world. She hated to wake her with this news. She'd wanted nothing more than to let Lennox sleep and relax in this little place where no one knew they were there. And now, that was ruined.

"Lennox? Babe?" Kenzie sat on the side of the bed and rubbed her back. "Lennox?"

"Hey. Why aren't you in bed?" Lennox turned on her side to face her. "And why are you dressed?" She smiled at Kenzie.

"I have some bad news."

"What?" Lennox awakened fully and rolled over onto her back, sitting up. "What happened?"

"Someone leaked to the press, and they know we're here. There are a bunch of reporters already outside."

"Shit!" Lennox exclaimed. "Who even knew we were here? I didn't tell anyone."

"I might have let it slip to Mary that we were staying at Peyton's place."

"You think she would have–"

"There's more. There's a *source* the press is quoting, and I told Mary stuff yesterday, when she came in to apologize. She's the only one I've talked to about it, and I think she might be their source."

"I haven't said anything." Lennox lifted herself up and off the bed in one swift movement, reaching for her clothes on the ground. "Why did you?"

"I thought I was talking to a gay cast member. I thought I could trust her."

"You were wrong, obviously. Shit, Kenzie. There's no backdoor to this place. We have to go out the front. Get your stuff. I'll try to pack and find us a hotel."

"Hey, stop." Kenzie pulled back on Lennox's hand to get the woman to face her. "It's okay. We don't have to rush. I'll call Carson back and tell him to get us the hotel and the car. He's already calling your publicist to figure out how to address this. We can slow down."

"The slower we move, the more of them will be out there. Trust me, I know. I've been dealing with it all week."

"So have I, Lennox," Kenzie reminded. "We're going through this together."

"No, we're not." Lennox threw her shirt on and stopped. "You went through it over here, in a hotel where you had security usher you out the back door of the hotel and onto the set. I had people lining up at the gate of my house – which is on every damn Hollywood star map, and snapping pictures of me as I left or returned, following me around town as I tried to take care of the crap I needed to move my life here for the next month, and then shattering my car window because I'm, apparently, a gay whore that didn't deserve my ex-boyfriend." Lennox slid on underwear and shorts.

"What? Lennox, what?" Kenzie took her hand. "What are you talking about? Someone smashed your window? Why didn't I hear about this?"

"Because I didn't want you to hear about it. I didn't want you to find out that my life has been hell ever since you left that damn summer camp." Lennox moved to the bathroom, and Kenzie stood completely still, not knowing what else to do. "Kenzie, come on." She touched Kenzie's back. "Look, I'm sorry. I'm just tired. Can we go? Have Carson get the hotel and the car, and let's just get somewhere else."

"Fine."

Kenzie called Carson back. He had booked three different hotels and leaked two of them to the press on purpose. One room was in Kenzie's name, one was in Lennox's, and the other one was with a new alias for the two of them when they wanted to travel together. When the car pulled up outside, they had barely been able to make it out through the still growing ground of press outside the door. They hadn't even had to call the police for help because the street had been clogged by the press vans and other cars, so the cops showed up and knocked on their front door just as they were ready to go. They had opened the door to two officers, explained the situation to them, and the police helped them part the crowd as they made their way toward the car. Their bags would be brought in for them later, once they could send someone, and Kenzie held tightly to Lennox's hand as she moved first through the cameras and microphones. She normally wouldn't have led them. Lennox had always been the one to speak for them or lead her through something. But Kenzie felt not only responsible for their situation but protective over Lennox, the woman she loved, and who had, apparently, been treated like shit ever since Kenzie had kissed her in public and started this whole thing.

Once in the car, the blackout windows gave them some privacy, but Lennox immediately picked up her phone and called her publicist. Kenzie sat still as she listened to the two of them try to figure out how to handle the situation. Kenzie heard Lennox suggest that maybe she should leave London, and that got Kenzie's attention. As her head snapped around to say something, Lennox's hand took her own and put it in her lap.

"I can come right back. I can even fake leaving or something," she said into the phone and pled with Kenzie with a silent stare. "Yeah, okay." Lennox hung up and continued her stare at Kenzie. "It might be for the best, Kenzie. London is notorious for letting the press run all over people. They'll keep working until they find us. If I leave, it will be easier."

"Easier?" Kenzie turned to stare out the window as

they drove along London streets. "Maybe easier, but not better; and not what I want, Lennox. You just got here. You literally just got here. It hasn't even been a day yet."

"I know. Let's just get to the hotel and see if anyone finds us by tomorrow." She leaned forward and addressed the driver. "Is anyone following us?"

"Yes, ma'am." He replied with a British accent. "I'm supposed to drive another two kilometers, and then, there's a drop off location in a blind alley. They won't be able to get through, and you'll be moved into a different car," he informed. "Don't worry; I work private security. I've done this before," he said, and Lennox leaned back.

"Good." Lennox rested her head on the back of the seat. "God, I just wanted a few days alone with you. Was that really so much to ask?"

"We can still have that, Lennox."

"Maybe." Lennox closed her eyes and let out another deep breath she had been holding. "It'll never be like how it was, though."

"What do you mean?" Kenzie squeezed her hand.

"At Peyton's little camp," she answered and opened her eyes to reveal they were welling up with tears. "We'll never get that back, Kenz."

Kenzie watched Lennox stare out the window until their car made two rapid turns at near-red lights and pulled into a slim cobblestone alley. There was another car waiting for them, and they climbed out and into it quickly before it backed away and joined the traffic on another street, taking them the rest of the way to their hotel, which was on the outskirts of the city. When they arrived, they were driven around back into the area for delivery trucks and let out of the car. The driver, another professional security Carson had hired, accompanied them to the doors, and then, to the freight elevator. He took it up to the fourth floor with them before checking the empty hallway and then moving them to the regular elevator, which they needed their room keys to activate to get up to the penthouse suite. He left them with their room keys and told them that he would be the one returning in a little over an hour with the bags. He gave them a name he would use when he called up to be let in. It was all very spy thriller, and Kenzie couldn't help but think that the reason Lennox was so calm, as she stared out the tinted windows toward the city, was because she was a slumdog and had done all these things in her movies.

"Lennox?" Kenzie stood still near the elevator over thirty feet away from Lennox, who was at the window on the other side of the large, open living room and kitchen space of the suite.

"Yeah?"

"I love you," Kenzie said.

"I know," Lennox replied and continued staring.

***

After their luggage had been brought up for them, along with food to get them through the night, Lennox sat on the couch, flipping through the channels on the TV in the living room, while Kenzie sat beside her, wondering how they'd gotten here. They hadn't spoken in over an hour, since Carson's call about what he wanted her to do. When he'd heard Lennox's suggestion that she leave London, he pushed Kenzie to that end. But Kenzie resisted, and Lennox sat there silently until he hung up.

"Babe?" Kenzie chanced after Lennox finally turned off the TV.

"Yeah?" She'd been watching story after story about them as they unfolded on various British entertainment shows.

"Do you want to go to bed? You didn't get that long of a nap earlier, and it's been a long day." Kenzie ran her hand through Lennox's hair.

"It's still kind of early." Lennox pointed at the time just below the TV. "Are you even tired?" She turned to Kenzie.

"Not really, but I can probably go to sleep if we go to the bedroom and try." Kenzie ran her thumb back and forth along Lennox's neck and felt her girlfriend relax into the touch. "I know things aren't great right now, but it'll get better soon."

"Soon?" Lennox closed her eyes and then laid her head down on Kenzie's lap. "It won't go away soon enough, Kenz. You have three days off. I wanted to spend them exploring the city with you."

"I know. I'm sorry." Kenzie ran her fingers through Lennox's blonde hair and put her free arm over her waist. "At least, we've both seen the city before; we've done the tourist thing."

"I haven't," Lennox announced.

"What?" Kenzie stared down as Lennox opened her eyes.

"I've been here at least twenty times. I don't know, maybe more." She met Kenzie's eyes. "I've always been here for work. It was mostly press junket stuff. I've never had a shoot here. I'd fly in for a couple of days, do over a hundred interviews, and move on. I've never seemed to have the time to see stuff when I traveled for work."

"You've never just taken a couple of days here and gone around like a tourist? Not even with Peyton?"

"I've been to Peyton's house here once before, and I stayed there for the night so I didn't have to stay in a hotel. She was here at the time, but we didn't leave. It was Fashion Week. She was here for Dani. I had an interview, and then, I had to go to Paris to do more."

"Lennox, have you ever just been a tourist in all these places you've visited?"

"When I was little, I guess. My parents would sometimes pass us off to nannies, and they'd take us places. We mostly went to amusement parks, if the weather permitted, or children's museums."

"Babe, we should go see stuff."

"I wanted to. I hoped we could explore together and

dress in camo if we had to, but that's near impossible now, Kenz." Lennox sat back up. "Maybe I should just go back to LA for a week or two and then come back. I can take Peyton's jet to a different, less known airport, and drive the rest of the way. We can find somewhere to stay outside of the city, out of the way."

"You keep suggesting you leave, Lennox. Do you want to go?" Kenzie slid away from Lennox on the sofa.

"No, baby." Lennox turned and moved into Kenzie, sliding her legs under the woman swiftly. "Kenzie, I told you what I want to do. We just can't do that right now."

"We can, though. They don't know we're here. We can head out tomorrow. I'll rent us a car to drive us, and we can wear hats. I have one you can borrow."

"Kenzie, not tomorrow, okay?" Lennox placed her hand on Kenzie's cheek. "Let just talk about it later, okay?"

"Yeah, okay," Kenzie gave in.

"I guess I am kind of tired. I'm going to bed, okay?" She kissed Kenzie's forehead and stood.

"Sure. I'll be right behind you."

"Okay."

Lennox walked into the bedroom. Kenzie stared after her, wondering where her girlfriend had gone. Maybe it wouldn't make that much of a difference if Lennox went back home. She wasn't exactly here right now, anyway.

CHAPTER 29

LENNOX'S first full day in London was spent in the penthouse suite of a hotel. In theory, that was the best way to start her first full day of vacation with Kenzie – stuck in the same space, but Lennox was off. She had a hard time being trapped like this. When she had gotten her first big break, she had been hounded. But when she went public with her relationship with Noah, she'd been stalked. The press never left her alone, and her fans followed her whenever they saw her out and about. At the time, she didn't live in a gated community with other celebrities, and she couldn't get away from it. She'd holed up in her house by herself most of the time because Noah was off working. It took months for the attention to calm down and for her to feel comfortable leaving her own house again. Lennox hated that time in her life. And while it didn't impact her relationship back then, she wasn't sure about today. This was different. Back then, she was just a girl who fell in love with a boy. Today, she was a woman who fell in love with another woman. She had been a liar and a cheater to many, who'd assumed Lennox had always loved women and had guys around as beards. She'd cheated on Aaron in the public's estimation, because the timing lined up that way.

She couldn't seem to look away from the TV or the stories online, where the comments called her a slut, a whore, and a sinner. That last one, at least, Lennox could push out of her mind because she didn't care, and it didn't bother her. The other comments hurt, though. Especially from the ones that said they'd been a fan and loved her work, but now they'd never see anything else she was in because of how she had lied to them or how she had, apparently, treated her ex-boyfriends. Little did they know, huh? Lennox kept trying to tell herself that. They didn't know her, and they didn't know what had happened in her past. They certainly didn't know anything about her feelings for Kenzie, or how disappointed she was in herself for treating Kenzie so poorly after Mary leaked parts of their private conversation.

When they'd woken up that morning, Kenzie had made them breakfast of toast and fruit with some coffee. She'd called down to the front desk to see about having something more substantive delivered to get them through the rest of the day before she called the director of her film and asked for a meeting the following day about Mary. Kenzie had been pissed. Lennox could tell she had been holding it back, and probably more for Lennox than for herself, but she was angry, and she still had to work with the woman. She had also called Peyton and Dani and asked if they thought there was any way anyone at the camp could have said anything. They'd both insisted it was impossible. The women there had known about Dani and Peyton for years and hadn't said a word. If they'd wanted to make some extra money or get more famous, they'd seen enough to write a book on Dani and Peyton.

No, it was Mary Matthews. She was a supporting cast member on Kenzie's movie; and while she'd had a good year, Lennox didn't see her lasting long in the business. She just wasn't talented enough. She did it for two reasons, in Lennox's estimation. She wanted to borrow fifteen more minutes of fame, and this gave her an opportunity. She went unnamed as the source at first, but would soon unveil who she was and give some kind of an exclusive interview. The other reason, Lennox could only assume, was because she had rebuffed Mary and pushed her away at the club. Lennox hadn't been gentle either. When she'd seen Mary – someone she'd only just met – staring at her like she was the hottest thing in the place, she'd known what she was after. But she'd been wrong in thinking that the woman had tact – or, at least, some self-control – because Mary had been on her in seconds and had Lennox shove her back. Those things, combined with Kenzie trusting her, gave her an in. And she'd taken advantage of it to their detriment.

"How about a movie?" Kenzie asked her after they finished their dinner and did the dishes provided in the suite.

"I was thinking about maybe just spending some time alone," Lennox returned and moved to the living room.

"You've spent most of the day alone," Kenzie said softly. "We've hardly spoken all day, Lennox."

"What are you talking about? We've been talking non-stop."

"No, we've been talking with other people on the phone, but that's not a conversation between us, Lennox. Talk to me, please. Tell me how you feel. Tell me about why the bitch, who threw a rock through your window and posted it online, isn't in jail? God, just tell me anything." Kenzie sat down next to Lennox on the sofa.

"We've switched places." Lennox opened her laptop and placed it on her lap.

"What?"

"Before, I was always asking you to tell me things. And now, you're begging me to talk," Lennox explained.

Kenzie turned to face her and waited. When Lennox said nothing, Kenzie stood and started walking toward the bedroom.

"Kenzie, wait. I'm sorry."

"It's fine. Just take the time you need. I'll be in the bedroom, running lines with myself, I guess." She hadn't turned around.

"Kenz, watch a movie with me, please," Lennox requested. "Tonight, can we just watch a movie and pretend we're in a theater, surrounded by people, because we're anonymous and we can go out in public and not get harassed? You can put your arm around me, and we can make out a little." Lennox smiled when Kenzie turned back. "I promise, we'll talk tomorrow about whatever you want, okay? Tonight, I could use a little normal."

Kenzie moved back to the sofa, picked up the remote control, and turned it to the hotel's ordering system before looking over at Lennox's computer.

"Are you writing?" she asked.

"Oh, I needed something to occupy my mind today, so I worked on something." Lennox closed the computer.

"Can I read it? What's it for?"

Lennox leaned in and realized she had been a bitch to her adorable girlfriend all day. She kissed Kenzie's lips gently and then nodded toward the TV.

"Normal tonight. You can read whatever you want later."

Kenzie smiled and kissed her again before sliding her arm around Lennox's shoulder, allowing Lennox to sink into her, fold up her computer, and put it on the empty sofa cushion.

"What movie do you want to watch?"

"Anything I'm not in," Lennox said and received a deep laugh from Kenzie. "How about porn?" she added and earned an even better laugh.

She then lifted her head up and watched Kenzie's eyes close in laughter, and the sound of it made Lennox feel free, even though she had been caged all day, and – to some extent – her entire life.

"I am not watching porn with you," Kenzie finally said.

Lennox moved to straddle Kenzie on the sofa, much to Kenzie's surprise and apparent delight, given the smile on her face.

"I love you. I just realized I haven't said that today. And today, of all days, I should say that to you."

"I love you, too." Kenzie placed her hands on Lennox's hips.

"Tomorrow, you have to meet with your director."

"Yeah. I can move it, though."

"Can you?"

"Yes, but not if you want to watch a bunch of dirty movies all day."

Lennox laughed and lifted her shirt up and off her body, leaving herself naked from the waist up.

"I was thinking maybe we could be tourists," she said and tugged upon Kenzie's shirt.

"What? Are you sure?"

"No." Lennox moved both of her hands into Kenzie's soft hair. "But I'm willing to try. I want to explore with you, Kenzie Smyth."

"There's no one I'd rather explore with, Lennox Owen."

Lennox's lips met Kenzie's before Kenzie pulled back and removed her own shirt, grabbed Lennox by the waist, and took a nipple into her mouth.

***

"I thought you two were staying inside indefinitely," Peyton said to her while Lennox finished getting dressed and Kenzie showered.

"I know. I feel like if things would have gone differently, we'd be in bed right now."

"You *can* be in bed right now."

"I mean, if it had been our choice… If we had been able to just live our damn life without everyone interfering – we'd be in bed for part of the day, and then, we'd go to dinner somewhere, like a normal couple."

"But you're not a normal couple, Len. You and Kenz are anything but normal. You've been famous forever, and she's in the prime of her career right now. This will blow over, sure, but you guys won't ever really be anonymous or be able to just go to dinner anywhere people have TV or the internet, without risking being recognized. That never bothered you before, though. What's up now?"

"I'm getting threats, Peyton."

"You're what?" Peyton exclaimed.

"You and Dani probably are, too."

"From the religious nuts? My security team goes through my mail now, just in case."

"I've had a few of those, but I'm getting others, too. I don't know… It just makes me nervous, and I don't want to bring Kenzie into that."

"Is she getting them, too?"

"No, just the religious-nut ones. She's actually in a lot better shape than I am about this." Lennox smiled at the thought. "She's keeping me together."

"I knew I liked that girl," Peyton remarked. "Do you need to borrow some of my security guys? I can get you a team if you want."

"That's the last thing I want."

"Tell me about it."

"We're going to go out today. I'm going to wear a hat with sunglasses and pretend I'm an American tourist, with my American tourist girlfriend, and put the rest of this stuff out of my mind."

"Sounds like a good idea. But, please be safe, okay?"

"I will."

"Okay. I love you."

"I know. Love you, too."

Kenzie emerged from the bathroom and entered the bedroom, with a towel wrapped around her, and her wet hair dripping onto the tiled floor.

"I'll just be a minute, and we can go," she said.

"Or, we could take a few minutes," Lennox suggested with a suggestive wink.

"How is it I'm the gay one, but you're the one who's all about sex with girls these days?" Kenzie laughed at her own joke.

"Not *girls*. Girl. *Woman*." Lennox pulled on Kenzie's hand to get her to stand in front of her. "And you know why."

"Because you love me."

"Yes." Lennox pulled on the towel to get it to drop and gawked at Kenzie's body. "And because you are the only one that has ever made me crave touching someone." She reached out and placed her hand between Kenzie's breasts. "When I touch you, the rest of the world disappears, Kenzie. And when you touch me, I'm in another world altogether; we're alone there, and it belongs to us."

"I'm going to ask Peyton to write me something."

"What?" Lennox laughed as she met Kenzie's eyes.

"You always make these beautiful speeches, and I don't have anything to give you in return. Peyton's a songwriter. I'm going to ask her to write something for me."

"Kenz, you don't need Peyton to write anything for you. Tell me how you feel right now," Lennox encouraged.

"Cold." Kenzie kissed Lennox's forehead and picked up the towel before moving to her bag to grab something to wear.

Lennox laughed as she watched her move.

***

Two hours later, they had finished up at a museum Kenzie had chosen, and while they were impressed by the art they had seen, they found the museum rather boring. The fact that they were out in public, though, and that no one had recognized them, was enough to sustain their smiles as they sat down at a small bistro to eat a late lunch.

"Do you realize this is the first restaurant we've ever been to together?" Kenzie asked her as their drinks were placed in front of them.

"I hadn't thought of that. But, yeah, I guess you're right," Lennox returned.

Their conversation and moods were light as they ate and drank and smiled at one another over their meal. Lennox noticed it first, but Kenzie was right behind her with a nod in the direction of the table where a teenage girl held her phone facing them and was either taking a picture or a video.

"We should go. If she posts it, the press will be here in under five minutes," Lennox said. "Let me get the check." She looked for their waiter, but he was standing in front of the computer, looking away from them. Not wanting to wait any longer, Lennox stood. "I'll be right back."

"Okay." Kenzie watched her walk away and lowered her head to try to keep more people from noticing them.

"You're Kenzie Smyth, right?" A voice questioned her in a British accent. "I read you were here. And that's Lennox Owen, right?" Kenzie looked up just as she pointed in Lennox's direction with her phone.

"We're just getting our check." Kenzie reached for her phone and opened the app to order a car for them, since they had walked the short distance from the museum to the bistro.

"You two are a couple, yeah?" the teenage girl pressed, and Kenzie looked up just in time for her to snap a picture of her. "Yeah, I knew it. I thought she was with Aaron Wilkes. So, was that a lie, or did she just cheat on him with you?" she asked.

Kenzie focused on the tablecloth and the feel of the fabric beneath her fingertips.

"I'm a big fan of Aaron's. He's totally sweet. I can't believe she'd do this to him. I'd never cheat on Aaron if I had him. Then again, I'm not a lezzie, so I definitely wouldn't do *that* to him."

"Can I help you?" Lennox asked when she approached the table, now standing behind Kenzie with her hands on Kenzie's shoulders.

"I was talking to your girlfriend and asking her how you could cheat on Aaron."

"Well, my girlfriend and I aren't answering any questions. We're leaving." Lennox squeezed Kenzie's shoulders.

"You must be a good fuck or something, for her to leave him for you," the girl said.

Kenzie's hand flattened on the table, and Lennox watched as she balled it back into a fist and wanted to say something but couldn't.

"Baby, let's go." Lennox placed her hand on top of Kenzie's, trying to get her to link their fingers. "Kenz?" She sat down in the chair next to Kenzie and watched her blank stare across the room. "Baby?" She took her hand and placed it on Kenzie's cheek. "We have to go, okay?"

"What's wrong with her? She got some kind of problem or something? Wait until they see this." Her phone was aimed at Kenzie.

Lennox didn't think. She stood, grabbed the phone, tossed it to the hard floor of the restaurant, and stomped on it.

"Now, no one is seeing anything. Leave us the hell alone," she instructed. Then, she opened her wallet, pulled out a respectable amount of currency, and threw it at her. "That should cover a new phone." She looked down at Kenzie. "Baby, come on." She grabbed Kenzie's hand more forcefully this time and pulled her toward the door. "Who the fuck raises a kid like that?" she said once they reached the sidewalk and then turned to see a camera aimed at her. "What do you want from us?" she half-yelled into it. "We're just trying to have lunch together. Can't you all leave us alone for one day?"

The car, Kenzie had apparently and thankfully ordered for them, had arrived, and Lennox moved the somewhat catatonic Kenzie inside before sliding in after her. It sped off and drove them the silent twenty minutes back to the hotel.

CHAPTER 30

"Baby, talk to me," Lennox said as she sat Kenzie on the sofa in their hotel room. "Are you okay?"

"I don't know," Kenzie finally uttered.

"Hey, there you are." Lennox touched her cheek.

"I froze, Lennox."

"I know, baby. It's okay."

"No, it's not," Kenzie argued. "It's not okay. She said things about you, and I wanted to tell her how wrong she was, and I couldn't. I just froze. Who does that?"

"It was the right thing to do."

"How?" Kenzie turned to her. "How was letting some teenager talk about my girlfriend like that the right thing to do?"

"Well, the wrong thing to do was to crush her phone under your foot and then berate the one member of the working press that showed up just in time to film your outburst. So, I'd say, of the two of us, your reaction was the best."

"That's never happened to me before. People recognize me, they ask for a picture or an autograph, but I've never had someone just walk up to me and judge me before."

"It doesn't matter." Lennox laid her head back against the sofa. "We tried, and we failed. We have to accept defeat."

"What?"

"We went out, and it didn't work. We'll have to deal with whatever story comes out about this and stay caged up for the next few weeks to avoid it happening again."

"I don't want that," Kenzie proclaimed.

"Well, neither do I, Kenz, but it's the hand we've been dealt. I'll stay here in the hotel, assuming they didn't track us here, and you go back to work."

"So, you're going to spend the next four weeks just staying in here?"

"What else am I supposed to do, Kenz? We go out there, and people feel comfortable saying things like that to us, and thinking something's wrong with you, and pissing me off to the point where I–"

"Something *is* wrong with me, Lennox."

"*Nothing* is wrong with you," she fought.

"I'm not like everyone else."

"And that's why I like you," Lennox replied. "Because you're nothing like everyone else. You're my Kenzie, and there's nothing wrong with you."

"I froze, Lennox."

"It's okay. A lot of people would have done the same thing."

"You didn't."

"Well, I've been dealing with this longer than you have."

"Since you first started acting?"

"Not exactly."

"Since you started dating me?" Kenzie asked, knowing the answer.

"It's not been fun."

"So, what do we do about it?" Kenzie asked.

"What I said. I'll lie low for a while, you'll finish filming here, and we'll go to New York, like we said."

"And you think New York is going to be better than this?" Kenzie questioned. "What do you think Dani and Peyton are going through right now?"

"They had a plan for this. We didn't," Lennox argued. "We were fine in our little bubble, and now…"

"And now, what?" Kenzie worried and knew she couldn't keep that off her face.

"And now, I don't know."

"What do you mean you don't know, Lennox?"

Lennox turned to face her.

"Maybe it would be better if I go home for a while?" she proposed. "And, before you say anything, it's not what I want, but this is more than I expected, Kenz. I wasn't prepared for this."

"You've had relationships in public before, Lennox."

"Not like this, Kenzie." She ran both hands through her hair.

"Because I'm a girl?"

"Because I'm crushing phones, Kenzie," Lennox professed. "I am not a violent person, but I wanted to beat the shit out of that girl today. And I'm angry all the time these days. It never used to bother me before, having the cameras around, but it does now. I think it's because even with Noah – and I did love Noah at one time – it never felt like this, Kenz. It never felt so real, so forever." Lennox ran her fingers along Kenzie's cheek. "I'm also much older than I was back then, and I've been through this before. It's not the same, obviously. It's worse *and* it's better at the same time."

"I don't understand."

"It's better because it's you, and I love you. I know that like I know my own birthday. I know I want you forever, Kenzie. It's worse because the comments aren't all good, like they were before. And people are saying things and doing things that didn't happen back then," Lennox paused. "I think I'm over it."

"Over it?" Kenzie's heart stopped beating in that moment, waiting for Lennox's response.

"Not over you, baby." Lennox tried to offer a small smile. "Over *it*. I'm over this business." She laughed, but it wasn't real laughter. It was laughter out of sadness. "I'm ready to just be done with it. And, unfortunately, people don't seem to be done with me."

"You want to be done with acting?"

"I don't know. Maybe. It feels like it." She leaned her head back against the sofa again. "It's a recent development in my life. I haven't exactly thought it out."

"Since me?"

"Not exactly, but you are a driving force."

"Because I didn't want you to take *Phoenix Rising*?"

"No, Kenz." Lennox turned her head but didn't lift it. "I've never been anonymous. There are pictures of me two days out of the hospital, with Will walking hand in hand with my mother next to my father, who was carrying me," she let out. "I think part of the reason I fell in love with acting the way I did, was because my parents seemed to enjoy it so much. And when Will clearly wanted no part of it, they shifted their focus to me. I was their only hope of carrying on the family tradition. Then, we lost Will, I took Jamie in, and I kept doing it because it was all I knew. I hadn't gone to college. I didn't have any other marketable skills. I am slumdog to my friends because I know a little about a lot, but that doesn't get you very far." Lennox hesitated, and Kenzie watched her seem to process before she spoke. "I'd been putting off signing on for another project for a while. My agent was starting to get annoyed, but I didn't even want to read a script. Then, I met you, and I felt like maybe I could, I don't know, take some time off, relax, and just be with you and be happy."

"But you're not happy?"

"Kenzie, you make me so happy. And none of what's going on out there is your fault. But no, right now, I'm not the happiest I've ever been; no. I wanted to be cooped up with you, yes. But not like this; not like we're just waiting for them to find us, and we have to move again; and not where I'm so tense, I can't even relax."

"It won't go away, Lennox. Even if you never act again, they'll still be outside. They'll still try to find us."

"I know," Lennox said in a low voice. "Let's just get through today and worry about the rest tomorrow."

"I don't want to just get through the day with you, Lennox."

"I know. I'm sorry. I'm in a bad mood. Do you mind

if I spend some time on my own in here? I feel like I need to think a little."

"Okay."

Kenzie stood because she didn't know what else to do. She went to the bedroom and closed the door because Lennox had always respected her space, and she would offer her the same. She also went to the bedroom because she needed to cry, and she didn't want Lennox to see her tears.

***

Lennox came into the bedroom later that night. Kenzie didn't say anything as she headed straight to the bathroom. They hadn't eaten dinner together, nor had they spoken since Lennox had asked for space. When Kenzie heard the shower turn on, she left the bedroom to grab a snack from the kitchen. She hadn't been hungry earlier but knew she wouldn't be able to sleep if she didn't eat something. On her way to the kitchen, she discovered Lennox's laptop was open on the table. Worried she might be reading more stories about their romance, Kenzie walked to the table and went to close it. What she saw instead, though, was a screenplay. Kenzie lifted her head to check to see that Lennox was still in the bathroom, and placed the computer in her lap. She felt guilty about reading Lennox's words without asking, but, technically, Lennox had told her she would allow her to read anything. So, with that thought, she turned her attention to the words.

"This is for my show," she said to herself softly, hoping not to be heard.

She scrolled to see that Lennox had written an entire episode of her show. She'd known Lennox had written some stuff down and that she'd had ideas, but she hadn't realized the woman had written an entire episode. Feeling more curious now, Kenzie went to the recent files section and found that Lennox had written not one but several episodes of Kenzie's show. There were four completed scripts, starting with the first episode of season two. Kenzie wanted to read all four, but that wasn't fair to Lennox. She really did want to read them, though, and she worried that now Lennox might not let her, given how tense things were between them. So, she opened her email on Lennox's computer and sent the files to herself. She wouldn't read them right away. She would wait for Lennox to offer and just keep them in her email for later when she'd want to re-read them. She had this feeling like she'd love whatever Lennox had written for the show and, in particular, her character. She also felt like she needed these in her possession to have some part of Lennox with her at all times. She knew how crazy that sounded, and she felt like the worst girlfriend in the world for snooping.

She headed back into the bedroom with a banana and some water, leaving a bottle and an apple on Lennox's bedside table, knowing the woman hadn't eaten earlier. When Lennox returned from the shower, she noticed the snack first and smiled at her girlfriend. Kenzie thought Lennox looked beautiful in her towel and with wet hair. Lennox took a long drink from the water and set it back down before taking a bite of the apple and sitting down on the bed, offering it to Kenzie. Kenzie shook her head but offered a small smile. Lennox leaned over and kissed her cheek.

***

"Lennox! Lennox!" They'd found them. It had taken the press two days, but they'd managed to figure out where they were.

Kenzie had had a brilliant idea to take Lennox to set with her for her first day back at work since Lennox had arrived, thinking the woman needed to get out of that hotel and that it would be nice for her to introduce her girlfriend to some people on set. Kenzie had met with her director and explained what had happened with Mary Matthews. Mary had admitted that she'd been the source but had claimed to the director that Kenzie hadn't said anything was off the record. It was an obvious lie. Sure, Kenzie hadn't said those words, but Mary wasn't a reporter. She was a colleague, and she knew they were having a conversation between friends. Kenzie requested that since they only had two more scenes to film together, that they do those last, because Kenzie did not want to see her right now. That gave Kenzie some satisfaction but not enough, and that was especially true when she and Lennox left the hotel through the back entrance, which should have been secure but wasn't, and they were swarmed by cameras immediately.

"Kenzie! Kenzie! Over here!"

They slid into the back seat of the black SUV and drove off. Kenzie watched Lennox's smile – which had been bright at the idea of going to set with her – disappear instantly, and her vacant stare returned as they drove off. Her phone rang a few minutes into their drive, and Kenzie caught Lennox's publicist's name on the screen.

"Hey," Lennox greeted without emotion. "Yeah, I know. Can you find us somewhere else?" She paused to listen. "I'll have someone grab our stuff from there while we're on set." She paused again. "Maybe we can just sleep in Kenzie's trailer," she suggested and then listened. "Yeah, I know. I know." She looked over at Kenzie, who was staring at her. "I know. I don't need a lecture." Lennox caught Kenzie's concerned stare and turned away. "I'll talk to her about it again, okay?" She then leaned toward the window, away from Kenzie. "I will. I'll call you back. Get some sleep." She hung up, apparently, without waiting for a response.

"You want to switch hotels again?" Kenzie asked.

"Well, we can't go back there. They'll find a way to get up to our suite and mess with us somehow." Lennox turned to face Kenzie.

"Were you serious about staying in my trailer?"

"At least, there's set security there, and we won't have to drive anywhere."

"My trailer is tiny, Lennox. I'm not you. I don't get the giant ones, with queen beds and full kitchens. You want to stay there for a month?"

"I get it." Lennox turned back to the window. "Forget about it. I'll call her back when we get there, and we'll change hotels again. Maybe I can just find us a short-term rental or something near set instead."

"Is that what you want?"

"I want to go home, Kenzie," Lennox blurted out without thinking and turned with large eyes immediately to face Kenzie. "No, that's not what I meant, Kenz. I'm sorry. This whole thing just has me turned around, and I'm saying stupid things."

"I thought I was your home," Kenzie replied softly, not knowing what else to say.

***

Kenzie left Lennox in her trailer and went to do hair and makeup. As she sat in the chair, she said nothing while the people working on her chose to talk to Nora instead, who was in the chair next to her. Her heart wasn't in her work that day. It took her several takes to get it right, and then several more for her to really get it done well. When they called lunch, Kenzie made her way back toward her trailer and was stopped by Marco.

"Kenzie, hey."

"Hi, Marco."

"Listen, I heard Mary told you about this whole Lennox Owen conversation we had, and I wanted you to know that I wouldn't have said any of that had I known you two were together."

"Okay. Thanks." She tried to move past him.

"And just out of curiosity, are you the reason she didn't take *Phoenix*? I mean, for real?"

"Her reasons are her own, Marco."

"No, I get it. It's just that the article mentioned that,

and then I read one that mentioned that she wanted to take a break from acting. But, she's Lennox Owen; she's been acting forever. Is she really going to take a break?"

"I don't know," Kenzie answered with frustration and again, tried to continue on the way to her trailer.

"I guess it just sucks." He walked alongside her as if she had invited him. "Part of the reason I'm doing the show is because of her. I was so excited about working with her. Now, I hear they're going to hire some unknown, which means the show probably won't be as big as they'd thought, and not as good for me, you know?"

"Sorry," she apologized without really meaning it.

"Do you think there's any way you could get her to reconsider?"

"You want me to ask my girlfriend to take a job that would take her away from me for years?"

"You could go to New Zealand."

"You do know I'm on my own show, right?" Kenzie tossed back. "And I'm not going to try to convince her to do something she doesn't want to do. She's her own person. And if she wants to take the job, she can and would. But she doesn't want it. She turned it down for the right reasons; not because of me. And even if I wanted to convince her to take it, I don't think I'm the person to try right now. All I seem to do is make her unhappy these days." She let out all at once and promptly turned around to see Lennox holding her trailer door open for her.

CHAPTER 31

LENNOX heard Kenzie's voice and decided to get up and open the door for her, because she needed to start apologizing for how she had been acting. When she did, though, it was just in time to hear Kenzie talking to Marco. When Marco noticed her, he gave a small wave and walked off without saying anything to either of them.

"Hi," Kenzie offered softly and hung her head. "How much of that did you hear?"

"Mainly, the part where you think I'm unhappy and that you're the reason," Lennox said and took a step back so that Kenzie could come inside.

Kenzie followed her and bumped almost immediately into her luggage, which had been brought over and stowed by the door next to Lennox's. In the small space, it only made it worse, and she regained her footing to see Lennox moving toward the twin bed and sitting on the edge. Outside of the desk and table combination, that was blocked by the luggage and the boxes of Lennox's stuff she'd also had delivered there until they could get to another hotel, the bed was the only place to sit on in the trailer.

"Am I wrong?" Kenzie asked as she sat down next to Lennox and saw Lennox's laptop open at the end of the bed.

"You're not the cause, Kenzie," Lennox told her.

"But you are unhappy?"

"I wanted to have this time with you. I wanted to have time where we could be at the beginning of our relationship – the honeymoon period – before everyone found out. Dani and Peyton had that, and I wanted that with you. And since everyone found out, things haven't exactly been smooth-sailing."

"I know."

"I found out, while you were working, that Aaron gave an interview. It's on YouTube, and he told them that we were together for a month and never had sex, so his guess was as good as everyone else's as to why. But he winked when he delivered that part, so now they're all going to assume it was either because I was gay and using him, or you and I were already together, and I was using him or cheating on him; I don't know, maybe both."

"I'm sorry."

"I know you're sorry. I'm sorry. Sorry doesn't change it, though, Kenz." She paused and turned to her. "Things aren't good right now. I don't know what to do, but it's not your fault."

"It is, though, Lennox. It's because of me that this is happening. I kissed you in that club, we walked out holding hands because of that, and I'm in London for work, so you're here, too, and they're stalking us."

"It's not your fault, okay?"

"What do we do?" Kenzie asked.

"I booked a flight home," Lennox replied.

"You what?" Kenzie's head snapped to her.

"Kenz, I love you, and I want to be with you." She took Kenzie's hand. "But I'm going through something right now, and I've got to figure things out. I have no idea what I want to do with my life if I quit acting. And I know that I want to quit. But the thought of doing nothing or having nothing else I'm good at, is killing me. And add all this stress and the fact that someone else took a video of me crushing that girl's phone, and one of me yelling–" She stopped herself and took a deep, weighted breath. "I'm not myself, Kenzie. And I want to be myself."

"So, you're running?"

"Kenz…"

"You told me not to run, but you're running." She stood and faced Lennox.

"This is different. You ran away and didn't talk to me for weeks. I'm going home; I'm not running away from you."

"But you need to be *there* to figure things out? Why can't you be with me?"

"Because being here is making it worse, Kenzie. Can't you see that? They're hoping to catch us in a moment, and they have. They want to see us kiss or watch us hold hands or fight so they can put it on their shows or sites. And I don't want that for us. I don't want to be splashed on every tabloid like some freak show because I'm in love with a woman and we both happen to be actors. It's never been like *that* for me, and I don't want that for me or for us. If I'm there – at least, they can't get us together; at least, they can move on to the next story. And when you get back to LA, things will have–"

"LA? You're not coming to New York with me now?"

Lennox stood up but kept her distance.

"If I go back to LA, I can meet with my manager, my agent, my publicist, and… hell, maybe my damn lawyer or something, too. I can try to figure out my career."

"What's there to figure out, Lennox? You're a writer."

"I'm not a writer, Kenzie. I just write. There's a difference."

"You wrote four episodes of my show. How are you not a writer?"

"How do you know that?" Lennox took a step back, but due to the small space, the back of her legs hit the bed, and she stopped.

"I saw them on your computer the other day," Kenzie confessed.

"You saw them on my computer?" Lennox reached over and closed her laptop.

"I didn't read them. I just saw them."

"But how did you see them? I was working on one, Kenzie. One. How did you know I have four?"

"Because I looked in your recently opened documents and saw there were four. But I didn't read them, Lennox. And I'm sorry I even looked, but I don't understand why you don't–"

"Kenzie, you can't just snoop through my stuff like that. That's not how this works."

"I know, and I'm sorry." She reached for Lennox's hand, but Lennox pulled away. "I didn't read them."

"Then, how do you know I'm a writer? I could be terrible, Kenzie. You have no idea if I'm even good, and you're suggesting I become a screenwriter."

"I know you're good because you're you," Kenzie returned. "You're so talented. You had a great idea for the show, and I know how you talk to me."

"Kenzie, let's just stop." Lennox held out her hand palm-forward toward Kenzie. "I don't want to talk about this anymore."

"Why not?"

"Because I don't," she objected loudly. "I think I want to leave it here, because if we keep going, I'm going to get more upset. And I don't want to leave like that."

"Leave? When are you going?"

"My flight is at five. I should leave now."

"Today?" Kenzie's face registered surprise.

"It's for the best. The faster I get out of here, the faster people will leave you alone, and I can go home and try to clear my head."

"You're running?"

"I'm not running. I told you, this is different."

"Lennox, I love you."

"I love you. Me leaving doesn't change that."

"So, how does this even work? You're in LA, and I'm here, and then I'm in New York… Do I get to see you at all?"

"I'll get home, and we can figure out a schedule with the time difference so that we can call each other."

"So, I get a few phone calls a week now?"

"Kenzie, please…"

"No, Lennox," Kenzie pushed back. "No, I don't want that. I want you here with me. That was the deal."

"Well, we have to adapt, because this isn't working for me, and I don't think it's working for you, either."

"It's different, yes," Kenzie agreed. "But I'm dealing with it because of you."

"I'm not." Lennox shrugged. "I'm not dealing with it, Kenz."

"Because I'm not helping? Because I'm not capable of helping? Because I freeze?"

"What? No. This has nothing to do with that."

"Just go." Kenzie's eyes were welling up with tears, and her voice was breaking. "Go, catch your flight."

Lennox nearly broke, too. The sound of Kenzie's broken sobs almost made her reconsider, and she hated herself. She didn't want to leave Kenzie. She wanted nothing more than to spend every day of her life with this woman. But, the way things were right now, she couldn't. She was struggling, and she wasn't happy. While that wasn't Kenzie's fault, Lennox knew she needed to get away right now. And, as much as it was hurting Kenzie, for her to leave like this, Lennox knew she needed it.

"Baby, I don't want to leave like this, okay? Let's sit down and talk."

"No. Go." Kenzie stood her ground and pointed to the door. "If you don't want to be here, I don't want you to be here."

"You don't mean that." Lennox moved into her and held her face. "Don't leave it like this."

"You're leaving, Lennox. I'm the one trying to make it work this time, and you're leaving. If you need to go, then go." She stepped out of Lennox's embrace and then around her to sit on the bed and stare at the floor.

"I called a car. I'll have the driver come to get my stuff," Lennox said and held back tears. "I'll call you when I land."

"Why?" Kenzie asked but didn't really ask at the same time.

"I love you."

"I know," Kenzie returned, and Lennox registered the intense pain that came with leaving someone she loved because the circumstances they'd found themselves in were too much for her to handle.

***

Lennox did call Kenzie when she arrived home hours later, but Kenzie didn't answer the phone. Lennox thought about not leaving a message, but she did, and she hoped Kenzie would call her back when she woke up the next morning. She tried to use the time difference as an excuse. Maybe Kenzie was asleep or hadn't heard the phone. She had likely set it to 'do not disturb,' given how many calls they'd both received recently. And Lennox wouldn't fault her for that. That was one of the reasons Lennox had to leave. Things were too hectic, with her being in London. This way, they could talk every day and let the attention die down around them. By the time Kenzie was back in LA to begin the next season of her show, there would be at least two more giant celebrity stories out there that would move them down the priority list. Even Peyton and Dani were about to get out of their hibernation and do their first interview as a couple, so that would shift the attention off Lennox and Kenzie for a few weeks, at least. That was her hope, anyway, as she finally gave into sleep herself. She rolled onto her side, and her arm lifted instinctively for Kenzie's form, wanting to wrap the other woman up for the night and kiss her shoulder before saying goodnight. But Kenzie wasn't there, and Lennox only had herself to blame.

Waking the next morning, Lennox decided to try again and was met with Kenzie's pre-recorded message for the second time. She decided she needed to give Kenzie some time. Lennox knew her. Kenzie took longer than most to process information, emotions, and changes like this. She'd give her the day and try again that night. And if Kenzie didn't answer, she would try again the next day, and the one after that. Because, as much as she needed time herself to figure out her life, Lennox knew she needed Kenzie more.

"Mother fuck, Lex! You just ran out on her?" Dani rarely swore.

In fact, of the two of them, Peyton Gloss – America's shiniest, cleanest superstar was the one who'd toss out a swear word every so often; but Dani Wilder – she rarely swore. Lennox couldn't even remember the last time she'd heard Dani swear. But, the first words out of Dani's mouth, when Lennox answered her call, were a semi-yelled swear.

"Dani?"

"I just heard from Peyton, who called Kenzie when *she* heard on the damn news that you had returned to LA and left her there."

Lennox tried to make sense out of that sentence and determined that Peyton had caught an entertainment show or something that Lennox had left London, and she had called Kenzie to find out what happened; probably because Lennox hadn't picked up her phone at all that day.

"I didn't leave her there, Dani."

"Really? That's what Kenzie seems to think."

"She's not answering her phone when I call her. It's been two days, and she won't talk to me."

"Why would she? You basically ditched her in a foreign country when things got hard, Lennox."

"Hey, I didn't ditch her, Dani. And you don't know what it was like."

"Pretty sure I have an idea, Lennox. I have about fifteen reporters outside my house right now, and that's the lowest number I've seen in days," Dani defended. "Did you really tell her you booked a flight two seconds before you left for it? I mean, Lennox…"

"I had to get out of there, Dani. It was so claustrophobic. I wanted to be locked away with her, yeah, but not like that; not with people just waiting for our next move so that they could capture it on their phones and post it online. She's not built for that."

"Don't blame her for this," Dani began. "She's been holding up fine. You're the one that's struggling. And that's okay. Things haven't exactly been perfect over here, and I love Peyton, but spending every moment with her, while waiting for the story to die down, makes me want to kill her sometimes. But I'd never leave her like that. I'd never make her deal with it alone."

"You guys were ready for this, Dani," Lennox argued.

"I wasn't. It's not like we planned on going public the minute I set foot in London."

"Well, you probably shouldn't have stuck your tongue down her throat on the dance floor then, because those pictures kind of give it all away."

"Did you just call to give me a hard time, Dani? Because my girlfriend isn't talking to me right now, I have no idea what I want to do with my life these days, and I miss the crap out of the woman I love. So, if you just called to yell at me, then hang the hell up."

"Hey, Len, that's enough." It was Peyton's voice. "I just walk into the room, and you're yelling at my fiancée. You wanna dial it back?" She must have been on speaker.

"I didn't call her," Lennox fired back. "And I'm in a shitty mood right now."

"Fix it, then," Peyton replied. "Fix it and stop yelling at Dani because *you* messed up."

"I didn't mess up, Peyton. This is what I need right now," she insisted. "I think this was the right decision."

"Right or not, according to *your* girlfriend, you handled it like shit, Lennox. What the hell is going on? This isn't like you."

"I'm scared, Peyton."

"Of what? Of Kenzie? Of being in a real relationship for maybe the first time ever?"

"Everything is just so much." Lennox wiped a tear from her eye and leaned back in her chair, closing her laptop in the process.

"You're in the beginning of a new relationship with a woman when you've never done that before. And you're Lennox Owen and Kenzie Smyth, so everyone cares about it. But, Len, that's no reason to leave your girlfriend in another country when you told her you'd be there with her and for her."

"I know. But if we're apart, they'll leave us alone; at least, more than they are now. I've been home for a few days now, and there have been a few reporters outside, but not nearly as many. It's already dying out, because they can't get their shot of us together."

"But what happens between now and when Kenzie gets back to LA?" Dani asked.

"We're still together. We didn't break up. I just couldn't breathe there, guys. We went from her hotel, the first time I was there, to your place, to another hotel, and her tiny trailer. And there was the prospect of another hotel, and another one, and it was too much. I couldn't breathe."

"If you're still together, why is she not returning your calls?" Dani questioned.

"She's mad. I get it. I left the wrong way. I should've stayed longer so we could talk more, but I couldn't. I was angry and getting angrier all the time, and I was taking it out on her; and none of it was her fault. I know I messed that part up. But I've left messages every day, apologizing for that and asking her to talk to me, but she won't call me back."

"She's listened to your messages," Peyton explained.

"Then, she's heard me crying into the phone on more than one occasion, trying to apologize, and hasn't bothered to call me back. Are you guys harassing her, too?"

"We're not harassing you," Peyton defended. "I love you, Len. Dani loves you. We just want you to be okay, and we want Kenzie to be okay, too. And, right now, neither of you seem like you're okay."

"I'm not okay," Lennox admitted and wiped at another tear. "I miss her, and I think I messed it up."

"She'll call."

"And what if she doesn't? What if I've really messed this up?" Lennox asked.

"Oh, sweetie," Dani exclaimed.
But it wasn't advice, and it wasn't reassuring.

***

Two days later, Lennox woke after having not slept much since she had returned to LA. She had finally been able to get some sleep and had been dead to the world, apparently, when a call from Kenzie came in. Lennox had shot out of bed and quickly got to her voicemail so that she could listen to the message.

"Hi," Kenzie paused. "I know I should have called you back sooner. I'm sorry." She sighed, and Lennox worried about what might come next. "You just left, Lennox. I know I left before, and I hate that I did that, but you left, too. What does that mean? What if we just keep leaving each other? I can't do that. I can't keep going through this – having you and then not having you." She paused again, and Lennox heard someone call her name. "I'm working a lot right now, trying to wrap this part of the shoot early, if I can, so I can get to New York. My friend Kat is going there for work in a couple of weeks, and I want to see her before I start the other part of the shoot. I think it might be a good idea if we take some time apart." She sniffled, and Lennox wondered if she was getting sick or if she was crying. "I get that this is a lot and that you have things to think about, so I will give you that time. But I can't do the nightly phone calls with you while I pretend everything's okay and that I don't want you here with me or that I'm not still upset with you for leaving like that. I love you, Lennox. I don't want anyone else. But if you need time, then I'll take time, too. Just… please try to figure it out quickly, because I miss you, and it hurts, Lennox." Kenzie was crying. "It hurts not being with you." She hung up the phone.

Lennox was in tears, too. She'd caused this, and she didn't know how to fix it.

CHAPTER 32

"KENZ, what do you want from me? I haven't heard from her in two weeks. I called her twice, and she hasn't called back," Peyton delivered.

"It's my fault. I told her I didn't want to talk while we were apart," Kenzie explained as she sipped coffee across from Peyton in Peyton and Dani's kitchen.

"Why'd you do that?"

"Because it seemed like I was contributing to the problem. She needs time alone, and I thought if I pressured her into talking every day or trying to figure it out faster or determining what's next for us, it wouldn't end well."

"Do you want it to end?" Peyton asked and sipped on her own coffee, but Kenzie noticed her bright blue eyes and lifted eyebrows and knew what that question *actually* meant.

"I don't want us to end, no. But I can't force her to plan her life faster for me or to spend time with me if it's hurting her. I want her to be happy. And if she isn't with me, then..."

"Kenzie, I've never seen Lennox so happy in my life. I watched her fall in love with Noah and thought she was happy. And then I saw her with you, and I realized that's what Lennox happy really looks like."

"But, if us being in public is a problem for her, I don't know how to fix that."

"Can I be honest with you?"

"Please," Kenzie encouraged and set her coffee on the island.

"Your publicists are dumb," Peyton said, and Kenzie gave her a look of confusion. "You haven't said a word; and neither has Lennox, outside of that momentary outburst. The reason it's so mysterious to everyone and they're so interested is because you're not talking about it. If you give an interview to confirm you're together and tell the story of how it happened, that will stop the rumor mills about how you met and when it all started."

"I can't exactly call Lennox and ask her to do an interview about us right now," Kenzie returned.

"Why can't you do it?"

"I've never had a relationship in public before. I've never commented on my private life before. People don't even know I haven't spoken to my mom in years. My IMDB page just says that my dad died and my mom is still around but has re-married. I never talk about this stuff… And I'm not good at talking about it, either, Peyton." Kenzie paused and stared down at her coffee. "When that girl with the phone started asking questions about us, I froze. I didn't know what to say or how to say it, and Lennox had to rescue me."

"I'm not going to tell you what to do. I'm saying that I think that's part of the reason Len is unhappy right now. Lennox has always been the golden girl. She and I actually shared a cover for Vogue once, like ten years ago, with the caption 'America's golden girls' on it. We were both sweet and innocent; and when we did start dating – it was weird, because, suddenly, no one knew how to report on it. We were supposed to be sweet and virginal and not date. We definitely weren't supposed to have sex." Peyton laughed. "When she started dating Noah – it was a match made in heaven, and they treated the two of them fairly. She was the smart, beautiful movie star with the gorgeous smile who was always nice to everyone. And he was the handsome, smart movie star with that mega-watt smile who was always nice to everyone. They had no problems with the press."

"I know."

"And with Lucas – he was the playboy, but he was a charmer, too, and no one really knew what was going on. Lennox was the good girlfriend, who didn't mind when her boyfriend was out late at night; sometimes with other women around. She put most of the focus on her career at that time, and no one seemed to notice. When they broke up, there wasn't some big story or anything. It was just known. They broke up, and there was no drama; nothing big to report."

"And with me, it's *only* big."

"Lennox Owen is interested in a woman. That is big news," Peyton confirmed and took another drink. "But, Kenzie, Lennox is also dealing with what she wants to do next. I've known her heart wasn't in acting for a while. She had to realize that herself. And I'm glad that she has, because I know she wants to do something different, and you helped her get there."

"No, I didn't."

"Yes, you did, Kenzie." Peyton laughed lightly. "You helped Lennox in the same way Dani helped me to figure out I wanted to make a pop album and not another country one back then. She never said anything specific. She didn't tell me to make a pop album; just her presence was somehow enough. And you've done that for her."

"I love her."

"I know you do. She loves you, too. She'll figure it out, and you'll figure it out. You guys will find your way back to each other."

"What if we don't?"

"That's not something I'm prepared to imagine." She stood up and carried her coffee as she walked. "I have something for you. I've been bored a little in here, since Dani and I can't have sex constantly forever."

"Peyton!" Dani's loud voice could be heard from the

other room where she was doing yoga.

Peyton laughed. Even Kenzie laughed for the first time in weeks.

"Anyway, I got inspired by the better parts of your relationship with my dear and sometimes dumb friend, Lennox. I wrote something for you guys." Peyton ushered Kenzie along toward her in-home recording studio. "Sit down. I recorded it yesterday, since I knew you'd be visiting. It's just me and a piano, but you can get the idea." She pressed one of the thousands of buttons on the giant table Kenzie had no clue how to use, and stood back. "I'll leave you alone. Come grab me when you're done. Oh, and the lyrics are over there if you want to read them." She pointed to a piece of loose-leaf paper off to the side of the table and left the room.

A few seconds later, the soft sounds of the song's intro began. Kenzie listened to the words Peyton had thought to write about her relationship with Lennox, and she cried.

***

"You'll follow my rule?" Kenzie asked.

"Yes, we've signed the paperwork," the producer confirmed.

"And if this leaks, you'll be sued." Carson pointed at the producer to confirm.

"We understand."

"Good. You sure you want to do this, Kenz?" He turned and asked her.

It had been twelve days since Kenzie had listened to Peyton's song. And it had been far too long since she had spoken to Lennox. But it had taken her this long to find her words, and she was finally ready to speak them out loud. She'd worked with Carson on the strategy, and they'd chosen this producer and reporter to do the work, but the words were all Kenzie's – and that was the most important part. Kenzie nodded at Carson and the producer.

"Let's begin." The producer motioned for Kenzie to sit in the chair.

They'd already done her hair and makeup and placed the lapel microphone on her button-down sunset-orange shirt that made her eyes pop. Her hair was half down and half pulled back, because Kenzie wasn't sure which Lennox preferred, so she decided to try both at the same time. She swallowed nervously, wiped her hands on her jeans, and waited for the reporter sitting across from her.

"So, you would define yourself as gay?" the reporter asked after they'd been chatting about Kenzie's career, upbringing, and a few other pieces of small talk before getting into the real reason for the interview.

"Yes, I'm gay."

"And you're currently dating Lennox Owen?" the reporter asked, and her facial expression told Kenzie she wasn't sure how Kenzie would answer the question, as if she'd been set up to give this interview of a lifetime and would be let down.

"Yes."

"There are a lot of rumors out there about the two of you. I know everyone is interested in your story. Can you tell us how you two met?"

"We met when a friend we share hosted a fun week-long getaway for the 4th of July."

"A lot of people have speculated that you met much earlier than that."

"I know. I've heard the rumors, but we met that week."

"And Lennox is also gay?"

"That's for Lennox to tell you; not me."

"And she's not doing the interview with you because…"

"Because she's in LA, and I'm here for work."

"Okay." The reporter laughed lightly.

"You two met that weekend, and was it love at first sight?"

This was it. This was Kenzie's chance to get her words out.

"I think I've loved Lennox Owen since I first laid eyes on her, but that was long before our week in July," she began. "I first saw a picture of her years ago, and I knew there was something about her. This was before I even knew I was attracted to women." Kenzie felt sweat form on her palms and her heart rate begin to increase. "I never thought she would have feelings for me. When I saw her there, she helped me with my bag. And I thought, 'I can't believe Lennox Owen is carrying my bag.'" Kenzie smiled at the memory. "We talked and talked; and I fell for her immediately, yes, but I still never thought she would return my feelings. I thought I was condemned to be miserable. But then, things started to happen, and she did return my feelings. I won't get into the specifics, because those moments – those amazing, miraculous moments, belong to us. That's the thing that gets me. Everyone is interested in our relationship because we work in this industry. I can understand it to a certain extent, because I'm a fan myself. I've followed actors and actresses and wondered about their lives. But Lennox and I are just two people who love each other and want to be together. Lennox has never cheated on anyone she's been with, and those rumors are false. She and Aaron Wilkes were never exclusive, and they were apart for much of the time they were casually dating." Kenzie ran her fingers across the fabric of her jeans, imagining it was Lennox's skin. "No one should have to live under that kind of microscope when all they're trying to do is find love. Lennox is being punished for loving me, and I hate that. It makes me sad, and it makes me sick, because she's the best person I know. She's smart, and funny, and when she listens, she really hears you. She's so kind and supportive, and I love her. Lennox Owen is the love of my life. And… I'm not the best with words, sometimes, so I'll just say something and wrap up this speech." Kenzie paused and stopped moving her hands. "All the love songs, Lennox. All the love songs."

The reporter was clearly confused at that last line, but she didn't comment on it.

"So, let's talk about what's next for you, Mackenzie," she said instead.

***

Lennox stared at the screen in disbelief for over five minutes. Kenzie had sent her an email. They hadn't spoken in weeks, with both of them trying to respect the wishes of the other. Lennox had picked up the phone at least ten times a day, thinking about calling her, just wanting to hear her voice. Every time, she had stopped before hitting send, because she didn't know what to say. She had spent all these weeks doing what she'd said she'd do. She figured out her life. The story of their relationship had died down, and the reporters had all but left her alone. She'd followed Kenzie online to see if they were still giving her a hard time, but since Kenzie had gotten to New York, they had left her alone. There had been a few pictures of her with her friend Kat, and there were some rumors that they were lovers. But Kat's boyfriend, who was also in New York at the time and was seen making out with her in public, kind of pushed that rumor to the trash pile.

Lennox took a deep breath in and opened the email that had no subject, silently praying that Kenzie wouldn't be officially ending their relationship over email but also expecting that that might be the case because Lennox had been such a terrible girlfriend. When she opened it, she noticed the attachment and the few words from Kenzie in the body:

I finally got my words out, Lennox. I did this without your permission, so it won't go anywhere unless you agree. But if you're okay with it, I'd like this to be seen. It says what I want to say. I hope it says what you need to hear.
Love,
Kenzie

Love, Kenzie? Lennox let out the breath she had been holding since she had started reading and re-reading the email before opening the video attachment and watching it.

***

It was two days later when Kenzie had all but given up on her relationship with Lennox. She'd sent the email with the interview, letting the woman know that it wouldn't go anywhere unless the network and all its employees agreed that it wouldn't see the light of day unless Lennox approved it. That had taken some time to arrange. Everyone wanted the exclusive, but most had a problem with having to wait or possibly having to shelve it if Lennox Owen didn't sign off on it. What Kenzie found interesting was that no one had asked her why Lennox hadn't approved it already. If they were a couple, madly in love with one another, hadn't they spoken about this prior to Kenzie doing the interview? Hadn't Lennox already given her approval? Kenzie had expected that question or many more like it, but she had to hand it to Carson. He was a decent publicist, after all, if he could curtail those questions and make sure the interview went down the way Kenzie wanted it to.

She had been glued to her phone and hadn't slept well since, hoping Lennox would call; even if it was late at night, and it was just to talk. Kenzie needed to hear her voice. She had gotten so desperate, she'd gone to her movie collection and done a marathon of Lennox Owen films, and then, spent the last two nights getting stuck in a YouTube black hole, watching video after video of Lennox in behind-the-scenes features from her movies and interviews of her on late-night shows. She had called Peyton to see if she had heard from Lennox, and had been disappointed and worried to find that Lennox hadn't contacted her best friend in days.

Work had continued, and she had been forced to work with Mary for one day after all, since it couldn't be avoided. Luckily, they were in the scene together but didn't have to interact much, and that was Mary's last day on set. She had left, offering an apology Kenzie hadn't been certain the woman had meant, and Kenzie's work on the film was also complete. She returned home to LA, called Peyton again, just to see if she'd heard anything one last time before she gave up and curled herself into a ball, preparing for tears that wouldn't likely come anymore. She had shed so many already, she wasn't sure she had any left. And it was with that thought that Kenzie heard her doorbell ring. She hadn't been expecting anyone, but she often had scripts delivered to her door by her agent, hoping she'd read them, so she'd gotten used to the bell ringing unexpectedly. She left her bedroom and walked down the stairs of her two-story modern home. At the door, she looked through the peephole and, seeing no one, she opened the door and looked to her welcome mat, which indeed had a heavy-looking envelope on it. Kenzie picked it up, recognizing it as a script, and closed the door. She pulled open the yellow envelope and slid out the gold-fastened script.

What she hadn't been prepared for, was a script from season two of her show. They would start working on it soon, but it was too soon for her to get the premiere episode script. Kenzie flipped through the pages haphazardly, as she sat on her plush sofa, and then set it on the coffee table, figuring she'd read it all later. As she stood up to return to her bedroom, she noticed something. Just as she did, the doorbell rang again, and she lifted her eyes to it. She looked back down at the title page and smiled. Bringing the script with her, Kenzie moved back to the front door, and, without looking through the peephole this time, she opened the door slowly. Lennox stood there with a single red rose and a hopeful smile on her face.

"Hi," she greeted.

"Hey," Kenzie returned with a wildly beating heart. "Did you deliver this?" She held out the script.

"I did," Lennox replied, still holding on to her smile.

"Did you write this?" Kenzie continued to hold it out.

"I did," Lennox confirmed.

"Is it real?" Kenzie asked.

"It is," she said. "Can I come in?" Lennox held out the rose.

Kenzie hesitated for a moment but took it from Lennox's outstretched hand and allowed her to enter the house, closing the door behind them. They stood in the entryway for several moments in silence before Kenzie motioned with the rose, clasped in her hand, for Lennox to move inside toward the open living room.

"Do you want something to drink?" she asked to stall for time.

"I'm okay," Lennox replied and stood in front of the sofa, apparently waiting for Kenzie to sit first.

"Okay." Kenzie sat.

Lennox sat next to her but made sure to leave enough space between them.

"I watched your interview," Lennox told her and placed her hands nervously in her own lap.

"You didn't call." Kenzie bit her lower lip and released it. "I assumed you were done with me."

"I'll never be done with you, Kenzie." Lennox smiled. "I wanted to call, but I had some stuff I needed to take care of first. And then, Peyton texted me that you were coming back to LA today, so I thought I'd come by. She gave me your address. I hope that's okay."

"And did you take care of that stuff?"

"Yeah." Lennox smiled again, and it took everything in Kenzie not to hug her, not to bring her in, and not to kiss her. But they needed to talk before anything else happened. "So, I had a lot of soul-searching to do… And, as much as I wanted to talk to you, because I missed you… Kenzie, God, I missed you so much… And I would pick up the phone and almost call you, but I needed to do this part on my own. I'd been so angry with how everything happened, and I was taking it out on you, and it wasn't your fault, and I need to–"

"Lennox, stop." Kenzie placed her hand on top of Lennox's in her lap. "Let's just start from now. We both know we didn't handle things well. And we'll have to work on that together; but we've apologized enough, I think."

Lennox intertwined their fingers as she looked down at their joined hands and smiled.

"I talked to my agent and everyone else you have to talk to in this business, and I told them I didn't want to act anymore. Well, at least, right now anyway."

"You're taking a break?"

"I'm taking a very long break," she corrected. "I told them no new parts for at least the next few years. I can always change my mind, but I don't think I will."

"Because?" Kenzie asked with a slight smile.

"Because I have a new job."

"You do?" The smile grew.

"I asked my agent to get my scripts in front of some people, and he knew one of the staff writers on a certain zombie TV show – because Hollywood is really just a small town; and I had a few meetings. You were right. You hadn't even read my stuff, but you were right. They liked what I'd written and wanted to talk about me being a story writer at first."

"At first?" Kenzie chuckled and moved into Lennox slightly so that their thighs were touching.

"I think part of the reason they hired me is because of who I am. I'm under no delusions that I'm just that great of a writer. But I'm on staff now, Kenz." Lennox pointed at the script Kenzie had placed on the table. "That's mine. It's the first episode of season two, and it's real. I have to go to work tomorrow in the writer's room." She laughed. "It's crazy, but I've been doing that since I got the job, and it feels amazing going to work now. I just sit there with the writers, and we talk ideas and throw them back and forth, and then episodes get assigned, and I worked on this one with Marcy Jenkins, and she's so great, Kenz. She took my initial script and helped me re-work it. And I'm on staff at your show." She shrugged with a smile. "I wanted to ask you before I accepted. And if you say you don't want me to work there, I'll tell them I can't take it after all."

"Lennox, you're going to work on my show." She stated and laughed. "Two months ago, I was worried I'd lose you to New Zealand for four years. And now, you're going to work on my show."

"I am?" Lennox lifted an eyebrow as if to verify Kenzie's words.

"You are," Kenzie confirmed. Not being able to help herself any longer, she placed a hand on Lennox's cheek. "I missed you so much."

"I watched the interview, Kenzie."

"I made sure they only shot me from the mid up so you wouldn't see my sweaty hands gripping my jeans." She bit her lower lip again.

"If you want everyone to see it, I don't mind it being out there." Lennox moved herself in even closer.

"You don't mind? I thought you would want it to go out because it clears everything up. You didn't cheat and–"

"I don't care about that anymore," Lennox interrupted and placed an arm over the back of the sofa. "Maddox sent me some pictures from the summer, and I noticed some things," she began. "I noticed the pictures of Dani and Peyton. And they're so happy together. They fit, you know?"

"I know."

"And then, there were these pictures of us, and I looked at them and noticed the same thing about us. We fit. We looked so happy together, Kenzie."

"Because we were."

"And I know it's no summer camp for grown-ups, but LA isn't so bad." She smiled. "I want us. I want us to be together. And I talked to Peyton about some of the stuff she had to go through each time the media tore her up for dating someone else, and the comments she's gotten since she and Dani came out, and I just have to accept the fact that some people will never believe us no matter what we say."

"So, you don't mind the attention anymore?"

"I think we should wait a little bit and then do an interview together," Lennox suggested and moved a strand of Kenzie's hair behind her ear. "Let's get back to being us. And then, when we're ready, we can set the record straight together. And if people still don't get it or have a problem with me, then I don't care. I let it get to me before, Kenz, and I almost lost you. I won't risk that again."

Kenzie smiled and closed her eyes at the realization that her plan had worked.

"I love you," she said when she opened her eyes to stare into the deep blue ones looking back at her.

"I love you, too." Lennox pressed her forehead to Kenzie's. "I won't run again."

"Neither will I."

"All the love songs, Kenzie."

"All the love songs, Lennox."

EPILOGUE

"YOU can't be doing that right now," Lennox told Kenzie.

"Doing what?" Kenzie turned to her and checked, her face showed confusion since all she was doing was standing there.

"The lip." Lennox pointed an accusing finger at Kenzie's face. "You know what that does to me, and we're not exactly in a place right now, where I can act on it."

"Still?" Kenzie chuckled at her and linked their hands, offering Lennox's a squeeze.

"What do you mean still? Of course, still," Lennox shot back with a playful glare. Then, she leaned to her side and whispered near Kenzie's ear, "Always."

"You two ready?" the reporter asked as she sat down in front of them. "And also, your microphones are live." She pointed at their chests where they each had a lapel mic attached to their shirt, and Lennox turned just in time to see Kenzie's blush creep through.

She smirked at it, knowing she was the one responsible and liking it, as the reporter, Kenzie had spoken with before and then not permitted to release her original interview, began hesitantly; likely wondering if the same thing would happen this time. Lennox knew it wouldn't, though. She and Kenzie had been together for nearly a year. It had been eight months since she'd shown up on Kenzie's door with the first draft of a script and a rose, hoping against hope that

Kenzie wouldn't send her away. Kenzie hadn't. And while their romance had been rocky after the initial magical start, and they'd had a lot of talking to do that day and the days that followed, they'd settled into their life in LA, and then their life on set, as Lennox often accompanied Kenzie there and on location, even when not required for her new role as a writer.

It had taken some time for Lennox to get used to being a writer and not an actor. Kenzie noticed it probably more than others, but there was trepidation there when Lennox received questions from directors or the actors themselves. She had gotten so used to others telling her they didn't want to hear her ideas, that she would hesitate before sharing them, even when prompted. Lennox had Kenzie, though, and Kenzie was always there to help. She would read Lennox's words out loud as her character when Lennox was struggling to find the right dialogue for a scene. She'd have Kenzie say different words in the sentence when she just needed to hear it in her voice to find the right one.

When the show first started back up, Lennox had received stares everywhere she went on set and at the studio, when she met with the rest of the group in the writer's room. Many people assumed she was working on another project nearby, guest-starring in the show, or was only there to visit her girlfriend. Lennox often let the stares go, and when the questions came, she answered them honestly. She was writing for the show, yes. But, typically, she was only there to spend time with Kenzie. It seemed silly to some, probably, that she would sit in Kenzie's on-set trailer for hours, waiting for Kenzie to have a fifteen-minute break so that she could see her before she had to go back to work, but Lennox lived for that.

She could have waited at home, sure. In the beginning, they'd spent every night either at her place or at Kenzie's; so it wasn't as if they didn't see one another. And when Kenzie had to go on location, typically just outside of the city, Lennox would go with her, and they'd share Kenzie's trailer or a hotel room. But that simply wasn't enough for either of them. If Kenzie was working fourteen hours that day, it only gave them enough time to fall asleep next to one another; and they both wanted more. In those breaks, Kenzie would return to find Lennox writing or catching up on books she'd always wanted to read but had never found the time. Lennox would smile the moment the door opened, knowing her girlfriend would be appearing, and they would talk about their mornings and Kenzie's work along with Lennox's progress on a scene.

If they had more than fifteen minutes, they would sometimes spend their time doing something else, and Lennox always adored Kenzie's blush after, when she would start to think about the fact that people were walking all around their very not-so-soundproof trailer. She'd remind Lennox of that fact every time and suggest that they save their more intimate activities for home; and then, they'd do it again the next day.

Lennox had admired the changes in Kenzie over the past near-year. Kenzie was still Kenzie at her core, and that would never change. There were still moments where Lennox would catch her running her fingertips over something to attempt to regain her calm, and often, it was Lennox's skin she used. Kenzie would touch her forearm in public but her stomach or thighs in private. She'd taken to holding Lennox's hand and running her thumb back and forth slowly when they were walking down the street and photographers found them heading to lunch or grabbing coffee together.

Outside of that though, Kenzie had become much more assertive. And while she'd probably always struggle in social situations, she had been much more outgoing since they'd met, and she hadn't shied away from going to non-work-related events and parties they had been invited to as a couple.

They'd spent their first three months in LA either at work or at one of their houses, and Lennox no longer felt trapped by the press or their circumstance. The attention they had received initially had died down; though not considerably. They still had cameras in their faces, following them wherever they went, and that wouldn't likely change anytime soon. But the question-shouting had all but stopped, unless it was a random one that they ignored about where they were going or how they were that day. The comments about Lennox had died down as well, and Lennox would often go back to that time in her mind when she had let them get to her. It would hit her when they'd be out and someone would flash their camera. Lennox would look over at Kenzie and think about how she had almost lost her because she'd let people's words affect her. She would feel ashamed and embarrassed for a moment before she'd catch Kenzie's scent on the wind or her small smile. And then, she would remember that they were here; they were together. They had both made mistakes, but they'd worked through them and were stronger for it.

Lennox felt Kenzie begin to slide her thumb over her hand, as the reporter situated her note cards in her lap, and she glanced over at Kenzie, noting she was getting nervous.

"Hey, what's my favorite color?" Lennox asked her in a hushed tone.

"Evergreen," Kenzie replied, and her thumb began to slow.

"And what's your favorite song?"

"All the love songs," Kenzie returned, and her thumb stopped entirely as she offered Lennox a small smile.

"Let's begin with that, if that's okay." The reporter picked up on their conversation, though likely not on the fact that this was how Lennox calmed Kenzie in moments like this.

"Okay," Lennox returned, not knowing exactly what she was referring to.

"Your favorite song is Peyton Gloss's song, *All the Love Songs*?" she asked Kenzie. "She's said she wrote that about the two of you."

"She did," Kenzie replied.

"So, the references to fireworks over the water and swinging from trees, snakes in a field and lifetime crushes – I believe the lyric is, '*lifetime crushes turned to bright red blushes and intense rushes*,' that's about the two of you?"

Lennox smiled at the memories Peyton's lyrics always evoked and squeezed Kenzie's hand at the thought of how long they'd probably loved one another without having any idea that that was what it was and that it could ever turn into what they had now.

"Peyton has always had a way with words," Lennox spoke. "She's been my best friend forever, and she knows me better than anyone. Well, almost anyone, now." She glanced at Kenzie, who was watching her as she continued. "She had known that Kenzie had a crush on me and, apparently, knew that I had one on Kenzie… but I didn't even know that," she added. "We hadn't met in person. We'd never spoken. We were just two people who worked in this business, so our pictures and stories were everywhere. She'd seen my stuff, and I'd seen her stuff, and we had crushes. It feels like there should be a better word for that, especially now."

"Why's that?" the reporter asked.

"Because it was always more than a crush," Kenzie replied this time. "When I think about how I felt about her before I ever met her today, I know it wasn't just a crush."

"It was more," the reporter clarified.

"It was always more. And when we met, I knew it. But I never thought Lennox would feel the same way."

"So, Peyton was kind of your matchmaker?"

"She was. And she *loves* taking credit for that." Lennox laughed.

"Let's talk about that first meeting." The reporter shifted. "It was at Peyton's big summer event last year. She holds one every year for her celebrity squad," she said, and Lennox resisted the urge to roll her eyes at the word *squad*. "How did you two officially meet?"

"Lennox helped me with my bag," Kenzie answered. "And I nearly tripped on the gravel in the parking lot," she admitted and laughed at herself, and Lennox loved that laugh. "I didn't know she was going to be there. I hadn't prepared for meeting her."

"Surprising, running into your big-time crush?"

"To say the least," Kenzie returned with another small laugh.

"Lennox, can I just say something? You haven't stopped smiling since Kenzie walked into the room. Is that common for you?" the reporter laughed as she asked.

"Yes," Lennox stated.

Kenzie had been at a meeting with her agent prior to the interview, so she had dropped Lennox off to get her hair and makeup done and joined her later.

"It's very noticeable," the reporter pointed out.

"She's pretty noticeable," Lennox argued and smiled at her girlfriend again.

"How did that happen, if you don't mind me asking? You haven't spoken yet about the part of this that confused people the most, I think."

"The part that I'm a woman?" Kenzie checked.

"Yes." The reporter smiled wide. "People, I think, have been waiting for that confirmation that Lennox Owen is gay or bisexual. But you've not shared anything on that particular topic. Is there a reason?"

"Not a reason, no. I don't feel the need to define that about myself to make other people feel better or to give them a way to describe me that's easier than who I really am. I've been in love with a man, and now, I'm madly in love with a woman. If you look at the definitions in a dictionary, you could call that bisexual."

"But you don't?"

"I understand that many people – and maybe even most people, want to label themselves because it allows them that sense of belonging and identity; and I support that all the way. I never thought about falling in love with a woman. I watched Peyton go through almost the same experience. It's not my place to tell Peyton's story, but I was there when she and Dani first met and fell in love. And the only thing that made it different from the other times she'd been in love – at least, from my perspective – was that she was finally in love with the right person. That's what it feels like for me with Kenzie. When I met her, I knew it. I knew I was done – I'd met the person I was supposed to spend my life with. And while it was something I had to understand about myself at the same time I was falling for her, it wasn't ever something that gave me pause. She is the best thing that has ever happened to me, and I wouldn't ever risk not having what we have because of her gender."

"Wow." The reporter seemed unprepared for that answer.

"She's great with words," Kenzie spoke up, and Lennox noticed the blush return to her cheeks.

"Kenzie, what was it about Lennox that first attracted you to her? You obviously knew of her, but what happened in the beginning there, that made you think you were falling for her?"

"She understood me." Kenzie shrugged. "I struggle sometimes in situations," she admitted as Lennox felt Kenzie's hand tighten around her own, and she knew what was about to happen. "I have Asperger's. I'm on the autism spectrum, and I can be awkward and have a hard time getting to know new people. It's one of the reasons Lennox and I even met." Kenzie smiled at that, and Lennox couldn't believe she had finally told someone else.

They hadn't discussed her revealing this, but Lennox felt Kenzie's hand loosen, and knew she was okay.

"Peyton didn't know. Well, she still doesn't know. She'll know now, I guess. But she did know that I had trouble meeting new people. She invited me last summer to help me get to know more of her friends, and she kind of sent Lennox to check on me."

"Check on you?"

"I'd gone off on my own. There were a lot of people there, and I'm not great at small talk. Lennox found me, we talked, and she understood me. She let me take my time and didn't pressure me to be more than I was or different than I was, and she made me laugh. I felt more comfortable and started to open up to her more than I had to anyone. And she's still the only person that I think really understands me." Kenzie turned to Lennox and smiled. "And that's not anyone's fault. I'd hidden this part of myself from all of them. I'd hidden the fact that I was gay from people, too. I don't hide anymore. And Lennox was the one that gave me the courage to embrace who I am."

***

Kenzie swung the cabana before climbing inside and leaning against its back, staring out at the water. There was a hustle and bustle around her, and while she wished she had the ability to keep up with it all, she no longer felt the need to try to be something or someone that she wasn't. She needed a break, and she'd take it, using the time to refresh her energy level and return to the ever-growing crowd. It had been a few months since their interview had aired, and while they still had the religious nutjobs telling them they were going to hell for loving each other, the rest of the chaos that had once threatened to break them had all but disappeared. Part of that was because there were new stories out there, and part of it was because there was a big wedding coming up, and it had leaked, so the news had shifted off them entirely.

"There's my girl. How did I know I'd find you here?" Lennox stood in front of the now slowly swaying cabana and climbed inside, choosing to straddle Kenzie's outstretched legs and move into her.

"Because you always find me here." Kenzie placed her hands on Lennox's hips. "Dress still fit?"

"Yes, I've tried the thing on about fifteen times since

yesterday. Peyton is a level three bridezilla." She rolled her eyes at her friend. "How are you doing?"

"I'm okay." Kenzie ran her hands up and down Lennox's back under her white T-shirt that had *'2nd Annual Summer Camp'* and the dates of the weekend on it. Kenzie knew the back of the shirt said, *'Maid of Honor.'*

Peyton had issued shirts for all of them. Each one was detailing their role in the wedding this weekend. Maddox, for example, had *'Photographer'* and then *'stay out of my way'* and *'no photobombs'* written underneath. That one had been particularly funny to Kenzie. Her own shirt said, *'Bridesmaid'* on the back. Then, under that, Peyton had written, *'and Lennox's girlfriend, so even though she's hot, back off.'* Lennox had laughed until Peyton handed her a shirt of her very own, where she'd spotted the *'Maid of Honor'* and then *'property of Kenzie'* under it in the same size letters. Then, Kenzie had laughed. Peyton's shirt was also white and had *'I love DW'* with a red heart in the middle to represent that love, and Dani had one with Peyton's initials as well.

"How are you?" Kenzie asked her.

"I'm okay. She hasn't gotten to level four yet. If she gets to level five, though, I'm running for the woods, and I'd like you to come with me." Lennox lowered her lips to meet Kenzie's gently and then hovered there. "It feels strange, being back here."

"But also, kind of perfect," Kenzie added.

"Yes, definitely perfect." Lennox pressed her lips to Kenzie's once more.

"Do you think you can sneak away for a bit?" she asked and gripped Lennox's hips again, running her thumbs over them.

"I might be able to arrange something," Lennox teased. "But if we're discovered, and she finds out I've been slacking off, I will blame you."

"You'd throw me under the bus like that?" Kenzie laughed and kissed Lennox's collarbone.

"Absolutely." Lennox laughed back. "Hey, at our wedding, can we just agree to not make people wear lame shirts like this?" she asked after another kiss to Kenzie's collarbone. "I'm thinking we'll make them wear pants with the words on the butt instead; or, at least, just Peyton, for making us wear these things."

Kenzie laughed quietly against Lennox's skin. It hadn't been the first time Lennox had brought up the idea of a wedding. The first time had been months earlier, when they'd officially moved in together. Kenzie had sold her house, choosing to move into Lennox's much larger place, and they'd made it their home. Lennox also sold her old apartment in New York after retiring from acting, needing a change of scenery. Instead of crashing at Peyton and Dani's or getting a hotel, they had been considering buying a place together there so that they could go back and forth and have their own place. They'd spend more time on that after the wedding. But, the first time she'd even made a comment about their potential wedding, was after they'd made love and were lying in bed, holding on to one another and trying to calm their ragged breathing. Lennox had made a comment that she hoped their sex was still just as good and, most importantly, frequent after they got married. Kenzie's heart raced faster than moments before when Lennox had given her a particularly intense orgasm, and Lennox laughed as she felt it against her chest.

The second time she had brought it up had been a month or so later, when they had been with Peyton and Dani, planning their wedding. Lennox had commented about not wanting carrot cake to be anywhere near their wedding cake, because there would be no vegetables on or in her cake. Kenzie had laughed and given a nod in agreement, but she hadn't said anything else. The third time had been when they'd seen Peyton and Dani's dresses for the first time. Peyton had emerged first, and they'd been sitting next to each other on a comfy love seat, sipping mimosas neither of them wanted but had been offered. They'd told

Peyton how beautiful she was and how she'd chosen the perfect dress, and then done the same with Dani. And, as both women changed back into their street clothes, Lennox had leaned into her, kissed her cheek, and said she hoped Kenzie would choose a strapless dress because she loved Kenzie's shoulders. Kenzie had kissed Lennox's lips at that but, again, said nothing.

The fourth time had come when they had arrived back at their favorite summer camp for the weekend-long wedding celebration. The wedding party had arrived a couple of days earlier, along with the staff that was building the outdoor event for Peyton and Dani. Lennox and Kenzie had been given a private cabin at the nearby campground and had been upgraded to a queen mattress as Dani and Peyton had gone all out for their wedding party and their guests. Lennox had stated she wanted a small wedding. This was fine for Dani and Peyton; it suited them well. But Kenzie and Lennox were not Peyton and Dani, and Lennox suggested a ceremony with maybe twenty to thirty people. She mentioned having to fight with her parents about that, because her mother would likely want hundreds at her daughter's wedding. They hadn't exactly repaired their relationship, but they'd called each other more often since Lennox had shifted careers and announced her retirement from acting. They'd met Kenzie once while in LA, and it hadn't gone terribly, but they'd returned home the next afternoon. That was the full extent of their interaction with their daughter's girlfriend. Kenzie hadn't given voice to a reply at Lennox's words that day either, but she did pull her in for a deep kiss that ended with her on top of Lennox, sliding her hands inside the jeans she'd already unbuttoned. Today, though, Kenzie kissed Lennox's collarbone again and then lifted her face up to stare into Lennox's eyes as the woman looked down at her in utter adoration Kenzie had come to recognize.

"Okay," Kenzie agreed.

Lennox's look of adoration turned into realization. She

moved back, resting herself on the back of her calves, and stared at Kenzie. Kenzie watched as Lennox took it all in.

"Okay?"

"And I think our first dance should be to our song," Kenzie suggested and took both of Lennox's hands in her own, pulling Lennox back to her.

It was Lennox's turn to nod and not respond. But, the shocked expression and a smile on her face, said enough. It wasn't a proposal. No, that would come later. They wouldn't take anything away from Dani and Peyton's weekend. It was a promise, though. It was a promise that the proposal would happen, and that they would have that day together where they celebrated their love and commitment in front of the people closest to them. They couldn't do it here. Peyton and Dani had loved this place so much, they were holding their own wedding here. So, they would find somewhere else, but it would happen. And Kenzie was no longer afraid either of them would run. Lennox, apparently, had the same thing on her mind, though.

"Where should we have it?" she asked with a light kiss to Kenzie's lips. "I'm thinking New Zealand," she joked and promptly laughed at herself.

Kenzie allowed her to laugh as she wrapped her arms around Lennox's waist and hugged her closer.

"I'm thinking London," she joked back and earned an even louder laugh from Lennox.

And, God, Kenzie loved that sound.

Made in the USA
Las Vegas, NV
19 April 2025